ONE
LAST

—THE LEGACY OF A PRINCE—

RAINY
DAY

THE RAVENHOOD

LEGACY

KATE STEWART

USA TODAY BESTSELLING AUTHOR

Editor: Donna Cooksley Sanderson
Proofreader: Bethany Castaneda
Cover by Amy Q Design
Formatting by Champagne Book Design

Dear Reader,

Spoiler Warning—If you have not read all *THREE* books in the series, now would be the time to catch up to avoid any confusion. As this is a legacy book, several references throughout this novel run through the entirety of the storyline, which could be confusing if you aren't privy to the last installment—*The Finish Line*, which is the blueprint of The Ravenhood series.

Though the following is written predominantly during Flock, I strongly advise reading all three novels before starting this legacy book.

TRIGGER WARNING:

Our dark cloud's presence echoes beyond his last chapter. That said, many things are implied off the page but also written in the script that some will find triggering or disturbing. Still, I found it necessary to include them to fully encapsulate our raven's struggles, especially those of Dominic King. Any hero of our time would be burdened with far more than they could withstand, and Jean Dominic King withstood it all for the very best reason—love.
That said, I hope you feel every part of this, as I did while writing it.

All my love,
XO
Kate

Plese visit Spotify for the playlist for
ONE LAST RAINY DAY (THE LEGACY OF A PRINCE)

To the heroes we so desperately need.
Come out, come out, wherever you are.

ONE LAST

THE LEGACY OF A PRINCE

RAINY DAY

PROLOGUE

INTUITION ISN'T SOMETHING I'VE BEEN GRANTED THE SAME way others have—a gift that sparks up at certain times for guidance. It's never been that way for me. For the entirety of my life, it's been my daily fuel and has never failed me.

Not once.

So how did I get here?

How in the fuck did I get here?

"He's a man with too many secrets and no one to share them with."—Cecelia, *Flock*

ONE

THE PURR OF SEAN'S MOTOR SOUNDS AS I TIGHTEN THE LAST bolt. The heavy repeat of his engine and crunch of gravel help detract from the noise that's been echoing in my head for the last twelve fucking hours.

It shouldn't surprise me anymore—laying witness to acts of disgusting, power-drunk men in a position of so much authority that they become bored. Once that happens, they start testing the limits to see just how much they can get away with. And they do, drumming up and living out the sickest of fantasies—most involving preying on the weak and defenseless.

So, no, while it shouldn't surprise me—no matter how hard I try—I can't ever find a place inside myself to fully numb to it. I'm not a praying man, but as of late, I find myself begging for that numb every fucking day.

Relieved Sean's here to distract me, I peer at him around the hood of the Mazda I've been working on since I gave up the possibility of sleep. He saunters toward the bay with a relaxed posture to envy and a shit-eating grin on his face.

"Get that piece running?"

Stupid question.

"Not a stupid question," he quips, tossing his cigarette down before grinding it out with the heel of his boot. "If you managed the unmanageable, I would go so far as to call it miraculous."

Unlocking the hood prop, I drop it down as he situates himself behind the wheel to get his answer. Rounding the car, I move to the other side of the driver's door where he sits in the shredded pleather seat, one boot planted on the garage floor. Plucking my shop towel from my jeans, I wipe my fingers clean as he turns the key, and the ancient car instantly sparks to life. Grinning, he lifts his chin toward me. "You'd be a half-decent mechanic if you were a little less scary and more conversational."

I roll my eyes as he continues.

"That's what, three or four sentences and no reply?" He jests, killing the engine before climbing out and snapping the door shut. "I rest my case." He scrutinizes me. "Where did you go last night?"

I shrug. "A drive."

"Yeah? See anyone?"

I jerk my chin.

"Isolation isn't always good in your case. My door is only feet away from yours."

"Wasn't in the mood to talk."

"Yeah, toddlers behave the same way when they get upset."

He reads my posture and sighs. "Going to be that kind of day, huh?" He shakes his head in irritation.

The truth behind this rare friction between us is that Sean believes he wants to know what's circulating in my head. For me to air my shit out so he can pick it apart because he thinks he might be able to help. But because I know him just as well, letting him in on the secrets I'm guarding would only tear his insides to a near irreparable state and leave him in the same predicament I'm currently in. For now—until I can unleash on those responsible for how I'm feeling—I'm stuck in the most hellacious type of prison.

For now.

But soon . . .

"What, man? What?" Sean asks, sensing my struggle against the leash that continues to tighten as I fight against it by the day. He fishes out another cigarette. "Come on, man. Give me *something*."

The flick of his Zippo calms me a little. The familiar sound reminds me that I am not alone in this and never have been.

"You may think you're locked up tight enough, Dom, but it's starting to leak everywhere. You are making this," he gestures between us, "hard already. If you keep a lid on what's important *now*, you'll make what's coming impossible."

I don't bother defending myself because the *situation* is what's impossible.

Rarely do I ever sit on secrets with Sean, but I can't utter a single word because if I do, curiosity will get the best of him. He'll demand to lay witness to what I have. Once that happens, *no one* will be able to stop things from going into motion.

Sean doesn't have the kind of control needed to keep himself in check—not when it comes to this. It's getting more unbearable for me as every second ticks by. Something I've repeatedly failed to make my brother understand. Every time Tobias dismisses me, he fails us . . . them—all of us.

At one point, I prided myself on being the one capable of gaining access to anything I desired. Now it feels like a fucking curse—with a weight I'll never be able to lift.

I just have to hold on a little longer. Just a little longer, and then I can serve up what I've been bottling up for the last few months since I started my task list.

A list that—for all intents and purposes—pivoted in a major fucking way as soon as I figured out how to tap into what's been hidden beneath a veil of dentist-whitened smiles and fake patriotic lifestyles. Lives masterfully manufactured to resemble the increasingly elusive American dream. When in reality, I'm laying witness to the hobbies and favorite pastimes of fucking monsters.

The evidence I'm gathering against the powers that be would take down our fragile ecosystem in less than a day. What's whirring around in my psyche is equivalent to the magnitude of ten atom bombs, and I can't utter a fucking word.

Not yet.

"Hungry?" Sean asks, knowing he's not getting anywhere.

Have I eaten? Am I hungry?

"Fuck, man. Two words. Give me two more words, or I can't leave you like this." He exhales a stream of smoke. "The hostility is rolling off you."

Swallowing my response, I step away from his unwavering intrusion. As it stands, I can't make a move without the support of my brother.

Sean breaks up my struggle with a hint of hope as he glances at the plastic clock hanging past my shoulder. "Shit, rain check. I'm going to be late if I don't get going."

The plan. We have a plan.

The last leg of it starts today with his return to Horner Tech. As soon as said plan is executed, nothing and no one will stop me from flipping the overly-polished table to expose the filth beneath. As if privy to that thought, Sean flips his keys into his palm and pushes off the car. As he readies to leave, I find myself wishing he would stay for no other reason than to distract me. Needing company is not me. Never been me. But right now, I need . . . something.

"Orientation?"

"That's one word," he quips, his eyes calculating. He doesn't trust me alone with my thoughts. I'm not sure I can trust *my own* much longer. "Give me one more, Dom."

"Ready?"

"Does it matter?" He says, running a hand through his hair. "Time to play my part. See you at the house in a few."

TWO

BASS THRUMS THROUGH THE SPEAKER ON MY WINDOWSILL, filtering down into the backyard of our new townhouse, where twenty or so of our most trusted loiter below. Entering my password, I hope to buy another hour from joining them before I'm summoned. I'm nowhere near the type of headspace needed to entertain, and I quickly dive in to avoid it when my burner rattles with a response to a text I sent from the garage hours ago. His replies are becoming more delayed with each passing day.

> **You good?**
>
> **B: Define Good.**

His response has me grinning, which feels foreign and has it dissolving as quickly as it came.

> **When I figure it out, Big B, I'll let you know. Making a list.**
>
> **B: Checking it twice?**
>
> **Yeah, call me Santa, and everyone on it has been naughty. When can we talk?**

B: Don't move.

Translation—my leash remains.

Like I said, we need to fucking talk. A conversation. It's important.

B: Patience.

That I don't have. Not anymore.

B: You never did. Can't get away now.

Can't or won't?

B: Wait for me.

You don't know what you're asking.

B: Not asking.

"Motherfucker," I grit out, tossing the burner on my desk. Screen blinking for a command, I decide to forgo the rabbit hole I've been deep diving in. Just as I find a little reprieve in milder, more mindless work, Tyler barks my name before opening my bedroom door.

"By all means, come in," I snap, regretting the fact that though we're grown men, our ambitious plans for the next few months made it a no-brainer to room together temporarily. A decision I'm regretting with the traffic downstairs thanks to Sean and the constant interruptions by both since we moved in.

"Pretty sure you want to hear this," Tyler supplies. "We have company."

"Pretty sure I gathered that," I jerk my chin toward the speaker streaming my playlist more in an effort to drown said company out.

"Not that kind of company," he counters, leaning against my door frame.

Rolling back in my desk chair, I grab my stash box and unload a few supplies. "Yeah? Enlighten me."

Tyler stalks further into the room, coming close to hovering above where I sit, his hesitance speaking volumes as he starts to preface his news with caution. "Look, man, whatever shit you have going on—"

"Already had this speech today," I interject, plucking out a blunt paper.

"I don't think you're in the headspace to handle it."

"Then why bother knocking?" Summoning some patience, I start to unroll the wrap. "Out with it. I'm good."

"You're not fucking good, and until you come clean with what's going on, we can't help you."

"I already reached out to France," I relay to kill the interrogation. He knows if I went to my brother, it's nothing he can help me with, and with that understanding, he switches gears.

"Sean brought back a new employee from the plant."

"Good on him," I sprinkle shredded bud into the prepped paper. "Blonde or—"

"*Cecelia*," he interjects, weighing my reaction through the few tense seconds that follow. I school my expression through the adrenaline spike, and he continues as I hit my keyboard. "So, we can handle this one of two ways. I can go feel her out, or you can. But either way, this greatly complicates shit."

Already logged into her email, I scan the last one sent from Roman yesterday morning. It's filled with everything from his gate code to his house staff schedule, giving her full access.

Though his mansion sits off a private road, and only the front is gated, it was erected like a fortress—especially in the way that the trees surrounding the property were cut back far enough that anyone who attempted to get in would be spotted by his meticulously placed security cameras. Through a strange fucking twist of fate, we own adjoining land, which grants us backyard access, but the house itself is too far away from any decent cover to get in and out without tipping him off. Any attempt to mic that house would raise flags we don't want raised.

I have zero doubt that Roman designed it that way.

Though we had every intention of tapping the house, we abandoned those plans after the dust settled on construction. The reason being Roman rarely, if ever, sleeps there. His permanent home is his condo in Charlotte, which we've successfully tapped along with Horner Tech's corporate office. Those taps have since proved useless aside from the ability to keep tabs on his schedule and whereabouts, making it easier for the birds on his permanent watch. One of which is a current headquarters employee.

"Thought we had birds on her?" Tyler prompts.

"I took over her surveillance the day after I got home because we were moving in on Roman. Which is why the old watch didn't alert us when she packed up yesterday and drove here. *Fuck.*"

"Did France know?"

"That I took over?" I cut my eyes up at him. "Why . . . do you think he would of fucking objected?"

"Only if you fucked up and dropped the ball, which you clearly did," he draws out as he crosses his arms. "Even so, you miss *nothing*, Dom, so what or who distracted you?"

The monsters. The noise. The rabbit hole I sought out, dove headfirst into, and that followed me out, only to haunt my every waking minute.

"She hasn't been here in eight fucking years, and he doesn't even live there," I excuse in shit defense. "Didn't think that would change anytime soon. Besides, when's the last time you had eyes on her, *jarhead almighty?*"

"Fine, let's quash the blame game and worry about the eighteen-year-old time bomb standing in our yard." He gives me a thorough once over. "Or should I worry about the one sitting in front of me?"

Ignoring him, I X-ray Roman's proposition to his estranged daughter, sifting through the details. Kicking back, I resume rolling my blunt as my mind races and Tyler's questions start. "Why is she here?"

"He's going to pay her college tuition and top it off with an inheritance for working at the plant . . . for a fucking year."

"Jesus Christ, Dom. You need to place another call to France."

Fuming about my fuck up, I jerk my chin. "He's not receptive to anything right now."

"I think, on this, he'll want to be privy. It changes things."

"It changes nothing," I snap. "Everything will go to plan." Because if it doesn't, I won't be able to control the shit festering inside me much longer. "Nothing changes," I reiterate, hearing the difference in my tone, which sounds every bit like an order—something Tyler doesn't take kindly to after following so many militantly over the years. There's a warning in his posture even as he summons the patience to press in on me for what's behind my resignation.

"Dom—"

"Remember when you came back from your only overseas trip," I twist my blunt tight, "and you didn't want to talk about it?" I don't bother looking up as I seal it closed. "Same scenario."

"That bad?"

"Worse," I swallow, wiping my desk free from debris. "These aren't acts of war."

"Jesus, man, I get it. But on this, we can't—"

"We fucking have to. Not a word, Tyler, to *either* of them. Sean can't handle the mind fuck, and my brother's too far gone in the game he's playing overseas. If we tell him, his mind will be *here*, and it can't be. Not right now." I let my statement linger for emphasis, and he doesn't miss it. "It's up to us. Trust me on this."

Tyler takes a full minute to mull it over but finally agrees. "All right. For now."

My answering glare echoes my request.

"Don't," he jerks his chin. "Don't question me."

"Then don't make me."

"Have I ever?" he barks, letting his arms fall to his sides. "Let's concentrate on the situation at hand. I don't think you should meet her, but I'm betting you'll go against my advice."

"What's she like?"

"From what I've gathered in my two-second assessment, curious, innocent, observant, and to keep it one hundred, *way too* fucking beautiful."

A low-lying fury starts to prickle in my veins as I run through a list of scenarios, namely Sean's current agenda to mix our business with his pleasure.

"I'm not the one you need to warn on the last part."

"*Goddamnit, Sean,*" Tyler groans, "I get that this came out of left field, but we have no contingency plan for this . . . Jesus. All right," he exhales audibly, "I'll do some additional recon on Roman to see what his motive might be for bribing his daughter back into his life. It doesn't make sense other than a last attempt at a relationship with her, right?"

"She just graduated," I relay thoughtfully, "Roman was there."

"At her graduation?"

"I didn't read into it. Maybe I should have," I admit.

"Well, it wasn't in my fucking newsletter," he snaps, exasperated. "Dom, you should have—"

"I don't need to be reminded of what my job entails," I grit out. "I'm aware of the cost of fucking any part of this up, but we're covered. I'll make sure of it."

"And *this* situation?"

"I'll think on it."

"Sure you don't want to put in another call to France?"

And risk my brother's life as he plays a dangerous round of roulette with a French thug sporting a God complex?

Fuck no. I earned and deserve the position I'm in. It's my call, and we both know it. He reads my decision.

"Choice is yours. I'll go feel her out." I give him a slow nod before he disappears, the promise of a future argument apparent in the tight snap of my door behind him.

Standing, I light my blunt before walking over to the blinds. Lifting one, I spot her lingering at our fence, her back to me, outlined and illuminated by the sinking sun. Pulling from my blunt, I watch her take in her surroundings, scanning the mountain ridge just as Tyler approaches her. When she turns to him, I drop the blinds in lieu of getting my first real look at her.

There's no point. I can't and won't appreciate the beauty of any complication that threatens our agenda. We've worked too hard and waited too long for the days, weeks, and months to come. Our plans aren't changing for any reason or anyone, especially Roman Horner's teenage daughter.

Despite what some say, not all birds are attracted to shiny, spinning things.

THREE

A FTER SMOKING THE WHOLE BLUNT TO CALM MY SHIT TO THE
point I can face my fuckup, I mimic a progress report under
the bird who's been on Cecelia's detail for years on the off-
chance Tobias checks in. Reasoning with myself that it's the only
way to keep my brother's focus where it needs to be, I shake off the
accompanying unease as I hit send. Pushing away from my desk, I
stalk downstairs and am caught halfway by Jeremy making his way
up with one of his regular girls in tow.

"Sean's room, motherfucker," I warn as he flashes a buzzed smile
while sweeping his conquest past me. Spotting me as they brush by,
I ignore her drawn-out stare and any others I attract as I cross the
living room toward the sliding glass door.

In the next instant, I'm surrounded by bass and mixed smells
of smoke wafting through a once-familiar crowd—people I grew
up with, who now feel more like strangers to me. Mixed greetings
die on their collective tongues with one glance in my direction, and

I'm thankful for it. It should bother me that I instill that hesitance, but I prefer it.

When I first arrived home from MIT, I found myself in the position to defend my place amongst some of the inked due to my four-year absence, despite my summers spent at home. That lasted a matter of days because I made it so. It had nothing to do with flexing but an obstacle in the way of getting to what's important, which brings me back to the matter at hand—my current hindrance. Scanning the yard, with a few twists of heads and moving bodies, I catch sight of the interloper standing next to Sean, their posture intimate.

As if she *feels* my summons, she turns her head, and our eyes collide. The second it happens, an odd premonition runs through me as a whisper snakes its way into my psyche. Shaking it off, I stalk toward her and enter her personal space, refusing to mince intent with useless words. Sean's attempt at interception does shit to dissuade me from making my point, and before uttering a word, she already knows her place with me.

Our sparring begins and ends with a brief back and forth in which I make it a point to embarrass her. It's only when I make it crystal that she's not only uninvited but unwanted that she drunkenly acquiesces. "Whatever, I'll go."

Turning to head back inside, she grips my forearm to stop me. Her invasive touch feels like a burn as I resist the urge to rip my arm away while whipping my head in her direction. Defiant dark blue eyes—matching those of my enemy—clash with mine while she downs the rest of her bottle before dropping it at my feet. "Oops."

It's then that my mission runs with clarity through my veins as we continue to stare off. As it happens, a slight remorse brews because she's completely unaware of the threat she poses.

Tyler was only partially right in his assessment but missed something vital.

Her beauty is fucking tragic.

If her presence here so much as alters any small part of the ground plan that has to roll out in the next few months, I'll have no issue doing whatever it takes to erase her from the equation.

Just as the thought crosses my mind, she ends her tirade, intent on having the last word. "You know, you could say it was nice to meet me. You are kicking me out of your party. It's the polite thing to do."

"Never been accused of being polite."

"It's common decency, arsehole."

The feel of her fingers wrapped around my forearm begins to gnaw away the last of my patience. Sean reads my rapidly changing demeanor, cursing before scooping her over his shoulder. His eyes linger heavily on my profile for some acknowledgment while mine remain locked on Roman's daughter.

"And what a pretty arsehole you are," she slurs out. Laughter spills out around us, cutting through some of the thick tension, and despite myself, I can't help the slight upturn of my lips in response. That is until she makes her last declaration. "I am trouble, you know . . . just ask your brother."

Dangling over Sean's shoulder, she keeps her steady gaze on me as Sean hauls her through the sliding glass door to protect her from getting the worst of me. When she's out of sight, Tyler sidles up to me, putting voice to the question we both already know the answer to. "What was he thinking?"

"That he'll get his dick wet while convincing us he's doing us a solid," I clip out, staring in the direction Sean fled.

"And no one thought to tell him otherwise?"

"We did," I glance over at Tyler. "He just wasn't paying attention."

Tyler's wheels begin to turn as I recall a long-ago conversation that took place next to a roaring campfire when we were just teenagers. A night that is—or should be—easily accessible to all of us, verbatim, because it's the night we truly began.

"We're going basic with our strategy," Tobias relays, staring thoughtfully into the flames.

"Meaning?" Tyler asks.

"We've got to play this just right. The only way to defeat a man like Roman is to play sleeping giant," my brother replies in a tone that has us all perking up.

"Think Helen of Troy," I offer, reading his line of thought and knowing all of us are well-versed in the Greek myth thanks to Mrs. Green's annual eighth-grade lesson.

In the story, Helen, the wife of King Menelaus of Mycenaean Sparta, was seduced and stolen by Paris, Prince of Troy, and remained with him, which sparked a ten-year war. My point in bringing it up has nothing to do with the love story but the tactic used by way of the Trojan Horse. Greek soldiers were able to gain access and take the city of Troy after a fruitless ten-year siege by hiding in a giant horse supposedly left as an offering to the goddess Athena. By using the same type of tactic, we could take methodical, measured steps to get to Roman.

Instead of rehashing that, I put a voice to my less complicated solution. "But it seems like a lot of trouble to go through when we can just eliminate the problem."

My brother's reaction is predictable and instant, a rare fear in his eyes as he weighs my words while assessing me. Saying it out loud forces him to acknowledge the side of me he's been getting glimpses of but fears out of paternal concern. A side of me he's terrified exists because it means, at one point, it will put me in the line of fire, where I fully intend to be. He speaks his objection a breath later. "I know you're not fucking suggesting we kill the man in cold—"

"Eye for an eye." I shrug. "Our parents burned to death. Don't you think that calls for aggressive action? You, yourself, told Delphine you were sick of all the talk. The meetings are a joke, filled with nothing but pussies who like to bitch while she refills their coffee. Might as well be a book club for all the fucking good it's doing."

Taking it a step further, I lay out my simplified plan. "You know, if we boil down enough tobacco and dab the right amount of concentrate on his fucking car door handle, within minutes of it seeping into his skin, it's game over. Heart attack on the autopsy report. Presented with the right opportunity, it's a hundred percent untraceable."

Though shrouded by the woods, there's just enough firelight to make out the color draining from his face as he speaks in both alarm and *warning.* "He's not a smoker, so there's the first hole in that stupid idea, and that's not who we are," he grits out, "and not who we will be, Dom. That's not what Maman and Papa wanted. There is a better, more diplomatic way to handle this, less merciful than death." He gives me an adamant shake of his head. "No, what we're going to do is change things for the better. Once we take Roman down, there's a hundred like him to take his place. They exploit people like our parents and discard them once they become a liability." He looks at each one of us pointedly. "What are we going to do about them?"

"Not our problem," Sean says from where he rocks in his camping chair in his football jersey, beer in hand, high lingering from the pep rally.

"We're going to make it our problem," Tobias declares, "that's the whole point of all of this. It's not just about our family or this town. Not anymore."

Shoving his hands in his pockets, he turns and stares in the direction of the newly-erected construction of Roman's house—a mere length of a football field away from our spot—his voice in a faraway place when he adds, "we're going to do this in a way that will honor them."

Sean pops another beer as he puts in his two cents. "This seems ambitious. I mean, come on, man. Look at where we're at—bumfuck nowhere."

"That's exactly the point." Sean's focus flits to me because of the amount of bite in my tone. He's still straddling realms, living in the created world and the one Tobias has envisioned and wants us to help re-create. Despite my warnings that Tobias isn't going to take us seriously if we don't step up, Sean's under the impression we're already in due to relation. He has no idea just how wrong he is in that respect.

"You want to end up just another line cook at Daddy's restaurant?" I remind him. "What's going to happen when they call in that bank loan?"

Sean's eyes flare, but he remains quiet, picking at his beer label as I turn and fix my gaze on Tyler, whose situation is just as grim. "Are you going to be a career soldier?"

Tyler glares over at me, his father's fate his own worse fear.

The truth is, none of us wants to trace the footfalls or repeat the fate *of our parents. While Tobias and I have suffered greatly, our brothers haven't been much more fortunate. Tyler's endured the worst by way of remnants of his father, who left US soil as one man and came back another. Sean's in the midst of witnessing the toll it's taking on his parents just to keep their restaurant running and collective heads above water.*

Their fear of repeating a similar path is one of the main reasons why Tobias has our attention—but he's given us plenty of others. He was the first to break the small-town mindset chain and get out. The not-so-subtle changes in him during his trips back are what's kept their curiosity stoked. I satiated mine by digging into why my brother's more relaxed demeanor started to disappear over a short time.

This made me more determined to ditch any ritualistic teenage bullshit and man up before I was expected to. Not that I had much of a choice or that he's noticed.

"This is exactly why we're here," Tobias asserts, "to get our priorities straight."

"My priorities are perfect," Sean lifts his hands and begins to tick off his fingers to spite us both. "Pussy, pussy, pussy, pussy, and . . ." he holds a finger on his thumb, "yup, I'm going to have to go with pussy."

I laugh despite my annoyance with Sean as Tobias's eyes flare in warning. "This is another reason why I called this meeting. You want a girlfriend? Have one, but pillow talk and this fucking club are never to go hand in hand. What the other birds do is not my business, but as far as we are concerned, women don't have a place at this fire, not yet. And not until they are vetted by me personally. End of."

"I thought you said women are a sanctuary." Sean snarks, testing Tobias again before sipping his beer.

"They are," Tobias spits, "away from business. Personal attachments are the greatest liability. And the first one who fucks up on that front will pay dire consequences." He again looks to each of us in an attempt to drive his point home before adding, "no fucking exceptions."

As the conversation progresses, I try to diffuse the tension that continually rears its ugly head as we all snap back and forth. The resentment for Tobias's long absences only to come back calling shots has him getting twice as much venom as he's giving. I can barely conceal my own grudge, especially when my aunt's drinking is tossed into the mix.

"So, if I'm getting this right," Tyler diverts, posture rigid, "we need a wooden horse to recruit an army to hide inside it and the opportunity to slip into the city."

Tobias dips his chin in confirmation.

"I'm going to be a third-generation Marine," Tyler declares, which is no surprise to any of us. "It's a given, and if there's one thing I know how to do—it's how to build an army."

Sean speaks up next, putting his petulant bullshit aside. "Me and Dom will cover the garage, and once it's up and running, I'll figure out a way to get us through the gate." He ruffles my hair, and I slap his hand away as he finishes, "and we all know this asshole's going to Harvard or Yale or some shit."

"Guess that makes you the horse," I clip to my brother.

"No, little brother," he counters as we stare off, our tension much harder to ignore due to our earlier fight. Mostly because he refuses to let me join him in France and thinks I'm blind to what he's started in Paris. Of the company he keeps and the constant danger he's putting himself in.

"You're the horse," he declares as he looks between the three of us, "as of this moment, I no longer exist."

After hashing out a little more strategy, I join my brother, who stands a few feet from the fire.

"What about Helen?" He stares back at me with unguarded surprise.

Until minutes ago, I was his gifted teenage brother and a tool capable of getting him out of tight situations along with doing recon that helps him gain ground where he needs it. To him, I'm supposed to be satisfied with the breadcrumbs he selectively decides to feed me while he keeps me a safe distance from his overseas dealings. At this point, I'm keeping my own secrets and choosing when and how I reveal them.

My crumb of knowledge about Cecelia is minor in comparison to the extent of what I've made it my business to know. Like Tobias, I saw her today, an innocent, young tender, with rebellion clear in her eyes as she shoved a book down her pants to spite Roman. His instilled *bigotry apparent as he glanced around the library as if the walls were splattered with shit.*

Staring back at me, Tobias speaks up in both order and warning that we aren't going there when it comes to Roman's familial ties, and knowing my brother, never will. "We're leaving Helen out of it."

Tyler stands next to me nearly a decade later in quiet contemplation as the party continues to bustle around us, our gazes in the direction where Sean fled with Cecelia in tow before I glance over at him. Within seconds, I see the recognition, his memory just as long and sharp as mine, his hearing ... *supernatural* and the highest card he has to play—which he does, regularly. He proves it as he speaks up, dread in his tone as he pinpoints it perfectly by voicing an ironic, specific warning. "Beware of Greeks bearing gifts." He runs a palm down his jaw as he glances over at me. "Jesus Christ. *Helen* just fucking landed in Triple Falls."

Therein lies the tragedy.

Helen's story didn't end well for her, or anyone else for that matter.

Tobias's warning rings sharp in my mind for the first time since that conversation because I felt the buzz start the second I locked eyes with Cecelia—and still feel it lingering. Knowing Sean's reason for bringing her in without him trying to justify it, there's no fucking way I'm looking this gift horse in the mouth—or anywhere else for that matter—because I know without a doubt if Cecelia has a part to play in this, it won't end well for any of us.

"What's your call?" Tyler prompts.

"Have everyone at the garage in twenty."

She's in it now, brother.

Herds of townspeople glide along the endless rows of vendor tents. Most all of them are wearing smiles, blissfully unaware that there is a war going on. That beyond some of their trees and state parks, there is a group of men fighting on their behalf so that the local economy can thrive, so the poachers don't get the best of them.—Cecelia, *Exodus*

FOUR

MORE SUN SEEPS THROUGH MY CLOSED BLINDS AS I SIP FROM a cup of fresh brew, focusing my blurred vision on my screen split by various camera views—two trained on Roman's backyard after tapping into his security server. The second—courtesy of the camera attached to the back of the truck of our lady bird in waiting—gives an ample view of the road leading to the newly discovered warehouse. The last is from the bolted camera on the roof of the warehouse. A warehouse owned by the target we're currently running a long game on—Anthony Spencer. One of a handful of Roman's enemies who made the first cut. Enemies who have their own empires we plan to rob and dismantle before burning them to ashes.

By eliminating our competition, we're making fucking sure we're the ones who get to serve Roman justice and make bank while doing it. We haven't made our pattern to take down Roman's adversaries apparent to him yet. Still, he'll be clued in soon enough when a few of the moguls he has an old beef with in neighboring high-rises start disappearing one by one due to methodical design, erasing all opportunity they could have had to get to him before we do.

He'll know *someone's* coming for *him* soon enough.

Frankly, I can't fucking wait until he starts scrambling to find out *who*.

Time. It's all just a matter of time.

I argued this tactic out with my brother as a condition since he refused to let me eliminate Roman outright. My reasoning? The least we could do is fuck with him psychologically while ensuring we're the ones who make him pay. Though Tobias resisted the idea at first, his vindictive streak won out.

Jeremy's Fleet Heating and Air van comes into view as he flies down the gravel parking lot and lines up next to where Tyler is parked. Hopping out, he searches for and spots the camera. Clicking on his earpiece, he flips me the company mascot between each word. "Testing. Testing."

"You're an idiot," I utter, unable to help my grin.

"Afternoon, Princess," he coos, chin lifted to the camera. "How's that cushy chair treating your ass?"

"Keeping my balls nice and cool, bro," I quip as Russell jumps out of the passenger side, opening the van doors behind him. "Maybe if you had done your math homework just once in your lifetime, you wouldn't be the man with calloused hands for more reasons than one."

"Don't flirt with me right now, Dom. This is serious business we're conducting. But tell me something, and be honest," he turns and thrusts his ass out toward the camera. "Do these uniform khakis make my ass look fat?"

Russell shakes his head with a chuckle as he studies the warehouse and speaks up. "So, who found this one?"

Jeremy supplies the answer. "Tyler. It wasn't listed in the douchebag's company assets, but he found the address hidden in some of Spencer's ancient paperwork."

Tyler speaks up, already inside the warehouse. "Safe to say we can hear you, dipshit. Clear the line of bullshit. We're on the clock."

"What's your status?" I ask Tyler, eyeing said clock on my monitor.

"Already at the door," Tyler grunts. "Like I suspected, this is a pull-up ground lock, not padded, so if we don't take anything, he'll never know we were here. The lock is giving me hell to dislodge. Give me a minute."

"You don't have much more than that," I warn.

Russell pulls on his gloves before retrieving two crowbars and handing one to Jeremy as Jeremy scopes the isolated building in the middle of bumfuck nowhere, which sits just inside our county line. It's the warehouse's location that lured us in. That, and the fact that after more digging, we found out that Roman sold the land and warehouse to Spencer when he was offloading worthless property years ago, back when they were still doing business together. The question is why Spencer kept it and why it's titled as a personal asset. Jeremy speaks up, echoing my thoughts. "So, what's in this one?"

"That's what you're there to find out, imbecile," I grit out.

Jeremy turns to Russell. "He's *so bitchy* lately."

Russell stares at Jeremy as he always does, like he's a lab experiment that went awry, as Jeremy continues his rant. "I get it, Dom. We all could use a day off. In fact," he glances around, "we're missing a bird today. Bet Sean's tied up at the moment . . . ooh, maybe Cecelia gets down like that . . . it's always the quiet ones."

Just as Jeremy says it, my burner rattles with an incoming text from Sean.

> **S: Five minutes out. Got the gate code.**
>
> **I don't need a play-by-play, and we have that already. Get me something useful and look for my signal.**

"Gotta agree, she is hot as fuck," Russell adds as Cecelia appears on the poolside camera in a bikini, looking utterly fucking perfect in the sun, long chestnut hair blowing around her flawless face, her build that of a wet dream. The mere sight of her gnaws at me as she studies the surface of the pool, seemingly lost in thought. Jeremy latches on to Russell's assessment, breaking up my own. "As off limits as she may be, if I were the one tied up, I would probably let her do some *really drastic* shit to me . . . feathers, oil . . . maybe even *leather*."

Jeremy slowly gyrates on Russell to emphasize his point, and Russell shoves him away. "Get the fuck off me, freak."

"Playtime is over," I bark, pulling my eyes away from Cecelia, knowing the second Sean sees her, he's going to fail to give us anything useful—despite the assurances he gave Tyler last night. The second Sean hit the top of the stairs after driving Cecelia home, Tyler ambushed him, catching him and reaming him out in the hall just outside of my bedroom door. I didn't bother weighing in or taking part in the argument. After relaying things would be 'business as usual' at the garage to those in on our secret, I made peace with the fact that Cecelia's nothing but an obstruction we have to work around. Sean eyed me apprehensively just before I kicked my door closed on their argument and went back to work.

When Sean tested the water at the coffee pot this morning, I made it clear I wasn't interested as he tried in vain to give me some of the 'advantage' spiel he did Tyler last night before I tuned them out.

Ignoring the gradually brewing resentment for Sean and dragging my eyes away from Cecelia for a second time, I clear my head for the bird's fate currently resting in my hands.

"Thirteen minutes until deputy dipshit comes through," I remind everyone on the line as I scan the warehouse entrance. "Van three, where the fuck are you?"

Peter speaks up. "About to pull up now, man. Denny and I got stuck behind a fucking tractor."

Checking the camera attached to Layla's F150, I spot her leaning against her open tailgate—dressed provocatively as requested—in case we need her as a last-minute distraction for the security guard who checks the warehouse like clockwork.

"How's it going, lady bird?" I ask Layla, whose focus is on the direction of security's routine approach.

"All clear," she says, wasting no time in an effort to keep the line clear, especially with her fiancé in on this secret.

Just after, I catch sight of the third van as they pull into the driveway, flying in from the opposite direction of where Layla waits. Skidding to a stop next to the first two vans, Denny and Peter jump out and burst into motion, opening the back doors before pulling gloves on.

"Got it," Tyler says, opening the bay door. Within seconds, they collectively disappear inside.

For a solid minute, I hear nothing but bickering and grumbling. "It's dark as fuck in here," Jeremy gripes as a small crash sounds. "We should have brought flashlights."

"In case you idiots forgot," I snap, "There are no interior cameras. I'm flying blind."

Denny speaks up first. "We've got a dozen stacked crates and a few boxes. We'll need to grab the dollies if we want to clear it."

Jeremy chimes in. "Pry one open, man, and see what's up. We don't want Spencer's ancient comic book collection."

"He's not going to have security checking the building every forty or so minutes for a comic collection, *jackass*," Tyler snaps. "Pry the top crates open . . . gently."

"Twelve minutes," I warn.

"We need more crowbars," Tyler barks, "Russell, back of my van."

"On it." Russell flies into my line of sight, grabs a black duffle, and disappears back into the warehouse as Jeremy speaks up.

"I got the first crate open . . . What the fuck? Tyler, over here."

"Eleven minutes. Tyler, talk to me."

More shuffling ensues, the sounds of the crates being pried open coming through my speakers as Sean appears poolside on Roman's camera as Cecelia emerges from doing laps. Denny speaks up, stealing my focus. "Got another one . . . fuck, these can't be real."

It's Tyler's reaction that has me tensing. "Jesus Christ. These are military-grade, and they sure as fuck aren't toys."

Russell sounds just as shaken when he tosses in. "You sure this is Spencer's warehouse?"

My patience thins out. "Eight minutes," I snap. "Talk to me."

Tyler speaks up. His voice strained with barely concealed fury. "We've got six crates of M9s and M fucking 16s, man. Along with bulletproof vests and enough ammunition to take out ten goddamn city blocks. Guns no fucking CEO of *any* freight company should ever be able to get his hands on without the right connections."

Tyler makes it a point to walk just outside the bay door and looks up at the camera, at me, his warning clear. "By connections, I mean *my fucking type*. This is above our paygrade for the moment, and if these do belong to Spencer, he fucked up using a flashlight cop to guard this place because whoever these do belong to isn't going to let it go when they find out they're missing. What's your call?"

Mind racing, I ready myself for a deep dive as I open my second screen and begin typing. "Take the bulk of the guns and send me everything on them. I'm going to see if I can get a line on who's in the market to buy and which piggy has them for sale."

Tyler jumps into the back of his van and begins to dump the contents of six large black duffle bags before he turns and barks orders into the warehouse. "Get the fuck over here!"

"Five minutes," I bark, logging in on my second screen. Jeremy, Russell, Peter, and Denny leap into my visual, joining Tyler as he passes out the empty duffels while doling out frantic orders. "Guns only. Leave the crates we haven't opened and switch the bottoms with the tops so they look untouched. Not a single fucking box looks out of place. I'll sweep up, GO!"

Jeremy and Denny appear first with bulked-out duffle bags and load them into their vans as Tyler, Russell, and Peter load the remaining vans.

Clicking on the street view of the main road, I spot the security car half a mile away and give Layla the heads up. "Incoming, lady bird, stand by."

Layla gives me a fast reply, pulling up her tailgate to take her wheel. "Ready."

"Out of time," I clip as Tyler shuts the bay door, locking it from inside the way he found it. In seconds he reappears from behind the camera, leaping into his van. All three vans fire up and line up, flying toward the gate—a gate that takes fifteen seconds to open and close. Seconds we might not have.

"Lady bird," I say as the car draws a quarter mile away, "if you could pull out slowly in front of him to buy us a few more seconds, we'd appreciate it."

"On it," she says as I clip out my order to the rest of them. "As soon as you can clear that gate, floor it. I want you half a fucking mile in front of the mall cop . . . Layla, *now*."

The blare of a horn sounds as the mall cop lays on it while Layla cuts him off and plays her part, laying on her southern accent. "I'm so sorry. It's my first time driving this big truck!"

"Get the hell out of the way, lady!"

When the gate opens just enough, all three vans gun out of the parking lot, speeding in the opposite direction.

"Good job, lady bird," I say, watching the gate creep toward closed, heart thundering in my chest from the adrenaline rush.

"Anything for my boys," Layla replies fondly.

"If you truly mean that," Jeremy speaks up as if it's an offer. A second later, we're all privy to a pained grunt. ". . . ouch, Jesus Christ, Denny, I'm driving! Such a jealous man."

Jeremy continues to torture Denny as I tighten my fists, breath bated. "I was simply going to ask for a little trim . . . a haircut! Fuck! Layla, you do know you're marrying a Neanderthal, right?"

Layla laughs. "Counting down the days. See you at home, baby," she says to Denny before she signs off.

The security car appears seconds later and painstakingly waits for the archaic gate to open before leisurely turning into the warehouse parking lot.

"All clear," I report through all lines.

"Fucking hell. That was too close," Tyler rasps out.

Jeremy pipes up, spluttering more bullshit. "I swear to God, it feels like my balls just shrank a little . . . or maybe they grew. Denny, take a look."

"Jeremy," Denny grunts in his zero-bullshit tone, "you whip *anything out*, we both die today."

Shaking my head with a grin, I keep the amusement out of my order. "Get to the compound. Denny, put these deep underground."

"Will do."

Shoulders sagging with relief, I toss my earpiece as the news pops up as programmed on one of my screens. Killing it, I check the message Tyler texted about the guns we just lifted, hoping I made the right call as I prepare to descend into another rabbit hole to find out what the fuck Spencer is into—happy I'm nowhere in Tyler's current vicinity. Right about now, the magnitude of what we just discovered is hitting him, and the fact that dirty military—his Achilles heel—may be involved has me shooting up a silent prayer for those around him.

Glancing back at Roman's pool camera—which gives an ample view of the pool and a large amount of side yard—I catch Sean standing in the shallow end with a lit cigarette in hand. Cecelia treads water at a safe distance, her posture suggesting mistrust as she weighs up Sean while they converse. A conversation I can't hear because Roman hasn't updated his security cameras since he built the house.

As Sean lures her closer with his pretty boy charm, he makes it a point to lift his chin in acknowledgment to me. Just after, I command the camera's red light to blink twice, unsure if he'll see it. Lifting my burner, I shoot off a text to the bird waiting nearby to scoop him up. Knowing I need to switch my focus, I observe their posture for another few seconds and get confirmation of my earlier assumption. Sean's doing anything but fucking taking notes for the club's benefit, far more focused on details for his own.

Even so, facts are facts. For now, and because of Sean, we're one step closer to accessing that house.

I've often had an inkling that Roman built that mansion to use as an overpriced safe. His secrets hidden somewhere between the walls, which is most likely why he keeps his distance from it.

Time will tell.

When Sean lifts from the pool after our bird pulls up, Cecelia watches him saunter off, staring after him long after he's out of her line of sight. It's then that I get my first inkling.

This could work.

FIVE

EXHAUSTED FROM OUR WAREHOUSE RAID EARLIER, DIVING into the ether to research what we discovered, and then working a long shift at the garage, I glare at the asshole in front of me. He's testing my limits thanks to his invitation to the comatose girl on the couch behind him. "I'm taking her. So, make an excuse," I grit out. "I need to scope the house."

"I'll get to it," Sean assures.

"You were in her pool hours ago and got exactly *shit*. You've milked this already within the last two days, both of which you saw fit to put her directly in my fucking path."

"I'm not trying to piss you off," he swears.

"You're failing. I swear to God, Sean. If you make this about your dick—"

"I'm not," he snaps back, giving me an irritated jerk of his chin. "It's not like that." He glances back over his shoulder where Cecelia is still passed out due to taking a few hits of my blunt during our exchange in the lobby.

"It's just . . ." he turns back to me, "she's been questioning *everything* since minute one. She's young, sure. But *she's not* an empty head. From what I've gathered, she's no more a fan of Roman than we are. I think there's potential you can't see because you're too fucking pissed off to try and glimpse it." He exhales smoke too close to my face, and I knock the lit cigarette out of his hand.

Lit ashes scatter down his arm and jeans as he bats it off. "The fuck, man! Who the fuck are you right now?"

"I'm the guy you're currently *fucking* to get *into her panties*."

"Yeah, seeing as how you're becoming more unrecognizable to me by the day, and we have to handle this *just so*. You sure *I'm the one* in the way?"

He doesn't bother hiding the doubt in his expression as he continues. "I get why you're pissed, but the brother I know would never let someone this volatile near this situation. So, you tell me, should I trust you to handle this for all of us? Because from what I've witnessed, you scare the shit out of her already."

From what I've gathered, she seems mature for her age. Too fucking young to know better, but brave enough to cross borders to start to learn her lessons. She all but admitted during our back and forth earlier that she's using us, this situation, as an experiment for her own amusement to piss her father off or test herself. Probably both.

Because knowing your enemy is the most important rule in the book. Unlike Sean, I took the time to understand her typical behavior pattern. Holing up in a garage with a bunch of tatted mechanics getting stoned? Not on her resume. She even went so far as to call me "Frenchman," which means she's already been warned by someone who couldn't spot my brother in a fucking two-person lineup.

Even when I full-out warned her that being here wasn't in her best interest, she didn't pause before leaping over the line I drew, entering the garage, and making herself at home amongst us with Sean's encouragement.

So, while she might be asking the right questions for answers she'll never uncover on her own, this seems more a classic case of a good girl wanting to go bad or, at least, make bad decisions.

That's where I come in.

I don't scare her. I *intrigue* her.

My blatant disgust with her invasion of my life and space only draws more curiosity, which I will use to my advantage as soon as I can swat her new bodyguard away.

Shifting my focus back to Sean, I stare past his bullshit reasoning—the image of his fingers curling around her earlier in a slight hint of possession fresh in my mind. "Do I even need to say it?"

The flick of his Zippo is the only answer I get for a few seconds until he lifts eyes full of contempt. "Yeah, Dom, maybe you better."

"You willing to fuck us all over for her?"

"Yeah, I'm in love," he spouts dryly.

"You're fucking *something*."

"Maybe I am. Because she's got real heart, seems pure of soul, and has a fucking brain. We both know she's innocent in this," he emphasizes, "I guess keeping that in consideration makes me a real fucking *monster*."

"I'm driving her. Figure it out. I'm not asking."

He swallows the fact that I just pulled rank for the first time in our relationship and I discard any worry about what it means for us. He steps back and gives me a slight dip of his chin before stalking over to Cecelia to caress her awake. It's then I know who's in real danger, and it's not Cecelia fucking Horner.

Speakers bleeding with "Bundy" to drown out the possibility of conversation, I can't ignore Cecelia's fear-filled screech as it morphs into high-pitched laughter while I race toward Roman's estate. Even with my agitation prominent, I fail to fight off the threat of a smile, knowing she's high off this. Palms on my dash, hair flying around the cabin due to the open windows, I ignore the weight of her stare while she analyzes me as she has all night. A few of the lingering gazes between us *I incited* earlier as I licked my blunt wrap like I lick pussy. She attempted to engage me a couple of times before and since, which I would find more irritating if I didn't need that attention to hook her without niceties.

Unlike Sean, I am dedicated to *playing* my part.

But . . . I don't deny or lie to myself about the attraction that hums when she leans over to punch in her father's gate code as Tyler pulls up behind us. Despite her attempt not to touch me, her silky hair drags along my forearm as I get a good whiff of whatever she's sprayed on beneath her uniform.

My eyes drink in her profile for the few seconds she crowds my space. Tragically beautiful.

Even if I've surprised myself by being able to appreciate the look of her—unlike Sean—I have a talent for ignoring it since I got my first hard-on and have learned to make good use of it.

Shrugging off the allure of the bait that currently has Sean's balls in a vice grip, I slowly roll up the drive, scanning the surroundings and taking notes.

Though I've seen Roman's fortress from every angle and memorized the fucking blueprints before they hammered the first nail in, this is my first up-close look.

My suspicions are confirmed as I pull up. It's the distance from any cover to the house that makes getting it wired impossible without detection. Any attempt to do so would trigger an investigation on Roman's part to find out *who* and why. Something he's proficient in doing and doing well. Right now, he's aware of every one of his earned opponents . . . *save us.*

We know this due to years of successful surveillance. Like us, Roman pays those who do his dirty work well enough to keep his secrets.

This house has never been a hot spot for activity until now— and we need in.

She's the way.

Pulling through the circular drive to the foot of the stairs, I finally flit my attention her way.

"I don't know whether to slap you or thank you," she says, deep blue gaze rolling over me.

"You loved it," I counter before turning back toward the house. It's impressive enough, but in my mind, this is the place where my enemy currently dwells . . . sleeping mere feet away. The closest any raven has gotten in nearly a decade.

With the Glock resting in my glovebox, I could end this long game point blank while simultaneously gaining the freedom to un-leash on the monsters who've taken residence in my mind. But inside the house in front of me resides a monster who stole my childhood by plotting my parents' deaths for seeing him beneath his carefully placed veil. Who covered up their murders and brushed their chil-dren away like debris with a payoff. The same sort of payoff he seems to be offering his own child for arduous and unnecessary labor.

What could Cecelia possibly fucking mean to him if he's so willing to let her work in that factory after ignoring her for years?

Nothing. She can't mean anything to him. She may be another victim of his ruthless fucking mind as well.

Studying the house, I swallow the fact that my parents' expec-tations were probably so low that their humble ambitions had them living in a home only a fraction of this size. At this point, my brother and I could buy this mansion hundreds of times over without losing an ounce of sleep. Tobias put us in the position to make it possible. If he hadn't taken the risks he has—and still is in France—where the fuck would we be?

Light years behind where we are now. And still, neither of us has a real place we call home to this day.

In the few seconds that pass with these thoughts, I can feel Cecelia's slight hesitation to exit my car, as if she can sense what I'm feeling.

She knows.

Ignoring the second time the whisper crosses my psyche in the last twenty-four hours, I catch her eyes back on me after she exits the car and thanks Tyler. In the brief exchange, remorse again threatens, this time twice as strong as the rest of my known facts about Cecelia flit in.

Like me, she was neglected and sometimes left to fend for herself due to her mother's indulgent taste for variety in bed and bouts with alcoholism. Like me, Cecelia was also stuck raising an adult. A commonality that has me breaking our connection as Tyler bids her a saccharine-filled goodnight.

Even he's not immune to her.

The ink loses again.

And fuck both Sean and Tyler for it.

The ink *exists* because of her father.

Fuck them both for forgetting it.

I'm sure as hell not going to.

Tipping point approaching, I jerk my chin to Tyler. The second he closes his passenger door, I press the gas, fury boiling through me as I catch sight of Cecelia in the rearview, staring, still fucking staring.

"Easy, man," Tyler says as if he's speaking to a rabid canine. "I get that you're pissed off."

"You get nothing," I snap, taking the hard right onto the main road. "What's pathetic is you and Sean both think you have a personal stake in this, but right now, I'm paying the price because, in truth, you fucking *don't*."

"That's not fair, man, and fuck you for saying it. You know—"

"Do yourself a favor and save your speech."

In my peripheral, I see him tense in his seat as I start to drive like I fuck.

"Damnit, Dom, you're not the only one in the fucking car!"

He continues as I floor the gas while he tries to reason with me.

"I know she wasn't part of the plan, and you've been put in a fucked-up position, but this isn't the way to handle it."

He's reaching, and he knows it. Because of Sean, I'm being forced to entertain the daughter of the man who fucking murdered my parents for knowing he was a thief. Pulling back up to the garage, I brake hard, skidding my Camaro to a stop as the gravel kicks back on the body. With a glance toward the building, what's been festering since the moment I laid eyes on Cecelia starts to overflow. Tyler challenges me on that front as I turn to him in a state of rage. "You're going to make me say it?"

"You're too fucking smart for this, Dom."

"It's apparent you're not," I clip. "Get the fuck out."

"I'm not leaving you like this. Just park, hand me the keys, and talk to me."

"I'm not asking."

"He didn't know, Dom."

"What the fuck is going on?" Sean sounds from behind Tyler, alarm in his tone, no doubt for *her*.

Glancing over Tyler's shoulder, I lock eyes with the person closest to me and see red. If I don't leave right fucking now, the damage may be irreparable between us. Sean seems to glimpse it in my expression when Tyler finally exits my car. Sean starts at a dead run, calling my name as I race out of the parking lot.

In the next minute, I go black. It's only when I lose control of the wheel—spinning out in the middle of the road—that I come to, taking control enough to pull over. Stumbling out the driver's door, I find myself in a freshly cropped field as my chest heaves. Staring up at the starless sky above, I pinpoint what set me off.

Sympathizing with my enemy's daughter.

I might have demanded to take her home tonight to further our progress, but Sean brought her in. This has forced me to recognize her as something other than a target.

Seconds or minutes later, I hear the approach and repeat of his Nova and turn in time to see him exit, headlights illuminating him as he reaches back and fists off his shirt.

As he stalks toward me, expression grim, I catch the resignation in his eyes.

He fucking *knew* and *ignored* it.

"Body shots only," he clips, just as I throw everything into my first swing.

SIX

"RENEGADE" BLARES FROM MY WINDOW UPSTAIRS AS I PRESS from the bench in our side yard. Sean joined me minutes ago, wordlessly feeling me out as he started pull-ups. Within a few lifts, I spot the knuckle-sized bruises on his ribs that have already faded to a pale yellow. Regret snakes its way in because I've never lashed out like that, even if we've bruised each other in the past. Those were testosterone-driven scrimmages between punk kids. This time it's different, and I can sense the toll it's taking when I catch his weary expression. I go to speak, and he shakes his head. "Don't. We're good, brother."

Neither of us believes that, but my reply is cut off by the clang of the gate as Tyler enters the yard approaching the two of us. "We've got problems. Fatty got arrested."

Sean drops from the bar as I pause mid-press before pushing up the rest of the way.

"On what charge?" Sean asks, fishing out a cigarette.

"Solicitation of a prostitute," Tyler supplies, disgusted.

Sean gawks. "Pussy? Are you serious? Was he in our fucking van?"

"No," Tyler jerks his head. "So, it's still our secret."

Sean cups the back of his neck, eyeing me. "Thank fuck."

"He wants a meeting," Tyler adds.

"Of course he does," Sean snaps. "What's our other problem?"

He looks between Sean and me. "You know what it is."

Sean's posture stiffens in preparation. "We've already worked this out."

Tyler divides his glare between us. "I did not serve one too many consecutive years in the fucking Marines for the haircut," he barks at me before turning his venom on Sean. "And I damn sure am not going to sacrifice everything we worked for so you can get your dick wet."

Sean shakes his head. "She's not a threat to us, and you know it. I'm being careful. We've gone over this. It's not like I'm going to mark her, but it sure feels like *you're* pissing in circles right now."

Tyler presses in. Apparently, he's just as on edge as Sean and I are. He's bulked up recently, in more ways than one. He's more authoritative now, whereas he used to let a hell of a lot more roll off his shoulders. We've all got our own agendas in carrying out our tasks, and Fatty getting arrested is one fucking complication too many just mere weeks in. Tyler relays as much. "You're asking too much of me on this one. This is going to backfire. And when it happens—"

"*If* it happens," Sean cuts in, "and it won't, and we wouldn't be in this fucked up position," he looks between us, "if you two would have told me."

"You want to chime in here anytime, Dom?" Tyler snaps.

"Rules of war 101, bro. Know your enemy and his weaknesses," I relay to Sean as I set the bar down and lift, wiping my face with my shirt before taking a long drink of water. Looking up, I return Tyler's unwavering stare. "The mouse is already in the trap, man. Not much we can do."

"Oh, I can think of something. Many somethings. It's not too late to—"

"Watch your stream, man," I warn him, temper flaring that I have to remind him of the *why* we can't call France. "Now you're pissing on *me*. Your objection is noted, but, like Sean said, we've already worked it out."

Tyler jerks his head in refusal. "Our window is closing to rectify this. Do I need to point out that one wrong move will fuck us to the point of no return?"

"The fact that we have to defend ourselves to you right now is bullshit," Sean spits, snapping his Zippo closed before pointing his lit smoke toward him. "I'm cut from the same cloth and wear the same ink. I know how far back this goes because when you were doing push-ups and yelling 'hoo-fucking-rah,' I was out on these streets getting our game together. And don't think I didn't see you licking your chops the minute you saw her."

Lit cigarette dangling from his mouth, Sean picks up my dumbbells and begins to do bicep curls. "I know how to separate business and pussy, and I've proven myself *more than once* on that front."

Tyler calls him out on his utter ridiculousness as he does reps with smoke billowing from his mouth. "Need a cheeseburger to go with that heart attack?"

Dropping the dumbbells, Sean takes a deep drag of his cigarette before puffing rings toward Tyler as he issues more warning. "These circumstances are different, and you know it."

"They aren't," Sean argues, "as long as I treat this like they aren't, it's business as usual. And while we're on the subject of pussy, I don't think I'm going out on a limb here when I say you're in *desperate need*, brother."

This time Tyler postures up. "Fuck you."

"I know it's been a while since you've truly mingled with the fairer sex, so I'll clue you in," Sean cups his hands over his nipples in demonstration, "someone a little more petite in stature, fuller hips."

Irritated with the pointless back and forth, I cut my gaze at Tyler. "She's a fucking mouse."

Tyler rears on me. "That mouse is attached to a fucking *mountain lion*."

Sean steps forward to grab Tyler's focus. "You think I'm going to let anything or anyone stand in the way of a decade of planning?" He blows out a breath of frustration as he spotlights the twenty-ton elephant in the yard. "You think I would do *France* dirty? We're handling it."

"Doesn't seem like you're the one handling shit," Tyler asserts, not budging an inch.

"It's better this way," I shrug. "Plans change. We adapt. You know I'm not known for my *sparkle*. Just let pretty boy here do the heavy lifting with her, and I'll take care of the rest."

"That may be the way you run your fucking sex life, but it's not the way to manage this."

Sean's eyes bulge at the low blow meant for me and inches toward Tyler, forever the voice of reason. "That was fucking wrong on so many levels, man. You're completely out of line. You need to start seeing this the way we do—as an opportunity."

Tyler pounces. "You think I'm fucking stupid? I see how you look at her, and it's been *days*. You're no more in control than she is."

Sean's eyes flare in warning. "You're really saying this to me?"

Tyler glares between us, his fear tangible. It's clear then that he thought I would reconsider and call France. I can see him mentally sifting scenarios before stepping back and running a hand through his lengthening hair. Eventually, his expression shifts into one of resignation. "Only for you two. But I swear to God, when this goes south, and it will, you both owe me, and I *will* collect." He glances down at me. "Sorry, man."

I don't bother to reply because I'm too caught up in the fact that Tyler's blatant dig didn't sting as much as it should have, and that instills a sort of fear in me. Have I detached so much from basic human emotion that I'm becoming immune?

Sean's eyes alight, happy with his victory. He rests a crooked elbow on Tyler's shoulder, fingering the shell of his ear. "Now, go fix me some eggs. I find you a lot sexier in the kitchen. And if you play your cards right, I may be willing to take one for the team."

Tyler attempts to shrug him off, a whisper of a smile lifting his lips. "Fuck yourself, mutt."

Sean hooks a forearm around his neck, pulling him in, and Tyler's nostrils flare. "Jesus, you reek."

They both start off toward the back of the house, and Sean glances back at me, giving an exaggerated slow wink as Tyler grits out, "Get. The. Fuck. Off. Of. Me."

"Come on, baby . . . just the tip," Sean coos before they round the corner out of sight.

It's my first genuine smile in a week.

SEVEN

THE SETTING SUN LIGHTS FIRE TO THE SKY, SOAKING MY surroundings in an apocalyptic-looking orange hue as Sean pulls up. He steps out of his Nova in his Horner Tech uniform, using his night shift scheduled lunch hour to deal with our latest setback. Offering him the blunt as he approaches, he takes it as we stand between our cars in the gravel lot in anticipation of Tyler's delivery.

The bay door opens behind us, and seconds later, Russell pulls our newly wrapped Fleet Heating and Air van out of the bay. Jeremy rides shotgun, dressed in his matching uniform, a giddy grin splitting his face.

"Despite some hiccups, that right there is a beautiful thing," Sean muses.

Jeremy and Russell lift their chins to us as they pass with their marching orders for tomorrow—a collection mission to help pay the bills.

"Can't argue there," I say, watching them pull off.

Years ago, we set up several LLCs for all types of inked

technicians to make service calls to scope out locations for future heists. Not only has it helped us micro plan robbing our targets, but it also legitimized the businesses with service calls to avoid the LLCs being suspect once we move in. Since we've pulled the trigger on one of our first brain children, our warehouse is rapidly filling— so much so it's close to the time for a donation.

Sean passes the joint back interrupting my thoughts while bringing me back to the matter at hand. "What's your call on Fatty?"

"You already know the answer to that," I exhale, pissed Fatty is even an issue. Years ago, when I agreed to let him take part in our secrets, I had one reservation. Being privileged, Fatty never had enough skin in the game.

Sean shakes his head in disappointment. "Damn, man, he's been good for business. You know he's loyal. Not to mention he gets the best smoke," he says, taking said smoke back.

"We've got fuses lit everywhere," I remind him. "We can't afford these kinds of fuck ups so early on."

"Why do I get the feeling you're talking about more than Fatty?" His stare hardens, and my lack of reply only pisses him off. "Come on, Dom. I told you the ink will always come first. You, of all people, know I don't need to be checked or chained."

I drop the blunt and run my boot over it. "All right, then tell me how you see this playing out."

"In *our favor*," he claps my shoulder, "always, brother," he assures as Tyler pulls into the garage parking lot with Fatty in tow.

Fatty exits the truck, eyes darting between me and Sean as I take him in. Despite his nickname, he's no more than a hundred and thirty pounds, and that's generous. His pet name is derived from the fact that he always manages to score the best bud and rolls it like it's his business—which he eventually made it—though he's never gone without a day in his fucking life.

That truth is apparent as he's led toward us wearing designer jeans and shoes with a price tag that serves as a bitch slap to half the people in our town struggling daily just to keep the lights on. Sulking as he approaches, he looks every bit the sentenced motherfucker he knows he is due to his epic screwup. Cuffs invisible, but there.

Tyler extends Fatty's phone to me. "He's clean. His password is in your texts."

Opening my Camaro, I toss his phone in my passenger seat as Fatty starts pleading his case to me. "Dom—"

"You had one job," I cut in, tone deaf to any excuse he has prepared. "Tuck and guard the van, and don't draw any attention to it or *yourself*," I relay. "Fucking simple."

"I wasn't in it."

"Should we fucking thank you?" Sean snaps before voicing the question of the hour. "Fatty, what the fuck are you buying pussy for?"

"It wasn't like that man. I didn't even realize—"

Annoyed, I refuse him any time for the jury. "You've been printed. You're of no use to us. As you well know, we *don't associate with criminals*."

His expression lights with hope. "That's just it. My lawyer said we can probably get the charges reduced or dropped altogether because it was my first offense. You can still use me."

"You've been printed. You're out." I relay the verdict, done with the conversation. "No exceptions."

"Come on, Dom. Three fucking years . . . I've given you free green. I've done everything you asked."

"If you had done what I asked, we wouldn't be having this talk."

Fatty turns to Sean, as many so often do.

"Come on, Sean. You know you can trust me."

Sean backs me up, refusing him. "We can't have you close to us, man. Not now. Maybe later on."

I jerk my chin. "Don't fill his head with bullshit." I relay my decision again, temper flaring that he's still appealing his verdict. "You're out. Hope the pussy was worth it."

"Dom, you've known me since fucking high school. You know I'm loyal. Tell me what to do to make things right."

Fisting the collar of his overpriced T-shirt, I slam him against Tyler's truck to ensure he hears me. Tyler objects with an "easy, man," as I glare at Fatty, whose mouth is gaping because I've never been this aggressive with him—never had to be.

"What I need is someone who can follow orders to the fucking letter without putting my entire goddamn family in jeopardy. Do you have any idea how hard we've worked to get to this point? Don't open your fucking mouth, Fatty. That question was rhetorical. The answer is no, you fucking don't. You wouldn't know anything about that, about real purpose, because all you've ever lived up to is your nickname . . . a fucking stoner who has no concept of real responsibility. You think this is a negotiation? It's not. Everyone was counting on you. But you got cocky because, unlike the rest of us, this is just a hobby for you, rich boy. So, what can you do? You can remember I have your father's fortune, your mother's pension, and your baby sister's college fund in the palm of my fucking hand."

Fatty sags in my grip against Tyler's truck. "You don't have to threaten me, Dom. I won't say shit. I know I fucked up. This is on me."

I slam him back into the truck again. "You were saying?"

He swallows, and his eyes flare with the entitled anger I expect from so many like him, but he does the smart thing and keeps that shit close to his chest.

"You're right. Threats aren't necessary, are they, Jonathan Daniel George? So later, when that buzz lifts and you reach for your teddy bear tonight, remember I have your DNA and can use it to ruin your fucking life in a *real* way." Releasing him, I hold his gaze. "Don't forget. We silence bitter baby birds that never make it out of the nest. It would be in your best interest not to smoke that truth out of your memory. Get the fuck away from us and *stay away*."

Sean speaks up to console Fatty as he pulls out his keys. "That was fucking stupid, man. You were so close."

Fatty's reply has me perking up as he opens Tyler's passenger door. "It wasn't like that. *She messaged me*."

I thought as much, and now I have more work to do. Another undertaking to add to my list and, more importantly, a *rogue bird* to hunt.

EIGHT

SIPPING MY MORNING BREW, I EYE THE NASDAQ FEED scrolling at the bottom of my third screen. Satisfied with our portfolio's progress, I type in my last few commands on a new program I designed and fire it off. In seconds, a symphony of characters begins to populate in green across my second monitor. Grin spreading at the sight of it, I mentally pat myself on the back. In the last few hours—due to some digging on our crate discovery—I unintentionally ensnared a local fly whose vibration landed heavily on my web. This had me following him into a chatroom where he made an inquiry. From there, I located his IP address and sent an update for his VPN program. Within a minute, the fly clicked on the bait that I had disguised in the software he believes keeps his web activity hidden but, in reality, gives me access to every single fucking click and command he's ever made.

Homeland Security is a myth. We aren't protected, we're wired, and our behaviors are observed and collected as data to help orchestrate the strategy on how best to manipulate the masses.

The scariest part? It's fucking working.

It's no longer necessary for the CIA to run government experiments using hallucinogens to practice mind control. All they have to do in the present is invent trapdoors within the global technology used by the masses in the day-to-day.

Ironically, the one thing we need protection from is any side of government *we ourselves* are electing to power.

Suspicions confirmed after a few minutes of digging and observation, I decide to monitor this fly closely in the coming weeks—which only adds to my growing task list of things to be dealt with sooner than later. Interference at this point isn't possible due to the ever-increasing list I'm compiling by the day regarding the club and my plans for our future targets. But when the premonition hits hard again, I decide this particular fly will have to take priority at some point.

I log out after tapping into the fly's bank account to alert me when any bulk purchases are made, or any large sums are withdrawn.

My main priority for the moment is to help Tyler uncover Roman's motivation to lure Cecelia here.

A change of heart regarding the relationship with his only heir doesn't seem likely, nor does his regard for her financial future since he's allowed her to live impoverished her whole fucking life. Her forgiveness or desire for any relationship seems unlikely after so many years apart.

Then there's the psychology on Roman's side.

The first factor being his age. Aging men with icy hearts tend to start thawing when reminders of mortality begin to loom. His regret regarding his only child could be the key.

Tyler and I have hashed out this logic in the weeks Cecelia has been here and remain skeptical. Especially since Roman's still relatively young and hasn't had any recent health scares.

And for an arrogant, callous, selfish fuck like Roman, I'm not convinced his motive has anything at all to do with Cecelia. Neither is Tyler.

There's more to this.

Something vital we're missing and have been missing. This is why we're hellbent on making sure the picture we've been painting by numbers over the years to reflect an accurate representation of Roman isn't off by a single digit.

No doubt, Cecelia's just as confused as we are on Roman's motives—eight years too late—but money has always been the greatest of motivators.

The solution is in the problem—the *why*.

In order to get it, we need to tap that fucking house, especially if he's going to be sleeping there on the regular. Though her presence is a serious interference—and after failing to come up with a definitive motive—Sean's part ink, part cock-induced plan might have some merit to it.

My hopes are sitting on all my brothers at this point, both in ink and blood.

Both are disappointing me as of late, and I'm losing faith.

Though this plan can't be rushed, I'll be damned if I don't figure out how to try to expedite the process to suit my timeline. As far as I can see, I'm the only fucking one it's paining—on all fronts—to keep our current speed.

When my phone rumbles, my hopes are dashed that Tobias has returned my text when I see *TATIE* filling the screen, and I reluctantly answer.

♛

Entering the lobby of the garage—after dealing with my aunt for the better part of my day—I'm thankful it's well after close, which gives me the privacy I need without raising other birds' suspicions. Heading toward my toolbox in the commercial bay, I stop when I spot Cecelia spread out on the couch, book lifted and obstructing her view of me. It's clear she hadn't heard my approach due to the earbuds she's wearing and the way she's sprawled out. Cheeks flushed, chest heaving, it's then I get why. Whatever she's reading has her fucking aroused, and I suspect seconds away from rubbing one out. Tempted to sit back and watch it happen for the ability to further fuck with her, my annoyance with her invasion wins and has me stalking toward her.

Cecelia catches sight of me as I near and jackknives, pulling her earbuds out as she sputters an explanation as to why she's here. "I'm n-not alone. I mean, I am right *now*. S-Sean just went to grab a pack of cigarettes and beers with the guys."

Eyeing the print size of the book to avoid looking at her, I realize the garage isn't the only one of my safe havens she's invaded recently.

"Where did you get that?" I ask, glowering at her from where I stand at the end of the couch. She nervously crosses her toned legs at the ankles, no longer at ease.

Good. She shouldn't be so fucking comfortable in any of my spaces.

Glancing down at her book, a barely-there smile lifts her lips before she speaks. "The library. I checked it out the other day and snuck out another. It's kind of a tradition." I'm all too aware of her little tradition. She was taking part in it the first time I saw her— which was supposed to be the last. Right now, I fucking hate the fact that it wasn't.

"Stupid fucking tradition considering the books are *free* . . . and the library is off limits," I growl, knowing what a fucking idiot I sound like. "Also, this is not a community playground, despite what Sean might have told you. Find somewhere else to *spread out*," I spit, eyeing the scrap of fabric she's excusing as a dress.

She scoffs. "You're seriously saying the *public library* is yours?"

"The whole fucking town is mine, Cecelia."

Her perfect features distort into anger, intensifying her beauty as she stands quickly, losing grip on the hardback, which lands with a *thwack* on the floor behind her. Turning to retrieve it, she bends at the waist, inadvertently giving me a show. Between tanned, toned thighs, I spot a strip of cobalt blue panties. The thin material shifts with her movement giving me a peek of her pussy as she painstakingly bends inch by inch to retain some modicum of modesty and fails. Inwardly groaning, I keep my gaze fixed where it shouldn't be as she rethinks her strategy. Bending at the knees, she palms the couch to stay upright, back ramrod straight as I clear the other side of the coffee table and snatch it up before she reaches it.

Eyeing the title, *The Bronze Horseman*, I smirk and look up at her, making sure my exhale hits the gap between her thighs as I slowly stand, palming the couch and mimicking her ridiculous movement. "Might want to return the eight-year-olds dress you borrowed if you plan on spending time in a place filled with heavy machinery. Then again, don't bother. This particular stop won't be frequent for you."

"You're like a dark cloud. You know that? Can't spot a single sun ray for shit with you hovering."

"Just so long as we're clear."

"That you're an entitled, raging prick," she utters under her breath, "we're *crystal*."

Bending to eye level—the tips of our noses close to brushing—her deep blues dilate as I invade her space. "Assume what you will about me, or better yet," I press the book into her heaving chest, and her glossy pink lips part. "Stick with your bullshit fantasies of virtuous heroes in a nonexistent reality. You're much safer *there*."

Turning, I grab what I need to fill my toolbox before stalking out the side door. Every hair on my body stands on end as I adjust the hard-on straining against my zipper. Once again, I've been forced away from my second home in order to avoid more exposure to her and the way she stares at me—too fucking much, for too fucking long. At first, it seemed innocent enough and served its purpose. Now it's grating on me because no matter how many times I avoid her curious stare, I eventually look back at her. When I do, I'm re-minded of why I've been avoiding her for the few weeks she's been here—a reason my body no longer refuses to ignore.

The need to fuck her.

More than that, I want to do it in a way that punishes Sean's prized new pet while making an example out of her, so he finally gets the goddamned memo.

Sean's smitten, it's obvious to everyone, and it's just a matter of time before he fucks her—if he hasn't already. But soon, he'll be made aware of just how much he fucked up. No matter how perfect our enemy's daughter is—and I can admit that much—she's getting in the way of our agenda and, more importantly, our friendship.

Even if she's nothing more than a defenseless mouse caught in a trap we didn't set, she's got Roman's blood pumping in her veins. I'll make it a point to make fucking sure Sean starts to see it that way because his assurances are getting weaker by the day.

Stalking through the graveyard of cars at the back of our shop, I spot the one I have in mind. I head over to it, pissed I didn't drag a shop light out with me as the sun threatens to set—the need to keep my distance taking precedence.

With Cecelia, I don't like who I am or the effect she has on me when we're around each other.

She's a rare type of flame far too close to my fuse—which is shortening by the day, some because of her invasion, most of it due to the constant nightmares looping in my mind.

Despite my actions, I take little pleasure in how I've treated her. Like Tobias, I see women as innocent bystanders of our cause. This makes them an inconvenience after we use them for our selfish purposes—which is why I don't hook up often. My progression in that department is stunted because of what I have to offer—what I've always had to offer when it comes to women—*nothing*.

At this point, it's about protection. Cecelia's allure is just as fucking dangerous to us as it is to her. Opening the hood of the Buick, I add another task to my list—to prove it to Sean before she does.

NINE

"**A**N ALARMING NUMBER OF WAREHOUSE ROBBERIES HAVE taken place in downtown Charlotte in the last three days, costing freight shipping mogul, Anthony Spencer of Export Execs an estimated 1.8 million dollars in merchandise," the radio anchor reports as I pull up to the warehouse.

Idling in my Camaro, I scan our bustling compound as the reporter drones on. "Authorities believe that Spencer is being directly targeted, but the police have no leads at this time. They ask if anyone has any information—"

Killing the engine, I exit as Peter backs his Fleet van into the warehouse next to Jeremy's, which is being unloaded to add Spencer's merch to our stock of goods.

Loaded dollies are carted toward the warehouse as Denny stops them taking inventory before they're hauled in. Russell pulls the last van up as satisfaction runs through me, and I shoot off a text to Tyler in wait for Sean.

All birds safely in the nest.

Jeremy exits the driver's side of his van and makes his way toward me, pride evident in his eyes. Peter is on his heels, and his expression is lit with the same sentiment. It's earned because it's one of Peter's first major scores while being a part of our secret.

"Where's Sean?" I glance back at the open security gate.

"Cecelia asked him to teach her how to drive, and they took off," Jeremy supplies stalking toward where I stand just outside my driver's door. "We grabbed the vans and came just after . . . but did you see her in that fucking dress? I don't think I'd show up for roll call if I had *that ass* in my driver's seat, either."

Russell joins us with Peter on his heels, both seemingly just as high from the take—as they should be. Everything we stole was lifted without sounding a single fucking alarm until after the fact.

Just after, each bird drove the loaded vans to different safe houses to lay low for a few days until we could get them here without detection. Just in case they were spotted in conjunction with the robberies and suspicions were raised.

The extra steps are necessary since the local police are still in Roman's palms due to years of overgenerous contributions. But our time is coming. This latest long-awaited egg is finally hatching as Sean resumes digging at Horner Tech—inevitably coming up as empty as he did the first time he worked there.

To me, we're continually beating a dead horse with that route. Any evidence of Roman's cover-up was no doubt destroyed and swept up the night my parents perished in that fire. So, while Sean being back at Tech is a waste of time, all isn't lost because his current station has him keeping an easy watch on Cecelia.

It's Roman's chokehold on her regarding her inheritance that's making it hard for Sean to gain full access to the house. Roman berated her by email on day two for having Sean over, stating that visitors are to be kept to a minimum. We've decided not to press it because we don't want him investigating the company she's keeping.

In the last few days, I've made peace with the fact that Cecelia will be more of a fixture at our garage until the right opportunity strikes. That was until Sean decided to invite her *tonight* of all fucking nights—prolonging our delivery to the warehouse. Which is why we were having words before *and after* she rolled up.

For now, we have no choice but to allow her into our space and mix her in where we can. This means exposing her to *all of us* and keeps her curious, noticing too much for my comfort.

Which reminds me . . .

"You hear the news?" Jeremy boasts, stepping up to me as I eye the ski mask still hanging from his back pocket. "It's every-fucking-where, and they don't have shit."

"The news," I nod, "Yeah, okay, let's start there."

Jeremy's brows pull in confusion, as does Peter's, and Russell stiffens when I turn to him and hold my index finger at eye level.

"What are you doing?" Jeremy asks, darting his eyes between me and Russell, a goofy grin plastered on his face.

"Think of my finger as the news, Jeremy," I utter, moving my pointer back and forth just in front of Russell's nose. His eyes follow, his own expression confounded.

"Watching the news, Jeremy?" I snap, slowly running my finger back and forth along Russell's line of sight.

"Yep," Jeremy says. His quick reply is jovial, as if he's in on my joke.

I run it past Russell one last time and hold it before sucker-punching Jeremy with my free fist.

"Mderfucker!" Jeremy grips his nose as Russell and Peter burst into surprised laughter.

"Da fuck, Dom?!" Jeremy groans, tone muddled, eyes watering.

"See what happens when you pay attention to the *diversion* instead of what's going on in your own fucking *reality?*"

Jeremy examines his bloody fingers. "You could have used a different tactic to get your point across, *dickhead.*"

"I could have," I say, snatching the ski mask from his back pocket and holding it out to him to reiterate my point, "but now you know *why I didn't.*"

Guilt-filled eyes lift to mine as he draws the conclusion intended.

Cecelia spotted the ski mask hanging out of his back pocket earlier while they were shooting pool and spoke up about it. A conversation I hadn't gotten to have with him yet, and just made unnecessary. Even if Jeremy played it off expertly, it drew more suspicion from her.

"Sorry, man," Jeremy grits out, "I fucked up."

"You think?" I draw out in monotone.

"Won't happen again, hand to God, man. My fucking bad."

"Yeah, next time, leave the fucking uniform at home, especially when you didn't even need it . . . and you know *who* the news is controlled by," I remind him. "You're better off believing conspiracy theorists at this point. At least there's some merit there."

"So, Tupac is alive and well and living in Cuba?" Jeremy snarks.

"You know better because they exterminate all the truth tellers."

"You Nostradamus now?" Jeremy antagonizes due to his swelling nose and battered pride.

Stepping into his space as he retreats, I command his gaze. "Yeah, I'm a prophet, and here's my prediction. When those doling out the selected forecast have everyone panicking about the price of an apple and a tank of gas so they can sneak more control through proposed legislation—having already taken freedoms *fought for and won decades ago*—we're all fucked." I palm his chest and lightly shove him. "That's why *we* can't get too cocky or parade around like idiots. There's too much at stake."

He nods, wiping his nose with his mask as I put him in a headlock and roughly knuckle his scalp. "And we already *know* they don't have shit." Breaking my hold, Jeremy looks over to me, eyes assessing as I give him due props. "Other than your shitty oversight, you did good."

His expression lights up at my rare praise before I turn to Russell and Peter, "you too."

Peter beams as he looks over the dollies full of merch being unloaded by recruits as Russell utters a low "thanks," seemingly lost in his thoughts.

Pun intended, Russell is a rare bird who's no doubt still mulling over my words. He's made it clear his goal is to run his own chapter at some point, so he's always paying careful attention to our words, actions, and strategies—especially mine. Of all our circle, he and I have the most in common.

Like me, Russell comes from a family of immigrants who came to the US to seek a piece of the illusion. His mother was born and raised Japanese; his father was a military brat raised on the Yokota Airbase. The second his dad was of age, he married Russell's mother and brought her back to the States to seek his piece of the American dream. What Russell's dad failed to realize—by not reading the fine print—is that if you gain sudden fortune of any kind, it better be in the *multi*-millions. Because once Uncle Sam is flagged, he'll be coming for his portion, which is only a few percentage points short of the lion's share. And if you spend your American Uncle's money, he becomes a loan shark, and if you don't pay, the reimbursement is freedom. The judge made an example out of Russell's dad, leaving him fatherless for most of his formative years. We're a lot alike in that Russell is also more of a man of action and rarely feels comfortable saying more than a few sentences unless he's surrounded by us—his *chosen* family.

Looking over at Jeremy and Peter, I can feel the excitement of what's brewing between us, all growing up in similar circumstances. Feral kids with no one looking for or calling us home while we did the best we could with our dealt hands.

Jeremy sniffs, his nostrils coated in red as remorse kicks in for the shit I just pulled. He's bound to fuck up here and there, as we all are until he can fly solo. Same as Peter, whose fresh ink is in the midst of scabbing over.

Tyler enlisted Peter in a jail cell the cops had locked him in, in the hope it would scare him straight. He was an unprinted juvenile on the verge of a life of crime—which made him a prime candidate for us. What the cops didn't know or care to recognize is that an empty stomach is a major fucking motivator. Peter had turned to thieving to keep the electricity on in the sad excuse of a trailer he resided in—which Tyler had relayed 'had a gaping hole in the floor.'

His short stint in burglary was an attempt to feed his infant sister after his abusive Dad bailed.

Glancing between the three of them, I hate the fact that we have these particulars in common. Unlike Fatty, the birds surrounding me have major skin in the game. And it's our job—*my job*—to ensure any mistakes made at this point are few and reversible, and I've barely had a spare second to put the time in with any of them since I got back to Triple.

"Get some rest. We're just getting started," I warn, pulling out my keys.

"Where you off to?" Jeremy asks, sucker punch forgiven.

"Shit to do." More importantly, a *bird* to find.

"Hey, Dom," Peter speaks up, hesitation evident before he lifts a shame-filled gaze to mine. "In our haul, I saw some coloring books and—"

"Take it," I say, looking between the three of them. "Take whatever you want or need. Just make sure you log it with Denny."

"Thanks, man," Peter says, eyes alight, heading toward the compound with Jeremy. Russell hesitates before turning.

"Something on your mind, man?" I call to his back.

He stops his retreat into the building and glances back at me.

"I'm just . . . thanks, Dom."

"It's what we do," I tell him. "Remember that if guilt-induced insomnia hits anytime soon."

His lips lift. "Trust me. It won't."

"Good to hear."

We share a grin before he turns to head inside. Watching him walk away to join the others in celebration, a sense of pride floods me.

It's working.

We're taking care of our own. It's no longer planning and daydreaming about our future. We're living it. All of the plotting and the effort to get to this point is proving worth it. Deciding a celebratory blunt is in order, and that there's only one bird I want to share it with, I check my phone to see Sean hasn't responded to my text. All hopes of celebrating with him dashed as I pull up the tracking app attached to his Nova to see he's parked on some dead-end backroad.

No big fucking mystery as to what he's doing—Cecelia.

Behind the wheel, I fire up my car as my phone rumbles, a text from Tyler filling my screen.

T: Got a bite on the line.

A little weight eases from my shoulders as I reply—at least Tyler's focused.

By all means, reel it in.

TEN

THE FOLLOWING NIGHT, SEAN STANDS JUST OUTSIDE HIS DRIVER'S door, his phone to his ear. I kick back against my Camaro in wait, scanning the towering mountains in the pitch-black sky. He coos into the phone, catching my gaze before giving me a drawn-out wink. "You know I could tuck you in *properly* if you'd let me."

Uninterested in his performance—which seems to be for my benefit—I jerk my chin to get him to hurry it along so we can get to work.

"Agree to disagree," Sean replies, ignoring my prompt. "You never did tell me about your dream this morning."

He waits patiently for her response. "I haven't given you enough already? Ouch. You're going to pay for that . . . me too. See you to-morrow. Night, Pup."

Sean clips his phone closed before locking it into his Nova, his other hand holding the Glock he's had trained on Clint since I pulled up.

Tyler found our dirty bird.

It took a few days to lure Clint in after Tyler set the trap, but Sean stepped in, taking responsibility once Tyler identified him.

Clint whimpers, kneeling at our feet, looking every bit the strung-out junkie he is. Lit by our collective headlights, his sunken eyes dart around as he tries to construct an adequate excuse to help him out of his current situation.

Sean rips off the masking tape that's muffling Clint. When I step forward, Sean gives me an adamant shake of his head. "This is on *me*."

I dip my chin, though I'm dying to unleash. But rules are rules, and when it comes to Sean's own recruits, it's his call. Sean kneels in front of Clint, casually draping the gun on his thigh. "You thought we wouldn't find out, Clint? Is that what you thought?"

Clint—already on the verge of sobbing—speaks up, "I j-just n-needed—"

"Oh, I know what you needed," Sean snaps. "It's one thing to poison yourself to the point you got cut out of secrets. It's another entirely to spread that poison." Sean leans in. "Think we wouldn't pinpoint how Fatty got pinched and printed? Did you think we would kick him out and leave it there? You yourself should know that we don't half-ass anything. That's how we keep our secrets."

Sean pulls a prescription bottle from his pocket and shakes it in front of Clint's face. "You know what that sound is, Dom?"

"What's that?"

Sean obnoxiously shakes the bottle in a taunt. "That's a junkie's mating call."

Spittle runs from Clint's mouth as he speaks. "I'll get clean. I'll do whatever you want."

"Hear that, Dom?" Sean snaps with disgust. "He'll do whatever we want. His girlfriend OD's three weeks ago and barely survives, but *this* is his wake-up call." Sean uncaps the bottle before balancing the small pill on the tip of his finger, and Clint's eyes follow. "You got hooked and poisoned everyone around you. But then you lost your spot with us and your respect. No bird wanted to deal with you or let you in on their secrets, so you took it upon yourself to sell Fatty out to steal from your own . . . I'm going to give you one fucking chance to confirm what I already know."

Clint nods and sniffs. "Fatty and I were smoking a spliff at his place a few days before," his expression falters, as do his words, as the fear of his confession eats at him.

Sean dips his chin as Clint sputters out the rest.

"I-I-spotted one of the vans at his place. It was under a tarp, but I knew what was going down because I'd done the service calls in the past, and I'd been trying to get in on it . . ." he harshly exhales, closing his eyes as Sean presses the Glock to his forehead.

"And?"

"No one would let me ride passenger, so I scoped Fatty's house waiting on him to leave. I wasn't going to take it all, just a little off the top . . . I swear."

Sean shoots him a withering stare, fed up with his hesitation.

"But h-he wouldn't leave the van, so I got him distracted . . . I-I knew the girl and offered her some money, but I didn't know she would get popped *that night* . . .," he shakes his head, "that was pure fucking coincidence. I didn't mean for him to get picked up. I was trying to buy time to get some merch to sell. You've got to believe me, man. I wouldn't—"

Sean presses the Glock in harder so Clint's head is forced back a few inches. "You fucking did. And Fatty lost his chance at getting inked in the process. That's so fucking cold, man. Must've stung when you found the van empty. You cost us a decent bird with that bullshit."

Sean sighs, looking over at me as Clint sputters more meaningless apologies.

"I'm so fucking sorry, Sean."

"The saddest part is—that *knowing how we work*—you thought you might get away with it." Sean nods toward me, and I grip Clint's head as Sean forces him to take a pill.

Clint gasps before Sean clamps his mouth closed, uncapping a water and forcing Clint to drink and swallow. Sean taps out another pill, and Clint fearfully eyes the bottle. As Sean moves in, Clint holds up his bound wrists in a useless attempt to protect himself.

"S-Sean, please. I can't."

"What? Don't like OXY anymore? Isn't this what you were going to steal from your brothers for?"

Clint looks up at Sean, his expression pathetic. "Sean—"

"Stop saying my fucking name. You think I don't know the psychology in that? You think it's going to change my mind? Make me think twice?"

Sean exhales slowly in disappointment. "I know you're flesh and bone. I know you consist of heart and soul. But yours went in the wrong direction. It's way too late to plead your case. Open up." Sean force-feeds Clint another pill and caps the bottle before standing and lighting a cigarette. Snapping his Zippo closed, he runs his thumb along his lower lip as he weighs his next words.

"Goddamnit, man. I don't fucking enjoy this, Clint. None of us do, but your junkie judgment had you ignoring one of the most important fucking rules and betraying the promise inked on your skin, and we can't let that go. You know that."

He drags off his smoke, posture resigned. "This is so much more important than me or you—than any of us. I took you under my wing. I gave you everything I had, and you do me like this? The rules are simple. No drugs, no guns, and no innocents. We don't buy, trade, or sell people, and we sure as fuck don't sell out our *own*, but you were willing to barter your own brother to get a fucking fix."

Clint shakes his head in denial as I approach from behind and cock my own gun, pressing it to the back of his greasy head. "I wonder if anyone will miss him."

Clint screams in protest. "Wait! Wait!"

Sean looks over to me. "Should we wait, Dom? He's already picked his poison, haven't you, Clint? Over yourself, over the people you love, over your fucking brothers."

Clint attempts to hang his head, and Sean fists his hair, forcing his gaze back up. "No, man. Nobody gets to fuck me with their eyes closed."

"Sean, I'll fix this. I'll get better."

Sean's eyes deaden, and I know playtime is over when he speaks up. "It's funny that you're pleading with *me*. And I get it," he gestures toward me. "Dom looks like a menacing motherfucker, but *me*? I paint a different picture and mostly represent it until you fuck with what matters to me most and well . . ." Sean tosses his cigarette down and grinds it out with his boot before uncapping the bottle and palming another pill, his expression lethal, ". . . this is where I start looking scary."

Clint opens his mouth with a soundless gasp, spittle running down the sides before Sean forces another pill into his mouth. Clint spits it out, choking out his pleas. "F-fuck man, p-please. You know me."

"Thought I did," Sean says, tilting his head. "Are you even salvageable, Clint? I guess that's the question being posed now, right? Good from bad, right or wrong. Are you the bad guy, or am I? Maybe I'm both. But I'm the one who brought you in, and therefore you are my responsibility. Clearly, my judgment was skewed, and your fucking memory is lacking because you forgot that when you fuck with one of us, you fuck *with all of us*. Time's up."

Clint's eyes widen in horror as Tyler pulls up in *his* car and exits, dressed like midnight, ball cap pulled low. Tightening black gloves on his fingers, Tyler takes a spot next to me as Sean shakes the bottle in front of Clint's face to regain his attention.

"How many is too many?" He leers at Clint. "Should we play roulette with your life the way you did with my club? Wouldn't want you to miss your fix, open up." Sean shoves the pill in Clint's mouth, and Clint again spits it out as he sputters useless apologies. "I'm sorry. I'm so fucking sorry. I didn't mean for it to go this far."

Sean scoffs. "Tell that to Fatty. Hope this high is the lowest you ever get, man. I truly do. How will I ever be able to trust you with that ink again?"

Tyler steps forward, his expression void of all emotion as he stares down at Clint in full executioner mode.

Clint's eyes light, hope in his tone. "I can p-prove it. In m-my glovebox is my second burner. You'll see my text to her. You'll see the whole conversation. I didn't talk to anyone else. It was just me and her, I swear. And all I offered her was money. She never knew *why*."

"You better fucking pray it's enough," Sean spits, exhausting the last of his wrath.

Tyler reads Sean's budding inner struggle and nudges him aside. "Let me take it from here."

Sean replies with a nod as Clint screams for him while Tyler drags him to the passenger side of the Honda before shoving him into the passenger seat. Retrieving the phone from the glove box, Tyler hands it to me, and I pocket it. At Clint's driver's door, Tyler glances between the two of us as Clint's screams echo to us, muted by the snap of the car door before Tyler pulls away.

Sean's Zippo sounds, and I turn to see him scrubbing his face before cursing and hanging his head. I step up to him, knowing his conscience will eat away at him in the days to come.

"This is war, brother," I remind him. "First fucking battle of many."

"I know, man. I get it, and we're counting on the loyalty of the one variable we can't control . . . *people*." His statement lingers, resonating with so much fucking truth as he looks over to me, the toll of what just transpired clear in his posture.

"I was so sure about him, and now . . ." he looks back toward Clint's retreating car. Sean's always believed intuition is his greatest gift, and I don't correct him, because, in that respect, he's impeccable at deciphering the good eggs from bad. He can read people easily, anticipate their needs and manipulate them for our benefit if necessary. The truth is, he's an empath to his core. His kryptonite is that he feels every part of what just happened . . . while I can remain objective and detached. This situation won't affect me a second after I drive away, but Sean won't forget it anytime soon. He'll lose sleep over Clint's fate and carry the weight with him.

"Do you believe him?" I ask as he exhales a long stream of smoke.

"It doesn't matter if I do, does it?"

For Sean's sake, I find myself hoping what Clint gave us is enough as we stand side by side, watching his taillights fade until they disappear.

ELEVEN

"**I**'M HEADING OUT," SEAN UTTERS LOW, TOTING AN overstuffed laundry bag down the stairs as I refill my coffee cup. He searches my expression for a verdict on Clint, and I shake my head in response that I don't have one yet.

My guess is that his excursion for clean clothes is his excuse to escape club business for the day. He's been sulking since we watched Clint's taillights disappear a few nights ago. He hit the bottle hard when the headline popped up of a local missing man whose car was found in a busy shopping center. I decide to make it a priority to let him know one way or another as soon as I've done my due diligence. As often as Sean and I have collectively pulled the trigger on the deserving, it's completely different when a fellow bird's fate is at stake.

"Want some help?"

At the front door, he tosses a hesitant look my way, and I gather that he's already got help lined up. Dipping my chin, I give him the out he needs. If he wants to bury his grief and dick in Cecelia, it's his prerogative. When he opens his mouth to speak some useless excuse, I wave him off. "I've got shit to do."

He pauses just after he opens the front door, searching for words that might mean something to me. Just after he realizes they won't, the door snaps shut behind him.

Taking the stairs two at a time after a late shift at the garage, intent on returning to my passion project, I stop mid-step when a raspy moan reaches me. Through the rails at the top, I find the source pinned to the small patch of wall at the end of the hall between Sean and Tyler's bedroom doors. Head thrown back, eyes closed, one of her legs is draped over Sean's bare shoulder as he greedily eats her pussy.

My blood simmers at the sight of it. Just as I predicted, Sean medicated his feelings with Cecelia. In his decision to drown in her, he also opened his bed and our fucking home, which changes things. Fury starts to boil just beneath my skin as I speculate about his motivation. Sean's Nova wasn't in the drive when I rolled up, and neither was hers, so how the fuck did they get here?

My guess is Tyler, who probably dropped them off and had sense enough to leave just after.

Sean had to have heard me pull up, but by the way he's eagerly feeding, he might not have. It's Cecelia's cries that break up my circling theories when she grips Sean's hair and starts to buck against his mouth. Eyes still firmly shut, Sean pulls back, tilting his head up at her while spearing her with his fingers, giving me a glimpse of her exposed flesh.

My cock jerks at the sight of it, of the ecstasy etched on her face. Blood pounds in my ears as the rest gathers below. No matter how much I want to, I can't fucking look away—so I don't. Knowing that if her eyes open, she'll catch me, I remain where I stand as she gets lost in Sean's coaxing.

"Want to come, Pup?" Sean utters, his voice coated in lust.

"Please," she whimpers as he coats his fingers with her arousal before massaging her as she bucks into his hand.

Sean dives back in, and Cecelia erupts, face flushing as she pants out his name, her thigh shaking around his head as she digs her bare heel into his back. The sight and sound of her coming unleashes a desperate fucking need inside me. Hairs rising on the back of my neck, my angry dick pulses in my jeans, demanding attention, and I refuse it.

Unshackling myself, I hit the bottom of the stairs just as Sean's door closes. Paralyzed where I stand, Cecelia's muffled moans resume from behind it. Senses acute, my cock threatens a revolt as I catch the sound of the running refrigerator along with the tick of a tiny clock on a nearby shelf.

Refusing to entertain the obnoxious throb in my jeans, I stalk toward the sliding door and into the side yard. I glance around as if something nearby might bring me some relief.

Taking the bench seat, I lift the bar and start a dead press. Mentally warring, I continue to press in an effort to erase the images of her lust-covered features—the sight of her landing strip and dripping pussy, and the fucking sounds that came out of her as she orgasmed.

Even if he wanted me to see it—to face my attraction for her—he couldn't have manipulated the timing that much.

Then again, we're masters at deception.

Sean doesn't do anything without thinking it through. Maybe he's fighting her effect on him, desperate to believe the lies he's telling—and losing. Perhaps this once, when it comes to her, he doesn't have the fucking answer.

None of us do.

Instinct guides my every move and decision at this point in my life. Always has. It was not until I reached adulthood that I could fully recognize it for what it is. As faithfully as I follow, I sometimes wish it was more subtle. It's anything but—always thrumming through me with unexplainable force while, at times screaming at me to obey. Refusing to give me any fucking peace.

Like now, as I'm roused from a much-needed dead sleep with the familiar inkling that I'm being watched, and without opening my eyes, by who.

That knowledge jolts me alert, and my eyes pop open to see her standing just outside the guest bathroom. Even feet away, it's easy to make out the lust in her expression. Seeing she's just as turned on as she was hours ago, I remain motionless, conveniently but unintentionally spread out for her viewing pleasure.

Taking her time, she soaks in every bared inch of me before settling her gaze on my cock. A cock that's already betraying me as it stirs at the sight of her looking freshly fucked, lips swollen, wearing nothing but Sean's T-shirt.

Her own alarm bells kick off as she senses my stare just before her desire-filled blue eyes fly to mine and widen. The now familiar electricity passes between us, my answering stare full of dare as I flick my gaze to my cock. A cock that now stands full fucking mast. I lift my chin a fraction just as she sputters out an apology before scurrying away like . . . a fucking mouse.

As Sean's door quietly closes due to Cecelia's hasty retreat, I can't help but feel for the son of a bitch for his latest bold move. Intentional or not, he's been baiting me with her since she got here. It's past time for his wake-up call and hers.

Gloves off, sweetheart.

TWELVE

"**C**HA-CHING."

The ping jars me from the image of Cecelia running her hands along my dick when we faced off in the kitchen yesterday. I'd done my worst, and even in doing it, the hum of attraction was there, only strengthening with our latest sparring match. This one heavily incited by me. She'd given just as good as she got, but Sean's latest test backfired in the end. He'd purposely left her in my path, again, and failed to make his point, again. She's nowhere near ready or has the strength to endure the trials of being in our world. The more he tries, the more his efforts have proven futile.

The Dead Sergeants ring out through my earbuds as I eye the new balance in our piggy bank. Scanning the Nasdaq feed when the exchange opens for the day, the local news simultaneously pops up, streaming on another screen. Satisfaction thrums through me when I search for and discover Spencer's company stock is plummeting according to plan. Once we've gathered enough evidence to bury him for the guns we found at the warehouse, it's RIP for Spencer and onto the next target. Just as I think it, my phone rattles with an incoming text from Tyler.

T: Meet you at the garage.

Annoyance flares when I catch another whiff of the fucking carrot cake Cecelia plastered to my head yesterday, and I decide another shower is in order. Moving to push away from my desk, I pause when I catch a headline flash across the screen.

LOCAL WOMEN'S SHELTER RECEIVES A STAGGERING DONATION.

Killing the streaming music, I turn up the volume just as the anchor cues the reporter on site.

"I'm standing outside "Chance Two Woman's Shelter" with director Loretta Dawson, where just days ago, an anonymous donor had a truck delivered. The truck was filled to the brim with supplies and non-perishables that will stock their pantry well through the new year. An unexpected but much-needed donation. Can you tell us a little more about that, Loretta?"

Sean's old Sunday school teacher steps up, a mix of nerves and excitement in her expression. *"When the truck pulled up, we were just blown away. We've received some generous donations in the past, but nothing of this magnitude. We were close to shutting our doors even after our annual fund-raiser last month. We're so thankful to whoever found it inside themselves to gift us the ability to keep the shelter going and potentially change dozens of women's lives."*

Satisfied, I lower the volume before cracking my neck and pushing away.

Muscles screaming due to pulling another all-nighter, I dread the long hours ahead. Heading toward the bathroom, my personal cell buzzes in my hand. Pissed it's not my brother—who's left my last two texts asking for a call unanswered—dread blankets me when BLUE RIDGE MEDICAL fills my screen.

In the bathroom, I study the dark half-moons under my eyes in the mirror as I answer. "Hello?"

"Dominic King?"

"This is he."

"I'm sorry to call so early. It's just that your . . ." I hear the flip of a page, "Aunt Delphine. Well . . . she's early for her chemo appointment and in no state to drive herself home."

Cupping the back of my head, I inhale a deep breath for patience. "How early?"

With her reply, I scrub my jaw. "Can you keep her there? I can be there in an hour."

Hearing the woman panic at what's sure to be the longest fucking hour of her life, I thank her and hang up before starting my shower. Once stripped, I palm the tiles, letting the water rain down my back as I close my eyes. "Jesus Christ."

It's the only prayer I can muster.

Somewhat revived after a brisk, cold rinse, I pull on my King's tee before kicking into my boots. Taking the stairs with what little energy I have, I'm halfway down when Sean glances up from where he stands behind the kitchen island—the news still running on the living room TV. "See it?"

I nod as he grabs a mug from the cabinet, scouring me as he pours me a cup before pushing it over the island in offering.

"Another all-nighter?"

I grunt, taking a hearty sip before the bitching commences.

"Need you whole, man. Can't keep burning the candle at both ends."

"I don't see anyone else around here capable of handling my workload, my way, and someone has to organize the mess that was left for me."

"According to your impossible standards," he snarks. "Did we really fuck up so badly holding the fort down while you were in Boston?"

"You feeling needy?" I ask between sips. "Want a compliment?"

"If I'm in need of anything or *anyone* right now, it's not you. By the way, thanks for fucking that up for me. She snuck out last night without a word and won't text me back this morning."

I lift my cup in salute. "Anytime."

"So, it was intentional."

"As intentional as you leaving her here yesterday without playing guard dog." I shrug. "Maybe you didn't drill your point into her good enough with your little make up fuck."

"I believe you heard evidence to the contrary."

"You're confusing me with someone who gives a damn. I've got more important shit to deal with right now than your fuck life."

"Say what you will, man, but even with Tyler on our collective asses, *you're* the one currently sabotaging progress."

"She needs to know her place."

"I understand why this is hard on you, but you can't keep holding her ignorance against her when she doesn't know what you're really about. If you'd give her half a goddamn chance, I think she'll surprise you." He palms the counter. "If you're honest with yourself, she already has."

"You understand?" I walk around and stare out of the kitchen window, scanning the cloud-covered mountain ridge beyond our backyard. "Yeah, I don't think you do."

"Then we need to talk about this."

"What we need to do is get to the fucking garage. Tyler's waiting."

Sean sets his cup in the sink next to me as I dump mine in a travel mug, grabbing the pot and filling it to the brim before capping it. Sean turns to me, and even as pissed as he is, his expression leaks with concern.

"Want me to drive you?"

"I'm good."

He bites his lip ring briefly before pinning me. "Are *we* good?"

He tries to get a read on me as I duck my head and grab my keys—over the Cecelia conversation altogether. "What do you want to hear?"

"The fucking truth. I'm not going to lie to you. There's potential there, not just for me, but for us, collectively long term."

I pause the travel mug at my lips. "Now you're thinking long term?"

"Isn't that the point of this? I see it in her, and I think you're pissed you can see it too."

"I see a mouse."

"Whatever, have it your way. If you wanted me to back off, you've made your point crystal fucking clear. Just so you know, you could have saved us all the dramatics and just told me outright."

"My fist didn't clue you in?"

He runs a hand through his scattered hair, perplexed. "I thought we fucking settled this."

"We did. Not my problem she couldn't hack it. It was your little experiment that went awry. That's on you."

"Right. Fuck it." Sean pulls his keys out and turns to leave, and I glance back out of the window to the world that awaits. A world I want no fucking part of if I can't play the role I want to within it. That's where Sean comes in. He's been my liaison to the outside well before my perpetual state of unrest. While the rest of my brothers remain focused on their agendas, Sean's always kept my back first and foremost. Even if his current motives with Cecelia are fucking selfish and asking a lot, he won't betray me when it matters most. Of that much, I'm certain. "We're good."

He pauses and studies me for sincerity. "You mean that?"

I do. Even if he's decided to make Cecelia a hobby, Sean doesn't do long-term. Whatever he has brewing with her will fizzle out one way or the other. So, what do I give a fuck if he's getting something personally out of it? It's part of who he is and what he needs. Something I've never identified with but always understood about him. If he's going to be distracted by any woman, who better than the one that will lead us closer to destroying Roman?

"Yeah, Romeo," I quip. "But just so you know, she's just another in a long line of Rosalines."

"Think what you will, but I'm straight up telling you otherwise . . . and I'm not sure you are or can ever be good with it. As much as I like her, and I truly fucking do," he admits, running his hands through his hair. "It can end now. This impasse she's decided on can be an out, so I'm leaving the ball in your court to decide."

He lingers to make sure his following words are heard, along with his warning. "But if you do decide to let her through, I'm bringing her *all in*."

His declaration has me pausing all movement. "And the consequences?"

"On me," he declares before turning and stalking out the front door.

Stunned by his willingness to vouch for her, especially after her meltdown yesterday, I follow and lock up. After cranking our engines to warm them up, I glance over to see him smiling through our lowered windows while classic rock begins to filter through his speakers.

"Let's wake you up."

I crank up my own music to drown his noise out, and he shakes his head in annoyance. In the next second, he's spinning tires to lead us out of the neighborhood, and I put my Camaro into gear and follow.

At the stop sign, I pull up next to him so our hoods are lined up. After three collaborative revs of our engines for a countdown, we both rocket into motion, claiming both lanes of the main road. Sean grabs the advantage when I'm forced behind him by an oncoming car. I can practically hear his sarcastic rebuttal when I floor my Camaro and bullet past him. The long double tap of his horn is an unmistakable "fuck you" as we fly down the road. Sean starts to gain on me when another oncoming car forces me to slow and roll into his lane. The driver lays on his horn, a "fucking idiots!" screamed as we zoom past. Sean guns it as I straddle both lanes, anticipating his every move, his hood dangerously close to my bumper as I block his maneuvering to stay ahead. I glance in my rearview, chuckling. "I may be seeing two of you, brother, but you're *both* behind me."

When we approach our last right turn, I allow him to dart past me, and I quickly decide to cut the corner of a dry field, tires skidding back onto the pavement as I reclaim my lead and give it everything I've got. Sean repeatedly sounds his horn as I chuckle, already tasting my victory.

We take one last dicey turn, and Sean recovers faster, gaining ground and flipping the bird out of his window as we go hood to hood on the straightaway. Opening up, I go full throttle, knowing horsepower has everything to do with the last stretch, and this is where I have slightly more edge. My engine wins as I gain a full car length before fishtailing into King's parking lot and stopping on a dime. Sean pulls into the space next to me just as I exit. He lingers at his driver's door, addressing me over the roof of his Nova. "You're fucking ridiculous. You know that? The rules are simple." He slices his hand left and right. "Stay between the mayonnaise and mustard."

"Since when are you a stickler for rules? Oh, yeah ... only when I'm dusting your ass. If you spent a little more time under your hood than under skirts, you might actually fucking beat me one day."

Sean shuts his car door and joins me at mine. "Day isn't over yet, asshole." He claps me on the back as we head toward the lobby door for Tyler's update. Tyler's made it his mission since our warehouse heist to get to the bottom of the *who* by utilizing his military contacts.

Our major setback with this is that if we attempt to dish out justice on something of this caliber, it could bring attention to our secret. Just as I'm sifting through the odds we're up against, Tyler pulls into the parking lot. We both head toward his truck for an update when I hear my name called.

THIRTEEN

Sean and I both turn to see Ginger getting out of her Chevy sedan. We'd missed her idling there when we pulled in. Doing my best not to show how her unexpected presence is fucking up my morning, Sean leans over to me in a whisper as we start walking her way.

"You fucking with Ginger again?"

Our collective boots crunch gravel as I take in Ginger's dress, appreciating her beauty as I always have. "We hooked up when I first got home. It was a *one-time*, welcome home fuck."

"Well, welcome home, *you're fucked*," he chuckles, adding a back clap as I glare at him in warning. Ginger steps up to us, dark red hair flying in the breeze, brown eyes darting between us as Sean takes the lead—his shit-eating grin firmly in place. Normally he wouldn't take so much joy out of my discomfort, but it's clear he's in it today for payback—for Cecelia. That idea gnaws at me as Sean speaks up, addressing her.

"Hey Ginger, lookin' beautiful this morning."

She gives him a soft "Thank you," before cautiously focusing back on me, her expression letting me know I haven't managed to mask shit. I've made her feel unwanted. Needing to say something to ease her discomfort, I fucking fail to produce the words before she speaks up. "Can I talk to you for a second?"

I lift my chin to Sean, who takes his cue and painstakingly walks backward, eyes darting between us. Ignoring my scowl, he addresses Ginger.

"Just got a new place, don't know if Dom told you, but you're welcome *anytime*."

"Thanks, Sean." Sean joins Tyler as he glances our way, lifting his chin to let me know the news he has is time sensitive before he greets Ginger with a friendly wave. I nod to let him know I'm coming.

"I won't take much of your time," Ginger assures, pulling my attention her way.

"It's good . . . you good?" I'm so fucking bad at this. I've never been able to do small talk, not even when I've wanted to. At one point, years ago, specifically with Ginger, I wanted to. I don't bother to attempt it anymore. Where I continually fail, Sean would've already talked a prior hookup into a more intimate setting and gotten balls deep, making her forget the reason she showed up. A talent he possesses that I'm at times envious of—if only for *this* fucking reason.

It's also why I've shared with Sean in the past when an opportunity presented itself. He takes pleasure in the whole fucking charade while I refuse to. When it's run its course, he's always been the one to let them down gently before I fuck it all up with the blunt truth or my inability to use words when it matters most.

That is why Tyler used it against me in the yard that day. It's fucking humiliating, and that point is driven home as Ginger patiently waits on me. She's always been a rare exception, and never held my weakness against me, not once since we were just kids.

Looking over at her now, I can tell there's more behind why

she's here before she voices it. "I'm fine, Dom. This isn't about us," she assures before biting her lower lip.

It's then I notice she's sweating, and it's too early in the day for it. To ease her mind, I grip her shaky hand and see her take her first full breath since she approached me.

"What's wrong?"

"Dom, I hate asking, but I need your help."

I tighten my fingers around her hand, knowing it's not me she's scared of. Anger starts to simmer for whatever motherfucker put this type of visible fear into her. "Ask me anyway."

Closing Ginger's driver's side door, I add another task to my never-ending fucking to-do list as she smiles at me through the glass before starting her car. As she pulls away, my phone rumbles in my pocket, and I curse, knowing it's the hospital, without bothering to look at the screen. Only thirty minutes or so into the hour I asked for, Delphine's already terrorized the hospital staff to the point that they're calling. Glancing through the lobby glass, Tyler spots my summons as I start making my way toward my car. He steps out, making his way toward his truck. "Raincheck, it's important. I'll get back with you in a few. Don't stray too far."

"Where you off to, man?"

"A drunk and disorderly *French menace* walks into a hospital *days* early for her chemo appointment . . . I'll get back to you with the fucking punch line."

"Shit. Need help?"

"I'm handling it."

"Let me know if that changes." When I don't reply, he curses as he secures his burner phone in his glove box before circling his truck and firing up behind the wheel.

He's debating following me. I'd bet my fucking hot wheels on it. Delphine is his other Achilles heel, and he's horrible at hiding it, at least from *me*.

Tyler fires up his truck as Sean flies out of the lobby. "Hey, assholes, where the fuck are you going? In case you forgot, I don't *work here anymore!*"

"You do today," I say before taking my wheel, knowing Russell will pull up within half an hour. Firing up my car, I sip my coffee for much-needed fuel before speeding off, my shoulders already tight.

It's going to be one of those fucking days.

FOURTEEN

STARING INTO THE DARK LOBBY OF THE GARAGE FROM MY SEAT, I run my knuckles down my wheel, tightening my hold on the burner phone. "I'm asking you to give me an inch, a fucking inch. I can't just sit back while—"

"You can and you will," Tobias snaps. "One at a time, Dom, and we need to concentrate on who's *first*."

"You don't know what you're asking me. Every day you deny me to act is a day wasted." Another life stolen, innocence lost, and a monster's victory. But I can't let on too much about how it's affecting me. He's rested the club's fate in my hands, and if he catches wind of how much my side project is fucking with the job, he may very well snatch it out of my grasp. I need some semblance of control. If Tobias takes the day-to-day away from me, it will be a fate worse than the one I'm living. His silence on the other end of the line tells me he's contemplating that decision.

"Stop. Don't even think about it," I warn.

"If you know what I'm thinking, then why are we having this conversation?"

His accent is getting thicker, and for some reason, it irritates me. Maybe it's because I don't want him claiming home to be on that side of the ocean. Though at this point, he's lived more of his life in France than he has here.

"We can't risk it, Dom."

"What they're doing . . . what they're fucking getting away with—"

"Has been happening for endless years and isn't stopping anytime soon."

"I get your logic," I admit begrudgingly.

"Do you?" His tone is full of condescension.

If he's speaking to Tyler as often as he is to me—and Tyler gives him more reason to worry—I might have already lost my place.

"Don't fucking do it," I snap. "I'll do your bidding. I haven't moved in on shit. That's why we're fucking arguing."

"Prove it is the right decision. Your time will come, brother."

"And how many times have I heard that?" I snap, running my knuckles down my wheel in a way that burns. I hear the clink of ice to glass and know then that he's also not putting a real voice to what's got him so worked up.

"Any progress on finding him?" I ask in an attempt to get something from him. Our conversations are rare as is, and I know it's so he can stay focused. For whatever reason, he's chosen our club's tipping point to search for his birth father, and I'm trying not to begrudge him for it.

"No," he replies. "A whisper of something, then silence for fucking days, sometimes weeks."

"Elusive, huh? An inherited trait, *no doubt*."

"I'm trying, Dom."

"Try harder."

"You've been no help to me recently," he snaps.

"A little busy here," I say through clenched teeth.

"Tell me," he urges, not as the shot caller but as my brother. His emotional whiplash tells me he's just as on edge as I am.

"My job has been a little hectic lately, but our pension is looking pretty fucking spectacular."

"Good to hear," he muses. "How are things at home?"

Delphine.

"The definition of insanity." I scrub my face thinking about my aunt rotting away in that house—how I watched her pour a drink from the porch just after parking her in her recliner earlier today. She's shackled herself to that house for as long as I can remember now. It's as if she's serving a self-imposed prison sentence.

"Don't let her miss a treatment," he orders.

"I've got it," I snap.

Silence. The clink of ice.

"Try not to resent me too much, brother," he finally says, recognizable guilt coating his tone. He's either on his third or fourth drink and getting antsy due to the time away—mostly from me. The paternal concern is starting to kick in. What he doesn't realize is that I'm just as fucking worried about his situation. On that, I'm done obeying orders and formulating a plan instead.

"You *tell me* about home," I prod.

"I'm talking to home."

"You *do know* the definition of insanity, don't you?"

He circles his glass, and I realize he's drained it already. That knowledge grates on me.

"It's repeating the same actions over and over again and expecting different results. That's where *waiting* has gotten us."

He releases my name like it's a nuisance as a text comes through my personal cell.

Ginger: He's here.

"Don't let my shit keep you from sipping your guilt away, brother, seeing how it's worked out so fucking well for the rest of the family. I have shit to do."

Smashing the phone into my dash, I toss its remains on my passenger floorboard. Reveling in the timing of Ginger's text, I allow the residual anger to snake its way into my vision. Downshifting,

I fly in the direction of her apartment. Once parked, I grab what I need from my glove box. As I do, recent, concerned looks of every single one of my inked brothers flit through my mind . . . along with Tobias's warning. Pressing send on a last-minute text to Sean, I slam my door closed and make a beeline for Ginger's apartment door.

Ginger opens the door just as I approach, and I see the source of her fear standing next to a littered coffee table. Nearby, a baby no older than a year bounces in a chair. Rage engulfs me, and I zone in on the motherfucker who barely has time to drop his glass pipe before I'm on him. Clamping a hand on his neck, I drag him toward the open front door.

"What the fuck?!" He shrieks, attempting to turn his head as I keep him bent but walking.

"Dom!" Ginger's sister, Marie, screams my name as if she has some ability to reason with me.

"Pack his shit," I bark at Marie as Ginger holds the door open so I can take the trash out.

Stopping just outside of it, Marie starts to berate Ginger, and the greasy piece of shit in my grip gets it together enough to start questioning me. "What the fuck, man?! Who the fuck are you?"

Gripping his hair, I pull his head up enough to scan the parking lot.

"Which one is yours?"

"The S10, fuck, please ease up, Jesus Christ!"

"He's not answering today," I inform him before pinning him to his rust-eaten Chevy. "I already called."

"She didn't tell me she had a man, dude. I swear." Inside, I hear the baby start to scream along with Marie, and my hackles rise.

Sean speeds into the parking lot, and in seconds, he's by my side, his voice barely audible to the pulse thrumming in my ears as I stare at the fucking junkie who was about to hit a pipe with a baby mere feet away.

"Dom," Marie screeches as she bounds into the parking lot with Ginger on her heels. "Dom, please don't hurt him!"

I slam him against his truck, leering at him as Sean's words finally start registering.

"Easy, man. This isn't the time or place."

"You've overstayed your welcome," I inform greasy. "This isn't your place. Ginger wants you gone. So *go*."

Marie turns on Ginger. "I told you it was just a couple more days!"

Ginger stands her ground. "You said that two months ago! I found a pipe in Toby's car seat this morning!"

Greasy, who hasn't taken his eyes off me, starts to sputter as I slam him into the side of the truck again. "You're smoking that poison around a baby. Are you not aware that shit can seep into his clothes, his skin?"

"Please, Dom, don't hurt him!" Marie shrieks.

The crackhead's smoked, false bravery decides to speak up on his behalf as he questions Marie. "Who the fuck is this guy?"

Sean supplies the answer for her. "You don't want an answer to that. It's best if you leave, man, and take him at his word. He's not a fan of repetition."

Keeping the fucker pinned to the truck, I pat him down before yanking his keys from his jeans and pressing them into his chest.

Marie must have taken a hit of the same bravery as her first threat comes out. "Let him go, or I'm calling—"

I flit my gaze to her. "You sure you want to finish that sentence, Marie?"

She backtracks as Sean turns toward her, his expression just as unforgiving as she cowers. "You know I wouldn't. Just, please . . . let him go."

Focusing back on the sweat-slicked junkie, I see him for exactly what he is—a complete and utter waste of a life. "Your dick seems to be clouding judgment around here." Slamming him against the truck again, he fades, going limp in my hold.

My voice of reason speaks up beside me. "Ease up, Dom. What's your name, man?"

"Jeffrey."

"Jeffrey was just leaving, weren't you, Jeffrey?" Sean gives him an easy out, a script to repeat, which he does not follow.

"Seems he's having a hard time grasping the concept, so we'll make it easy." I turn to Marie. "I'm only going to say this one more time. Pack his shit. He's taking it with him. We'll wait, won't we, Jeffrey?"

Jeffrey, who is full of bad decisions, has the gumption to look bored. "Yeah . . . sure."

I turn to Ginger. "You said two months?"

"Around that, yeah," she replies with a shaky voice, her eyes darting nervously.

"Has he given you a fucking dime for anything—rent, utilities?"

"I don't care about that," she waves her hand.

I turn on her. "Then maybe you *deserve* an unwanted houseguest if you're willing to be so hospitable."

She quickly speaks up. "I just want him away from my nephew."

"I wasn't hurting him," Jeffery offers in a shit excuse.

"Jeffrey," Sean shakes his head, "don't talk."

"Nah, let's chat. How much cash do you have on you, Jeffrey?"

Jeffrey fearfully glances at Sean for more help and finds none. "I dunno."

"Hmm, Sean, how much do you have on you?"

Sean answers instantly. "Around three hundred and change."

I turn to Ginger. "Ginger? What about you? How much is in your wallet?"

"I just filled up, so around forty dollars. Why?"

"Because only a loser without a care in the fucking world is unaware of how much money they have in their pocket, and that's because they're content with someone else doing all the heavy lifting."

Reaching into Jeffrey's back pocket, I pull out his pathetic Velcro wallet and glance over at Marie. "I see your tastes have changed drastically since high school, and you're only getting classier with age." Ginger snorts as Marie glares at me. "I told you to go pack his shit."

"Dom—"

"Go soothe your screaming baby and pack his shit!" Sean snaps at her, and her eyes widen in a way that she knows arguing is futile. She turns on her heels as I fix my stare back to the cesspool she's chosen to play father figure. I release him enough to keep him pinned with my elbow while I sort through his wallet. I pull out his license and hand it to Sean, who studies it. I pluck out a bag of powder inside the billfold and toss it at his feet before holding the wallet open for him.

"I'm guessing this is the full sum of your net worth right here. This is all you have?"

"Yeah."

"Take the money out and give it to Ginger."

"It's all I got."

"Technically, it's not," I correct. "What's the street value of the powder?"

"Eighty dollars," he replies, searching all sets of eyes on him for help that's not coming.

"Eyes on me." He lifts blown pupils to mine. "Give the money to Ginger."

He hastily snatches the money from the wallet and thrusts it toward her. I can practically hear the crack in his back as I reprimand him for bad manners, and the bills float to the ground before Ginger has a chance to reach them. Jeffrey whimpers when I press my forearm against his neck. "Now, Jeffrey, simple mathematics will tell you you're leaving with twice as much as you just gave her. But my guess is that you're going to smoke your entire net worth before you reach the highway."

Marie bounds out of the apartment with a trash bag, her son on her hip. His tiny chest bounces with his hiccups due to the strength of his cries. My resolve only strengthens as I rip my eyes away from him while I try to rid him of the monster that sleeps too close to his crib.

"Is that everything, Marie? We don't want to give him an excuse for another house call."

Sean reaches for the bag as she answers me. "It's everything."

I keep my eyes trained on the crackhead as Sean drops his shit in the back of his truck. "You're packed, but if anything is missing, you can live without it."

Jeffrey dips his chin in reply.

"Need to hear you say it," Sean instructs as I press in, and he winces, agony etched on his features.

"Right. R-Right, if anything is missing, I can live without it."

Releasing him, I step back as Jeffrey quickly grabs his only priority—his bag of dope—and grips the handle of his truck. Eyeing me for my next move, I step back and allow him the space to get in. It's when he's safely inside and fires up his truck that I tap his window with my Glock. Jeffrey's eyes bulge at the sight of it before he hesitantly cracks his window a fraction.

"Don't call. Don't write. You won't be missed." Jeffrey nods, and I step away as he floors the gas, speeding out of the parking space and biting the curb hard with his exit.

Marie turns to Ginger with a glare, adjusting Toby on her hip. "I fucking hate you."

"You're next," I tell Marie. "And if you so much as utter another disrespectful word to the person putting a roof over you and your son's head, it will be *now* rather than later." She opens her mouth and thinks better of it before stomping off and slamming the apartment door. Ginger turns to me, the relief on her face enough even if she voices it. "Thank you."

"He'll be back," I warn, "and she'll let him in while you're working. When that happens, *text me*."

She nods half a dozen times, her expression filled with gratitude. "Okay. I will. Thank you. Really, I'm sorry—"

"You know *he* isn't the problem, right?" I tell her.

"I do, but she's the only family I have, even if she's a nightmare."

"I can relate."

Sean chuckles at my reply—one of the rare few who gets the joke as Ginger eyes me in a way I used to welcome when in need of a distraction. I can read her invitation before she voices it. "Do you want to come in?" She looks between me and Sean. "Uh, both of you? I've got some beer."

"I've got shit to do," I tell her. She nods, expecting the answer I gave.

"Okay, well, I'm around if you change your mind."

"Text me if he comes back," I turn and stalk toward my car.

"Night, Sean. Thank you."

"No problem, Ginger, see you," Sean says before catching up with me.

"She grew up a stunner, didn't she? Your first crush in junior high." I don't take his bait as he continues, trailing me to my Camaro.

"Something tells me this favor was sentimental in nature, but you always did have a thing for redheads."

"I grew out of her a long fucking time ago," I tell him honestly. What I don't say is that I grew out of this town after my freshman year in Boston. Coming back hasn't at all felt like a homecoming. Years out of Triple Falls did exactly what my brother predicted it would do. It boosted my ambition to a different level—pivoting my aspirations on a much bigger scale—which only adds to my unrest. If Tyler feels the same after his years away, he doesn't voice it. Aside from his few trips during my college years, Triple Falls is all Sean has ever known. But if given the choice, I don't think he'd ever venture too far away from the county line. This town is in his blood. I don't fault him for it, but it distances us a little in mindset, which only adds to the growing gap between us. "I didn't need you playing good cop. I had it fucking handled."

"Then why did you call me here?" A question he answers for himself. "We both know if he had fifty more pounds on him, this would have been a shit show. You have got to get a handle on whatever is festering inside you. And if it's Cecelia—"

"It's not. I've made my decision. We're moving forward."

"You sure, man?"

Gripping my door handle, I glance over at him. "Whatever it takes."

FIFTEEN

"**G**ET THAT ASSHOLE OUT OF MY POOL," CECELIA ORDERS Sean from the lounger they've been bickering on since we got here.

I press my lips together.

Sorry mouse, the water feels too fucking good.

Sun-drenched and weightless for the first time in fuck knows how long, I crack open my beer and survey the yard. Tyler makes quick work of unpacking our cooler as Cecelia gives Sean hell for not having her back during our little showdown.

"Tell me you didn't miss me," he prompts, crowding her on the chair.

"Irrelevant. If I can't trust you to have my back when I need you, what's the point?"

Doing my best to drown out their drama, it's Sean's last confession that has my ears perking back up. "I thought I was doing the right thing, but I don't know what that is when it comes to you."

"What does that mean?"

"It means, for both our sakes, I should probably leave you alone, but I'm not fucking going to."

There it is—the truth he refuses to spare either of us as he kisses her to drill his point home. As I thought, he's been fighting himself when it comes to her—while I've made a firm decision the predicament will remain his and his *alone*. Tipping my beer, I survey the sparkling pool and surrounding grounds while I tune in on their back and forth.

". . . Father has security cameras set up everywhere, and he's already threatened me about having company. This isn't going to bode well."

Which is precisely the reason for our ambush today.

Surprisingly, Sean lets her in on the camera surveillance solution, *me*, but not the when.

Sean really does trust her, and due to my decision to let her through—if only to hasten serving up Roman's justice—means she'll be privy to a lot more in the coming days and weeks. But whatever Sean's thinking about regarding Cecelia long term is delusional. On that, I decide to let my brother be the one to break it to him when the time comes.

At the moment, Roman is boarding a plane for a day trip to one of his Detroit plants, which gives us just enough time to get in and out. When the subject is redirected to me, Sean pleads my case. "Look, he isn't easy. But he's here because he wants to be."

Part truth, part lie.

"Is that supposed to make me feel better? The guy is a motherfucker."

Tipping my beer to again hide my grin, Tyler intervenes. "Good. Mom and Dad made up. Time to celebrate." He sprays them with a beer as Cecelia's laughter rings out, and Sean and I lock eyes as I ready myself to play my part.

My turn to make nice.

He scoops Cecelia up honeymoon style and delivers her to me by jumping them both into the pool. Breaching water, she sputters out her scold as they begin to coo at one another until Sean's cellphone rings. He immediately exits the pool darting a glance my way before he answers with a, "Hey, Dad."

Right now, *Dad* is being played by Jeremy. He's giving us the all clear, stating Roman's plane is climbing toward an altitude he can't be reached—and we can't be monitored.

Feeling the weight of her familiar stare, Cecelia inches toward me, where I lean against the shallow end wall. Her eyes roaming over me in an unmistakable way.

"I suppose you want an apology," I say, close enough to drink in every detail. She's pure temptation—long, drenched, slightly fire-kissed hair, perfect fucking features, bee-stung lips, palm-sized tits, toned torso, ample curves—a literal wet fucking dream. The triangle of material between her thighs hovers just above the water as she inches toward me.

Despite the grudge I have against her maker, she really is the most beautiful fucking girl I've ever laid eyes on. Along with a mix of things that would allure any man—innocent and forbidden.

A mouthwatering combination of fire and water.

But despite my body's constant reaction to her—*not for me.*

"I won't hold my breath," she scoffs.

Downing my beer, I hold up a finger. "Okay, I think I'm ready ..." I exaggerate my exhale. "I'm sorry I told Sean I caught you staring at my dick."

She surprises me by tossing her head back and laughing, and I can't help my return smile. Her eyes widen at the sight of it before she speaks up.

"You are a rare bastard."

"I prefer motherfucker." Her eyes bulge. *Yeah, I heard you, mouse.*

"At least then, it would be somewhat factual. Isn't that right, Tyler?"

We both glance over to Tyler, who shoots me the finger, adding in a "Fuck You."

Cecelia and I share a grin as her navy eyes dance along my

profile, dipping further with every word she speaks. "You had your door open. I was surprised, to say the least."

"And the other five minutes?" I quip.

"Do women actually sleep with you?"

"No, never. They're too busy screaming my name. Except the last girl, she was a corpse."

No offense, Ginger.

"You are unreal. Psychiatrist's dream indeed."

Her eyes glaze as a little silence lingers—as does her appraisal of me. "What are you thinking about?"

Her guilty gaze drops. "Nothing."

This girl has no chance of making it in our world if she can't play off something as simple as sexual attraction. Though I can, I find myself in a new but predictable pattern as I fight my cock's reaction to her. Thankful when Tyler leaves his lounger and Sean nears with a nod for the both of us, I turn and push out of the pool. Out of time for the patty cake portion of the plan, I begin walking toward the back door, and Cecelia speaks up. "Where are you going?"

"Have to use the can."

"You could ask."

The clank of the gate closing at the side of the house cues me in, and I turn and lower my shorts.

"Oh my God," Cecelia sounds up behind me with fast directions, "through the door past the study, down the hall on the left. Savage."

Candy from a baby.

"I might like that better than motherfucker."

Sean joins her in the pool, promptly stealing her attention.

Closing the back door, I glance around before stalking through to the front door and opening it where Tyler stands in wait, our packed duffle bag in hand.

Within seconds we're in Roman's sad excuse of a security closet, six surveillance screens stacked atop each other on small shelves.

"You were right. He's got them angled to capture every possible approach."

"It's the reason he built it like this. No ambush is possible without being flagged. Which means there's something in this house worth finding."

"Then why wouldn't he update his cameras?"

"Because he had no real plans of living here."

"So why bring her here?"

We're still no closer to finding out why a month after her arrival.

"Exactly," I say, unzipping the duffle.

Tyler flips through the screens, stopping as Sean corners Cecelia in the pool and begins fucking her.

"Lucky bastard," he groans, as my eyes linger a little longer on the twist of her features before he kills our view. "Now, let's hope the fucker has some stamina because, as you know, it's been a *whole week.*"

He rolls his eyes due to the number of arguments we've had with Sean in trying to keep him at bay until we could figure out how to use their little love quarrel to our advantage. Though he made it my call, he's been vocal about the time it's taken.

Taking what I need from Tyler's backpack, I drop my soaked trunks and start toweling off.

"Jesus, man, some fucking warning would have been nice."

I pull up my sweats. "Just trying not to leak all over the floor. Don't want you to have to mop up."

"I'm talking about the fucking hard-on," he grits out, eyes pinched closed as I glance down at the inconvenience of interacting with Cecelia.

I slap his jaw playfully, and his eyes pop open in a glare. "You poor thing, I guess you didn't get *the talk.* I'll make it brief. One day, when you're a big boy, *little Tyler* will grow three sizes too big and want to do some pushups when he sees a beautiful girl."

"Play it off all you want, but I physically *felt* that chemistry you two were stirring up in that pool."

Shrugging, I bend and dig into the bag, snatching some of the mics and a flash drive.

"You're not going to deny it?" Tyler asks.

"I don't lie to myself, but that's exactly what it is. *Chemistry* because I *can't* and *mentally taxing* because I *won't*. But that's all it is . . . an old-fashioned case of wanting to fuck what you can't have because it's bad for business and will destroy relationships . . . but you wouldn't know anything about *that*, would you?"

He holds my inquisitive gaze a millisecond before recovering. "Clocks ticking. I've got the first floor."

Making my way upstairs and into her room, I head straight for the laptop on her bed, plug in the flash drive I filled with spyware, and start the download.

Glancing around, I spot a bag of books from a major retailer. Unable to help my grin, I unload it on her bed. She hasn't been back to the library since I told her it was off-limits. She's avoiding me when and where she can, as I have her. A receipt floats out—landing on top of the pile—and on the back of it is a handwritten list of books she wants to read.

All of them romance.

Lucky for her, Sean's just her type.

It strikes me then—as it often has over the years—that most of the population craves that type of connection. By now, I should have felt some deep seeded need inside of me that longs for a spiritual bond to go with the sexual. Maybe by allowing myself to remain stunted, I inadvertently got rid of that urge.

Tyler's voice jogs me out of my thoughts. "All good up here?"

Shoving the books back into the bag, I situate it the way I found it and pocket the receipt before pulling the flash drive from her computer. "It is now. Got three mics in."

"Downstairs is good to go, and I got the rest of this floor while you were sniffing through her panty drawer."

"Fuck off with that," I say as he flicks my ear playfully when I push past him and head toward the stairs.

"Tell that to your dick," he mutters.

"He's a big, big, boy but even with his ego, he makes good decisions."

"Time will tell," he taunts, trailing me as I start to take the stairs two at a time and stop on a dime just a few steps down—the hairs on the back of my neck spiking in awareness while an uneasy feeling spreads through me.

"What?" Tyler asks, all traces of animation in his tone gone as I glance up to where he stands at the top of the stairs.

"Sure Roman is on a plane?" I ask, unease running from my soaked head to my bare feet.

"Fucking positive." His brows pinch in confusion. "What's happening right now?"

"I don't know," I say, scanning the foyer. The feeling starts to dissipate as I start back down the stairs. "Nothing."

"You sure?" Tyler prods.

No.

"Yeah. Let's go."

"All grown-ups were once children . . . but only few of them remember it."—*Le Petit Prince*, Antoine de Saint-Exupéry

SIXTEEN

A KNOCK ON MY DOOR JARS ME AS I EYE THE CLOCK ON MY monitor and know the only person it could be at this hour. The only bird whose nights are as restless as my own. Tyler enters a second later, hands filled with a solid black box.

"Delivery," he chimes, a glint in his eyes.

"From?"

"France." He sets the box in front of me. "Mind if I stay?"

"Yeah, but stay anyway," I jest. I go to look for my letter opener as Tyler produces a pocketknife. It's unique but severely dated. "How fucking old is this thing?"

"Ancient, but it still gets the job done," he states, his interest in the contents of the box rather than relaying the backstory of the knife. Placing his expression as excitement, my interest sparks. Carefully, I slice the taped bottom and release the inch-thick protective cardboard. Pulling away the bubble wrap, I unveil a large black mailer sitting atop the contents with a small note taped to it, handwritten by my brother.

For your list.
Frères pour toujours

A ball lodges in my throat at the sight of the words.

"Maman!" *I yell, running into the kitchen as light flashes and the giant's footsteps rattle the windows.*

"Dominic?" *She whispers, wiping her face, her eyes red and puffy.*

"Maman, the giant is going to eat me!" *I look over my shoulder to see Tobias chasing me.*

"Oof," *Maman says as I run into her, and she drops a picture on the table.* "Slow down, Petit Prince," *she says, pulling me into her lap.* "What giant?" *She asks Tobias.*

"I was just trying to stop him," *Tobias says.*

"No," *I shake my head as more of Maman's pictures fall on the floor.* "He said to be very afraid that the giant foot was coming to eat me!"

"I said the giant would only eat you if you got out of bed." *He smiles as the giant's foot sounds comes closer.* "See," *he makes big eyes at me,* "he's coming."

"Tobias!" *Maman says.* "It's just a storm, Dominic," *she whispers.* "Nothing to be afraid of." *She looks at Tobias.* "Why are you trying to scare your brother?"

"I was trying to keep him in bed," *Tobias tells her,* "because he doesn't listen. Ever."

"And you'll keep him up all night," *Maman sighs as I point to one of the pictures.*

"That's Tatie!"

"Yes," *she whispers, pulling me closer to her as I point to another picture,* "That's Papa!"

"Uhhmm," *Maman says.*

"He looks funny," *I giggle.*

"He never cut his bright red hair," *she says, tickling me. I point to another picture.*

"Who is that?"

"That's you," she points to the baby. "And that is your brother holding you," she says, holding out the picture for Tobias to see.

Tobias shakes his head.

"Take it," she says. He snatches it out of her hands but doesn't look at it.

"You were mad at him then, too," she laughs.

"For what?" Tobias says, sitting in the chair next to us and looking at the picture.

"For being born," Maman says.

"That's stupid," he snorts. "You can't be mad at someone for being born."

She laughs. "Well, you were. Because you had just thrown him in the trash."

"You throwed me in the trash?!"

Tobias doesn't answer.

"He was as big as you are now," Maman tells me. "He was only mad because he did not want to share my hugs."

"I should throwed you in the trash," I tell Tobias.

"It's throw, imbecile," Tobias snorts.

"Hush, both of you," Maman sighs, looking over to Tobias the way she does when she is about to spank us with the big spoon. "Family is important," she says as she puts the pictures in the box. "No matter how mad you make each other, you will always be brothers." I pick up the pictures to help her put them in the box.

"Careful, Dom . . . Merci," she kisses my head.

"You can keep him. I'm leaving," Tobias says, standing.

"You can't leave," I wiggle off Maman's lap as she tries to hold me still. "You can't leave Tobias . . . we don't have any money!" I pull on his arm to stop him. "Papa said we don't have any money to keep a roof and water! How will you brush your teeth? How will you poop?"

Tobias and Maman laugh.

"It's not funny!" I yell. "Maman, he can't leave when it tunders. The giant will eat him!"

Maman pulls me back into her lap, and I squirm against her when *the house shakes.* "It's okay, Dom. It's only thunder, not the footsteps of a giant."

"You can't leave now," I tell Tobias. "Not with tunder."

"Thunder," *he says, the way he does when he sounds out words when we read.*

"Thunder," *I say back, and he smiles, his chest puffing as he rolls his eyes.*

"If you leave, we will be brothers wherever you go, right, Maman?"

"Dom?" Tyler says as I stare through my brother's signature.

"That's right, Petit Prince."

Always brothers.

For others, it's most likely seen as a simple sentiment between siblings. Beneath the apparent, it's been Tobias's way of telling me I come first since he left for prep school at sixteen. Through the long years of enduring his absence since . . . I've struggled to believe it at times. Our call earlier being one of those times.

"Fuck, man. The suspense is killing me," Tyler bustles next to me. I lift the heavy machine out of the box and examine it. It's as sleek as a stealth bomber. The material seemingly indestructible.

Checking for a power button, I find none, but figure out the crux of why in seconds. Opening the laptop, I place my hands where the keyboard would be, and it lights up instantly. Typing what I know Tobias meant to be the master password, it sparks to life at the speed of light. The keyboard glitters red beneath my fingertips, the placement perfection. The screen itself looks like something out of a fucking sci-fi movie. As if you can reach in and physically touch the display and mechanical parts powering animatedly behind it.

"Holy fucking shit," Tyler exclaims in rare animation as he grabs the slim black envelope and tears it open. "Instructions?"

I can't help my chuckle. "Not for this."

Within two commands, a menu of programs appears, and I choose every one of them. What I imagine is a junkie's type of rush seeps through my veins as they download in seconds—programs that would typically take hours.

Tyler plucks a thick, lone certificate from the envelope, and I don't have to see the front of it to know what it is.

"You didn't grab this while you were in Boston?"

He turns my MIT degree toward me, and I jerk my chin. "I didn't walk."

"Why the fuck not?"

"Wasn't important."

"To you," he states.

"He wasn't there."

"This says it all," he shakes the certificate. "So, I'm guessing you didn't leave a forwarding address?"

"No point."

"He paid for it and wanted to see it. I'm willing to bet that when he did, it was one of the proudest moments of his life."

The sentiment hits so hard that my throat burns. Whether the gift is a manipulation to placate me or not, I know Tyler's words are truer than my own. My brother has never shied away from his pride in me, no matter what company is present. Not ever. He knew Tyler would be the one to hand my degree to me, and this was his way of displaying that pride as both brother . . . and father.

"He ordered this over a year ago," Tyler cuts in, his words striking deep. "Even with my connections, it took me months to find capable enough hands to design it—and more than one set—because this is the only one of its kind. We made fucking sure of it."

Emotion threatens as he continues.

"Dom, you may think our club is his greatest accomplishment—"

"You can go now," I say, draining the rest of my cold coffee, my heart pounding harder with his assurances. He ignores me as usual, forever playing big brother, even though he's only got me beat in age by months.

"It may not seem like it at times, but you're the only one that helps him make sense of his life when he can't. He's been where you are. Just as frustrated, just as eager to dole out punishment and forced to wait . . . and do you know why?"

For us.

For us to grow up, *man* up, to understand the importance of what we're doing. For us to align at the right fucking time. For the here and now.

"You've made your point," I manage to get out without emotion in my tone.

"All right, man," Tyler rounds my chair to get a better look, eyes brimming with satisfaction. "Just . . . to finally see it, it's fucking unreal."

"A million-dollar laptop," I utter, turning back to the screen, equally awestruck.

Tyler scoffs. "The downpayment."

"Fucking serious?"

He grips my shoulder. "I questioned whether or not to let you have your new toy this late, but orders are orders, and he wanted you to have it as soon as it got here." Taking in my appearance, he shakes his head with a grin. "You need some fucking sleep, but I can see by that smile you're trying so hard to hide that there's no chance of that happening. I'll cover your shift at the garage tomorrow."

"I'll owe you," I tell him, running my fingers over the most sophisticated equipment on the planet—the possibilities endless. Tobias might not be greenlighting my plans, but he just gave me the perfect fucking tool to carry them out when the time comes.

It's a promise.

A promise of future permission, and it's enough for now.

"You're his greatest investment," Tyler sneaks in as my eyes start to burn. I can't help, nor do I give a fuck about what emotion he hears when I finally speak. "It's fucking perfect. Thanks, man, really."

He tosses a new burner phone on my desk before walking toward my door. "Don't thank *me.*"

SEVENTEEN

STALKING DOWN THE HALL TOWARD SEAN'S BEDROOM, I'M stopped outside when I hear his low chuckle and, a second later, realize he's not alone when a soft reply is whispered.

Cecelia.

Figures. They've been inseparable since they made up poolside a week ago. "That must have been some dream, Pup."

"Why do you say that?"

"You were moaning. What was my girl doing?"

A pause.

"I don't remember."

"Huh," he says in a way I know he's calling bullshit. "That's a shame. I would've loved to have heard those details."

"Some dreams just aren't good enough to remember," she offers, even I can tell she's lying. Not a second later, she catches me where I stand, watching them in their early morning spoon. It's when her eyes widen and then narrow that my suspicions are confirmed. "How long have you been standing there?"

"Do you live here now?" I counter. "Because if so, we're out of milk . . . Sean, a word."

Sean's sparkling eyes dim as he groans in protest. "This can't wait?"

"If it could, I would've spared myself your pillow talk."

Cecelia cuts in. "It's fine. I need to get going anyway."

She lifts the sheet closer to her chest and frowns at me. "Do you mind?"

Unmoving, I motion dismissively. "Take your time."

Sean chuckles. "Come on, man. It's too early for your shit."

Snaking her arm out, Cecelia snags her shorts from the floor and tugs them on beneath the covers while shooting daggers at me. "You're a real asshole. You know that?"

After managing to get her shirt on the same way, she stands and slides on her flip-flops.

"While you're out, grab some coffee too, and don't be cheap."

Rolling her eyes, she looks back down at Sean and plants a knee on the bed, hovering within reach. "See you at work?"

"Yeah," he whispers, "and *after*, so don't make any plans."

"All right." She dips and kisses him, and he cups the back of her head, making it last, no fucks given about the audience. Her eyes flick to mine before she pulls away. After grabbing her purse from Sean's dresser, she moves toward the door, and I give her just enough space to squeeze through. She attempts to get past me without contact and fails.

"Sweet dreams," I utter low enough for her to hear when she pushes past me. Her eyes flit to mine briefly before she stalks toward the stairs. Turning back to Sean, we sit in silence until the front door closes and her car starts.

Sighing, he moves to sit at the edge of his bed before grabbing his jeans from the floor. "You just can't help yourself, can you?"

"Sounds like a question you need to direct to your mirror."

He fastens his jeans before walking over to his dresser, rolling on some deodorant before snatching and pulling down a fresh T-shirt. "So, what couldn't wait?"

"You *really do* feel for her."

Sean pauses before tucking his wallet into the back pocket of his jeans. Grabbing his keys, he looks over to me, the answer clear in his eyes as Tyler appears at his door. "Good, you're both up."

Sean runs a hand through his hair. "What the fuck is up with you two assholes creeping into my room so early this morning?" His eyes scour Tyler with concern. "You just getting in, man?"

"Yeah. I've been working on our *crate* issue."

"And?" Sean prompts.

"Let me rephrase, we've got different problems," Tyler says, his exhaustion apparent.

Sean tucks a fresh pack of smokes into his jeans. "So, basically, business as usual? Oh, happy fucking day."

Tyler nods. "And it's just getting started."

"Mind if I get a coffee and have a smoke first?" Sean asks.

"No time. I'll meet you outside." Tyler exits the bedroom and heads downstairs, and Sean glances over at me, resuming our conversation.

"Yeah, I do feel for her, and I've been honest about it, so that makes *one* of us."

"The fuck?"

He shakes his head. "I'm not blind, man. Seems to me you're both fighting the inevitable." He lifts a brow. "Want to talk *that out*?"

"Sure, pencil that in for fucking never."

This past week, Sean's infatuation has led to more run-ins with Cecelia. A few days ago, she caught me in the midst of a deep session, pacing my room. Undeterred by my openly hostile reception, she offered me the bowl of ice cream in her hand.

One long look at her profile as she stepped into my room to leave it on my desk, silenced every bit of the roar inside my head and chest and had me losing focus. I thanked her by slamming the door in her face. Sean reads my lingering silence as an admission that sends his wheels turning in the wrong direction and jacking his jaws. "You in need of another field session to work some of that aggression out, *Major Malfunction*?"

"Cute. Will you be using all your girlfriend's quips against me now that *you're* strung out?"

"Yep, this is a case of full-on *penis envy*," he taunts.

"Sure it's not you who's envious?" I playfully slap his face. "Because I think we both know who she was *dreaming* about."

With that, he pounces, managing to dodge my first light fist, landing his own sucker punch before racing into the hall. I lunge for him as he swings and narrowly misses me before leaping onto the stairs. When he's halfway down, I tackle him at the landing, and we both slam into the drywall, hearing it crack.

"Get your fucking dick beaters off me," Sean groans, gaining his bearings before throwing a blind fist behind him, catching me in the throat and momentarily stunning me. My hoarse threat reaches him as he pushes off the wall giving chase. "You better run."

Sean bursts out of the townhouse with me hot on his heels and comes to a dead stop a few feet out. He curses before glancing back over his shoulder at me when I see Tyler's expression—and whom he's waiting with.

"It is lonely when you're among people, too." —*Le Petit Prince*, Antoine de Saint-Exupéry

EIGHTEEN

GINGER SITS PASSENGER IN TYLER'S TRUCK WHERE HE STANDS next to his open door, holding an ice pack to her cheek, her lower lip caked with dried blood.

Fury clouds my vision as I stalk toward her and pinch her chin between my fingers, slowly turning her face to survey the damage.

"I'm sorry, Dom. I didn't know where else to go. He's on a rampage, and Toby," a sob bursts from her as Sean speaks up from behind me.

"Dom, listen to me. You can't go off. Now is not the time."

He steps up next to me, his instructions for Ginger. "Ginger, I hate fucking saying this, but you'll have to go the legal route."

"Jeffrey's cousin is a Triple Falls cop," she discloses softly. "I've already tried."

"Fuck," Sean exhales, snapping his Zippo closed.

Tyler gently tucks her back inside his truck. "Give us a few minutes, sweetheart. Okay?"

Ginger's eyes remain glued to mine through the glass after he shuts the door.

Tyler ushers me away from her as we huddle in the yard, my pulse thrumming in my ears.

Sean audibly exhales a plume of smoke. "Can't we just wake up and eat our Wheaties like normal folk?"

"Not what we signed up for," Tyler answers, eyes on me for a decision.

Sean waves him off, looking between us. "Yeah, yeah. What's the plan?"

Tyler picks up where Sean left off, his words for me. "Dom, she's going to have to go through legal channels to get him out. There's no other way."

"There's a way," I clip, pressing back against the rage threatening to overtake me as I sift through possibilities.

Dread covers both their expressions as Tyler presses me. "What are you thinking?"

"Get her to Layla, and don't let her go home." Tyler nods and, without another word, walks back to his truck before backing out.

Ginger's eyes stay glued to mine as Sean speaks up beside me. "I can see a thousand scenarios going through that fucking head of yours." He exhales more smoke as I stalk toward my Camaro. Sean opens my passenger door, opting to stick with me until he knows it's safe to leave me to my own devices, dread in his tone. "Wonder which one will cost me less skin."

♛

Splintering the front door open instead of a polite knock, my birds flood in from behind me. Scanning the space, I'm met with the sight of Jeffrey's friends scattered throughout Ginger's living room and kitchen in different states of a fucking high. One with Toby's baby bottle tipped up, drinking from the nipple.

Cloaked from head to boots in black, my inked brothers begin to pluck away Jefferey's tribe one by one. Russell drags one kicking

and screaming through the front door just as I zero in on the motherfucker and his wide eyes. In a flash, I'm gripping him by the neck
and his jeans, lifting him chest level before dropping him onto the
littered coffee table—which shatters beneath him. In seconds, the
apartment is cleared, and the only remaining screams are those of
the baby down the hall, echoing his mothers. I lift Jeffrey by the
collar to see him conscious with only a few cuts—which won't do.

His eyes widen when he realizes who is staring back at him
through the ski mask. His scream cut off with my first blow.
Knowing time is of the essence, I rain down on him as many times
as I can, feeling his flesh give way to my knuckles to make sure he's
unrecognizable until Tyler rips me away.

"That's enough, brother," he urges before dragging Jeffrey's unconscious body through the door. Marie follows, begging Tyler to
release him—a fucking lost cause. Pulling my gloves from my pocket,
I slide them on and dial the number with my burner phone while
making my way toward the baby's room.

Pushing open the door, Toby's screams ring in my ears from
where he stands in his crib. Diaper weighed down, tear streaks—
both new and old—coating his filthy cheeks.

Tamping down the rage at the sight of him, I pull my mask
up as I approach before lifting him from his crib. He stares back at
me, terrified, as I run my gloved hands down his back in a soothing
motion. "Shhhh, little man, it's okay. It's okay."

"Please don't take him, Dom." This comes from Marie, who now
stands at the door, her plea echoing throughout the quiet apartment.
Time ticking, I hear the operator on the other end of the line speak
up as I walk over to Marie and hand her Toby. "No more chances."

Putting the phone on speaker, I toss it into Toby's crib as the
operator's voice fills the air. "Sir, are you there? Sir . . . we have a unit
on the way now with an ETA of four minutes. I want to confirm
that you asked for child protective services. Can you tell me the age
of the child? Can you get them to a safe location? Sir? . . . Sir?"

Marie gasps, face twisting in panic as I pull my mask down.

Stalking past her and clearing the front door, I jump in and close the double doors on a van full of screaming drug addicts.

Limbs heavy, I pull on the blunt while making both a literal and physical attempt to drive some of the restlessness out of my body. Tension starts to marginally disburse with every long pull on the blunt. Sinking further into my seat, I click on the radio.

"It's 1 AM in Western North Carolina. And now for Today's forecast and your local news on the hour. You can expect clear skies for most of the day and a high of 87 with the slight possibility of a late afternoon shower. Now for the news . . . wow, get this, folks. Eight men were just arrested for public intoxication and indecent exposure. The men were found naked and disoriented, walking down a median on Highway Eleven. Each had conflicting stories on their whereabouts prior to their arrest. One of the men was reported as saying they were captured by birds before they were disrobed and left on the highway. Consider this your PSA to take it easy on the Moonshine. Let's kick off our next half hour of uninterrupted music with my man Marvin's "What's Going On?" Feels appropriate."

Grinning at the stoplight, I grab my cell to call Sean and let him in on the secret we handled while he was working his shift at Tech and pause, tracking his Nova instead.

Grandad's Apple Farm.

Tossing the phone, I decide this is another secret he won't be privy to. When he got no word from us after he clocked in for his shift, I'm guessing he assumed we weren't making a move today. He's so preoccupied that I doubt he'll bother to ask.

Downshifting, I decide that the longer I wait for everyone to get on the same page, the less gets done. We've got a severe kink in our system that needs to be worked out before we can take things further.

Sean's words about counting on people's loyalty are ringing truer than ever. Over the years, he's been a part of everything, and his continued and voluntary absence from the day-to-day lately has me questioning whether his ink matters as much as it used to. Sting ringing in my chest, I floor the gas and let the road guide me until my vision starts to blur. Even then, I push through as the truth of it settles in my gut. The truth that life moved on when Tyler and I left, and no one waited for either of us.

Just as no one is waiting for us now.

NINETEEN

TYLER APPEARS IN THE DOORWAY BEFORE TOSSING SOME paperwork on my desk. Pulling my earbuds out, I scan the report as he gives me the CliffsNotes.

"Marie didn't implicate us, even though Toby's now in Ginger's temporary custody. Marie took full responsibility for all of it and has to make state-mandated efforts to get him back."

"I have zero fucking regrets," I toss the paperwork aside.

"It was risky," Tyler adds.

"Yeah, well, that's our daily bread."

"We need to get going."

I nod, logging out of a few windows. We're meeting at the warehouse to discuss what inventory we want to barter with before taking it to trade with other chapters at the Meetup.

"Any word from Miami?" I ask, clicking out of a dozen active windows on a few screens.

"Still haven't paid dues since we denied them in on our big secret."

The big secret being our new connection with birds infiltrating government agencies to help cover their asses in the future. We decided not to take the risk since they've always skated moral lines and have no intention of stopping.

"Fuck them."

"My sentiments too, but something is definitely up."

"They coming?" I ask, making a few more clicks.

"The invitation was sent, but they've missed the last two."

"Might be time to send a few birds to fly south."

He nods as I roll back in my chair and glances at my desktop. "What were you working on?"

He reads my hesitation and grins. "Now I *have to know.*"

Standing, I move the mouse to hover over my last open window before clicking it and turning up the volume. In the next second, Cecelia's voice fills the air.

"*If I'm being forced to pay, literally, for your oversights, then I will have my say with you. That woman told me over and over that I was your daughter, and I had no idea how to convey that meant nothing!*"

Eyes widening, Tyler steps into the room and shuts the door.

"When did this go down?"

"About an hour ago."

"Sean hear it yet?"

"No, but I'm sure he's aware. This was brought on last night due to a confrontation at the plant. Cecelia's been bullied."

Tyler nods. "Sean mentioned it."

"You didn't tell me."

"Didn't think you would care . . . any visual with this?"

"No, this mic is in the dining room."

"Damn." Tyler crosses his arms, listening intently as Cecelia goes off on Roman. "*. . . asked you for a single thing, aside from extending support to my mother, who worked herself stupid to make sure I had everything I needed, and you couldn't be bothered to do that. I'm asking you to make this right, not for me, but for them. If you want to continue to dangle your fortune over my head, then do it, or better yet,*" *take it away and give it back to them. Because if it's their money I'm inheriting, I don't want it."*

Tyler's smile widens with every word. "She's really laying into him. I would love to have seen his face."

I stand and grab my boots, kicking into them at the foot of my bed as he turns to me. "You still aren't sold on her."

A statement—so I don't bother with a reply. Tyler lets me off the hook where Sean wouldn't.

"I get it, Dom. I don't think I could separate it either if I were in your position, but she's good people. And whip-smart."

I don't correct him that recently, I have been able to separate Cecelia from her father. Not just because of my attraction to her, which there's no fucking denying. For that, I blame the gift of vision combined with my underutilized cock.

What I haven't told Tyler is that even though this fight went down an hour ago, I've been listening to her berate Roman on repeat since it happened. My issues with Sean's absence lessening as I did. He's been utilizing his time with her wisely—not just dicking her—but teaching her what we collectively stand for, like any other recruit. Teachings she's obviously taken to heart and ring clear in her stand with Roman.

"I don't have to be right about her," I tell him truthfully as Cecelia continues to criticize him for a lot more than being a shitty business owner. "It's better if I'm not," I grab my keys as her emotional baggage starts to shift her rant.

"I'm sure it's a lot to deal with, but this one is close to you. It's right under your nose."

Lowering the volume at the doorway, I glance back at him. "But yeah, I'm still not sold for more reasons than one. She's too fucking young."

"But you're considering it." Another statement, but this time I speak up.

"I wouldn't go that far." I push past him where he lingers at the monitor. Her voice echoes down the hall as I take the stairs two at a time. Pushing out of the front door, Sean's constant pleas with me to hear her out circle through my mind as I start up my Camaro and flip on the radio to drown the new noise out.

Cecelia shrieks next to me when I bank on the shoulder and speed back toward the gas station. She was just as confused as I was when I picked her up. I'm still unsure as to why I felt the need to leave the compound and drive straight to her house to collect her. The worst part was calling Sean when I was already sitting in Roman's driveway. The 'I told you' in his tone cut short when I hung up on his smug ass.

Pulling into the gas station, I stop on a dime and glance over. "Need anything?"

She explodes on me, utilizing my new pet name. "You *motherfucker!*"

"Not in the mood for foreplay right now, but how about a Mountain Dew?"

She stares back at me, coiled up and ready to strike, no doubt due to my impromptu driving lesson. "I'll take that as a no."

Fighting my chuckle, I exit the Camaro and walk into the gas station. Glancing over the counter, I spot Zach in his invisible cage on the filthy fucking floor, books spread out, as he scribbles out his homework. Every bit of the high from sparring with Sean's new girlfriend evaporates when I take in his attire.

Making my way over to the cooler, I open it to hear Cecelia asking for the key to the restroom at the head of the store. Thankful her little piss break will buy me some time, I walk up to the counter to stare into the eyes of the attendant, whose nervous gaze meets mine before he glances over his shoulder at his son.

Zach's posture stiffens as he continues to work steadily on the floor as Tim's alcohol-laced breath hits me when I set down my drink.

"Need wraps."

He nods and turns to the display. "What flavor?"

"Cherry or pineapple."

He glances back at me, brows drawn that I'm not asking for my usual. "I don't have those."

"Then why don't you check your little stock room," my reply more an order than suggestion. Moving around the counter, Tim again looks back at his son, who doesn't lift his eyes. As soon as Tim is out of earshot, Zach pops up from the floor while I stare at his threadbare shoes.

"Hey, Dom," he greets, head lowered. Shame and embarrassment. Two things I've lived with for too many years and could recognize in anyone.

Redirecting my inspection, my anger flares further when I see the same tattered backpack next to his books.

"The fuck happened to the shoes and backpack?"

Zach keeps his chin tucked into his chest. "Uh, the shoes were the wrong size."

"Doesn't explain why you aren't wearing the *right one*. And the backpack?"

"Dom—"

"Look at me," his eyes lift, but his neck remains lowered. "Lift your chin, Zach," I grit out.

When he does, I get a clear view of the finger-sized bruises on his throat. They're faint but damning. Turning, I walk down the aisle and pin Tim to an endcap just as he walks out of the stockroom.

"Get out," he wheezes.

"So, daddy finally found the money I've been tucking into his son's backpack *for years*."

"My son is none of your bus—" I squeeze harder, interrupting his rant until he's ripping at my hand for air. The only sound in the store coming from the lotto machines. Neither man playing has bothered to look back. Good on them.

Time is ticking, and I know I need to back away, but one look in Zach's direction—of the fear in his eyes—has me finishing what I started.

"You robbed your own goddamn son, Tim, and for what?"

"It's none—"

Squeezing tighter, I cut him off. "We're over that, far past formal introductions and pleasantries. I know you used to run with my brother, and that you know I know that. So, at one point, you had potential, but we both know how you wasted it and have no one to blame but yourself."

"Dom, you know it's been hard for me since his mother left—"

"Who the fuck could blame her? Have you seen your fucking reflection lately?" I tighten my grip on his throat to make sure I don't get a response. Releasing him, he remains where he stands, neck marred, which brings me little satisfaction.

"I'm going to make this easy since you seem like a pretty simple man. The money I'm about to give Zach to replace the shoes and backpack you stole and anything extra belongs *to him*. For needs you can't meet because you're a worthless, selfish fucking drunk. Anything else I decide to gift your son better fucking remain in his possession."

Not so playfully tapping his jaw, I walk over to where Zach stands, his own profile ghastly white, and hand him one of my burner phones after programming my cell in. A now-shaking Tim keeps himself busy restocking the endcap I destroyed.

"Memorize this number and call me. Every goddamn day. If he touches you when I leave, *call me*—if you have to, come to the garage. Do you know where it is?"

Zach nods, eyes soaked in fear as I pull out a wad of bills and place them in his shaking palm, rage seeping into me at the fear that's been instilled in him.

"This isn't how it's supposed to be," I relay as twin tears he's been fighting finally spill over his cheeks.

At the sight of them, it takes every ounce of my strength to speak instead of act. "Zach, look at me."

He does, and I fight within myself to keep what's threatening to unleash locked down. "This is not your fault. It's *his* fucking failure." Zach swallows. "Do you hear me?" I stare into the eyes of a terrified boy who's been living impoverished and seemingly punished for merely existing in a drunk's selfish world—no doubt feeling like an unwanted burden, an obligation. A boy I've watched grow up over the years and was forced to abandon when I went to Boston. A boy who's habitually abused by the adult he's been forced to call his father. "It was his decision to become who he is, and it's going to be your choice not to be anything like him. One you'll make every day. Understand?"

Zach gives me another nod, his tears flowing freely. Tears that tell me he's suffered horribly, which pushes me to my limit. I snatch my drink from the counter and know I have to bail when a sob escapes him.

"Get me a wrap, okay?" I slap a twenty on the counter. It's when I see the bruised fingerprints on the back of Zach's neck that I step back over to Tim, who refuses to meet my eyes. Forcing my way into his personal space, they fearfully snap up. "If you abuse him again in *any way*, I will fucking *kill* you."

Tim gapes at me as Zach turns and pauses, gauging his father's expression when I stalk back over to grab the papers.

"Thanks," I collect them and see my hand is visibly shaking, "be good."

"I will." Zach nods, and I can tell he wants to say more but doesn't. Knowing that fear will have him in a chokehold until he believes any part of what I told him.

He's eleven, so it won't be too much longer until the resentment kicks in and the anger follows. What scares me is who he'll become when he gets angry about the venomous hand he's been dealt in a world that's fucked him. Dressed in rags, surrounded by bigots who continually shame him for doing nothing but breathing in and out and trying to survive another fucking day with a growling stomach.

Will he start to retaliate against it? Will there be a fucking soul there to hold him back? A person aware of the war that will rage between his heart and mind to help him understand the way my brother—who's *still* trying to reel in my resentment for Delphine— helps me?

Exiting the station with worry for the future of the replica of a younger me on the other side of the glass, I'm stopped short when I see Cecelia hemmed up at my hood, being harassed by one of the regulars at the machines.

"No, the car isn't mine," she replies politely, "excuse me."

When he blocks her path, I feel the anger I just tempered flare again as the asshole speaks up, stalling her with small talk, his posture predatory, "I used to race back in the day. Just wanted to—"

Wrapping my fingers around his neck, I use the leverage to swat him out of the way. Cecelia's eyes widen when he smacks into the side of the building before landing on his ass. She gapes at me as I snatch the bathroom key from her grip with my order—my patience thinned out. "Get in the car." Lifting my gaze back to the store, I meet Tim's eyes through the window before making my way back inside. Tim makes himself busy as I hand Zach the keys, elevating my voice. "See you both soon."

TWENTY

ELPHINE'S PILL BOX AND TRASH CAN IN HAND, I STOP OUTSIDE of Tobias's old bedroom door and twist the lock from inside in case Cecelia uses the bathroom and gets curious—which is likely since she bulldozed her way inside the house after I ordered her not to. Satisfied when the knob doesn't give, I return to the living room where Delphine sits in her recliner, Cecelia hovering uncomfortably nearby as I set the pill box on her table and the trashcan within reach.

"All separated. Take them, Tatie, or you'll get sicker," I order, spotting the French translation Bible forever resting in her lap. "Too late for you, witch."

We share a chuckle before she speaks up. "If there's a back door into heaven, maybe I'll find it for you too."

"Maybe I don't agree with His politics," I add, unwilling to get into another spiritual debate.

"Maybe He disagrees with yours, doesn't mean He can't be an ally. And you forget I know you. And stop separating my pills. I'm not an invalid."

Taking in her frail appearance, I can't help my reply. "You're doing a good job getting there. Don't drink tonight. I'm not searching the house, but if you do, you know what will happen."

"Yeah, yeah, go," she dismisses me as I swipe the remote and begin clicking through channels.

The mood intensity shifts behind me before Cecelia speaks up, her question for Delphine. "Should we stay?"

"Not my first time. Go, the night is young, and so are you, don't waste it," Delphine gives in a typical reply, though her weak tone betrays the strength of the declaration.

Fighting the urge to snap out my rebuttal, I mutter it instead. "You are too."

To say that whatever feelings I have for my aunt are complex would be a gross understatement. In the last handful of years, we've come to an understanding of sorts. In no way do I view her as a parent, but a parent is what she's tried to resemble as of late— more recently in the months she's convinced herself her death is imminent. Only escalating her illness with the way she treats her body, Delphine's been trying to pass down what nuggets of wisdom she feels are fitting for me. To her credit, I've been listening.

For the most part, our efforts have proven worth it. We've salvaged what relationship we're capable of—unless, during our conversations, I'm reminded of her cruelty early on.

Admittedly, seeing her so weak and terrified has beaten a lot of the resentment out of me. Even though a raging alcoholic, she was once a force to be reckoned with. A force that, at one point, Tobias and I found impossible to manage. Amidst her drunken ramblings over the years, some of her logic as Tobias, Sean, Tyler, and I strategized, was brilliant. We put it to use—especially her insight on fighting the machine we all loathe. In that, she's inadvertently been a part of rearing the soldiers we've become, even if she lost the war of having her own role in our movement.

If and when Delphine loses this last fight, I'm unsure of how I'll feel or what, and the idea of that has me mindlessly filtering channels as Cecelia softly whispers, "Romans 8:38-39."

A flip of pages sounds between my continuous channel clicks as Delphine recites the designated passage. "For I am sure that neither death nor life, nor angels nor rulers, nor things present nor things to come, nor powers, nor height or depth, nor anything else in all creation will be able to separate us from the love of God in Christ Jesus our Lord."

A brief silence ensues before Tatie speaks up with a shake in her voice, her question posed to Cecelia. "Do you believe that's true?"

Turning, I'm slammed into by the sight of Cecelia kneeling at Delphine's feet as she offers more words of comfort. "Those are the only verses I've memorized. So, I guess, maybe, I want to believe it."

Delphine's eyes slowly lift to mine, and Cecelia's deep blue gaze follows. The second we connect, a tidal wave of awareness crashes into me. That's when I see it, fucking *feel* it, and I'm not the only one. A heartbeat later, Delphine confirms it with a French whispered warning. "Elle est trop belle. Trop intelligente. Mais trop jeune. Cette fille sera ta perte . . ." *She is too beautiful. Too smart. But too young. This girl will be your undoing . . .*

Whoosh. Whoosh.

"*What happened to your parents?*"

Cecelia's question during the drive back to King's reverberates through the cabin of my Camaro as I exit, leaving her in the passenger seat. Feeling her heavy gaze following me as I stalk away, I don't bother to acknowledge Sean, who stands shrouded in the dark just outside the bay. His own calculating stare adding weight to hers as I make a beeline for my toolbox while my heartbeat thunders in my ears.

Whoosh. Whoosh.

Grabbing my toolbox from the garage, I press through the

backdoor heading through our littered graveyard of forgotten cars toward the Buick.

Whoosh. Whoosh.

There's always been an undertow-like grip in Cecelia's gaze. A grip and drag I've successfully managed to dodge—until tonight—when she glanced up at me from where she knelt at another unknown enemy's feet, her empathy and humanity on full display.

Whoosh. Whoosh.

That exchange was a bitch slap, forcing me to finally acknowledge everything I've been purposefully overlooking when it comes to Cecelia.

Propping the hood of the Buick, I plug in the extension cord attached to the shop light before sifting through my tools. Intent on losing myself in monotonous work, I toss them around as those seconds threaten to burn into memory while the goddamn whisper I've heard multiple times snakes its way in.

She knows.

The fuck she does, but our earlier exchanges indicated otherwise as she picked up on every unspoken word between us.

She undoubtedly felt my annoyance with the fast conclusions she drew during our earlier errand. Not a minute later—while stowing away my gun—temptation reared its unwanted head as my fingers brushed her skin, gathering the rapidly building electricity as it pulsated between us. Our lips so fucking close it would take little to no effort to erase the distance and finally get a taste.

Not long after—while rolling through the drug store pickup—Cecelia's jealousy emanated from the back seat, jealousy she didn't bother to mask as the pharmacist eye fucked me. She even took pleasure when Delphine slung insults toward the girl—as I did when I busted her, meeting her gaze in the rearview. That pulse pinged and lingered through the Camaro, even while Delphine rode passenger.

Sidestepping those urges was becoming first nature for me until those few seconds of eye contact in Delphine's living room.

The final straw was when Cecelia prodded me with the million-dollar question on the drive back to the garage. The answer to which would solve a lot of Cecelia's mystery regarding me.

"*What happened to your parents?*"

My inclination was to reply with something along the lines of, "your father found out about my parents' plans to expose him, so he staged a plant explosion to silence them while scaring the fuck out of anyone else with ideas of attempting the same."

That reply was suppressed even as it was constructed because of the concern in her tone—for *me*.

I could end this charade now if I wanted to. But something about the way she spoke to Roman earlier today had me considering Sean's pleas to try to see around the guilt by association.

What I didn't expect was for it to happen. But in those short seconds, what I saw—*felt*—forced that disconnect.

For the first time, I saw nothing but her.

When we met with RB—as I assumed—she'd passed judgment on us both in minutes. I called her out for it.

In truth, I set her up, then blamed her for her ignorance when she was just another victim of a system designed to keep us discriminatory and indifferent to each other's circumstances.

The difference is, I know Cecelia's circumstances . . . and now she knows mine—especially after forcing her way into my former childhood home and seeing the conditions in which I was raised. The second she stepped in, I *felt* the understanding washing through her. Just after, her misplaced determination kicked in to care for yet another unforeseen adversary.

Delphine.

Delphine, who never got over our parents' murder but could never put the vodka down long enough to do anything about it.

She was almost too slow on the uptake when I introduced Cecelia, if only to see how Delphine would react. When my aunt finally got on the page and realized who Cecelia was, the difference in personality and treatment was close to imperceptible . . .

for those who didn't know better. I did, and it was the difference I saw that shocked the fuck out of me.

There was no misinterpreting what was in Delphine's expression after decades of alcohol-induced tirades—guilt. She was littered with it after their little impromptu Bible study. But why?

Why in the hell would a woman who hates Roman as much, if not more than my brother and I, harbor guilt for anyone with Roman's blood pumping through their veins?

It's when Cecelia selflessly attempted to quiet my aunt's fears that my world fucking tilted, and I realized I'm just as guilty of having my own preconceived notions.

Believing that when it comes to Cecelia, evil is *inherited* instead of *taught*. Even if the former is possible, she's untouched by it, by him, by choice. She's rebuked her father in all the ways that matter.

It was then I glimpsed some of the blank canvas Sean's been begging me to see. Unlike countless others, Cecelia's anxious to understand the world around her—and the people in it. The why of it all.

She might be on some mission to play with fire and stick it to her father, but it's her own rebellion against the hand she herself was personally dealt that fuels her. In that, we're alike.

In that, *she's like us.*

Ensnared by her in that short time, realization struck—Cecelia Horner is filled to the fucking brim with *untapped* potential.

There's a sort of power brewing within her that not even she is aware of.

That's what I saw, felt, and rang through me with absolute certainty.

Not her age, beauty, or our undeniable chemistry, or even the danger she presents to us. The realization was so visceral that it had the hairs on my neck rising. Now that I've seen it, it can't be denied.

Tossing my wrench into my toolbox, I step back and stare

up at the night sky as Delphine's prediction rings clear. *"She is too beautiful. Too smart. But too young. This girl will be your undoing."*

A warning that had me speeding Cecelia straight back into the safety of Sean's arms.

Whoosh. Whoosh.

The wind kicks up, the breeze rolling through the junkyard as thunder rumbles in the distance. A reminder that at some point in the future, a giant is coming to dole out retribution to those ignorant of its existence.

A giant that exists because *I took part* in its creation, and with each day that passes, it draws near. Dread cloaks me with the knowledge that when it finally arrives, it will be just as blind and unforgiving as I've been, and none of us will be able to stop it.

TWENTY-ONE

PULLING UP TO THE GARAGE AFTER MANAGING A FEW AGITATED hours of sleep, I join Jeremy, Peter, and Tyler at the high-top table tucked in the corner of the commercial bay. Russell approaches, wiping his hands on a shop towel, glancing back at the bustling lobby. Just inside, a preschooler presses his face against the glass door as Russell speaks up. "I have five minutes, tops before Mrs. George starts demanding to know when I'll be done."

Tyler dives in. "All phones in the safe?"

Jeremy nods, not bothering with any of his usual antics. "So, we finally talking about the gun—"

"Just discussing strategy for our upcoming *ball game*," I jerk my head toward a customer exiting a nearby car, "now that we know *who* the *players* are."

Jeremy glances back and winces as Tyler leans in, speaking low. "So, here's what we know. Spencer's company—like most major shipping companies—is *freight forward*. Meaning, when a requisition—or a *ball order*—comes in from any foreign country, a US military specialist assigns the order to a freight forward company for fulfillment. Processing the balls from that point to gain authority from the ordering country to see it through until the balls are received and accounted for."

Russell leans in on a whisper. "It goes that far? We're talking dirty military and corrupt foreign government officials?"

"Yeah, it does," Tyler supplies while scanning the parking lot. "And considering how rare these balls are, I knew exactly where to dig."

Peter gapes at us, "Jesus, who knew Spencer was capable of something like this."

Tyler's expression hardens. "It's clear by the way they irresponsibly guard the balls in that shit shack that they've been getting away with this for some time. Spencer's part is easy, which makes the case of his involvement open and shut. His hands couldn't be redder. The specialist handling the order is just as compromised as the buyer because there is some serious protocol when it comes to *ball* sales."

Russell audibly starts piecing it together. "I read a story the other day that *balls* that were supposed to be on a military base were used in a street robbery . . . fuck . . . so this means that Spencer and the specialist work with the dirty foreign official under the guise they're ordering balls for their *own* military, receives them, and then falsifies the ball's location on a foreign base in their country before shipping them back to US soil to sell to God knows who?"

Tyler dips his chin. "That's the sum of it. Solves a little of the mystery of how some who should never get their hands on these types of weapons acquire them. Though rare, this is one of those ways, and it's the action of these greedy fucks selling out their stars and stripes, disgracing the rest of us in uniform. So, when this type of shit is discovered by those serving with good intentions, it's a big fucking deal."

Russell glances over at Tyler. "Which makes this *personal* for you."

"Goddamn right it does," Tyler snaps. "Which is why I've tracked who requested the balls and what specialist *here* they're working with. I'm guaranteeing all involved are getting a share of the sales considering each of the big balls in our park are worth twenty to thirty grand each."

Peters' money-hungry eyes bulge. "Jesus. That's—"

"More than what's in your piggy bank, and that balance isn't changing anytime soon," I snap, cutting off any illusions he might have about profiting.

Mrs. George chooses that moment to poke her head into the garage. "Russell, I've got to be at my hair appointment by nine!"

Russell groans, muttering a low "told you," before amplifying his reply to her. "I'll have you out of here in fifteen, Mrs. George."

Mrs. George leaves us with a withering stare before retreating into the lobby as I pick back up. "More crates were delivered to the warehouse last night, and we still don't know who's coming for them and when, so the clock is ticking."

"Timing is everything here," Tyler tosses in.

"Always is," I toss back, "but before we make a move, we need to get the bulk of the balls into *our possession* because we don't want the kids buying them and playing with them in the streets."

"Right now," Tyler adds, "from their perspective, everything looks untouched. This gives us a closing window to get what we need, so it's all hands-on deck, because once we go there . . ." Tyler gives us each a pointed look, ". . . there's no going back."

Russell looks between all of us, his face paling as he gathers the enormity of the situation. "But if we draw the wrong attention and our plan backfires—"

"We'll summon the perfect storm," Tyler finishes. "We're talking a majority of the big players, including the FBI, ATF, and the military itself sniffing in our backyard."

"So, it's a good thing we've got feathered friends in high places," I add.

A tense beat of silence passes as the stakes set in. None of us expected to deal with something so high-risk this early.

Peter speaks up. "So, *what is* the plan?"

Glancing around, I make a quick decision and walk over to

the tool shelf, snatching three Solo cups from a sleeve along with a handful of washers from a coffee tin. Taking a side of the high top away from the rest of them, I line the cups up on the table and lift a single washer. Using my sleight of hand, I place it beneath a cup before scrambling them. The washer noisily drags on the table, all eyes on the cups until I stop and lift my gaze to Jeremy for his guess.

Jeremy sighs and points to what he's sure is the obvious cup, and I lift it. Empty. His eyes widen in surprise as I slowly start to re-scramble.

Russell groans in protest. "Hey Dom, you are aware we have a lobby full of people, right? No need for a visual demonstration to get your point across. Contrary to what you might think, *Jeremy* is the only *idiot* here."

Jeremy gapes at him. "That *really hurt.*"

Peter speaks up. "Dom, we get it. We're going to use illusion to get the job done. It's child's play. You going to sing us Ring Around the Rosie too?"

I pause my movements. "Have you ever examined the lyrics to that sadistic fucking nursery rhyme?" I resume my version of the shell shuffle. "Ring around the Rosie," I relay, "refers to the rash associated with the plague. Posy was a bouquet used to mask the smell of decaying flesh."

"Ashes, ashes, we all fall down," Peter rasps out thoughtfully, "damn, that is some sick shit."

"See how that works?" I draw out. "Everyone at this table probably knows the words." They nod in confirmation. "That's the crux of our lack of critical thinking. That sick rhyme and countless others have been passed down for generations because we've been careless as to what we teach one another." I eye Peter. "Bet you'll think twice before you sing that lullaby to your baby sister."

I stop my shuffle. "And when you have a spare minute, Google the origin of Jack and Jill and some of the others, and you'll soon find our Mother Goose was in favor of Munchausen."

Russell makes his guess and weighs in. "So, I gather we're going to have them all scrambling to find the balls?"

"No, brother," Tyler says, a devious smile lighting his face as I swipe the cups off the empty table and Tyler extends a closed hand over it, slowly lifting his fingers to reveal a palm full of washers. "We're going to eliminate the *game.*"

Stalking back to my Camaro when Mrs. George pokes her head out again, I leave Tyler to lay out our strategy of framing Spencer and his accomplices without drawing attention to the club. Retrieving my phone from the glove box, I power it on to see a waiting text from Sean.

>**Sean: Meet me at the lake, bring the usual.**
>
>**Got shit to do.**

The bubbles immediately start.

>**Sean: Yeah, you do, but you're taking the day off.**

TWENTY-TWO

"**E**NCORE, MAMAN!" Again, Mama.

"Patience." She tosses my pajamas on the bed next to me. "Arms up."

"Encore, Maman!" Again, Mama, I yell louder, lifting my arms.

"Such a demanding little lark," she says, pulling my shirt down before pinching my nose. "Count with me."

"Un, deux, trois," One two three, we recite together before she begins to sing. "Alouette, gentille alouette." Lark, gentile lark! "Alouette, je te plumerai." Lark, I will pull your feathers! "You sing too, gentile lark."

"Je te plumerai la tête." I will pluck your feathers off your head, I sing as she begins to tickle me.

"Je te plumerai la tête." I will pluck your feathers off your head, she sings back.

"Et la tête," off your head, she sings high.

"Et la tête," off your head, I drop my chin and sing low.

"Alouette," Lark! She sings.

"Alouette," Lark! I sing back.

She presses her nose to mine, our eyes getting bigger as we sing together. "O-o-o-oh!"

She pushes me back on the bed, hair tickling my belly as she kisses it, and I try to wiggle away.

"Encore, *Maman*," I yell as she chases my foot with my pajama pants.

"Et le bec," off your beak. *She pinches my lips.*

"Et la tête," off your head. *She plucks my hair.*

"Alouette!" Lark!

She stops, yawning.

"Maman," I yell. "You did not sing it all!"

"We can sing again tomorrow."

But we didn't. We didn't sing.

We never got to sing again.

"Maman," I whisper, speeding away from the lake, chest burning as trees blur in my peripheral. Irony strikes me that mere hours ago, I chastised my inked brother for taking stock in a nursery rhyme while I replay the one I'm most familiar with—a subconscious punishment.

Atonement demanded by my psyche to re-live one of the handful of vivid memories I have with my mother.

One of my last, when maman declared me her gentle little bird.

What would she think of me now?

What would she think of the fact that I've become a different bird entirely?

A bird of prey.

A bird fueled by retribution.

A cunning bird capable of acts so vile, that boy is almost unrecognizable to me now—a liar, a thief, a master of deception.

A bird capable of taking part in destroying an innocent girl in the name of vengeance.

But what transpired on that lake float didn't feel like that. *At all.*

It felt like the *opposite* of that.

"Dominic."

Cecelia's moans skitter down my spine as her coconut-scented oil seeps further into my skin. My cock stirs at the memory of her above me—and beneath me.

The lust-filled tidal wave that crashed into me by way of a deep blue stare.

Her parted lips—and the sounds coming out of them.

A long pull of her pebbled nipple in my mouth.

The feel of her flawless skin between my bruising fingertips.

Her velvet tongue thrashing against mine.

Her endlessly long legs cradling me as she sank down onto me before we clicked into place, the fit fucking surreal.

Today's forecast did not call for—or in any way predict—me fucking Cecelia Horner.

But it didn't feel like fucking. What that felt like was . . . otherworldly.

The snap happened so abruptly that the static that always accompanied us caught fucking fire as the noise stopped. I succumbed so quickly that I made my own will a laughingstock but was rewarded in a way that I experienced every single moment. With just a kiss, this bird totally fell under the spell of the shiny, spinning thing.

In offering her my fuse, she ignited me.

Fire and water, she's both burn and soothe.

The haze I've been immersed in lifted so fast. It was as if I had roused from a deep sleep only to open my eyes and see the world through a magnifying glass.

All of my senses became more acute as sensation and sound overwhelmed me—the lake waves breaking against the float, the sharp intakes and exhales of breath, the feel of my heartbeat, the electricity that flowed at my fingertips, the thunderous warning that rumbled through the sky. Though, I bat away any foreboding feelings induced by any idiotic fairy tale I conjured as she swept me into a fucking fantasy. I wanted her so goddamned much that I would have defied anything or anyone who tried to separate us.

"*Dominic.*"

For the first time since the nightmare I'd existed in for weeks began, I felt like I'd surfaced from being underwater and took a much-needed breath. A breath of realization that I am a living, breathing man. A man starved, due to self-deprivation, in dire need of the woman spread in front of me.

I took the breath allowing everything I felt to ring true, in the way I touched her, voicing the few words that came to me, my guard absent.

No longer feeling like I was watching just outside my own life but participating in it. I was capable of taste again and savored hers. Touch turned into worship. With every deep thrust inside her, the burdens weighing me down were forgotten.

Something so natural and straightforward for most . . . but so complicated for me.

If fucking was all we had done, I'd already be home, finding another way to fill my time—but it wasn't. I totally lost myself in her, and every second of it only ramped up the one before.

Fully hard from the recollection, I speed forward in the opposite direction of the sun as I attempt to race away from the fact that the best I've ever fucking felt in the whole of my existence was when I was moving inside Cecelia Horner.

Speeding past any route home—knowing I can't be anywhere near where she is—I pour every effort I have into putting those minutes, that stolen time, into its respective box.

Cecelia and I are practically strangers. But that interlude said otherwise, just as the whisper informed me the second I laid eyes on her and every time since. The last part of said whisper, I refused and denied even after I saw her for the first time without the grudge in my eyes.

She knows.

She knows you.

Tightening my hands around the wheel, I curse whatever fate brought her into my life because finally allowing it to happen, wanting it to happen, and in participating in it, I lost the most important battle I had yet to fight.

Goddamn Sean.

Goddamn them both.

"Goddamn you," I grunt as the clarity threatens to disperse while the weight of the secret I just took part in begins to take its toll. Chest thumping, I lick the remnants of the kiss I left her with—a kiss that lingered with a promise I'll never be able to see through.

A fresh wave of culpability crashes into me as another vivid memory surfaces. My eyes fixed on a buzzing tattoo gun before lifting to meet his where he hovers a foot away—his expression a mix of pride and obvious affection. Pride and affection I may never see again because in finding that bliss—and momentary peace with Cecelia—I might have lost my forever constant.

My brother.

Turning into the heavily concealed driveway, I speed past end-less acres of land and park at the foot of his porch. Taking the wide steps up to the ancient farmhouse, the door opens just as I lift my knuckles to knock. Denny's eyes roll over me in a mix of curiosity and concern for a second before he dips his chin and widens the door enough for me to step through. I palm my cell phone against his chest as I pass. He takes it, my intent for being here made clear as I make my way through the house, retreating into his guest bed-room. Within seconds I'm stripped bare, every muscle in my body shutting down with fatigue, my mother's voice ringing through as I collapse onto the mattress.

"*Il est temps de dormir, Petit Prince.*"

It's time to sleep, Little Prince.

TWENTY-THREE

MY REWARD FOR FUCKING MY NEMESIS'S DAUGHTER?
Eighteen straight hours of comatose sleep.

Sleep my body finally allowed me after temporarily forgetting my ink and possibly fucking away my brother's trust. The Cecelia-induced haze I was under dissipated the second my eyes popped open at nightfall the next day. After spending the better part of last night into this morning exploring Denny's endless acres of cultivated farmland, my determination kicked in to rectify the situation.

Feeling I've summoned what I need due to my literal pre-dickament, I step through the front door finding Denny in the kitchen. Spotting me, he wordlessly pours a cup of steaming brew before holding it out in offering.

Taking a sip, I thank him, and he replies with a grunt before spraying his counter with a label-free bottle to wipe it down. No doubt the concoction is his own mix.

What so many don't know about Denny—who always passes in the sharing circle—is that he's our most resourceful bird. He made it his mission to utilize the farmland he bought outright and mastered it in a way that would put all doomsdayers to shame. Whether chemist or carpenter, he fills whatever role necessary to self-sustain without help from the outside world. For that, he has my admiration. We're alike in the fact that he both craves and thrives in isolation while working overtime to exercise restless energy. Glancing outside his floor-to-ceiling windows at the blooming grounds of his personal compound, it's apparent he's as restless as ever.

Of all our birds, Denny is amongst my most trusted, next to his fiancé. Layla was brought in early on by another bird, Craig, who became a fast liability after getting inked and took pleasure in treating Layla like shit. His tirade ended a mere week after Denny was brought into the flock and laid eyes on Layla, choosing her as his first big heist. Their relationship since has been intense, to say the least. Denny's borderline obsession with Layla turned into full-blown possession when he not only marked her but ringed her finger soon after, making fucking sure everyone else got the memo. Suspicions are that Denny delivered the news to Craig personally.

Whether Craig's death was by Denny's design remains unknown, and we decided that if that was the case, it was his secret to keep because if so, Denny did us all a service. And like Layla, Denny's a master at guarding secrets with a heaving side helping of not asking before carrying orders out to the letter. If I could, I'd replicate him. "And where has your lady bird flown off to?"

Denny shrugs. "Figured you didn't want her asking questions, so I tasked her with an errand to give you a chance to make a clean getaway."

"You really do speak my love language, bro," I tip my cup toward him in salute.

Grinning, he pulls open a drawer producing my burner.

"Anything happen while I was out?" I ask, taking it.

"Yeah, we got what we needed," he confirms.

I nod. Pleased by the fact that they used my brief sabbatical to successfully lift prints from Spencer's accomplices. It brings us a step closer to marching Spencer toward the guillotine. "I'm going to take off."

I walk my cup over to the sink and rinse it, soaking in the view of his pond and the surrounding grounds. "What you've done with the place, man, it's incredible. A recluse's dream."

"It is, thanks," he says with a pride-filled grin.

"Appreciate you, man. Thanks for the hospitality."

"Anytime," he offers, walking me to the door.

"You hate company," I chuckle.

"Not the quiet kind," his lips lift before I take the stairs of his porch, pulling my keys from my jeans. He calls after me, stopping me at my driver's door. "You good, Dom?"

"*Almost* made a clean getaway," I jest.

"I only give a fuck because of the state you were in when you got here."

"It's nothing I can't handle. See you tonight."

"See you," he says before shutting the door, no doubt relieved I didn't want to talk feelings.

Pulling up to the townhouse a few hours later, I park next to Sean's Nova and gather the bags littering my passenger seat. Just as I hit the top of the stairs, Sean's bedroom door opens. Flipping on my bedroom light, I place my burner on the magnetic strip that blocks all digital signals before dumping the bag's contents on my bed.

A second later, Sean fills my doorway, assessing me as I start to line my empty shelf. "What's good, brother?"

"Not a lot since both my girl and best friend went AWOL."

"Well, you know me. If you've got a personal problem . . . it's best to keep it to yourself."

He chuckles, sauntering into the room. "You're such a dick."

"Yet, like all the others, you keep coming back for more," I deadpan.

I continue to load my shelves as Sean clears his throat. "'He slipped his shorts down enough so his ready cock sprang free,'" he recites, open paperback in hand. "'He was so hard, pre-cum dripped from the tip. He took it in his hand and pumped a few times.' I see we're expanding our summer reading repertoire," he muses, tilting the book my way.

"The romance genre alone grosses over *a billion* a year," I counter, "which is currently more than *our* collective *net worth*." Gathering more books, I turn to stock them and pause when I glimpse the hardback sitting on the shelf above.

"Clearly they're cashing in on *you*," Sean quips as I brush my finger down the severely cracked spine of my mother's copy of *Le Petit Prince*. A vision of her shutters in, nestled in her favorite tattered chair, the open book resting on the arm of it as the sun streams through the window behind her. This time, I'm thankful for the memory without the accompanying guilt.

"Or maybe *you're the one* planning on cashing in," he rasps thoughtfully, sorting through the books. Glancing back, I see his brows pull in confusion. "What is this, Dom?" His eyes narrow. "What the fuck are you doing?"

"Whatever it takes," I relay for a second time.

His mood shifts instantly. "So, you disappear for two fucking days and come back with a plan . . . to what? *Hurt her?*"

"'The ink will always win,'" I recite back to him.

"I told you, all in, Dom, and I fucking meant it."

"You seem to forget you don't make the calls."

"*You* made this call, and if I can lure her out of hiding, I'm inviting her to the Meetup tonight."

I dip my chin. "I'll drive her in."

"To protect her." Both statement and question.

"Sure."

"God damnit," he runs his hand through his hair, "if you're planning on hurting her—"

"Maybe you conveniently forgot, but it was *your plan* to use her to get to Roman."

"I won't let you intentionally fuck with her," he growls.

"The way you have *me*?"

He swallows, eyes dropping as I turn back to the shelves.

"We're going to end her father, Sean. There's no future for you and Cecelia. Make peace with it."

"I get that, but—"

"You fucking need to because France is eventually going to find what he's looking for, and when he does, it's only a matter of time. Once that happens, you can't protect her."

"And you won't?"

Annoyed, I push past him to grab a shower, and he grips my bicep to stop me. Jerking away, I glare at him. "In a matter of hours—by your design—she's going to know damn near everything and will most likely run anyway. So, this conversation is pointless. Are *you* prepared for that? Because that's the risk you're taking baptizing her by fire."

He hooks his thumbs into his jeans pocket. "It's the way we've always done it when a recruit is ready. She's earned my trust and the right to know who we are."

"But she never truly will, will she? Even after you stomp on her rose-colored glasses." Stepping toward my bathroom, I fist off my shirt. "I'm done debating this. Completely fucking done arguing about her. It was a mistake to bring her anywhere near us."

"That's your fear talking," he digs in.

"No, it's yours," I snap, "we need to focus."

Sean bites his piercing before turning to stalk out.

"You were right about her," I call after him, kicking off my boots, "I'll give you that much. I see her potential, just not for our club."

He runs a hand through his hair as he lingers just inside my door. "Align yourself to any agenda you want when it comes to her, but I was fucking *there*, and I *felt* that shit happen between you." He shakes his head, refuting my stance. "You won't hurt her. Not intentionally."

"You have no fucking idea what I'm capable of," I grit out as he leers at me.

"Yeah, well. Apparently, neither do you, asshole," he counters, stalking out, his parting words filtering in from the hall. "But lucky for you, *I do*."

TWENTY-FOUR

FIFTEEN MINUTES AFTER SENDING ANOTHER FRAUDULENT progress report regarding Roman's daughter into the ether, I pull up to King's, dreading the hours ahead. Karma has a good laugh at my expense when my headlights beam directly on Cecelia as I roll to a stop. Eyes fixated on the woman who has been occupying my waking thoughts the last few days, I rev my engine in signal. Silhouettes of the birds surrounding her scatter, heading toward their cars. The sight of her feet from my hood—dressed to murder my reinforced resolve—sends humming, rapidly heating blood straight to my cock. My thirsty eyes drink her in through the windshield where she stands motionless, just as absorbed by me, while some of my crumbling resignation starts to scatter from me like windswept ash.

Fuck.

If this is what infatuation feels like, it's meant for lunatics.

I can already sense the screws loosening themselves from the hinges of the door I swore I mentally slammed shut.

Hating the parts of me responsible for the hasty betrayal—and Sean for knowing better as he steps up to her—my resignation is further compromised when her eyes light with Sean's request that she rides with me.

After a brief back and forth, Sean catches my gaze for a beat before heading toward his Nova, his trust in me unwavering.

I decide to hate him for as long as I can for his unshakable faith in me—along with sharing his current obsession—while firmly sticking to the belief that labels are for weak-minded, insecure men. That a woman's affection and loyalty should be freely given, *never* demanded. In a sense, he's right. In another, he's a goddamn fool. As allergic as I am to the feeling circus, even *I know* women crave some show of possessiveness, even if I agree they should be given the choice.

Bass thrumming in time with my heartbeat, Cecelia approaches, and I lean over and push open my passenger door. The night breeze sweeps her scent through my interior as she buckles in.

Nostrils flaring, I tighten my grip on the wheel, furious with my inability to ignore the pull. I cut off her attempt to greet me by tearing out of the parking lot. Her musical laughter rings through the cabin as I race toward the Meetup. Feeling every second of the attraction-induced chemical high, my earlier warning to Sean reverberates, striking me differently. Within the span of an hour, her perception of me will be altered—if not changed altogether. Just as I think it, she turns down the radio in search of some truth.

"Are we ever going to have a real conversation?"

Not possible.

"We had one not too long ago," I remind her.

"That's not what I mean."

"Want to start with politics or religion," I muse, because what in the hell could I possibly tell her that rings sincere? Opting to give her some half-baked truth, I relay the ideal existence of a twenty-five-year-old mechanic. The man I might've been if I wasn't on the brink of waging war on monsters—one of them her father. Briefly, I imagine a day of life without the club, a day filled with simple pleasures.

"Eggs—runny, coffee—black, beer—cold, music—loud, cars," I floor the gas. She laughs out the rest. "*Fast.*"

"Woman," I trail my eyes down her frame and feel her soften next to me due to the sentiment. When she moves to grip the hand resting on my gear shift, I pull it out of reach. "I save that for when I can do something about it."

"And you think that's affection?"

"Isn't it?"

A pregnant pause as she realizes intimacy is not in my wheelhouse.

"What makes you happy?"

"All of the above."

"Runny eggs and coffee make you happy?" She prompts, calling bullshit.

If only my life were that fucking simple. "What if you woke up tomorrow and there was no coffee?"

She frowns. "That would be tragic."

"Next time you drink it, pretend it's the last time you can have it."

"Great, there are two of you. Is that some philosophy? Okay, Plato."

My lips lift. "You can discover more about a person in an hour of play than you can in a year of conversation."

Sensing the familiar heaviness on my profile, I glance over. "I was raised to appreciate the small shit." The understanding in her expression only has my need ramping up to get closer.

Because I do want her, but the reality I exist in makes that an impossibility. The current continues to thrum between us as knowledge batters me that once we reach the end of this drive, both the bliss and temporary peace I've found with her—*in her*—will most likely be snatched from my grasp. Making a rash decision, I turn onto a dead end that leads to a small clearing. Killing the engine, I'm struck stupid by the sight of her staring wistfully through the windshield up at the half-moon. Her lit profile has my fingers itching to run through her flame. Leaning over with a, "come here," I grip her hips and pull her to straddle my lap. Sinking in my seat, she surrounds me while I immerse myself in the temporary high, flexing my fingers through her silky hair. Lips painted red, and eyes shrouded in black, she stares back at me, temptation personified.

When she dips, it takes some effort to deny her kiss, but I do, knowing I don't have the luxury of time to lose myself. As she pulls away, her beautiful features twist in confusion. I'm just as confounded as to why I spent two days convincing myself that allowing our pull to overtake me to the extent it did at the lake was a one-*time* high.

"He likes the red," I offer in shit excuse, which serves as a reminder to us both. Guilt mars her face at that reminder, and it's then I know she's fighting her own battle—a war with instilled morality. Her next question proves as much. "How long have you known each other?"

The uneasiness emanating from her has me running my palms up her back as my traitorous cock starts to harden, giving absolutely no fucks about my stance where she's concerned. "Most of our lives."

"That close?" She asks, rocking atop the bulge growing beneath her, gauging the heated warning in my eyes.

"We're all close."

"Apparently so."

The rumble of approaching engines cut through the night noise, serving as a reminder that I'm on borrowed time. Cecelia glances over my shoulder as they fly by. "They're leaving us."

"We left them," I correct, my palms hastening up and down the material covering her back.

"And we left them because?"

"Because," I lift to kiss her—because I fucking want to—and stop myself just before impact. Eyes closed in wait, her fast, anticipatory exhales hit my lips as all replies die on my tongue.

Because in minutes, you'll be fully aware of the level of deception we're capable of, and your moral dilemma about being shared will be a non-issue.

Because once you do know, you'll distance yourself far beyond either of our reach.

Slinking back into my seat, she opens her eyes to find me smirking in satisfaction. She wants me just as much.

"You're an asshole."

And you're the most beautiful punishment I've ever been dealt.

"That's not news. Anything else you need to know?"

"I don't *know* anything."

"Sure you do," I thrust up, so she can feel just how fucking much I'm denying myself.

Knowing I need to start armoring up for what's ahead, I opt to continue playing with the electricity at my fingertips because I'm just that selfish motherfucker.

Stealing the rest of her breath, I grind against the heat I can feel seeping from her core and am rewarded by fast pants as she sifts through our conversation.

"You described most red-blooded men. Cold beer, ah," she moans as I continually thrust up, and she starts to give back as good as she's getting, swiveling her hips.

"Fast cars?"

Thrust.

"Black coffee?"

Thrust.

"Runny eggs and . . ."

"And?" I prompt, lifting her so she's suspended on my outraged dick.

"Me," she whispers hoarsely before flashing a smile that serves as a direct hit.

"Then you know enough."

Giving myself a minute more, I lift her shirt and groan inwardly when I'm met with the sight of perfect tits and peaked nipples. Every bit of remaining self-control I have threatens to abandon me when I dip and pull her hardened flesh into my mouth. As I greedily feed, she explodes into motion, grinding onto me as I momentarily lose myself. I soak in what I can of her scent, the feel of her, knowing it might be my last taste.

It's when she moans my name that I mentally start to force myself away, biting down on her exposed flesh before soothing away any sting with the tip of my tongue.

"That was cruel," she scolds.

My dick agrees, but at least my conscience won't eat at me like it tried to after the lake. If I ever lay another hand on Cecelia Horner, at least she'll have a better idea of whom she's getting into bed with—even if key parts of the truth remain purposefully tucked away. Sean was right in the sense that she deserves to know who's fucking her. After tonight, she'll be aware of the true nature of the devils she's dancing with, and after that, it will be her decision to stay on the floor.

"We'll have to pick this up—later," I say, knowing it might be the last lie I ever tell her—that after Sean pulls back the curtain, she'll most likely run. Glancing over as I turn the key, something inside me stirs at the possibility that she won't.

Vision muddled by black rage, someone grips my hand, and I whip around, fist drawn to see Cecelia's mortified gaze. Shaking her concern off, my wrist throbs as I offer her another lie. "I'm good."

I'm anything but fucking good.

Fury and adrenaline continue to war for dominance as Cecelia takes a cautious step away from me. Her expression is telling as Sean snakes a protective arm around her, pulling her into him to shield her—from *me*. "Let him cool off, baby."

Not fucking likely.

As predicted, the last hour has been a fucking disaster. Feeling Cecelia's terrified gaze trail me, I break through the cover of the trees, fighting the urge to retrieve my Glock and end Andre and Matteo— no matter who's left in the audience. I'm bending my wrist and flexing my trigger finger when Tyler appears, eyeing my injury. "Broken?"

I jerk my chin in reply. "Andre no showed."

"I know," he exhales, glancing toward the roaring bonfire. "I've been tracking them both all night."

Andre—the head of the Miami chapter—missed the window for our one-on-one. Which, in our club, is a blatant sign of disrespect. Meetups are more a guise for the deals that take place between the trees at the party. A time meant to set up the when and where to trade stolen goods of each Chapter's most recent takes—along with introducing any recruits. It's one of the few secrets we share. "They're not even hiding it anymore. Something's up."

"I'm pretty sure you made it clear you're onto them," he says, gesturing toward my hand. Knuckles still dripping, I have no regrets about disfiguring the fucking bastard charged with doing Andre and Matteo's bidding.

We've always known Matteo and Andre were killers for hire—psychopaths who take pleasure in their work—which we utilized for our benefit until recently.

"I'll switch cars and follow them back to the Florida state line," Tyler offers, "and put some birds on patrol to make sure they all get the fuck out of our neighborhood."

"That's all fine and good, man, but you're not hearing me. They took out another black-market contract yesterday—nondiscriminatory. They've switched to killing innocents for a higher paycheck. They've broken every rule of our club and are rubbing it in our faces with their presence tonight, with an added plan to weaken us."

"How so?"

"I think they tried to take Sean out in the race."

His eyes widen. "The. Fuck?" He tilts his head up as if summoning patience. "Before we act, Dom, you need to be sure."

Clearing some of the haze, I replay it objectively. Sean's car rounding the curve in the outside lane, one side mountain rock, thousands of feet of drop on the other. Florida's headlights disappearing from my rearview to run alongside me before gunning straight for Sean. When I realized his intent, I gassed my Camaro just in time to cut him off, forcing him toward Tallahassee, who crashed into the rocky cliff just after we cleared the turn.

"Positive. He knew the road and had to have mapped it before the Meetup. There's no other fucking way to interpret how it went down. If Miami had so much as tapped *either* of Sean's bumpers, our brother would not be breathing right now. They need to be dealt with—*swiftly*."

Tyler's expression hardens as he glances around to ensure no nearby ears are privy to our convo. "Make the call to France and text me the verdict."

I shake my head. "You can't go at this alone. We don't know the nature of the game they're playing."

"Don't underestimate me," Tyler snaps, warning lethal.

"I never have, brother. I'll text you his decision but keep me updated."

Eyes murderous, Tyler takes off in full executioner mode, and I know if granted permission, he'll see it through—and make it painful.

Clearing the trees, I stalk toward my Camaro and am stopped by a brunette at my trunk, her nails raking up my chest. Annoyed, it takes a few seconds for me to recognize her.

"Hey, Dom," Stephanie purrs, reeking of whisky and cigarettes. "Been awhile, and I've got a secret . . . I've been thinking a lot about you," she drawls.

"Funny, I've been thinking about everything *but* you."

"Don't be a dick," she pouts before hitting her knees and reaching for my belt. "This time, I'll let you come in my mouth."

"Jesus Christ, Stephanie," I bat her hands away before lifting her by the underarms to stand. "This isn't a good time."

"You didn't mind it last time," she slurs.

"That was what? Two, three fucking years ago?"

"I just wanted to play around a little and reminisce," she stumbles in front of me, and I grip her elbow to study her.

"I think it's time we both forget you have no lips and move the fuck on. Go find another babysitter to suck off. I don't have time for this shit." Using my grip on her elbow, I gently guide her out of my path.

She jerks her arm away, stumbling in the process, "Fuck you, Dom."

"Not if I had a spare dick, Stephanie. Now would be a good time to remember who you're talking to and tread more carefully," I warn. "If I were you, I would get back to the bird you came with. This doesn't look good on him."

Just as I say it, her name is clipped out a few yards away. Her head snaps in that direction as I take a seat behind my wheel and pull my burner from my glove box to shoot off a text.

ROGUE BIRDS: This can't wait.

My burner rings a second later as Stephanie is not so gently carted off by her bird, and I catch sight of Sean pulling off with Cecelia in tow as Tobias speaks up. "Talk to me."

"Miami is full-on defecting," I get straight to it. "They're taking black market contracts on innocents, Andre turned his back on me at the party, and they just tried to take Sean out."

"What the fuck?" The instant change in his tone lets me know I have his undivided attention. "How?"

"During a race. They were going to make it look like an accident. I don't even think Sean knows how close he came to dying tonight. I stopped them right before they got him. It was close, brother," I rasp out, a knot lodging in my throat. "Too fucking close."

"It's a mob move."

"Exactly my line of thought." What transpired tonight aligns with the mob mentality of taking out the lieutenant because it would be too obvious if they went after me first.

"Tell me everything," he clips out, the noise in his background silenced by the closing of a door.

I relay it all and end with my proposed solution. "Tyler wants permission for turn down service."

"Denied."

"They tried to take out Sean!" I roar, my patience tapped out. "This can't go unpunished."

A few tense seconds tick by before he speaks up. "You do know that Miami has actual fucking mob ties?"

"I know who the fuck they are, but they need a reminder of who *we are*."

"Where are *you* now?" He clips out.

"Still at the Meetup. Tyler's going to follow them to the state line. We're putting birds on patrol to make sure they don't overstay their welcome, but something needs to be done, brother. We can't let this go."

"I'll put them on permanent watch for now until I can have a face-to-face with Andre."

"The time for peace talks is over."

"This isn't your fucking call," he snaps. "If we take the bait, we become *baited*. I'll handle it."

"How do you propose to do that a continent away, *Frenchman?*"

Silence. I'm pissing him off. Good.

"I can't believe you're willing to let this go."

"That's not what I'm doing. But we don't shoot first and ask questions later. They know the ins and outs of our fucking club, Dom, which makes this a delicate situation. Before we move, we need to at least try to come to some sort of understanding."

"Fine. Whatever," I turn my key, and Tobias hears me start up my car.

"Where are you going?"

Blue lights race by just as I start to pull out, and I instantly kill my headlights before pulling between the trees.

"Dom?"

"Blue lights. Someone non-club must have reported the race. Hold up."

Just as I go to compose a text, I scan some missed messages.

R: Blue lights on Kanuga Road.

P: Already following. Sean's leading him away.

P: He's losing them.

My shoulders sag in relief. "They're on Sean and—" I catch myself in time not to blurt her name.

"And?" Tobias prompts.

"He's losing them," I sigh.

"Good. Go home."

"Not yet. I'm going to help flush the streets until I'm sure the rest of Florida is headed south. Tobias, we can't let this go. I can catch up with Tyler, and we can end this tonight. Miami—"

"You're needed home."

"So are you," I snap. "But you aren't fucking here, are you?"

He exhales harshly, circling the ice in his tumbler in his typical repetition of three. "How is home?" *Delphine.*

"Here's an idea, *call her*," I clip out and hang up.

"When someone blushes, doesn't that mean 'yes'?"—*Le Petit Prince*, Antoine de Saint-Exupéry

TWENTY-FIVE

"**M**Y RAINY DAYS ARE YOURS, DOMINIC. IF YOU WANT THEM."
She didn't run.

Even after witnessing me at my most hostile and being made aware of some of the depth of our deception, she stayed. Not only that, but she also met me downstairs when I got home from patrol after the Meetup, bandaged my wrist, and fucking bathed me before tucking me in. The only conclusion I could draw was that Sean had prepared her—and *well*. Well enough to the point that when he left the next morning, she chose to stay at the house *for*, and to be with *me*. A day I've re-lived with my right hand through one too many cold showers.

"It rains a lot here."

The weather in the days since has made a liar out of me. Evidence by way of the sun's rays currently lighting the room in the reflection of my bathroom mirror. Razor poised an inch from my face, I glare down at Sean's spitz, Brandy, who whines just inside my bathroom door.

"What the hell do you want?" I snap. She replies with an order-filled bark. Sighing, I rest my razor on the sink and jog the solid white hairball downstairs to the sliding glass door. Opening it enough to let the dog through, the heated summer wind breezes in as a reminder that the season has set in. Brandy races toward Cecelia, who's wearing the bikini I rid her of the first time I fucked her. Her back to me, she's bent over, pert ass thrust in the air in offering. I inwardly groan as Sean yells instructions from the side of the house, realizing the reasoning for her positioning as she moves a sprinkler.

"A little closer to the fence," he shouts.

"Here?" She asks.

"Yeah. That's good, Pup."

"Is the water on?" She scrutinizes the arched metal bar full of holes. "It's not working." As she further lowers to inspect the sprinkler, her bikini shifts, revealing a heaping handful of ass cheek.

This. Fucking. Girl.

Temptation mocks me mere feet away, along with the knowledge that there's not a drop of fucking rain in the forecast anytime soon. Each time I pull up the weather app, I hate myself a little more for it. The summer sun has decided there's no relief in the future for little Dom, who's currently growing three sizes too big in my boxers at the sight of a beautiful girl. A girl I now know a lot more intimately after a solid day in bed together but crave to fuck like it would be the first time.

"Now?" Sean asks.

"Nope," Cecelia calls back to him as I imagine a half dozen scenarios to approach her with how she's situated. She might not have run, but she did lay out ground rules. Ground rules I start to resent her for as the throb continues in my boxer briefs.

"Huh," I hear Sean say, knowing that tone. "Crank the dial up and see if that works."

"This thing looks ancient," she shouts, "It's probably broken, okay, try it—" her shout turns into a shriek as she's soaked by Sean's design. Sean's deep laughter rings out as she scolds him with an *"asshole!"*

Brandy begins to bark at the offensive sprinkler, the

dumbest damned dog in existence, which is why I mostly ignore the fact that she does exist.

"I'm going to cut and trim out front. Give me about thirty minutes."

"K," she calls, bending to pet Brandy as she eyes the sprinkler fanning water over the yard. Expression lightening, she stands and sprints toward the fence before turning and running to leap over it, soaking herself, a shriek bursting out of her.

Images of Sean, Tyler, and me doing the same when we were rugrats shutters in. As she makes another pass in my direction, the sight of her so full of carefree joy has my chest tightening. Despite her physical allure, she's the picture of purity. Even if she experienced enough during her start with her parents to be just as jaded as I've become, she isn't. It's by choice that she embraces the lighter side of living, whereas I welcome the dark, dwelling amongst the shadows and manipulating them to suit.

Like me, Brandy stands by observing her, equally captivated by what makes her tick, in an attempt to try and understand her.

Cecelia continues to run back and forth through the waves of water, urging Brandy to join her.

"Come on, girl," she coos, running back and forth in demonstration. When Brandy joins in, leaping over the sprinkler in time with her, Cecelia's melodic laughter crashes into my chest, further widening the crack she's managed to create.

Disgusted that I'm inching toward creeper status after watching one too many passes, the half of my face covered in mentholated shaving cream begins to burn. Ripping my eyes away from her, I make my way back upstairs. Patting my face down with a damp towel a few minutes later, I spot the summer of my discontent staring back at my reflection.

"Hi," she whispers, her eyes rolling appreciatively down my frame.

Hi?

Hi?

I narrow my return gaze on her.

If this is hard-up, I'm not going through it alone.

Turning, I grip her wrist, yanking her into the bathroom. Palming the wall next to her head, I crowd her as I trace the droplets of water skating down her glowing skin. Her eyes search mine for a reason for my aggression, but my cock lets her know as it salutes her and remains at attention—pointing straight at her. When she opens her mouth to speak, I press my finger against her lips as Sean cranks the mower outside. Her chest rises and falls as I lower my gaze to her pink-painted toes while deciding my course of action.

Gripping her shoulders, I position her in front of the toilet before shutting the lid and taking a seat. Draping the damp towel over my lap, I gather the rest of my supplies from the counter. Flicking on the faucet to refresh the water, I plug it before switching it off and lifting her foot, resting it on my knee. Wordless, Cecelia rattles in anticipation in front of me while I dispense some shaving cream into my hand.

Palm full, I slowly begin to cover every inch of her leg and thigh as I speak. "It takes an average of twenty minutes to ready a woman to the point of orgasm." Scraping the blade from her ankle up to her calf, I swish it in the sink and tap it twice before running it from above her knee to her thigh. A harsh exhale escapes her as I look up to see her dark blues hooding.

Once I've made a few passes, I swish the razor through before again tapping away any lingering excess.

Swish. Tap. Tap.

"Unfortunately, for women, twenty minutes of stamina is pretty average for a man, which would make our creator seem like one cruel motherfucker," I scrape another path up the length of her leg, "if said creator hadn't given us ways to remedy that. You see . . .," I glide the razor along the ridge of her leg, "what most men don't know—or give a damn enough to know—is that said creator did give us a number of efficient ways to get a woman where she needs to be. In fact, there are thirty ways . . . or more, depending on the woman."

Swish. Tap. Tap.

Knowing I have her undivided attention, I glance up and can't help smirking at the rapid rise and fall of her chest. "Should we try a few of them out?"

She nods half a dozen times as I resume.

"It's sad, really, that most men think of a tight fit as a reward, and for some, it's inevitable due to the size and girth of the male anatomy, but not all are as blessed as *others*." My own blessing agrees with a jerk as I make it a point to exhale along her freshly shaved skin, and goosebumps erupt. "But considering what a woman's anatomy is capable of, a tight fit is often a sign that the prep work wasn't done properly."

Swish. Tap. Tap.

"There's the inner thigh," I scrape the razor up to the top of her thigh as she palms my shoulders to steady herself. "This crease at the top of it," I run my thumb along the sensitive skin just below her bikini bottom from her ass cheek to her hip as her soft pants begin to fill the bathroom. "The armpit."

Swish. Tap. Tap.

"There's the ears, the stomach, and the hands." Pausing the razor, I lift one of the hands resting on my shoulder and pinch her pressure point as I gently brush my lips along the entirety of her palm, including the pads of each finger. She exhales my name as I draw the towel from my lap and pat away the excess cream. Brushing the tips of each pinky along her newly sensitive skin as I towel her off, her eyes close when the first moan escapes her.

"Such a beautiful, *sunny* day," I remind her of her fucking rules. Rules that hinder me from acting on any scenario in which my throbbing dick gains access to the heaven lingering inches from my face. Rules I respect and will continue to, but hate at the moment. She runs a hand through my hair as I turn her palm up, licking slowly along her wrist, catching her speeding pulse beating against my tongue.

"Then there's the crook of the arm." I demonstrate by sinking my teeth into the skin opposite her elbow, which earns me a more drawn-out moan.

Noted.

Bringing her other foot into my lap, I glance up to see the lust in her eyes. Her plump lips part as I tamp down the demand raging in my boxers.

"The bottom of the foot." Roughly, I run my thumb along the arch. "The Achilles tendon," I squeeze the back of her heel before moving up, pinching the tendon between my fingers as her nails dig into my shoulders.

"Between the toes," I whisper heatedly, painstakingly brushing a finger between the soft pads of her grass-covered toes.

"The inside of the ankle." Bending as I lift hers, I run my tongue along the outer bone to the inside before clamping down and sucking lightly. This has my name whispered with more urgency from her lips.

Noted.

Dispensing more cream into my hand, I run it up her toned leg covering every bit of skin. Her fingers dig into my scalp in demand. "Scalp, too," I say, stopping her explorative hand and placing it back on my shoulder before making several long swipes with the razor.

Swish. Tap. Tap.

"Dom, please," she whispers.

"Not in the forecast." Feigning indifference, I run the blade along her vibrating inner thigh. Using my free hand, I palm her stomach, spreading my fingers in a caress before running it up her torso and stroking between her perfect tits. One by one, I move the triangle-shaped curtains covering her hard nipples, exposing them to the air steadily blowing down from the overhead AC vent.

"Obviously, the breasts, which is a more in-depth process . . ."

"Dom, I—"

"But we'll get to those," I cut in.

Swish. Tap. Tap.

Shaving the rest of the path away, I slowly massage away any remaining cream. The second I lower the towel, she takes a step toward me, and I palm her stomach, slowly inching her back. "We're not done."

Rapt, she watches me refill my hand with a small amount of shaving cream before I pinch the top of her bikini bottom between my fingers. Pulling up, I expose her clearly defined tan lines while wedging the material between her pussy lips.

The sight of it has my cock jerking again in time with her rough intake of breath. Hooking and holding the bound material with my pointer, I lower my thumb and gently brush it along the top of her landing strip. "The mons Venus."

Using two fingers, I gently apply the cream on the sides of her bikini line before picking up my razor. When I press it to her skin, her breath stops altogether. "I need—"

"If only it were raining," I taunt, making my first swipe.

Swish. Tap. Tap.

"We can—"

"Shhh," I whisper, taking great care as I run the razor gently along the sides of her pussy. "Then we have the lips . . . but there are more than one set," I whisper, "actually, there's three. The ones you gloss, and the others," I smirk up at her, "*I gloss.*"

Blue waves of fire reflect back at me, the torrent tide threatening to sweep me in. Chest heaving when I wipe her freshly shaved pussy free of any remnants, I feel the snap in her before she speaks.

"Fuck the weather," she declares, straddling me on the toilet seat. She thrusts a demanding tongue in my mouth, and I deny her before swiping my own along her pouting lips. Taking advantage of the fact she's firmly wrapped around me, I lift and back her toward my bed. Gently depositing her, I take a few minutes to revisit the spots she appreciated most before I start to tick off the ones I hadn't yet gotten to.

The trimmer sounds up outside, giving me a timeline as I prop on my side next to where she lays flat. Chest heaving, pupils dilated, her body hums in response to every single touch.

"Where were we?" I ask, running a finger along her neck before sucking the skin behind her earlobe.

"The lips," she rasps into my ear as I stifle another smile. After tracing her mouth, I slide two fingers between her parted lips with my order, "show me how wet you are." She pulls them in deep, sucking feverishly as my cock threatens to self-destruct.

Fingers soaked—but knowing I didn't need the help—I slide my palm from her breastbone, down her stomach, and into her bikini bottoms only to confirm it. She's drenched. Gathering the wetness seeping from her core, I spread my fingers into a V and, with the pads of them, start lazily sweeping them from the bottom of her outer lips, tracing them to the top.

Gripping my head for a kiss, I deny her, and her back arches as pleas start to pour from her mouth. Taking special care not to graze her clit, her hips begin to buck for friction. It's when I glimpse the sheen of sweat covering her that I know I've got her hyperaware and ready.

Bypassing her nipples, I suck the skin of her breasts—the skin less sensitive but still stimulative.

"Dom, please, please," she rasps out.

"Trust me," I murmur, watching my fingers as her pussy weeps for me, her chest bouncing as I start to trace lazy circles around her areolas, avoiding her taut nipples.

She cries out when I dip further in, tracing her inner pussy lips, satisfied as she thoroughly soaks my fingers.

"Like our filthy little experiment?" I taunt as she writhes beneath me.

"Oh, God," she stutters, "Dom, p-p-lease, please!"

"Your clit is pulsing," I whisper hoarsely, not bothering to hide the heat in my voice, my cock straining against her leg, "and that's because you're concentrating on where you *think* you need me to touch you. But you don't. Watch my tongue, Cecelia." The whole of her body shudders when I repeatedly thrash my tongue against her nipple. Her moans become more desperate, her legs shaking against the forearm that I'm moving between her thighs. Stopping my fingers, I use my pointer and dip a little further to rim the opening of her pussy before sucking her pebbled nipple into my mouth. A surprised gasp leaves her when she starts to come undone a second later.

"Let go," I order around the nipple clenched between my teeth before pulling it in and sucking, *hard*.

"Oh fuck," she cries out, her sounds cut by her rapid breaths as she convulses. The sight of it is so fucking hot that my dick weeps. As she comes down, she stares up at me with kaleidoscope eyes in varying shades of deep blue, and I rest my palm to cradle the side of her face, gently sweeping my thumb along her hairline.

"That was . . ." she looks up at me in wide-eyed wonder, "that was crazy," she whispers before a gradual, lazy smile lights her face. "I can't believe I came . . . *like that.*"

"That's because the most important erogenous zone is *here,*" I double-tap her temple with the pad of my thumb before sliding it along her delicate cheek. "You were halfway there because of how attracted we are to each other and because of how incredible it feels when we do fuck."

Pupils dilated, her eyes soften as she sinks into my mattress, and I soak up every bit of the aftermath in her expression. "That's how it feels for you? Incredible?"

"Yeah, it does," I admit, which is why my dick hates me for the moment. The words are starting to come a lot easier, and worse, starting to flow out of me *unchecked.* The sound of the trimmer cutting off signals that time is up as I pull the top of her bikini back into place. "Dom, that was . . . seriously the hottest thing ever, and don't take this the wrong way, but . . . I'm still *aching* for you."

"That's not going away anytime soon. For either of us."

Her answering smile serves as a battering ram in my chest. Lifting her to stand, I turn her toward my door and slap her ass hard enough for it to sting.

"Ouch." She glances back, palming and rubbing her ass to soothe the reddened skin. "That stung."

"Good. And just so you know, the next time you come into my room on a day that doesn't *belong to me,* you're getting *fucked* with *extreme prejudice.* Oh, and . . . *hi.*"

TWENTY-SIX

G RABBING THE ALTERNATOR, I PULL OUT MY TOWEL AND WIPE away the debris from the reconstructed part before setting it in place. Tyler works silently next to me—lately more of an apparition than a roommate, only haunting our townhouse to collect bare necessities. It's obvious he's keeping secrets of his own. After spotting his truck driving through our old neighborhood when I dropped Delphine off after her last chemo appointment, I have a good idea about one of his choice haunts. My wrist smarts, and just as I start to tighten it in, a rumble sounds in the distance.

Ears perking up, my pulse follows as a breeze sweeps through my open bay door, cooling my sweat-slicked skin.

There's been no exchange of numbers or a promise for a call I wouldn't make. Cecelia left my bedroom that day with nothing more than a warning from me and an opt-in for her invitation, weather permitting, as it does now with a deafening lightning crack.

An unsettling feeling snakes its way in as I wonder in what fucking universe this could possibly work. Especially with my existing bedside manner and refusal to treat this situation differently. The rattling echo off the bay doors a second later has me losing partial grip on my wrench, which noisily clangs against the engine. Cursing, I manage to grip it before it hits the garage floor.

"Have you ever had a girlfriend?"

I gave her some bullshit, but the honest answer is no, and I have no intention of breaking that winning streak. Even so, since the day of our last encounter, I haven't gone a few hours without thinking of her—and it's done nothing but grate on me. I chalk it up to sexual frustration. Between that, the infuriating idle of my club, the festering friction with my brother and Sean, not to mention the sick fucks I continually keep tabs on—it's safe to say I'm close to reaching my limit.

Exasperated, I try to focus again when the wrench slips from my hand, clattering to the garage floor. Retrieving it and determined to dismiss the idea that this state is perpetual, I glance over to see Tyler observing me like a fucking zoo animal from where he works a bay over. Another lengthy bout of thunder filters through the shop as the next icy breeze brings the unmistakable patter of rain.

Bristling under Tyler's steady attention, I glare over at him. "What?"

"Tell me where you're at, Dom," he prompts in a coaxing tone. "Give me that much."

"You know where I'm at," I grit out, tightening the first bolt. "I'm caged until the one with the key unlocks the door." I secure another, my wrist giving me hell. "Any word from Miami?"

"France has birds on watch."

Rain begins to pour as I glance at an accumulating puddle just outside the concrete lip of the bay. "As much good as that's going to do."

"There will come a time—"

"So, I hear," I cut in dryly. "I'm over it, Tyler. I'm being a good, levelheaded little bird."

"There will, Dom."

"Sorry if I don't believe you or anyone else wearing the same ink right now."

"I get that things feel *off,*" he offers.

"That's just your roundabout way of saying *I'm off,*" I zero in on him. "You think I don't see the way you all look at me? Like I'm some bouncing live wire you're all afraid to get close to?" I shake my head in disgust. "If I am, it's because I'm filled to the fucking brim with a need to act—to expose the truth. Something we once had in common and had issues getting others to believe until proven. What's incredible to me is that lately, I've been put in the position to defend myself to my fucking own." I shake my head. "You would think at least one of you would understand my struggle. But it seems like everyone around is so locked up in their own fucking lives—their own shit—so afraid I'll upset the balance when upsetting the balance is the reason we fucking soldiered up in the first place."

"We are moving," he reminds me.

"At a snail's pace," I scoff. "It's like everyone forgot they were once angry too. So angry they altered their entire life path to take action, and what are we doing?" I toss my wrench in my toolbox in disgust as the little girl's screams in the latest video amplify—the noise crashing back into me in a breath-stealing rush.

I'll never outlive the image of her surrounded by monsters—defenseless, alone, and begging for help that didn't come. Turning on him, I feel the anger start to simmer just beneath my skin. "This isn't supposed to be about *us.* If we give into caring about only what we get out of this, we're no better than the people we're targeting."

"I get that, I do," he assures.

"Yeah?" I snap my head up. "So, tell me, brother. Where do you go at night? Because it can't all be about the fucking club."

He swallows. "It's not. Not always."

"That's what I thought."

"I'm still mad, Dom. I've also laid witness to shit that no human should ever see. The difference between us is that I can temper it a little better. But you continually seem to forget I've sacrificed a lot to start this fight with you. Don't write me off so fucking easily. It's insulting."

Sighing, I keep his stare and get a really good look at him for the first time in weeks. His posture is fatigued. The circles under his own eyes are darkening by the day like my own. "I am thankful for you, man, but it's stagnant water we're floating in, and it's," I groan and run my hands through my sweat-soaked hair in frustration.

"We have to trust that France knows what he's doing."

"What if he's just as lost as we are?" I ask, the thought terrifying. "Don't you find it pretty disconcerting that he chose *now* to search for his birth father? Seems like some sort of existential shit to me, and it couldn't be worse timing."

"He's wondering why it's been so hard to get ahold of you the last few days."

"Yeah, well, he can keep wondering because he's been ignoring me for his own selfish shit since he left."

"So, it's not this thing with Cecelia?"

I shake my head. "That's temporary. Everyone knows that, including Sean. So, ignorance is bliss, right? Maybe I'll fuck around with that mindset for a while."

Shoulders slumping, I shake my head. "Doesn't matter . . . things are changing, and apparently so are we, and nothing about any of this feels right."

"I believe you, Dom. You don't have to convince me of anything. And no matter how much shit changes or how much we change, I'm not going anywhere, okay?" He's only a foot away now, his back to the open bay as rain starts to pour behind him.

I nod in reply, a slight bit of tension easing off my shoulders.

"And you're right," he sighs. "He's being selfish with his quest, and the timing is questionable. But considering how long he's been at this without us, he deserves it. Hell, with what we're undertaking with no end in sight, maybe we deserve to indulge in a little escape if we can manage to find it."

My reply dies on my tongue when I spot Cecelia over his shoulder, standing outside of the bay in a solid white sundress, lust-glazed blues rolling over my profile. Static instantly lights my veins, along with a sweep of relief as I exhale the breath I hadn't realized I was holding.

"Yeah," I whisper hoarsely, unable to rip my gaze away, as Tyler follows my focus. "Maybe we should."

The next roll of thunder has nothing on the roar in my chest as thin cotton clings to my midday mirage, who's rapidly becoming soaked while charged seconds pass between us. A puff of temperature-invoked smoke billows from her heaving chest as her soaked dress outlines her erect nipples and every curve. I no longer have to wonder about the *how* because it's crystal clear she's here to collect.

She came. For *me*.

TWENTY-SEVEN

"I'LL FIND SOMEWHERE ELSE TO BE," TYLER MUSES, TURNING to stalk out as Cecelia sets into motion, passing him without so much as a glance. The slam of the bay door behind him leaves us cloaked in dim light as we collide. The impact is like a much-needed shot that rapidly seeps into my bloodstream—Sweet. Fucking. Relief.

Her moan vibrates my tongue as she surrounds me entirely—her scent, her skin, and her noises. My entire body is alight with need—my cock, already fully hard, strains to get to her through my zipper. Kissing her back just as feverishly, I lift her to straddle me, and she molds around me as if it's natural. It feels that way and has since our first kiss on that float. When we finally part, she looks up at me, pupils blown with desire. "Please don't stop, Dom. I *need* you."

Stunned by her easy admission, I prop her on the hood to relieve my screaming wrist and run my hands over her soaked arms as her eyes search mine. "Cold?"

"No," she murmurs, grinding her center along my cock.

It's been one too many fucking days without rain, without her.

"Dom," she pleas for relief, as if I'm the only one capable of giving it to her. Right now, in her eyes and her touch, she makes me feel like I am. God knows she's quickly becoming the only thing I want more than vengeance.

I can't have that yet . . . but I can have *her*.

My blissful ignorance.

So, for now, I'll get lost in the oblivion she offers because I need her too—if only for the peace she brings with her. I might be horrible at this, but she's got a way of making me feel like an expert.

She stares up at me expectantly as scenarios race through my mind of how the next few minutes might play out if I get greedy and take my salvation here and now. The thought of interruption likely, I reluctantly set her to her feet. Her hands continue to roam, plucking at my clothes, running along my abs as she lifts to press hot kisses to my neck. Unable to help my chuckle, I pull away, and she glowers at me. "Give me a minute."

She stares back at me, exasperated. "Seriously?"

"Be right back."

Stalking into the lobby, I pull my cell from the safe and dial the number, thankful when it's answered on the first ring.

"Hey, Cindy, need a favor," I glance over at Cecelia, who's running her hands up and down her arms, and narrow my eyes. Little liar. She is cold. "Twenty minutes? Leave me a little something? Thanks, Cindy, I owe you."

Walking back into the garage, I drink her in, hair-soaked, tan skin glistening even with the lack of light. She stares back at me, just as greedily but seemingly lost. After securing the bay, I take her hand and lead her out of the garage as I lock up before tucking her into my passenger seat. Firing up my Camaro, I crank up the heat and turn onto the main road as rain floods the windshield.

Flicking up my blades to clear it, I shift gears, leaving my hand on the gearshift. Instinctively, Cecelia covers my idle hand, and I pull it out of reach.

Glancing over, I see the sting of rejection as my cock dismisses it and speaks on my behalf, snapping out my first order. "Lift your dress."

She does, and I freeze when I see a thin strip of cobalt blue.

Fuck me.

"Show me what I've been missing, Cecelia."

She goes to pull her panties down, and I jerk my chin and bark. "*No*, leave them on." Retribution is in order for the number of fucking scenarios I've drummed up starring those panties. "Pull them to the side and spread your pussy with your fingers," I snap as I give the car a little gas, "show me."

Head tilted back, she stares over at me, eyes hooding as she gives me a glimpse of heaven.

"Wider," I bite out, on the verge of parking any-fucking-where close to get inside her. She does my bidding, and I don't get my fill when forced to snap my focus back to the road. "Dip your fingers in and give me a taste."

When she starts to lift glistening fingers in my peripheral, I snatch them into my mouth, sucking and savoring her taste, determined to drown in it. Her answering moan echoes through the cabin, whispering straight to my cock, which jerks in response. Doing everything I can not to drive recklessly, I release her fingers with a pop while mentally clearing my calendar, replacing everything on my to-do list with eating her until my lips and tongue are saturated by her.

Heartbeat thundering, I ease up on the gas—forced to slow around every curve as we head up the mountain, every stretch of mile agonizing. Allowing myself one more glance over, I witness a drop of water land and run down her exposed thigh and decide to replace it with the cum leaking from the tip of my dick.

When we finally reach the open gate, I race into the right turn, and she misses the sign, prompting me with her question.

"Where are we?" She asks, glancing around.

"Alone." Which is all that fucking matters. I don't want an audience anywhere near us. Whether it be a wall or a fucking bay door. As much as it turns Sean on at times, voyeurism isn't really my thing.

She made it clear the night of the Meetup—it's not for her, either. On that, we're straight. Privacy is a necessity because I want her to be as vocal as she was our first day alone together.

Wipers sliding the rain from view, I hear the mud and gravel collect on my tires as they grip enough road to get us past endless rows of ripe green vines to the left and right of us. Stopping just outside of the wine cellar carved into the mountain cliff, I exit and round the car. Pulling her out of the passenger seat and straight into me, I crush her lips in a bruising kiss. Trailing my fingers between her thighs, I nudge her panties to the side. Thrusting two fingers up to the knuckles, I squeeze her pussy lips between my thumb, ring, and pinky. Using the grip, I cradle them around my swirling digits to ready her. She breaks our kiss with her pleasured cry, parted lips against mine. Recapturing her mouth, I swallow her noise down in an attempt to partially satiate the beast.

Rain batters us both outside my passenger door as lightning cracks, the storm feeling like more of a *result* of *us*, than nature's permission.

Every drop of rain that falls unleashes me. Feral with hunger, I walk her into the open cellar, clicking on the light.

Just feet inside the open door sits the edge of a twenty-foot table littered with scattered flowers, jars, and floral supplies, no doubt abandoned after I called. Uninterested in our surroundings, Cecelia's hands snake beneath my T-shirt, fingers tracing my abs as she sucks the rain from my neck, using her free hand to grip my cock.

"Dom," she breathes as she drags her teeth along my skin, raking her nails down my chest. Inhaling a breath of patience, I swipe one of Cindy's offerings from the top of a nearby barrel and unscrew the top with my teeth while palming Cecelia toward the edge of the table.

"Pull your dress around your hips."

She complies, the material cinched at her waist before I press her flat to the surface. Eyes shimmering with anticipation, she gapes up at me as I blaze my own trail down her body. Flattening my hand on the table next to her head, I hover a beat before doling out my next order. "Open."

Taking a swig of the wine as she parts her perfect lips, I dip and funnel the wine from my mouth into hers, the "hmm" in her throat fueling me.

Pulling down the soft material at her shoulder to free her nipple, I flick my tongue against it as she clutches my head. Armed with another mouthful of red, I draw her nipple into the mix, and she arches against me. Pulling it in deeper, I suck hard, a reminder of our last time together. I'm satisfied she needs none as her beg drifts into my ear. "Dom, please, *please*."

Ensuring her thirst remains—as do her cravings—I splash some wine over her nipple before sucking it in. The spillage runs along her flawless skin, ruining the collar of her dress. Pouring more, I make my way down her torso, laving every trail I can catch with my tongue before stopping to lap at the shallow pool gathered in her belly button. Her eyes follow when I hit my knees, drag her to the edge and push her thighs apart.

Tipping the bottle, I free-pour over the thin cobalt strip covering her pussy, before sucking the whole of it into my mouth. Through the silky material, I tease her clit with fast flicks of my tongue. She begins to buck, needing more focused attention for release, but I deny her, opting to feel that explosion on my cock. Taking my time, I watch her writhe. I bring her to the edge as she does my bidding, my name tumbling from her lips half a dozen times—the sound of it pulls me further into our present cocoon. The only goddamn place I want to be. Ensnared by her melodic moans, she sweeps me up into a blue undertow as I set the bottle on the nearby barrel, freeing both hands to touch her.

"Dom!" she pants, "I need you *now*."

Feeling is mutual.

The hard concrete is unforgiving at my knees, and I know the table can't be comfortable—but I can't spare a fuck to give. Hooking her panties with my fingers, I tug them down her legs before snapping to stand, bringing her with me, and lifting the ruined dress over her head. When I toss my shirt aside, she grabs my injured wrist and gazes up at me while placing reverent kisses along it. Her expression and the act convey just how much she cares as the crack she formed in my chest widens a little further.

Words fail me as she continues to gaze up at me, completely bare, trust in her stare. In that moment, I want to warn her not to so freely give things I haven't earned and don't deserve. My heartbeat shifts, pounding in a remorseful rhythm as everything stops in those few seconds, and she stares up at me with faith in her eyes.

I'm deceiving her.

Brows drawing, she palms my jaw, trying her best to read the reason for my hesitation, but lust and hunger win.

Turning her to face the table, I rip my wallet from my pants and press her flat to the surface. Tearing the package with my teeth, I lift her knee to rest on the edge. After plucking the condom free, I press my fingers inside her, twisting them along her G-spot in beckoning.

"Fuck, please," she rasps out in a prayer for me to speed up as I keep at my task, feeling the tell-tale swell at the pads of my fingers before I'm satisfied. Withdrawing them, it's the vision of her glistening pussy that fucking undoes me.

Unfastening my jeans, I pull out my dick and secure the condom on the tip as her back rises and falls. The vision of her spread and ready force the words out.

"You're so goddamn perfect, Cecelia," I confess before bending to bite down on her shoulder, cheek flat against the table, I feed her my fingers and she sucks them eagerly.

Though I could ready her all day, the lust overrides me to the point that I'm still rolling on the condom when I thrust into her.

The surge of pleasure as I press into her has me roaring, "fuck!"

Covering her back with my chest, and pinning her crooked knee with my own, I flatten her hands to the table with mine and start furiously pumping into her. Pleasure sieges me as mewls leave her with every thrust. The table rattles as I piston into her, flowers falling off the sides as a few jars crash onto the concrete. After a few rough strokes, I pull back to my feet, watching my cock and her stretch around it as she desperately tries to hold on. Feeling her start to succumb, I snake an arm around her waist to lock her to me. She starts to shudder as I pick up even more speed. "Give it up."

Within a few targeted thrusts, she's shuddering beneath me, ragged intakes of breath interrupting her moan as her leg buckles. Gripping her hips as she crumbles, I secure her waist with my other arm and use both to lift her from the ground as I thrust her through the orgasm. She goes limp as it subsides, and my wrist starts to fail as I set her down. I gently turn her on her back and soak in the look of her. Her hair is tangled, lips swollen, perfect tits beaded, chest heaving, and her eyes are clouded with release. The roar intensifies as I lift her heels to rest at the edge of the table. Gripping her hips, I slowly drag her down the surface and onto my waiting dick, watching as, inch by inch, it disappears into her wet heat. Her breath hitches at the invasion, and I pause a beat, allowing her time to acclimate.

"Don't, d-don't you dare f-fucking stop."

It's all I need as I thrust into her like it'll be the last time—and chances are it will be. Pleasure coils up my spine as she gapes up at me, her eyes rolling up before they close.

"Open." Thrust. Thrust. Thrust. "Them."

They pop open as I bat away every bit of reasoning that threatens to break through the sensations bouncing between us, pressing past deep, past her limits and mine. Palming her thigh up to go deeper, I feel the same inevitable click I felt on that float—which goes past physical. Just as I start to drown in the sensation, she reaches up and palms my jaw, demanding acknowledgment.

That I do give her, slowing for long, tense seconds.

I don't hide it from her, but I don't voice it either. A beat later, I'm released. Feeling crazed, I rocket inside her as her hands roam over my chest and arms until she grips the side of the table. Seeming just as lust-driven, she matches my thrusts with the lift of her hips as the feeling bouncing between us intensifies tenfold.

If this is what passion feels like, it's too fucking good to ignore.

It's then I'm made aware there's no difference between fucking and making love—not with a connection this strong. I can make it as filthy as I want, but it won't lessen the effect. It's my last thought as she tightens around me, gripping me so hard as she comes, I succumb.

And fall . . . back into the state where nothing but the feel of us matters. Like last time, I'm not scattered, but present. With her.

Just as high, just as oblivious, just as blissed out.

As lost as I feel—and have felt—she continues to find me and bring me back.

A gift from her, one I won't ever deserve.

Partially collapsing on her, the exhale of her name sounds like sandpaper as she strokes my slick back, whispering sentiment I can't return.

"I missed you."

"But the eyes are blind. One must look with the heart."—*Le Petit Prince*, Antoine de Saint-Exupéry

TWENTY-EIGHT

"**S**O, THIS IS A THING," CECELIA DRAWLS, VOICE HOARSE, fatigued. "You have access to businesses all over town?"

"If we help fatten their bottom line we do," I whisper to her temple, running the pads of my fingers along her back. Her wine-soaked dress sits in a heap on the floor—as do my clothes—our collective focus on the expanse of leafy vines trailing up the slope of the mountain.

Cheek pressed against my chest, she straddles me on one of two built-in benches lining each wall of the cellar. Mere seconds after we came to from our first round, a drawn-out kiss led to a deep, slow ride on the bench. One we're still coming down from.

"It's so beautiful here," she whispers dreamily, fully relaxed. I can't say I'm not feeling the same sort of lull, my posture just as lax as I draw lazy circles on her skin.

"Wine's good," I glance at the barrel where an unopened bottle sits next to the breathing one I doused her with. "Want some more?"

"I'm not really a wine drinker, but I'll have some, if you will."

"I'm not really a *drinker*." I shrug. "A few beers here and there."
A beat of silence.

"Because of Delphine?"

It's not a stupid question, and for the most part, she's on point. "Some of it. Mostly because I need to keep my wits about me."

"In case of bird business," she concludes, tracing my ink. Another stroke of my fingers down her bare back elicits a full-body shiver. Satisfaction thrums through me at how responsive she is to my every touch. We're both a mess, hair picked through, sweat-slicked and sticky. I can't manage a fuck to give that we're naked and could be easily exposed to anyone who might pull up. One day in the near future, we will be, and all hell will break loose. Sean continues to play ignorant that day is coming, while I know what repercussions that revelation will bring. It's the thought of cutting her loose now to help mitigate that disaster that has me tensing.

"Am I right?" Lifting her head, she frowns when she sees my mood has shifted. She fails to smooth out my drawn brows with her fingers, and I swat her effort away.

"Such a moody man," she says in jest. That truth stings because it's all I've dealt with lately from those in my inner circle—Sean especially, who's currently keeping his distance in a way he never has. Sensing my irritation, she shifts from my lap onto the vacant bench beside me. "Dom, I was joking."

Up in arms, she reaches for what's left of her dress as I snap off the condom before grabbing my boxers and pulling them on. "No, you weren't."

It's the fucking truth. I can't seem to handle my shit anymore—my temper becoming impossible to regulate—especially when my mind drifts to the repulsive horrors I've been continually feeding it. Not bothering to gauge her lack of response, I grab the half-empty bottle from the decorative barrel and walk it over to Cecelia as she covers herself as much as possible—now on the defensive.

Way to go, asshole.

I fucked up the mood, as I so often do. This is where shit gets tricky. There's no quick parting after sex with Cecelia. It's not how she's built, and it's not like I want to end our time together, but this is unfamiliar territory—fucking lightyears from my comfort zone. Taking a long swig from the bottle with that truth in mind, she gapes at me. "Uh . . . for someone who just declared you don't drink much, you pretty much downed a quarter of the bottle."

"We have another," I thrust it toward her with brute force, and she takes it cautiously. Pulling on my jeans, I push into my boots before making my way to the passenger side of my Camaro. Slackening rain pelts my skin as I collect my stash from my small, fireproof box. The interior of the cabin lights up, and I glance up to see the sun peeking from the clouds before scanning the soaked grounds of the abandoned winery.

Thinking on my toes about how to try to turn things around, I turn my key and tap a song on my playlist. Bob Marley's "Three Little Birds" rings out, echoing across the mountaintop. Glancing back toward the cellar, I catch Cecelia smiling at me.

She's already forgiven me.

One of her gorgeous legs is propped on the bench, her bare foot resting on the edge, our wine bottle unceremoniously clutched to her chest—she's the picture of serenity.

So. Goddamn. Beautiful.

Returning her grin, I stalk back into the cellar, taking a seat at the end of the table to roll.

"This really is a dream, Dom," she swigs from the bottle, and I glance over to see her inhaling deeply. "Thank you for bringing me here."

"I wanted to be alone," I assert, knowing it dampens some of the romanticism for her. But it's important she doesn't get the wrong impression. Picking through loose bud, I hear another swish of wine as it eases to the bottom of the bottle.

"Wine drinker or not, this is delicious," she scans the label. "Point Lookout, that's where we are?"

"Yeah, the guy who owns it is a relative of Tyler's. He attended West Point."

"He really was bred from a loyal military family, huh?"

"All of them. Every single one," I tell her. "Except Tyler's mom."

"I'm guessing from your tone, that's not good?" She prompts.

"Not for Tyler's mom," I confess, tucking the weed into the ready paper.

"How so?"

I shake my head, catching myself. "Not my shit to tell."

"Ahh, more secrets."

"Yeah, so keep that shit to yourself," I snap a little too harshly. *Jesus, fuck, Dom.*

She takes another drink, eyes flaring before they soften as she lowers the bottle. "Want to talk about it?"

"Consider 'never' my standard answer for that question," I swipe away debris from the table.

"I'll try to keep that in mind," she rolls her eyes.

As much as I like sparring with her, it feels off now, considering what just transpired between us physically.

I'll never get this right.

Soaking the closed joint between my lips, I feel the familiar weight on my profile.

"I'll never get tired of watching you do that," she whispers heatedly, "it's sexy as hell."

There it is again, the discomfort. Though I can't really fault her because we both speak bluntly, Cecelia's bold truths provoke a raw type of honest response that pry into me. Keeping to my task, I catch another involuntary, full-body shiver in my peripheral. She's still cold.

Tucking my blunt behind my ear, I snatch the unopened bottle in one hand and hold out my other, nodding toward the wine she holds. "Cap that. Let's go."

"Already?" She deflates, eyes dropping while taking my hand and reluctantly standing.

Back in the car, feeling her disappointment from where she shivers next to me, I make a fast decision and turn right, treading slowly up the paved, steep inclined road that leads to the top of the mountain. The main tasting room and reception hall to our left,

Cecelia audibly gasps when she sees what's waiting on the right as it gradually comes into view. "Dom, oh my God, this is . . . *wow!*"

Transfixed, she exits the car in a dream-like state, and I grin and follow. I pass a handful of tables to join her where she sits on the waist-high rock wall lining the cliff. Before us is an endless view of the peaks and valleys of the Blue Ridge Mountains. We spend a few minutes in comfortable silence. It's when I light my blunt that she rips her gaze away, glancing over. "So that's your only true vice," she nods to the joint, "besides breakfast," she giggles.

"Don't drink too much," I warn. "Red wine has a way of sneaking up on you."

"I *am* feeling a little tingly," she admits.

"I don't fuck the unconscious," I warn.

"Wow," her eyes widen in mock surprise. "Such a gentleman," she muses before grabbing another eyeful of the landscape. ". . . you know, for a guy who thinks romance is a gimmick, this is pretty incredible."

"Not a gimmick, just not—"

"—something that interests you, yeah, yeah, heard you loud and clear the first time. At least we're past the fuck-you-eyes and grunting stage," she jests as I give her a warning look.

"Oh, nope, seems we've *regressed*," she giggles again.

Unable to help it, I shake my head with a grin.

"Ah, and progress in the next second, it's a tango with you, King, but I'm guessing you don't dance, either."

Offering her the blunt, she refuses it, and I take a long pull, answering on exhale. "You guessed right."

She turns back to the stunning view spread before us. "Yeah, nothing romantic about this at all," she deadpans. "This must be killing you, Mr. Gloom and Doom."

Instead of snapping at her that this wasn't intentional, I let it go.

Even if I think romantic love is mostly a chemically induced state, she believes in it. There's no need for me to be a dick about it or try to ruin her idea of it. Sean can give her all she needs in that department. I'm glad in that respect because she deserves to believe for as long as she can. Life has a way of ripping our ideas and hopes about the things that matter most to us to shreds.

We sit quietly for long minutes as I tug on my blunt. Fortune has a good fucking laugh at my expense when, in the distance, a solid rainbow appears.

Cutting her eyes my way, Cecelia presses her lips together until she loses her battle, bursting into a fit of hysterical laughter. "Talk about an epic backfire," she says through a laugh, "poor baby, this must be torturous for you."

"Shut up."

"Just waiting on a unicorn to do a fly-by and drop a crown in my lap," she muses. "Considering I've already snagged a temperamental Prince who rides a dark horse," she nods back toward my Camaro.

"Hilarious," I quip, pulling the last of my joint and stomping it under my boot before glancing back at the rainbow. "They're actually pretty common around here," I tell her, just as another faded duplicate appears behind it, both beginning and ending in a high arch over the expansive neon green terrain.

"Holy shit," she exclaims, "so I'm guessing *this* is common too?"

Stunned by the sight of it, I can't remember the last time I saw a rainbow, let alone bothered looking for one. Music drifts from my speakers as I immerse myself in the created atmosphere—intentional or not—while a light buzz settles into me. Tension easing up substantially, mind slowing as I remain present, I somehow manage to slip back into a scarce, tranquil state along with her. Turning to Cecelia, I watch her watching the show, her expression wistful. Maybe it's the wine and the bud, or maybe it's her, but I can't rip my eyes away. I've never been so attracted to a woman in my life.

Whoosh. Whoosh.

Sensing my stare, Cecelia slowly turns to me, her smile fading when I cup the back of her head and pull her close.

The ever-present buzz increases as I sweep my tongue along her lower lip, capturing a droplet of lingering wine on the corner before pulling away, our lips brushing.

Whoosh. Whoosh.

Whoosh. Whoosh.

Feeding from the charged current continually humming between us, she stares back at me, equally as ensnared.

Fuck it.

The kiss starts deep, going past what I went in for, lasting for long, blissful seconds, maybe more, as she clutches me to her. It's when my chest rattles in awareness that I break the kiss abruptly and stand. "Let's go take a shower."

Her eyes light as she reads the meaning between the words—that our time together isn't over as far as I'm concerned. Not even close.

And I'm right because it rains for the next two days.

"You become responsible, forever, for what you have tamed."—
Le Petit Prince, Antoine de Saint-Exupéry

TWENTY-NINE

SEAN AND I STAND ON OPPOSITE ENDS OF THE ISLAND, SIPPING morning brew, debating the news as if the stalemate we've been in since the Meetup doesn't exist. Though it's still apparent, the glimmer in his eyes is back, and it's no big mystery who put it there. Just as I think it, the source catches both of our attention as she halts all movement at the landing of the stairs. Fresh from Sean's shower, she idles in black boy shorts and a form-fitting tank—her expression that of a deer caught in two sets of headlights. To be fair to her, this is the first morning she's been alone with the two of us since this started. Sean glances toward me, a brow lifted in amusement, before making his first attempt to lure her toward us. "Hey, Pup, have a good shower?"

She slowly nods, her eyes darting to me and back to Sean.

"Coffee?" Sean asks in another effort to lure her down.

She nods again and slowly makes her way to us as if we're a problem she's trying to solve. Grabbing a mug from the cabinet, I place it on the island between our steaming mugs and pour.

The second she's within reach, Sean pulls her into him, his whisper easy to catch. "It's cool, baby. We're not going to bite." He kisses her cheek. "You smell so fucking good." She whispers something back as I scan her, her hair twisted and secured on the top of her head, her slender, delicate neck flushed red with embarrassment, shame, or both.

"I'm going to go grab a quick one," Sean croons in a soothing tone as Brandy trots into the kitchen, nails ticking on the tiles. "Want to go get some breakfast after?"

"Sure," she says, eyeing me briefly as I pour Brandy's breakfast into her bowl.

"Be right back," Sean gives her a slow wink before heading upstairs. Cecelia eyes me pensively where she stands at the fridge, grabbing the milk and heading toward the island.

"Hi," I whisper, discarding the bag, unable to hold my smile as she cuts her eyes at me, the 'asshole' clear in them. Moving to join her, I trail my gaze down the length of her.

"When are you going to make peace with it?" I ask as I approach, my breath hitting her nape as she uncaps the milk.

"I'm," her lips lift in a tight smile. "I have no clue. It's just different."

"Yeah?" I run my thumb down the slope of her delicate neck. "Did he fuck you last night?"

"Dom," she exhales a harsh breath of surprise.

"Did he make you come?"

"I'm not answering that," she expels with a shake.

Rapid breaths leave her as I pull out her hair tie, and it falls limp along her shoulders. The scent of shampoo hits me as I flex my fingers through the bottom, loving the silky, cold feel between my fingers. "Can he make your pussy sing like I do?"

The need to mark her builds as I envision her stretch around me. "Did he press your beautiful face to the mattress and bite your neck . . ." It's not a scenario, but a memory of the last time I took her ". . . suck your nipple purple, and thrust in so deep that you went into subspace, *flooding his cock* and *sheets?*"

"Jesus Christ, Dom," she scolds in alarm, her neck and profile flushing red, stopping her milk pour just in time to keep her mug from overflowing. Running my fingers through the damp hair at her neck, I catch the brief close of her eyes and the glimmer of blue fire when they reopen and focus on me.

Her choppy exhales increase as the sight of our last day together replays so vividly, and my blood starts to heat. Because of my attraction to Cecelia, my sexual imagination has gone into overdrive. She's been more than a willing volunteer for every experiment, not one of them going awry. I've tormented her with hours of foreplay, edging her, watching her beg, only to come back asking for more—nothing vanilla about it. I don't consider myself a man of kink, but a man with a sexual appetite who flirts on the edge of it. She flirts right back with me, and it pays off for us every fucking time.

Grazing my hard length across her back, I sweep her hair out of the way of my focal point, her nape, before pressing my lips below her hairline.

"Dom," she whispers on alert, "I'm, uh, I'm—"

"Shh," I whisper, "Sean can speak for himself about the biting," I taunt before sinking my teeth into the back of her neck. A moan escapes her as I graze the skin I made raw while snaking my arms around her.

"You're breaking the rules," she mewls in weak protest.

"Can't really hold that against me since it's my fucking *profession*," I remind her, fanning the pads of my splayed fingers as I palm her chest, running them over her taut nipples.

"Dom, we can't—"

"*We* aren't," I say, trailing my nose along her exposed shoulder, "*I am* because I've got home-field advantage. He should know better by now than to leave you alone in a room with me. *Ever.*"

"It's not that I don't want to," she exhales shakily. I bite my lips to hold my chuckle in. She's still easing into polyamory, and being the motherfucker I am, I'm not making it any easier on her. She chose this, we all chose this, and not one of us is complaining, especially her.

"So terrified that if I pulled down your little boy shorts," I cup her pussy through them, "your boyfriend will find me hammering into you," I squeeze it again for emphasis. "But do you *really know* what he would do?"

"No," she says breathlessly as I bite along her shoulder, marking her for him to see.

"Maybe he'd punish you," I whisper, "but you know you would like it. Because you like mine, don't you, *Pup?*" I hiss, feeling no guilt for this stolen time because Sean hasn't exactly been all hands off, either. I've caught him once or twice stealing moments alone with her when he can, but neither of us has fully crossed the line or the boundaries she created. It's nothing I begrudge him for and vice versa. Because of those boundaries, the situation has been easier to navigate. The hookups in the past were always planned, taking place outside our homes, and never had any impact on our club. This dynamic is entirely different from the others.

Those were clearly temporary, and though this one remains in the same category, it's the three of us who are collectively and purposely drawing the expiration date out. Me included because I can't get enough of her.

But even as I see an eventual end to this, I don't deny that it runs deeper because Sean is already attached, and I'm drawn to her in a way I can't ignore.

Running a palm along the material of her stomach, I dip my fingers into her shorts, and she grips my hand to stop it. "I'm on my period."

"Your clit doesn't give a fuck, so why should I?" Slipping my fingers in just enough to massage her through her panties, I demonstrate how much of a fuck I don't have to give. Starting with the slow rotation of my pointer, her head falls back to rest on my chest.

"God, you're such a bastard," she rasps out, as she starts to shake in my hold, where I have her pinned between me, my fingers, and the island.

"Not denying that, ask me to make you come," I order as she begins to move her hips, bucking into my touch. "*Ask me, Cecelia.*"

"Make me come," she concedes, turning her head in invitation for a kiss I don't take—a kiss I refuse to give her because that will only trigger me in wanting more. Our kisses have a way of igniting us past the point of return. A state of arousal I have no desire to be in if I can't act on it.

"That sounded more like an order," I nip the shell of her ear, "not a request."

"Dom, please," she whispers, and I know it's because she wants that connection. Ignoring her plea, I add a finger, massaging her in slow circles, her body jerking slightly as she chases the high. Breathless, she turns her head again, tilting her chin up, her lips so close she's able to brush them against mine.

"Don't," I grit out, my control on the brink of snapping.

"Kiss me," she rasps out, voice hoarse.

"No," I snap, my need starting to take over as her shoulders shudder and her clit beats against my fingers. Body molded to mine, I physically feel it when her orgasm starts to crest. She grips the back of my head, riding my fingers frantically as she chases the wave.

Pressing my cock into her back through the thin fabric of my shorts, I decide exactly how to push her over. "Next time I fuck you, I'm going to get you so wet that when I press your face against my mattress and spread you, you'll already be dripping onto your thighs."

"I-I-fuck, Dom," she pants as she pulls the hair at the back of my neck so hard my cock jerks.

"Give it up," I order as she tips over, shuddering against me until she's depleted and sagging. Keeping her tightly to me as she comes down, I whisper words that spring up and fly out unchecked. "You're the most *beautiful woman* I've ever laid eyes on, Cecelia, especially when you *come apart for me.*"

Releasing her to grab my coffee, she turns suddenly. I'm only able to see her narrowed blues before she pushes me back against the island, firmly grips the back of my neck, and crushes our mouths together.

Tensing, I open to object. "Cece—"

Taking advantage, she thrusts an insistent tongue into my

mouth and instant need sieges me. One second, one fucking second, is all it takes to sweep me in, to match the violent thrust of her tongue—which I do, lick for lick. Losing myself in the kiss, she keeps me locked to her and hostage. Her moans drive me fucking insane as she slips her hand into my shorts, gripping my dick—hard—and pumping eagerly. Running her thumb over the head, she "hmms" in satisfaction when I groan into her mouth. She releases my cock briefly, lowering her hand to sink her nails into my thigh. My legs damn near buckle as she forces me further back, pinning *me* to the counter while at *her mercy.*

Goddamn.

My bearable flicker is now stoked to white-hot flame. I grip her arms in an attempt to break free as she presses all her weight against me, digging her claws further into my skin, knowing what it does to me.

She maintains control of my mouth, feeding and fueling me until I'm in a frenzy, ready to fuck whatever she'll allow me before she abruptly pulls away. A smirk grows on her lips as she eyes the state of me. Seeming satisfied, she turns and dumps two spoons of sugar into her coffee and stirs. Turning back to me with one arm crossed over her torso, she takes a sip and scans me where I stand frozen, hard as a nail, and fucking furious.

Psychologically, I'm on my knees.

Physically, I could fuck a brick wall.

"I'm assuming you're halfway there," she lifts a finger and taps my temple twice, "because you know just *how good it feels when we do fuck.* So," she pushes off the counter and glances back at me, swaggering toward the staircase, "you can finish yourself off . . . oh, and *hi."*

"Why did you hate me?"

"Who says I don't hate you?"

Groaning, I glance over at the small digital clock on my

nightstand as the conversation from our first day together replays on a loop.

Blinking after catching sight of the blurry digital hour, I run my hand down my jaw with a groan. Cecelia's murmurs circulate through my restless mind for the umpteenth time since she left me in that kitchen after turning the tables—leaving me wanting more, *needing* more.

Closing my eyes, I'm struck by the ingrained image of trailing my palm along her spine and over the curve of her perfect ass, along with the echo of the blunt truth she battered me with on rainy day *one*.

"You stare at me all the time, too."

I've managed to dodge those intimate conversations since our first day, but it continues to taunt me anyway—invading me like she has since she drove into Triple Falls. This morning she called my bluff, and as she walked away, I knew that she'd been placating me. More than that, *playing me by* allowing me to think I have the upper hand. She knows exactly what power she holds and has been feigning innocent.

At my keyboard tonight, I found myself zoning out with thoughts of her. Of ways to try and keep her entertained in my box. Those thoughts eventually wandered to the various ways I want to fuck her. I've fisted my dick *twice* to expel the pent-up need to no avail, which left me simmering.

Catching another whiff of her scent, I turn my head, inhaling deeply, before pulling away and glaring at the source of my agitation. Gripping the pillow, I pull it to me and inhale, identifying the culprit for my unease. Smell evokes memory, which then helps to trigger all the other senses. Dropping the pillow like it's on fire, I realize it's her addictive aroma that's provoked every torturous minute of the last nine fucking hours.

Lifting my bed sheet to sniff, I catch another strong whiff of her. She's everywhere.

In my head, in my sheets. Even my libido is starting to play Fido. *Fuck this.*

Springing to my knees, I grip the fitted sheet and tug hard. The ends snap off the corners before I toss every pillow in the center of it, wrapping them up and fisting the bundle like a sack over my shoulder. Dragging it behind me downstairs, I hit the landing as another hint of her engulfs me, and I toss them to the foot of the stairs like they're on fire. Marching toward the kitchen, I'm stopped short by two pairs of curious eyes. Tyler stands frozen on the other side of the island, coffee mug halfway to his mouth. Sean is across from him at the stove, spatula in his hand. Stalking past them into the kitchen, I snatch a trash bag from underneath the sink.

"Morning, buddy," Sean says, his voice full of mirth. "Have an accident? Don't worry. It happens to the best of us."

Glancing up as I stuff my bedding into the bag, I see Tyler biting his lips to keep from laughing as I glare between the two of them.

"You do know," Sean drawls, lazily cutting through his eggs with the spatula to scramble them. "You can *wash* the pillowcases, right? No need to toss the pillows, too."

"Fuck you," I snap, tying the trash bag before heading up the stairs.

Laughter erupts out of both of them as I grip the rail and take them two at a time.

"He's so fucked," Tyler sounds through a chuckle. "I swear to God he was listening to K-Ci and JoJo last night when I popped into his room."

"It was on the radio, you dick!" I defend, stalking toward my bedroom.

I may have found the song in my cloud and replayed it once or twice.

"Doesn't surprise me," Sean coos up at me in taunt. "The meaner they are, the harder they fall."

"Don't confuse *your entrapment* with *me!*" I boom, taking the last few strides to my room and snapping my door closed behind me. Chest heaving, I palm the back of it as if the sheets might come back for me. "Jesus Christ, King, get a grip."

But I can't because deep down, I know exactly what this is.

She's trying to domesticate me!

Scanning my room for any remnants of her, I spot a hair tie on my nightstand and narrow my eyes. Grabbing my trashcan, I walk over to it, flick it off, and into the can—satisfied when I earn two points.

If this is longing or attachment, it ends right here.

Right now.

"Have you ever been in love? . . . It's not a stupid question."

"It is if you find love irrelevant."

"Why is love irrelevant?"

"Because it doesn't interest me."

"Never will," I say to absolutely no one as I stalk toward the shower and turn it on, spotting a tube of lip shit on my sink before swatting it into my nearby trashcan.

Love is a four-letter *curse.* No bird I know of—who's been struck by it—has ever flown quite the same way.

She may have the looks to rival every woman I've ever fucked, a pussy made for worship. She may even be a decent conversationalist and reading partner, but I. Will. *Not.* Be. Domesticated.

THIRTY

I'VE BEEN DOMESTICATED.

Somewhat.

To a small degree.

Minuscule, really.

What's worse is that I actually don't mind it *that much.*

Reason being is that it brings a modest level of routine to my otherwise chaotic existence.

Cecelia flips a page next to me as music filters from my speakers. Exhausted by the recent short bout of sleepless nights—when the sky fucking refused to break, and rain refused to come—I close my eyes as relaxation sets in. Hand splayed on my chest, I tap along to the song with my pointer. Maman loved Chicago. A few bars in, I feel the unescapable weight of a deep blue stare on my profile.

Cracking one eye open, I see Cecelia's book sliding from her chest onto her lap. She sits in nothing but stark white panties, her jaw slack as she gapes at me. In the next second, she tosses the sheet up before it hangs briefly midair and lands, blanketing her as she starts rooting around, searching the mattress.

"The fuck you doing?" I ask as she pokes my side with the pads of her explorative fingers.

"It seems I've misplaced the motherfucker I came home with," she says, her tone jovial before she lowers the sheet, a blinding smile in place. "Because there's no damned way I just busted him lip-syncing Peter Cetera . . . O.M.G. is that a blush? Are you blushing?"

Unable to hide my smile, I slowly extend my palm to her chest and flatten it before pushing her off the bed. She lands with a thud, her hysterical laughter filling my bedroom. Not at all something I'm used to—my chest tightens a little at the idea it could be.

Laughter subsiding slightly, Cecelia's head pops up into view. Lifting to her knees, she folds her forearms on the bed, brows raised. "Note to Cecelia, a little wine and a few puffs, and your closeted romantic comes out."

"Haven't had a drop, and you know it," I assert.

"Which only further proves my point," she quips with a shrug. "Your secret is safe with me, my menacing motherfucker, but I feel it's my duty—as I've been told numerous times recently—to tell you to 'own it.'"

"You're delusional," I dismiss.

"Can't blame you. As they say, 'they don't make love songs like this anymore.'"

"*They* are idiots."

"Ah, Jean Dominic," she coos, "but you have to admit, it puts you in *the mood*, right?" She snaps to her feet and turns sideways, thrusting her pert ass out and positioning her hands on her hips before she starts to gyrate. "It's all bump and grind these days," she bellows in a terrifying impression of a man's timbre before booming, "and 'get on your knees and *suck it* biatch!'"

She pops her ass out with each word for good measure which has me barking a loud laugh as she continues to gyrate, adding her arms in the mix. "Stop," I chuckle, "for your own sake—and mine— and don't *ever* do that again."

She turns and tosses a flirty grin over her shoulder while batting her lashes. "You really shouldn't try to deny your inner romantic, Jean Dominic, I've seen it, and I busted you sifting through The Bronze Horseman."

I shrug. "The plot is decent."

She climbs back on the bed and presses her nose to mine, drawing another chuckle out of me. Her bravado is due partly to the bottle we saved, and I tell her as much. "You're cut off."

"I drank it all anyway, and don't you dare try to divert, buddy. You've got more than one romantic bone in your body." She pops her brows and runs her fingers down my cock.

"I didn't read the whole thing," I lie.

"Uh, huh . . . sure you didn't, that's why the other two books suddenly popped up on your shelf." Stradling me, she presses our noses together and bugs her eyes. "I, too, take notice of things, birdman." She lowers her voice above a whisper. "You're in quite the mood tonight. Dare I say a good one?" I pull my nose away and grip her ass, squeezing hard in warning.

"Ouch, okay, fine, I won't push it. Besides, if you hold that smile a few more seconds, you might scare your face."

She takes her place beside me as the opening notes of "Hard Habit to Break" start to play. Angling her head so we share a pillow, she listens intently until the song plays out. "Nothing to interpret about that," she comments in mention of our budding routine, where we listen to older, more cryptic music from different eras to try and decipher the lyrics. She squeezes our laced fingers, looking over at me, eyes hazed. "God, that was beautiful and *painful*."

"Some of the best things are."

She turns on her side, propping her head with her palm. "Such as?"

"Growing up," I say, tracing the divot at the hollow of her throat.

"That's right," she grips my finger and kisses it reverently. "Someone is about to have a birthday." She glances back at my bedside clock, "in exactly four hours." Her eyes lower to calculating slits.

"Please don't embarrass yourself by making plans I won't show up for," I warn.

"Don't underestimate me, Jean Dominic," she quips, twinkling eyes making it apparent that a plan is already in place.

"Stop saying my name like that. I'm not a French poet." Brushing the hair away from her shoulders, it's easy to make out she's fully relaxed and seemingly . . . entertained. Something I can't say I've ever really accomplished with another girl outside of the physical.

But for how long? She can't be happy locked in my room. She needs—

"Whatever you're thinking, stop. It isn't true," she says softly, reading my apprehension. Something she's getting way too good at. Knowing I'm not going any further with the conversation, she takes the reins. "Spark one up. This time I'm smoking with you *and* playing DJ."

Lifting to sit, I do as ordered as she flips through the extensive digital library open on my desktop. Not a minute later, "Oh No," by the Commodores, another of Maman's favorite groups, starts to play.

She shrugs when she sees my surprise. "I loved it when you played it before." Turning it up on my keypad, she smirks, knowing we're at full capacity tonight at the townhouse—no doubt pissing the neighbors off. Even with Lionel Richie blasting through my room, I can't find a fuck to give. Especially when she animatedly leaps back onto the bed, pouncing me. Lowering her head, she runs her lips and tongue along my neck before reaching for a condom from my nightstand.

"I am not fucking you to this," I announce firmly, "I have my limits," I mumble against her active lips as she does her best to seduce me. "I've already watched one too many teen angst movies against my better fucking judgment."

"Two," she draws out as I turn her over and sink between her thighs, discarding the blunt she ordered me to light on my nightstand.

"Yeah, and that's *two* too many."

It was another of those rare days spent out of my head. Where we did exactly shit—aside from watching movies on my laptop and fucking—but a day I didn't feel like my world was coming to an end. She stares up at me, grinning like the romance-drunk fool she is. That look is unmistakable—a look she gives to me in front of everyone, unabashedly, fearlessly, whether we're at the garage or alone. A look my head and chest can no longer ignore. A look that's starting to feel like it's beyond chemistry.

My blissful ignorance stares back at me, her smile fading, that look ever-present.

Ignoring it is fucking torture—so I don't bother doing it or denying it anymore. I can't, to the point that I palm her face and lower to kiss her. When I close the kiss, she pulls back, dazed. "What was that for?"

For believing for the both of us that whatever the fuck is happening between us is real, because I can't.

The throb only increases as I take her mouth again, and she matches me, lick for lick. I'm hard in seconds, and I refuse to ignore it, this thing, this feeling, this state. Lionel serenading us or not, our attraction gets the best of me, and I let it guide me along with her moans. Just as I'm about to take her panties down, a pounding sounds on my bedroom door a second before Tyler's voice booms from the other side of it.

"Please, for the love of fucking God, no more love ballads tonight. That's all I'm asking."

Sean sounds out not even a second later with an "A-fucking-men, brother."

"First chance I get, I'm moving out of this fucking frat house," Tyler snaps before slamming his bedroom door.

Cecelia and I break apart, laughing hysterically. She buckles sideways, and when I realize her destination—*floor*—and manage to get a good grip on her, she takes me down with her.

We stay there, crumpled between her side of the bed and my bookshelf, her cradled in my arm. As the sun sets, the room grows darker, and neither of us moves. Whispers of streetlight stream between my blinds, hitting the wall behind my computer as we smoke a joint while listening to the Commodores. When the record plays out, Cecelia fills the long bouts of silence she knows I won't by telling me about her life before she was summoned to Triple Falls.

Since this thing between us became regular, I've done what I can to avoid this part—knowing the consequences of feeding into it and deciding it's inevitable.

Because I want to know. *Everything.*

So, I listen, feigning ignorance about the particulars I do. At the same time, she fills me in on memories—and the people that matter to her. She changes some of the fiction I've read about—the girl living in a parallel universe to factual—the beauty of what makes her tick while whispering a new reality between us.

"I'm sorry . . . I haven't shut up," she says sometime later. I don't even recognize how much time has passed, having sunk deeper into her melodic voice, her history, her antics, smiling or chuckling—even when she's not funny.

Especially then.

"Must be the weed," she offers as if her rambling hasn't been present the whole time we've been together. "Am I boring you?" Before I can answer, she's talking again. "I don't remember what I was talking about anyway."

"When you and Christy stole your mom's car in seventh grade," I prompt.

"You were listening," she muses.

"Not like I had much of a choice," I quip in jest, pulling her tighter to me so she knows it. I feel her smile against my skin as she tilts back, her eyes on what she can make of my profile before she presses a slow, sensual kiss to my neck. She wants me to know she cares and to feel it—and I do.

Stopping this is pointless, but encouraging it is the worst crime I could commit.

Tonight, I do neither.

When her soft murmurs start to fade in strength, I gather her up and lay her atop me on the bed. Burrowing in, she rests her cheek on my chest, securing her thigh around my torso—the act familiar.

It's how we sleep. The feeling of it settling in my chest, the kind of intimacy I've never allowed myself with anyone.

Ever.

Because of the exact fucking conflict going on inside me now.

"Happy Birthday, Dom," she whispers softly, running her fingers over my chest before drifting off. Somewhere between the drift of sleep and consciousness, I claim the only gift I want, palming her thigh and drawing it up to bring her snugger to me. Pressing and keeping my lips to her forehead, I inhale her scent and let myself fall into the idea of us and linger there—knowing that eventually, I'll be jerked away by the hard, unforgivable reality waiting for me when I hit the ground.

Rousing due to the feel of her hand on my cock, I open my eyes in time to see Cecelia flick the head of it with her tongue, the most devilish smile lifting her lush lips as she glances up to see my eyes pop open.

"Hi," she rasps out, a greeting that rings out more like a warning. Freshly showered, dressed in a tank top and panties, hair damp, she grips me hard as a confession starts to roll off her tongue between licks.

"In case you've ever wondered," she murmurs before flattening her tongue up one side of my cock and down the other, "If I was braver the night I saw you naked. If I knew then how good this felt," she draws out, her tone pure heat, "I would've walked into your room," she swirls her tongue over the tip of me "and done this." Clamping her swollen lips around my length, she takes me to the back of her throat.

Jesus Christ.

A low groan escapes me as she works me over, lips still swollen from the hours we've spent in this bed. Her skin marked, shoulder and neck rashes still raw due to my bottomless imagination.

"Fuck," I grunt, fighting my hips to keep them idle as her

addictive scent invades me. Intent on not missing a second, I gather her damp hair into my fist, absorbed as she takes hard pulls of my cock, keeping my base in a firm grip. Inhibitions forgotten, she keeps her confident gaze on me—on my reaction.

When I move to lift her up to me, she swats my hands away, making it clear she wants me at her mercy while she takes my pleasure for herself. She's coming into her own, realizing how potent her power is over those that desire her. With that knowledge, I let go, allowing her to take what she needs from me. The second I do, she sucks me so thoroughly that I see stars, tightening the fingers I have tangled in her hair.

"The perineum, or the taint," she ticks off as if doing a mental count. She brushes the skin just beneath my balls, fisting my sheets as she suctions before letting my tip pop out of her mouth. "Oh, did I say that *out loud?*"

I narrow my eyes as she rakes her nails gently over my balls—leaving me speechless.

"You *do know* that's one of a male's *most potent erogenous* zones, right?" She demonstrates it's fast becoming one of my own as she licks the skin beneath my balls with an explorative tongue before deep-throating me and pressing on it gently with the pad of her thumb.

I've created a monster.

"Cecelia," I grit out in warning as she rakes her nails down my thigh.

"Come," she commands, gripping my base hard and suctioning around the head.

"Fuck," I exhale as she swallows my release like it's the air she needs. Chest heaving, I stare down at her as she flattens her tongue along each side of my shaft. She carefully avoids my sensitive tip before releasing me and moving to hover above me, eyes glittering with satisfaction. "Happy Birthday, motherfucker, and good morning."

Releasing my smile, I run a thumb along her swollen lips. "You're doing a good job of convincing me it could be both."

"Take a shower and meet me downstairs," she whispers before placing a few worshipful kisses on my lips.

"Join me," I whisper back, matching her tone.

"I've already showered, so I'll see you down there," she bounces off of me onto the edge of the bed.

I grip her arm, pulling her upper half to me, brow raised. "Cecelia?"

"Yes?"

"What's waiting downstairs?"

"Coffee," she says, feigning innocence.

"I told you I don't want—"

"Shut the hell up, King," she eases from my grip and stands, pulling her shorts up before tossing my next order over her shoulder. "Make it quick."

When she closes my door behind her, my gaze trails up to the ceiling. Another year older. Another year to create the future I want. Another year to change it if I decide the life I'm living isn't enough for me—another year of opportunity not to proceed along the path I paved for myself and my brothers. The choice has been a no-brainer year after year. It's my frustrations in the last few months—and the lack of progress—that have me questioning the decision for the first time since I got inked. Standing in the bathroom, I study my tattoo.

What difference can *one man* really make?

A hundred years from now, will a single thing we do collectively truly matter?

Will every victory we claim be wiped away by a thousand steps back?

Running my palm over the heavily imprinted ink, I resign to try, as I have since the day the needles penetrated my skin.

My mind is mostly quiet due to the wake-up tongue belonging to a blue-eyed devil in disguise, or angel, depending on the minute. I'm in the midst of shampooing my hair when the shrill sound of the smoke alarm rings out. Managing to get some of the suds rinsed, I leap out and slip a little on the tiles as I snatch my towel. Gripping it around me, I race down the stairs and am stopped at the landing by the sight that greets me.

A hand-painted 'Happy Birthday Motherfucker' banner hangs above our kitchen island. To the side of it, Brandy sits, tail wagging, a cone birthday hat strapped beneath her furry chin. It's Cecelia's shrieks and Sean's hysterical laughter that grabs the rest of my attention. Cecelia scolds Sean a decibel higher than the alarm as she opens the smoking oven. Mitts covering both hands, she retrieves a cake as the smell of burned bacon wafts into my nose.

"Give it up, Pup," Sean chuckles, circling her waist and lifting her where she holds the cake before swinging her toward the sink where she releases it mid-bitch, ". . . told you not to distract me, to give me just five minutes!'"

She pushes against Sean's captive hold as he nuzzles her, chuckling deeply. Releasing her, Sean moves the burning bacon from a lit burner onto another as Cecelia catches sight of me, shampoo sliding down my chest. Brandy takes notice of me, too, barking just as the right side of the banner falls from where it hangs, sweeping a party plate full of runny eggs with it to the floor. It's a fucking circus and everything I never thought I wanted but glimpse in those chaotic seconds.

Sean begins to wave a broom at the fire alarm as Cecelia's expression falls, shoulders slumping in disappointment as she darts her eyes from the smoking cake to the burnt bacon, to Brandy, and back to me, lip quivering.

So, *this* is *adoration*.

It is such a mysterious place, the land of tears.—*Le Petit Prince*, Antoine de Saint-Exupéry

THIRTY-ONE

A MELODIC "CHA-CHING" SOUNDS FROM MY MONITOR SPEAKER, and I make a few clicks, settling in to watch my latest egg hatch. Money hasn't been an obstacle since my brother's gamble years ago at a French horse track. A gamble that made me a teenage millionaire and funded the startup of Exodus. Managing our funds since has become one of my favorite hobbies, which includes terrorizing corrupt fucks into feeding more into our machine.

Another day, another suit who played the game, won and lost it all because he missed a moral step or twenty along the way. They're a dime a dozen due to the economic order most abide by. It's those that don't—like us—that make targeting a breeze. Following fast accumulated fortune by dirty deeds led me to Timothy.

Clicking on the corner view of the floor of his high-rise office, I'm amped to discover I can make out his expression as he scans my carefully constructed love letter.

Timothy, a man of relatively new wealth and power, will go down one of two ways—one of them most likely *grave*.

Just as he finishes my intricately tailored manifesto for his new life direction, he tosses his breakfast into his trashcan. Searching deep, I find absolutely no fucking empathy if he chooses door number two.

If anything, I'll rest easier knowing his fourteen-year-old step-daughter is now safe from another late-night attack. The paycheck we're about to receive—if he opts for door number one—will only be a bonus.

A year ago, I would have thought this a much bigger victory. But now?

Compared to what I'm up against—along with the visions I'm minute by minute trying to tamp down from playing in a loop—Timothy's demise feels insignificant. Eyeing the clock, I decide to work a little on the Buick. Rolling back from my desk, I pull out my earbuds and tense, swearing that I faintly heard Cecelia call my name.

"Dom!" Cecelia bellows from below as the front door slams downstairs. I didn't imagine it or the shake in her voice. Pulse elevating, I rush out of my bedroom as she calls for me again, the urgency in her summons unmistakable. I'm halfway down the stairs at the landing when she spots me and flies into my arms. I barely manage to catch her, my back hitting the wall behind me as she buries her face in my chest.

"What's wrong?" She's full-on shaking in my arms as I flit through a list of scenarios while my heart continues to pound, the hammering beat in my ears.

"Cecelia, what happened?" Gently prying her away from me, I examine her from head to foot and see no sign of injury. The thought occurs to me that maybe she's discovered the truth about us—about me and her father. But she can't know, or she wouldn't be clinging to me this way . . . unless it's pity. It's when she looks up at me that I see nothing but appreciation. Beautiful features twisted, mascara streaks lining her face; I palm it between my hands.

"*What?*" I ask again, furiously wiping her tears with my thumbs. "What happened?" I prompt as her face falls again, and a sob bursts out of her, the sound of it cracking my insides.

"Jesus, tell me," I demand, my tone stern. I've seen her cry silently while watching movies or after finishing a good book, but this is completely different.

"Cecelia," I grit out, "I'm about two seconds away from—"

"You, what y-you do for them," she murmurs, pulling back. "I w-went w-with Tyler today to d-deliver the checks, and I," her lip quivers as she stares up at me, another tear giving way to another, her expression hitting with the impact of a sledgehammer—a mix of admiration and adoration, for me. "What you've done for them, Dom, it's incredible."

"Cecelia," I grunt as relief courses through me, "It's not—"

"No," she scolds, furiously shaking her head as Tyler saunters in behind her, his lips tilted in amusement. I narrow my eyes at him over her shoulder. He shrugs. "Don't look at me, man. She figured it out," he sighs, "she's been like this all day."

He lays a consoling hand on Cecelia's back while passing us on the way to his room. "See you soon, beautiful."

"T-thank you for today, Tyler," Cecelia sniffs, her respect-filled gaze following him until he clears the stairs before she zeroes back in on me.

"You don't get to downplay what you're doing, Dominic. You deserve to know how you're changing their lives."

She grips the hand I have palming her face, her need to express this to me outweighing any of her typical emotional sidestepping for my comfort. "You're saving them—" She crumbles again, and it's then I recognize just how personal this particular club errand was for her. Wiping more of her tears with my thumbs, it becomes clear that she's reliving years of repressed acknowledgment of the neglect she endured at her mother's hands. Gently gripping her arm, I usher her up the stairs and into my room, sitting her at the edge of my bed before kneeling in front of her. A few seconds tick by before she collects herself enough to speak—her eyes gloss over with memory.

"I w-was five the first time I remember it happening . . . the first time she got lost in her head and checked out," she sniffs, her voice raw. "It's like she forgot I existed . . . her eyes . . . it was like she was looking right through me. You could tell, you could *feel* her pain, so much pain," her voice cracks. "I don't remember how long it went on. What I do remember is her lying on the couch, day and night. She didn't move, Dom. She didn't change clothes or shower . . . When I tried to talk to her, it was like she couldn't hear me. I remember thinking . . ." she shudders as another lone tear tracks down her cheek. ". . . That maybe if I swept the floor and did the dishes, it might make her happy."

The gap in my rib cage widens as I imagine Cecelia trying to work a broom handle taller than she was and straining on her toes to do dishes in a sink she probably couldn't reach.

"I ate wish sandwiches," she admits sheepishly, body shaking as she struggles to quiet her cries enough to speak, "do you know what those are?"

"Yeah," I whisper, all too aware, "when you wish there was more in between the bread than just—"

"Cheese," she finishes as we share a sad smile.

"Until the cheese ran out, and then it was ketchup and bread." Her deep blue eyes finally focus on me, pinning me. "She tried, Dom, she really did. So hard. Her highs were amazing—some of the best memories I have. But her lows—her spells—they would always set us back so far that she'd spend her time between them playing catch up."

Her lips quiver as she stares at me long and hard, prying deeper before she speaks. "I know you know what it feels like to be invisible . . . to have a sick parent. To suffer and constantly worry about if the lights will get cut off, or if you'll have lunch money or eat at all. I saw it that night I was there. I *felt it* in the atmosphere of that house. The desperation," she holds a palm over her chest, "because it lingers there, it's in the walls, and I recognized it. I lived through it too."

She weighs my expression, and I have no idea what she sees as my heart thuds out of control—her confessions striking deeper with each one.

Whoosh. Whoosh. Whoosh. Whoosh.

"I-I'm sorry," she whispers, "I don't mean to unload on you, it was just . . . today did something to me, and as those people lit up, as the worry eased from their faces . . ." she relays, heart in every single syllable. "I had to come here. I had to tell you that you probably saved some invisible kid from a similar fate today. Kids like *us* . . . or someone like my mom who was sick, and is still sick, and too fucking broke to get the help she needs." Tentatively reaching out, she palms my face, slowly running a thumb along my jaw. "Do you know that's why I'm here?"

I shake my head because it's the truth. All I knew was what was in the email. Sean hadn't trusted me with this, but to be fair, I hadn't ever let him get far in telling me much about Cecelia. Though the house is equipped and tapped, I haven't listened in since the day I picked her up. Roman hasn't been back, so I've respected her privacy—even when curious.

"I'm here. I came to Triple Falls because she's sick. She went into a deep depression just after I graduated. She just couldn't function, so when Roman sent the invitation, I couldn't say no, Dom. I'm doing this for her. I'm here to get an inheritance, to do the same thing you're doing for so many others that need the help." She moves in and presses a slow kiss to my lips. "I just couldn't . . ." her blue eyes shine with a sincerity that levels me, "I had to come here and make sure you know that you're a good man, Dom—an *incredible* man."

Pulling her hand away, I shake my head in refusal. "I'm not, Cecelia, don't believe the narrative going on in your head. It's your emotions playing tricks on you."

"Bullshit," she retorts, shaking her own head, refusing my statement.

"Don't put me on some nonexistent pedestal," I warn. "I'll only disappoint you."

"Please," she begs, stopping my retreat, "please, just . . . just acknowledge that you're helping people. Desperate people who need it. Give yourself that much credit, okay?"

I nod, my throat tight. "Okay."

"I'm sorry I unloaded on you," she sniffs, wiping her rapidly flushing cheeks. "You probably think I'm crazy."

"You do leak a lot," I flash her a grin as she looks over at me without a trace of humor.

"I see your heart, Dom, I see it—and it's *beautiful.*"

Biting my lip, I stand. She glances around like she doesn't remember how she got here as I go through the same motions, chest raw and aching.

She stands and shakes her head ironically. "God, I'm a mess. I'm going to go clean up for my shift." Looking up at me, she lifts and presses a slow, emotion-infused kiss to my lips. I don't catch her parting comment as she walks out. I'm still standing in the middle of my room when she starts her car.

"I have lived a great deal among grown-ups. I have seen them intimately, close at hand. And that hasn't much improved my opinion of them."—*Le Petit Prince*, Antoine de Saint-Exupéry

THIRTY-TWO

CECELIA RUSHES TOWARD MY CAMARO AND DOWN THE PORCH, dodging a few rogue drops of lingering rain as I push open the door from inside the cabin.

As she settles in, her addictive scent greets me along with her soft "Hey."

"Hey," I echo, as she corners me with her usual "missed you" while securing herself into the ancient seatbelt.

"I won't scare you today," I lie.

"Liar," she spurts with a sarcastic laugh as I start rolling out of the driveway.

Glancing in my rearview, Roman's estate starts to shrink behind us—which is fitting, seeing as how our progress with him is still at a standstill. As I eye the mansion in the rearview, Cecelia follows my gaze, and I tense when she speaks up.

"What's this?" She asks, curiously eyeing the offering hanging from the rearview. "Oh, my God, Dom . . . is this what I think it is?"

"It's no big deal," I interject, "just—"

"—a crown made of honeysuckle vines," she admonishes as though I've just given her the Heart of the Ocean from the Titanic. I inwardly groan as she starts to gush.

"It's so beautiful," she murmurs.

"It's edible weeds," I counter.

"It's incredible," she dons herself in my peripheral. "Dom, you really made this?"

"Well, seeing as they don't exactly sell them at the Texaco, yeah. Stop acting so surprised. I'm not the anti-Christ," I snap.

"Since when?" She chuckles, and I turn to see the vines I fastened into a makeshift crown, flower buds out, perched and fitting perfectly atop her head.

"You look ridiculous," I jest, downshifting for speed before glancing to see her eyes lit with that same damned look.

"You made me a crown. I can't believe you made me a crown," her voice wobbles.

I palm the air in front of her. "Don't make a big deal of it. I was waiting outside Peter's house this morning and got bored."

"You were totally thinking about me," she sighs.

"Jesus," I mutter, "no good deed goes unpunished. Seriously it's not a big deal."

"Well, it is to *me*," she whispers, "but you know that. Thank you."

Knowing she's itching to touch me, I turn up the radio and downshift, feeling her eyes on me the entire way to the spot. I don't even have the car parked before I'm attacked, and she makes a *very big deal* of it.

This. Damned. Girl.

Typing out my command, I feel her ever-present heavy stare on my profile, summoning me from where I sit in my camping chair. Wearing nothing but board shorts, I've been soaking in some much-needed sun between the blanketed clouds after days behind my monitor. "You're never getting another present," I state, as she continually peruses me. "Facts."

"Oh, shut up. The novelty has completely worn off."

"Good to know," I say, typing out another command.

"That's a lie," she admits, gently securing her crown.

"Well then, keep 'em coming," I snark as a silent beat passes. Then two.

"What?" I ask, unable to ignore her outright—a feat that's become next to impossible.

"It's Sunday, Dom. Take some time off."

"To do what?"

"To rest," she sighs. "You work so hard. Between the garage and the day-to-day of," she eyes my computer, muting any mention of the club, "it's a lot."

"Glad you appreciate it," I smirk over my screen while grabbing an eyeful of her as she lays out on one of the picnic tables at our Meetup spot. Abandoned book beside her, honeysuckle crown on, her sun-bronzed skin glows under the sunrays peeking through the hovering clouds. She's in a scrap of a crop top which gives me an ample view of her cleavage—especially when she turns on her side, and her sculpted torso and long legs are fucking mouthwatering. It's definitely a screen saver worth opting for in lieu of the one in my room. She smiles as she catches me ogling her, long hair spilling over the side of the table.

The unguarded affection in her stare unsettles me but also makes it impossible to tear my attention away. No woman has ever held so much ammunition against me with a single look.

Sensing I'm taking her suggested break, she lifts from the picnic table and walks over to me, gently pulling the laptop from my grip before walking it over and securing it back into the Camaro. "Was that necessary?"

"Yes, because I have a confession to make," she states, stalking toward me, seemingly on a mission. Dread races through me as her lips lift, unphased by whatever reaction she sees. "Don't look so scared, Dom. It's not what you're thinking."

"I'm not scared."

"Lie," she taunts as she bypasses the table and drapes herself across my lap, long legs hooked on the arm of my camping chair. Running her hands over my sweat-slicked skin, she leans in. "Here's my confession . . . I know what I'm holding," she murmurs, "I know *his worth*."

The same confession I gave her during our first day together. A day when my resentment was fully ripped away, and all I could see was Cecelia for who she really is—the way I see her now, as a young tender with a heart full of affection and a soul spun from gold. As dramatic as that assessment feels—it's spot fucking on. She's a living, breathing reminder for me that there is good left in the world.

"You truly do work so hard," she murmurs, palming my shoulders, "you should play hard, too."

"I think you're aware of just *how hard* I play." I lift my hips for emphasis, but as usual, she refuses to let me bat the sentiment away. "That was so predictable. You're not that guy."

"You shouldn't think so much of me, Cecelia," I say on an exhale.

"Tell me why."

Because every fucking day you're mine is a day I deceive you.

"I'm a criminal, and I do what criminals do. Lie, cheat, steal, deceive."

"Maybe . . . but you also provide, gift, and inspire."

"That's laughable."

"You inspire *me*," she whispers, pressing soft kisses along my jaw.

How in the fuck does she manage to do this every single time? Evoke the raw in me? More importantly, why do I allow her to corner me into it? A gift of hers I'm not at all fond of. The sincerity in her words and expression demands no less than sincerity in return. She exposes me constantly, to the point that I want to search for a quick escape while simultaneously fueling me with the desire to get closer to her.

It's fucking witchcraft. And all she's being is honest.

Even if my own words are continually trying to fight their way out of me, I can't and won't utter them.

She presses along my shoulders, massaging them as best she can, and pauses between them to the tightness there. "What is this?"

I shrug.

"What causes this, Dom? What frustrates you so much that *your body* betrays what you mask so incredibly well?"

"Like you said, I work hard."

"It's more than that. What are you carrying?"

"You know I can't tell you."

"You can tell me *anything*," she counters. "I will keep your secrets. Every one of them. Especially the secrets we make *together*. I think, no, *I know* you know that, or you wouldn't have let Sean take me to the Meetup and give me the choice."

"Which you haven't made," I tell her, hating the direction of this conversation.

"It's a huge decision."

"I thought you would run," I admit honestly. "I'm still wondering why you haven't, and I'm not going to convince you not to."

The safest thing she could do is say no and get as far away from us as possible. If I wasn't so fucking selfish, that's what I would tell her. What I should tell her.

Self-preservation seems to rank low with her, and maybe she should be told. But her eyes mute me—as does her touch. I don't want her anywhere right now that's not with *me*—looking and touching. It feels too perfect, even as I rob her trust blind and soak in her misplaced loyalty.

"Tell me what this is," she whispers, running her fingers over the knots between my shoulders.

"It's frustration."

"About what?"

I shake my head. "Things I see, what I feel, what I believe, and mostly what I can't control."

"Such as?"

Thinking on it, I sink into her massage as she waits patiently for an answer. Even as she caresses me into a lull, my body and senses come alive, aware of every ticking second in the present—the rustling trees surrounding us, the feel of grass at my bare feet, the bees circling beneath a corner of the picnic table. It's my favorite gift from her—the ability to rope me back from the darkness into acute awareness amongst the land of the living.

Fucking voodoo.

She's given me so much of herself—her care and attention—that I mull my words over carefully and give her nothing but complete honesty in return.

"It's like the very first time you take off in a plane . . . you're speeding down the runway, exhilarated when you're caught by air, and ascending. Minutes later, you're so stunned you're flying through the clouds, taking part in an experience so incredible it's almost impossible to believe. As that initial buzz runs through you, you stare out the window and get your first good look at the landscape, only to see it's littered with lines that act as borders. So, you start reasoning with yourself that land itself is owned and measured, but you never once expected to *see* it and *how unnatural* it looks. The view of the lines kills the vibe entirely, the impact so jarring it destroys the idea of flying for you."

Cloud cover sets in, and I catch a glint of embarrassment in her eyes. "I get what you're saying, but I've never been on a plane . . . we never . . . you know, had the money."

I tip her chin up with my finger before tracing her jaw with my thumb. "There's nothing to be embarrassed about, Cecelia, I was only a year younger than you are now the first time I got on a plane, and it was to go to college."

"It doesn't matter," she says, shaking it away, "tell me."

"I'm glad you told me because it perfectly reiterates my point and is exactly where a ton of my frustration lies."

"How so?"

"Because of the division—the way the lines were drawn—so many aspects of your life were decided before you were born. Your accent, how and where you would obtain your education, your exposure to religion, hand-me-down bias from those who raise or influence you between your lines, and any advantages. No matter where or who you are, it's the same scenario for everyone, for better or worse."

"So, flying is the idea of America?"

"Exactly."

"But looking down is what? Government?"

"Looking down from above is seeing what many don't want us to see. Those continually laying down the lines—or controlling the people that do—want to keep us blind. Oblivious to the system that continually sets so many of us up for failure. A lot of us are so caught up in the struggle just to survive *between* the lines to fucking care where we fit into the grand design. So many others are distracted by fighting on the edge of their line to hold it that they never understand the concept of flying."

I let out a slow exhale. "It's so fucked. The mapping was done over two centuries ago, and we got it wrong. The more we forget flying exists, the more lines are drawn, and we get distracted by it, the stronger our cage becomes. It's because of the lines of control that true division was created in the first place, and it's escalating."

She stares at me long and hard. "So, how do we fix it?"

I slide my thumb along her cheek. "Who the hell am I to even begin to think I can solve that . . . but we could start by ignoring the rabbit that has us running in fruitless circles while gunning for each other's throats. Then maybe we could lift each other up to get a glimpse of the true view."

"Buy everyone a plane ticket?"

"Exactly, that's all I'm trying to do."

"Is that even possible?"

"I don't know," I admit honestly, "but it seems like we're not far away from where we started anymore, so it's worth trying, isn't it? Maybe so we can take back charge of the map, but . . ." I swallow.

"But what?"

"From what I'm seeing—what I can prove—it's fucking terrifying. There's a powerful group of people, several, who will stop at nothing to make sure we remain blind. We might have a chance if they're knocked out of the equation."

"Our country is broken," she asks, her eyes searching mine, "irreparable, isn't it?"

"Is that what you think?" A raindrop falls from the sky, skating down her leg, and I trace its path with my finger.

"Sometimes, when I look at you—how angry you are—sometimes, I think that's what you *think. I can feel it* from you."

The helplessness, utter hopelessness I've felt over the last months hasn't gone unnoticed by the one person I've refused to show any of my cards to, and still, she sees me.

Whoosh. Whoosh. Whoosh.

Because she does know me.

Whoosh. Whoosh. Whoosh.

The roar in my chest intensifies as she palms my jaw, demanding my eyes.

"Dom, when you . . . feel this way, you can come to me. I'll be there for you. I'll be the best friend you've ever had." Her blue eyes fill with concern, "You can talk to me, and I won't . . . I'll try not to ask too many questions. I'll listen, I'll be here for you, and we can—"

I cut her off with my kiss, so she can't see what's brewing in my eyes as light rain begins to pelt us both.

THIRTY-THREE

"**D**OM," TOBIAS CALLS FROM DOWN THE HALL BEFORE appearing at my bedroom door. Lowering my hardback, he eyes the title. "Freshening up on history?"

"I think of it as more of a 'what not to do' and 'how not to get caught' for dummies."

He grins. "Get dressed. I'm taking you out for dinner."

"I am dressed," I look down at my T-shirt and jeans, my muddy boots discarded somewhere on the floor beside my bed.

He grimaces. "You don't have anything nice?"

I quirk a brow. "Have we met?"

"Good point, come on." He jerks his chin toward his bedroom, which sits catty corner to mine. "I'll lend you a shirt . . . and pants . . . and shoes," he chuckles.

"I'm good."

"No, you're not," he flicks a finger toward me, "they're not going to let you in wearing that."

"Then I'll pass," I raise my book to resume reading.

"We're celebrating, little brother, and I'm not in the mood to fight about how," he grumbles. "So do me a fucking favor and just borrow some clothes."

"Fine," I acquiesce, following him into his room. Taking a step in, I glance around. It's the same as it's always been, same furniture, same setup. The difference is that he doesn't live here anymore and hasn't for nearly a decade. Most of those years, I've only looked across the hall to see it pitch dark and empty. "What are we celebrating?"

"You're leaving in a week for college. That calls for celebration."

"Which includes fine dining? You sure this party is for me?" I snark.

"Maybe for me a little too. Is that so wrong?"

"It is if I have to look like I stepped out of Men's Warehouse," I quip, dubiously eyeing the luggage on his bed.

"You're not selling out, Dom. It's just a fucking dress code." He flips open his luggage, and I cringe when I spot a cashmere sweater.

"You seriously wear this shit?" I pilfer through his suitcase alongside him.

"Yes, I do, and the difference in feel and fit is incredible."

"I'll take your word for it."

"Why?" He tilts his head. "There are perks to being a millionaire, and it's time you see the upside, or in our case, the flipside."

"You don't think I'm ready for MIT," I conclude.

He pauses before plucking a tightly rolled shirt from a row of them at the bottom of his suitcase. "I don't want you feeling like you don't belong."

"Let me save you the suspense," I widen my eyes, "I won't blend well."

"Dom, I'm not telling you to change, but things will be different—the people, the norms, the culture. It's a different environment."

"I'm not a fucking idiot, hence the acceptance letter. I know how to pronounce big words, too. Don't worry about me. Better yet, stop worrying about me."

He scoffs. "You act like it's a choice."

"It is. I'm all grown up now, so you can brush the dust from your hands. You're all done. I can take it from here."

"So easy, huh, this game of life? I'm halfway through my twenties and still have no idea how to handle certain situations. Ever hear the saying 'age is nothing but a number?'"

"Yeah, but I think you're more on a 'grass is greener' trip right now."

"It can be. Don't be so damned prideful little brother. I didn't even know how to properly fasten a necktie until I was in prep school. The man who taught me saw potential in me and altered some of the instilled perceptions I had about myself on a night that changed my life. So, just put the fucking shirt on, and try to keep an open mind."

"Fine," I snatch the shirt from his hand.

"You should iron it," he adds, shrugging on his suit jacket.

"That's a fuck no," I grumble.

He raises his palms in surrender as I fist off my shirt and slide the collared atrocity on.

Pinstripes.

Shoot me now.

We're closer in build than we've ever been, so it fits well enough. Trying not to gag, I shed my jeans before pulling on a pair of his chinos. When my shirt is tucked in, Tobias's expression resembles something akin to pride as he reads my discomfort and chuckles. "Okay, maybe we skip the bow I had picked out for your hair. Try not to look so miserable. We're going to have fun." His eyes dip. "Shoes too."

He pulls some loafers from his bag, and I jerk my chin. "Not. Fucking. Happening."

"Wear them," he muses, "I promise none of your friends will see you."

"Sean's not coming?"

"No, Tyler either. You'll be alone in college . . . at least at first," he reminds me.

The weight of that truth doesn't sit well, and he pounces on it. "That, that right there, is the whole point of tonight."

"Thought it was a celebration?" I start to unbutton the shirt. "Not really interested in your little experiment."

He swats my hands to keep me from undressing and sighs my name in frustration.

"Here's an idea," I mutter, "how about just allowing me to go through shit to figure it out for myself?"

With the snap of a cufflink, his patience follows. "Because you've gone through enough on your fucking own!" The light in his eyes dims as he runs a hand through his hair in exasperation.

"All right, big brother, no need to get emotional." I flash him all my teeth, and he glares at me in return.

👑

Three hours later, Tobias lays down a card for the three-thousand-dollar dinner bill—mostly due to his various wine selections. We've literally dined like our namesake. Our glasses never got close to empty—wine or water—as we were catered to like infants.

"So?" Tobias prompts, looking pleased while sipping his wine.

"So what?"

"So, was that not the best fucking fare you've ever eaten?"

"Sure." I shrug.

He tosses his pressed linen napkin onto his empty plate as silverware clinks around us, along with hushed conversation. Looking relaxed, it's clear he's in his element. After thanking the waiter for topping off his wine, Tobias pins me with his stare. "We grew up gutter rats, and you just ate from a tasting menu designed by one of the best chefs in the country. Why are you so pissed about it?" He shakes his head. "Tell me, Dom, what does impress you?"

"A woman's flexibility," I smirk.

He sips his wine, unimpressed. "That's Sean talking."

"I'll tell you what doesn't impress me—wasting three thousand dollars on fermented grapes and sautéed vegetables."

"That's Delphine, through and through," he dismisses, "tell me, Dom, where is your voice?"

I glare over at him.

"Don't be offended that you're a chameleon. You change colors to blend with the company you keep, and it only proves just how intelligent you are. But you've allowed others to give you the impression and current idea of what you deserve. You've been dodging looks your whole life," he surmises. "The glares from Delphine for being a reminder of our parents' deaths and the orphans she was forced to take in. The attention and cruelty you garnered for being a poor kid wearing ill-fitting hand-me-downs. The looks you draw now for lashing out because your grudge against the world is so obvious . . . Jesus, you haven't even noticed the three women to our left who've been eye fucking us for the last twenty minutes. So, while you talk a good game—and have a healthy amount of confidence to back it up—you don't exactly know who you are yet outside of the club."

He leans forward, eyes intent as I rake my fork over my last bite of pureed cauliflower.

"That's okay, Dom. It takes time—a lifetime for some—but it requires truly living and experiencing the world outside of books through your own perspective. Leaving Triple Falls is your chance to discover yourself outside our mutual purpose and decide what kind of man you want to be." He pauses, knowing he has my attention. "I'm sharing this with you because I felt completely fucking lost my first year in France. I had no idea who I was. You've surpassed me by miles in some respects, but I'm worried because you haven't evolved past the limits you were made to believe you have. You have to try, Dom, for yourself. I'm scared of how lonely you'll be if you don't."

"I don't get lonely," I counter.

"Because it's been such a constant state for you that you don't recognize it anymore. You prefer isolation because it's safe."

I remain mute as he leans in. "You can talk to me about this, brother."

"Why?" I snap defensively. "Because you're managing to pull off the scam so well?"

"No more than anyone else here is. But yes, I'm a chameleon and will remain one, and so will you."

"Is this dinner sponsored by overused slogans? Now it's 'fake it until you make it?'"

"No," he grits out. "Always fucking fake it. We've already made it, but if people catch wind of that, they'll only try to drag us down—make *our lives harder out of envy, spite, or both. So, keep the grudge but hide the fangs. But make no mistake," he warns, "most interactions between humans are just a formality. When people ask how you are, most don't give a fuck, and that's all that interaction with outsiders is, Dom—a formality. So, don't waste energy, time, or effort on the people with whom you're only meant to exchange formalities. It's when you can't fake it with someone who consistently shows up for you without motive that you'll know they're deserving of all three."*

I can't help my grin. "This monologue of yours is a bit cliché, don't you think? Like a mobster delivering life advice before getting whacked or run over by a milk truck."

He shakes his head, tossing in an exaggerated eye roll. "Your constant vitriol is exhausting, brother."

"I learned from the best, and it's not like this," I glance around, "is really that much of a stretch for you. You like this atmosphere and dressing that way," I point out.

He shrugs. "I like expensive wine and clothes, and things we never imagined we could ever afford and now can, so why aren't you at least allowing a little of that in? You haven't spent a fucking dime since we added zeros to our net worth. At the very least, you need to order a new fucking mattress, but you haven't, and I know why. Look at me, Dom."

I snap my eyes to his.

"Press through your mindset limit and decide your own potential. Once you figure that out, we'll forge a fire so fucking big—no one will ever be able to overlook it or escape it."

Twisting his glass stem, he stares at it contemplatively. "It's laughable now how comfortable most of the men of our time are," he ponders. "The men in your history book who really did something with their lives and raised actual fucking swords in defense of their beliefs. Who spilled blood in the streets without flinching, declared themselves outlaws, and sacrificed every comfort while fearlessly fighting to the death. While more civilized negotiations have become part of the progression from Neanderthal to the modern man—who use brain over brute force— there's something to be said for those men of the past. I'm pretty sure those trailblazers weren't getting regular mani-pedis."

We both chuckle as he plucks the bottle and fills our glasses, a buzz humming steadily through me. "So, take this time to live some life outside of the club because one day in the near future, we're going to be fighting in the streets—maybe in more expensive clothes, armed with better, foolproof plans, but fighting nonetheless."

"I'll drink to that," I say, taking a hearty sip. He grins as he lifts a finger for the waiter, who nearly trips over himself getting to our table.

"Yes, sir?"

Tobias pushes the check back toward him. "We're going to have dessert."

"Which one, sir?"

"Every selection on the menu. We're celebrating," he boasts proudly. "My brother is going to attend MIT."

"Ah," the man barely spares me a glance. "Excellent, sir, congratulations." The waiter takes off as we eye each other over the table.

"I don't think he gave a fuck," I muse.

"He doesn't," Tobias retorts jovially, "he's probably sweating about how much of a tip we're going to leave. Even a shrink shows up for money. Now look around."

I do. My last stop is the table of women currently looking our way. Making it a point to, I catch the come fuck me eyes of one of them as Tobias speaks. "They're no better than you are, Dom. Not fucking one of them. You're the biggest threat in this room. That's a fact, so believe it."

The woman's eyes dart away before I turn back to see him lifting his glass to toast. "To the long game."

"To the long game," I parrot as we clink glasses, the buzz intensifying.

"Let's play hard, brother," he winks before we drink.

Glass still tilted, Tobias's eyes light over the rim as he catches sight of someone over my shoulder. Tabling his wine, he abruptly stands. "Ah, finally, I wasn't sure you were going to make it."

"Sorry about that," the man replies, approaching our table with a mischievous gleam in his eyes as they shake hands. My own eyes trail over the man in recognition as he shifts his focus on me. Exuding confidence, he extends a hand in offering. "Finally, the prodigal brother. Nice to meet you, Dominic."

Tobias beams with pride. "Dom, this is—"

"Congressman Monroe," I say, already standing, extending my hand and shooting Tobias a confused look as we shake. In response, he gives me a conspiratorial wink.

Four hours and countless glasses later, Tobias turns just after exiting and slams me into closing the door of the town car he called after our vision blurred and doubled.

Releasing me, Tobias stumbles further back into the yard, drawing from his hip in declaration. "En garde!"

Gripping his nonexistent sword, foot stretched in front of him in a lunge pose, he arches his opposite arm over his head, fingers dangling above his crown. When I just stare at him, his shoulders drop as his expression goes limp. "It means draw your sword."

"I know what it means, but drawing my sword will only embarrass you in front of the handmaidens," I snort.

"All I'm hearing is that you're too impotent to draw your steel," he taunts.

"Don't project, brother, I hear it happens to all men with age, and I'm more of a hand-to-hand man," I declare, charging toward him. Feigning a successful dodge of the thrust of his invisible sword, I tackle him into the grass.

"Oof," he goes down, roaring with laughter until I gain the advantage and deliver an over-playful bitch slap.

His eyes flare in warning as he knocks me off. "Poor form, Dom. This is a gentlemen's fight."

We both stumble back to our feet, and I raise my sword and mimic his posture. "Never going to be a gentleman, but touché, or whatever the fuck," I slur. We drunkenly shuffle back and forth across the yard and up the porch stairs, clashing invisible swords while knocking over two of Delphine's clay-potted plants. As Tobias reaches for the screen door, I lurch forward, delivering the death blow, burying my sword until my knuckles hit his chest.

He grips his wound, eyes widening in mock surprise. "So ruthless, brother. A street fighter to your core, right through the fucking heart," he sniggers with pride.

"Gutter-rattith-forith-thou-killith," I smirk.

Opening the screen door, Tobias shakes his head, smile disappearing, eyes narrowing when he sees the state of me. "You ruined my two-hundred-dollar shirt."

"I consider it an improvement and deserved punishment for spending that much on a fucking shirt."

"You're a teenage millionaire, Dom. Spring for a new pack of V-necks and BVDs." Eyes glazed by drink, he pats himself down. "Do you have your key? I left mine with the valet."

"Nope."

"Fuck," he drops his head before rapping on the door. Not a second later, the porch light comes on, and it opens, Delphine's narrowing eyes darting between us.

"Look, Dom, it's the milk truck!" Tobias roars before we both throw our heads back, laughing hysterically.

Sighing out "imbéciles," Delphine widens the door to let us in. Scrutinizing us briefly, she adjusts her robe before turning to retreat to her bedroom.

"Non, Tatie, join us," Tobias calls after her, shrugging off his jacket. "I'm making breakfast for both of you."

"Non," Delphine protests.

"It's time," Tobias says, unbuttoning one of his sleeves and rolling it up as he and Delphine share a tense but silent exchange.

She nods toward me, "he is drunk."

"Then that makes three of us," Tobias snarks, "put on some coffee so we can talk before the rest of the crew arrives to collect him."

"Time for what?" I ask, taking the rattle stool beneath the counter as they start to silently work together. Anticipation builds as Tobias glances over at Delphine, and they exchange another loaded look before he palms the counter, his words for me. "It's time you know your history. How and where it all truly began—and where it's going."

It was one of the handful of times I've ever been drunk, but I haven't forgotten a second. In the hours that followed, I sobered considerably with every passing minute, sipping coffee while Delphine revealed my parent's history—details of whom they were involved with *and in* before I was born. She added specifics about her own path and what eventually led her to Triple Falls. Minute by minute, my mind became more blown by how much *they both* had been keeping from me. The details of Delphine's sordid past helped me understand so much about her and *why* she is the way she is.

Tobias laid out his plans, his own revelations taking me aback. Especially the secret that the congressman who taught him how to fasten a necktie is an *original raven* Tobias attended prep with. An original on the fast track to becoming *president*—and still is.

That morning, Tobias trusted me with his most heavily guarded secrets and his vision for our long game. The way he is trusting me *now* with the fate of the club.

He'll never forgive you.

Guilt swallows me whole at the act of betrayal I just took part in because, as of right now, one of our originals is on a plane headed for France.

The reason? I'm having my own brother shadowed, his whereabouts reported, so I can continue to fuck our enemy's daughter.

If Tobias spots him, he'll immediately be tipped off that something is amok—along with knowing exactly *who* ordered his tail—which will only hasten his return. On the off chance he doesn't catch it, at least I'll know if what he's telling me is true. If the real reason for his long absence is to find his birth father.

If I'm caught, Tobias will suffer the worst kind of betrayal and heartbreak at my hands. Something he doesn't fucking deserve.

Remorse consumes me whole as I shoot off a text that says it all—that I miss him. That I have regrets about the way things are between us. That I'm trying. That no matter what he's doing or how far apart our current paths are, one thing forever remains the same.

Always brothers.

My phone instantly buzzes with his reply—a reply that has my throat burning.

B: Miss you too, little brother.

He'll never forgive you.

"It is much more difficult to judge oneself than to judge others. If you succeed in judging yourself rightly, then you are indeed a man of true wisdom."—*Le Petit Prince*, Antoine de Saint-Exupéry

THIRTY-FOUR

I'M SOMEWHERE BETWEEN CONSCIOUSNESS AND RESTLESS SLEEP when my phone rumbles on my nightstand, and my eyes pop open. Premonition strikes hard as I check it to confirm what I already know.

Dressed in seconds, duffle bag in hand, I pause at the foot of the stairs before backtracking to Sean's room. Opening the cracked door, I spot Cecelia sleeping peacefully. Chest aching, I soak in the look of her where she lays on her stomach—hair fanned over her pillow, expression serene, lips slightly parted, the sheet resting just below the small of her naked back. Burning the image of her into memory, guilt threatens because the last time I saw her, I'd been in such a fucked-up state that when she popped her head into my room, I slammed the door in her face. As cruel as that act was, I refused to let her glimpse what was festering inside me. Aching with regret, I rip my eyes away and make a beeline for my Camaro.

Fifteen minutes later, I finish screwing the temporary tag onto the old Buick before taking the driver's seat. Adrenaline pumping, I fix the rearview and pull my solid black ballcap down. Though I'm thankful for the early morning blanket of cloud cover, I curse when rain begins to accumulate on the windshield.

Trying my luck with the wipers—the one aspect I overlooked while restoring the eighties model sedan—I send up a thank you when the rusted blades power to life. Pulling down the ancient gear shift at the steering wheel, I roll through the debris of the junkyard, following the narrow path I cleared in preparation. Narrowly maneuvering the Buick between the crushed, stacked sedans on my left and the side of the garage to the right, I'm feet from King's parking lot when Sean steps directly in my path.

He doesn't so much as glance up as he takes painstaking time to produce his Zippo before lighting the cigarette dangling from his lips.

Exhaling a steady plume of smoke, Sean remains idle, a foot from the hood of the Buick as I roll down the driver's window. Rain dings from the hallowed cars stacked next to me when he finally looks up and pins me where I sit in the driver's seat. "Where you off to, brother?"

With zero time for his theatrics and knowing there's no way he's moving without an answer, I exit the car and stalk over to him, anxiety ramping. "Get the fuck out of the way, Sean. Now is *not* the time."

"So, I'm guessing you don't want me riding shotgun?" He scrutinizes the Buick before turning back to me, tilting his head with his question. "What the fuck is this, Dom?"

"What this is, is time sensitive," I grit out, "in a way you can't fucking fathom, and I don't have time to satiate your curiosity or talk feelings."

"Tell me," he snaps in demand.

"Tell you what? That I'm just as guilty as you are now, and that he'll fucking never forgive us both! That's what you wanted, right? To have someone to share the blame with? You win. I fucked her, have been fucking her."

"Yeah, well, narcissists blame everyone but themselves," he drawls out, "but never perceived you as one of those." He takes another long drag, brows drawn in confusion. "Is this you spinning out?" He asks. "Is this what this is, Dom? I get that what's going on is heavy—"

"You have no fucking idea what's going on and haven't since she got here. That's on you." My anxiety ramps as I dart my gaze back to the Buick, shoving him back while using the one piece of mental leverage I've got to keep him distracted. "Since day one, you betrayed your ink and brothers and made it look easy—that's also *on you*. I'm done. So, stay the hell away from me, and while you're at it, *keep her* away from me too."

Hurt leaks in his voice with his next question. "Do you want me to give up on you?"

"I don't give a fuck what you do."

His eyes dim before he flicks his lit cigarette at the Buick and turns to stalk off. I'm back at the driver's door when I'm turned and pinned, neck snapping to the side after Sean delivers a punishing right hook. "You didn't mean that. *Any* of it."

My jaw thumps as his expression hardens to one of resolution when my mask temporarily slips, and he realizes he's right. "Stop protecting me and tell me how to fucking help!"

"Get the fuck out of the way!" I roar. "Goddamnit, Sean, let me go!"

"Then tell me you can *come back* from this," his eyes desperately search mine, and I give him a slow nod.

"Words, Dom."

"If this goes wrong because you held me up, I'll never fucking forgive you!" I already fucked up and narrowly missed this window because I got distracted by Cecelia. A window that's rapidly closing as Sean steals precious seconds from me. The thought that I might miss it entirely triggers a fear I've never felt before. Posturing up, I leer at Sean as I speak. "Please don't make me hurt you."

Sean steps back in shock, not bothering to hide the betrayal he feels as he rips himself away. Even as I break a piece of us—a piece of his heart—he pleads with me because I'm his only concern.

"Meet me at the goddamn junkyard when you're done. At least give me that much? Whatever it is, we'll handle it, finish it—*together.*"

With a dip of my chin, he turns and stalks off without another word, slamming a bay door closed so I hear it, an unspoken promise he won't follow or try to stop me as I race through the parking lot.

An agonizing hour and change later, I'm parallel parking the Buick while frantically scanning the street for signs of the fly's hatchback. Thanks to Sean's hold up, I managed to beat him here in a matter of seconds, which is confirmed when the hatchback comes into view. I send up another quick thank you to whomever or whatever is watching over me when a car pulls out in front of him on the other side of the barricaded street, and the fly takes the spot adjacent to where I'm parked.

Scanning for pedestrian traffic, I find none as the familiar vibration rattles heavily through me—so much so my hands start to shake as I press the brake and pull down the gear shift just as he starts to exit his hatchback.

Slowly backing away from the curb to buy time, I slam on the gas when he retrieves what's needed from his back seat and shuts the door. Before he can take a single step toward the auditorium, I pin him between the Buick's passenger door and his driver's door. His eyes widen when he sees the silencer attached to the Glock I have trained between his eyes.

"Good morning," I utter low, tugging my hoodie with my free hand to unveil the offering sitting in my passenger seat. He's dressed in his uniform, his security lanyard hanging around his neck. Unzipping the duffle with my gloved hand, I open it to reveal my offering.

"Take it in trade," I order, keeping his gaze and recognizing the void inside it. It's like staring into a bottomless pit. I commit his expression to memory because I might have lied when I answered Sean. There might not be any coming back from this—in one sense or another.

Time will tell.

"Think of it as a gift with my blessing," I prompt him.

His eyes dart to the stadium before flitting back to me.

"The trade isn't optional," I stretch my gun toward him, my intent clear.

"Who are you?" He asks, his timbre humanizing him. He could be any one of my brothers . . . but he's not.

I rattle off his handle, and understanding crosses his expression. He thinks I'm the one who's been with him nightly in the chatroom. A nauseating grin spreads over the fly's face as he accepts my offering, collecting the duffle bag and leaving his loaded backpack in my passenger seat. Duffle strapped on his shoulder, when he clears the window I fire three times in quick succession and slam on the gas. His lifeless body collapses onto the street in my rearview, confirming that no amount of glue will piece his diseased head back together. Waves of anxiety roll from me as I take all the alleys to get back to the main road, keeping a law-abiding pedestrian's speed even after I hit the highway.

"Dom," Sean snaps my name again to jar me into talking as he has since I pulled up. The noise roaring in my head keeps me mute as I watch the fire rage inside the Buick. The plastic steering wheel melts like puddling clay as I toss in the ball cap, fueling the flames while stripping down. Tossing in my T-shirt, Nikes, jeans, and boxers into the mix, I grab the running hose as the morning sun beats down on the two of us.

Mere feet away, Sean chain smokes, his anxiety building as I rinse myself with the bar of soap before using a cuticle brush, scrubbing to ensure there's no residual spray on me before I towel off. Reaching into my packed duffle, I pull my boxers on as I glance around the junkyard. Denny observes the fire, extinguisher in hand, the only bird here aside from the two of us. He hasn't so much as looked our way, wordlessly keeping his distance while diligently ensuring the Buick I arrived in never existed. After fastening my jeans, I toss the towel into the mix along with the duffle itself and dip my chin to Denny. A few more silent minutes tick by before Denny fires off the extinguisher, dousing the flames as Sean and I step back.

It's times like this that I'm thankful I bought the junkyard with my money rather than expensive clothes. An acquisition that, to outsiders, makes perfect sense in conjunction with owning an auto shop. I credit the inkling that I had to move in on this property for needs like this.

Once Sean's taken the hint that conversation isn't happening, we both watch on as Denny mounts the forklift and, seconds later, drives twin prongs through the body of the smoking Buick. It's when Tyler's engine sounds before his C20 flies into view that I ready myself, the truck skidding to a halt feet away.

"I didn't say a fucking word, Dom," he assures me, his eyes volleying between Tyler's truck and me.

"I know," I clip out.

Sean's still on my side for the moment, my most trusted, my brother by choice, and my best friend for the same reason. That truth resounds deep as he rattles next to me in fear. His concern—even after I've done my worst—eliminates some of the space between us. "The fuck did you do, Dom?"

"You're about to find out," I relay, getting a good look at him for the first time since I got here, the haze starting to disperse before I issue my warning. "Don't step in for me."

"What?" Sean's brows draw together a second before Tyler flies out of the cab of his truck and charges me, his right hook landing squarely, making my teeth rattle. Unable to withstand the force of it, I stumble back but lift my chin, readying myself for more. We've been at the junkyard for a little over two hours, which means the news has already broken with enough details to have Tyler drawing the right conclusions and steering him to my whereabouts.

Still clueless as to what just went down, Sean ignores my order and steps between us, trying to get Tyler under control. Truth is, if Tyler wanted to have another crack at me, he'd have already put Sean down and delivered it tenfold. Tyler has yet to show *anyone* in the club what he's truly capable of. Something I admire about him, even as my mouth stings like a bitch.

"What the fuck!" He roars, attempting to push past Sean, who divides us now after ignoring my request.

"Let him through, Sean," I snap.

Sean sighs and reluctantly lets Tyler by.

"You fucking know why," I relay, trying to keep my tone level.

"We had a goddamn plan!" He rages, and I can tell he's doing everything he can to keep from striking me.

"You made a plan that includes utilizing a *broken system* to do *our* job. That's not who we are. We don't make citizen's fucking arrests, Tyler. Maybe you spent one too many years following rules."

"So instead of raising those points, you go and fuck it all up?" He fires, his head swiveling toward Sean.

"Don't look at him," I bark, drawing the heat away from Sean, "I acted alone by baiting one of the hooks you were planning on casting a little early in a way that can't be ignored. But this can still play out to plan." I step forward, meeting his accusing eyes. "I just sped the process up a little."

"What the fuck is happening right now?" Sean demands between us.

Tyler shakes his head, his livid stare fixed on me as he speaks. "What's happening is our unhinged brother went rogue, endangering his fucking life and future while simultaneously trying to take care of our crate problem."

"I altered it," I insist in a shit excuse. "Kicked it into motion early out of necessity because my fucking hands were tied!"

"Yeah, and where are our hands now?" He snaps before opening his truck door as the Buick is crushed to dust behind him. Reaching into the cab, I know exactly what his plan is, and a second later, the news fills the yard.

"*—gunman found dead outside the North Carolina stadium has been identified as twenty-year-old Joshua Brown. Authorities have issued a state-wide search for a suspected second gunman, who investigators think might have had a last-minute change of heart. Firework shows* *have been canceled across the following counties, Gaston, Iredell, Lincoln, and Mecklenburg. Please be advised a second suspected gunman remains at large and should be considered armed and extremely dangerous—"*

Sean's eyes fly to mine. "Jesus Christ, Dom!"

"Don't look at me like I had a choice," I snap at both of them. They stare at me like I'm a different person than the one who rode bikes with them well after the streetlights came on, snapped cards in our rooms until the late hours, and explored every inch of the surrounding woods while sharing stories of the first time we got our dicks wet.

Maybe I'm not the kid they grew up with anymore.

Maybe I haven't been in a long time.

Maybe the look in their collective eyes is justified, and I focus on Tyler as I relay as much. "Neither of you wanted to see that I'm as capable as you are," I say, knowing he's well aware the *other* I'm referring to isn't Sean. "You can relay that to France when you update him to earn your brownie points."

Tyler's eyes flare in final warning, and I take it for what it is, along with the struggle inside him—knowing he's now crystal clear on the nature of mine. While they might still be straddling the line from the reality that exists—and the world we have plans to change—in my mind, I've been living full-time on the other side.

"We can't stand idly by, not when it comes to stakes this high," I declare, "You can look at me all you want like that, but you would have done the same thing because all three of us know when we wait for *someone to do something* no one ever fucking shows up."

Tyler full on rushes me, gripping my T-shirt in both hands. Nose to nose, he stares me down, and I don't waver. "We're the some-ones, Tyler. That's who we decided to be." He searches for the cracks in my psyche, but I haven't felt them yet. Right now, I feel nothing, and it must show because he steps back, seeming satisfied, before releasing me and hanging his head. "Goddamnit, Dom."

"You're wasting time already," I remind him.

"Those plans have to change," he snaps.

"They don't," I tell him as he looks up at me, staring through me, his mind racing with a dozen scenarios, tailoring each to further cover my tracks.

"Cameras?" Tyler prompts.

"Blacked out everything within blocks. No pedestrians on the street. I didn't speed. I don't think anyone made the car, and I didn't get out." I nod toward the dusted Buick. "We've owned it for years due to a mechanics lien."

He gapes at me. "How long have you been planning this?"

"A while." Since the fly vibrated on my web.

"Fuck!" Tyler slams his fist on his truck glaring at me, his request for Sean. "Get everyone to the garage. We're going on a field trip. I'll meet you there in fifteen minutes."

I move to get into Sean's Nova, and Tyler shakes his head. "Not you. Go to Denny's and fucking stay there until I text you home." He looks over to Sean. "He's grounded." Tyler snaps his gaze back to me, and I don't bother to object. He's the only one who can veto me, and there's no fucking way around it. "This is what it is, or I bring France home. Don't fucking test me on this, Dom."

Exhausted, I give him a sharp dip of my chin as he climbs into his truck and speeds off. Sean sparks up a cigarette, and I give him the words I know he needs. "I'm okay."

Denny pulls up, and I round the car as Sean remains idle, studying me intently for the same cracks Tyler sought. Opening Denny's passenger door, I jerk my chin. "Go. I'm all right, brother."

Seconds later, Sean's speeding off in his Nova. Denny remains wordless as I stare through the trees blurring out of his passenger window. On that drive, I realize I've finally reached the place I've been searching for. A state not quite as blissful as the peaceful place I've come to rely on but strong enough to recognize—*numb*.

I've bore witness to two prime examples that there are good men left in the world. Loyal men. Faithful men. Though thieves they may be because they've stolen my heart.—Cecelia, *Flock*

THIRTY-FIVE

Two days later, I stare up at my ceiling in the same position I've been in since Denny dropped me off hours ago—boots crossed, back on my mattress, palms on my stomach. The heavy repeat of his Nova jars me from the backdoors of my mind, and not a minute later, Sean's silhouette appears at my door—partially lit by the streetlights. He stands in wait, none of his typical 'little spoon' quips coming while the aftermath of the last forty-eight hours emanates from him.

"You've been busy," I say, knowing Tyler proceeded with our plans—along with improvisations—in an effort to sweep up after me. While I was on lockdown at Denny's, Layla paced next to me as reports flooded their TV screen of the statewide manhunt for the second suspected gunman, *me*, who's still at large. Hours after I fled, Tyler utilized the birds he trusted to divide and conquer. They made good use of the guns we lifted from the warehouse in a free for all of victimless gunfire—shooting up abandoned buildings and closed businesses. Starting in Charlotte, they webbed out in all directions—from the edge of the Tennessee border all the way to Nags Head Beach, leading those investigating on a wild-goose chase.

Sean palms my doorframe. "Stroke of genius to put those prints on some of the bullets."

We'd already devised the plan to put partial and full prints that we extracted from Spencer and the dirty military on his payroll on some of the shell casings so the guns would be traced back to them. The tactic is meant to keep all government alphabet agencies and military investigators as far as possible from our county line while searching for the guns now in our possession. After the evidence was not so subtly planted, Tyler flagged one of our feather feds as to which locations to look for those prints to get them all investigated and possibly indicted. Convicted is another story. In that, I have zero faith.

"They'll get off," I state, toeing my boots off before nudging them off my bed.

"Worth trying, right?"

"Where is he?" My question regarding Tyler's whereabouts and the status of the grudge he may still be harboring against me.

"Not coming back tonight," Sean relays, "but he has his ringer on."

For me.

I don't ask about Cecelia, but I can sense what's coming as he takes a seat at the edge of my bed. "She's wondering where you are."

"Let her," I snap in warning, looking over to him as he casts his gaze my way and swallows.

"You know she asked me not too long ago who my hero was—"

"Don't," I warn, throat burning.

"That answer changed two days ago," he relays without hesitation.

"I killed a twenty-year-old kid," the confession feels ripped from me as I say it out loud for the first time.

"You stopped an imminent mass murder," he insists, tone unwavering. "Denny unloaded his backpack, and it was fucking horrifying . . . he was going to open fire on families watching fireworks.

There's no telling how many lives you saved. Your hands *were* tied. Tyler knows that—we all do. I know you couldn't or wouldn't have done it if you thought there was any other way, and you didn't take him down until you were sure."

Quiet seconds pass as the burn circulating through my chest keeps me silent.

"Please don't torture yourself," he says on a long exhale. "I can guarantee that you need something or *someone* right about now, and maybe you can't put your finger on it. Or maybe you can—"

"She doesn't need to be anywhere near us, Sean. It's only going to get more fucking dangerous for all of us."

"I tried," he cups the back of his neck. "*That night,* I tried to break it off with her . . . and I failed. I couldn't do it. But I heard you," he hangs his head. "I heard you, Dom, and I'll respect whatever decision you make. But," he swallows, "please know I'm sorry, truly, for everything," He runs a hand through his matted hair, no doubt due to the ski mask he's been wearing for days to help cover my tracks. "I'll never bring this secret up again, but I wish you could have trusted me."

"I did . . . I do."

"Only when I forced your hand," he stands and looks over at me, eyes glazing. "I might have lost your trust, but I would hand you my firstborn, Dom, no questions asked. From here on out, I'm done asking about shit you don't want to answer, but I hope you don't have to make me because I want that trust back if you'll give it to me . . . and heads up, from now until France comes home, I'm not going to let you out of my goddamn sight."

It's no big surprise my sentence has been lengthened, no doubt one Sean and Tyler came to while en route to plant red herrings.

"Truth is, I want this time with you 'cause I miss you, man." I don't have to see his tears to know they're there. "And you know I'm not above playing fucking dirty to get it, so don't make me."

"I won't." My reply has him pausing for any sort of dishonesty.

"But just so you know," he says, contempt for Tobias clear in his voice, "or need a reminder. You're a living, breathing fucking human being and allowed to behave as one."

I don't bother to tell him I was granted that clarity by the one person in the world I shouldn't have gotten it from.

"And you might think I'm ignorant to it," he rasps out, "but the night of the Meetup," his Adam's apple bobs, "if he had reached me. If you hadn't stopped him, I wouldn't be standing here," his voice cracks. "I will never sell you out to France," he slaps at his tears, "he doesn't have to know. You don't have to cop to it. I'll—"

"I didn't mean it," my whisper is just as guttural, and he exhales harshly in relief, fingers twitching at his side. He wants a cigarette, but I already know what's coming before he puts a voice to it. "I'm in love with her."

"I know."

"So, if you're going to break her heart, you're going to have to do it alone." His voice is raw when he speaks again. "I'm just so fucking sorry I messed us up in the process." He stares down at his boots, running his forearm along his jaw. "I love you, brother."

He leaves the door open as my vision blurs, and I move to sit at the edge of my bed, staring after him before catching my half-lit reflection in my bathroom mirror.

Part human, part monster, and stuck in limbo for the foreseeable future.

I've always labeled the other side "monsters" because at least then I could justify slaying them. The truth is, those monsters are human beings capable of doing unspeakable acts outside of moral lines—where I dwell to stop them—but pulling the trigger was different for me this time, and we all know it.

Tyler knows it, Sean knows it, and even though I knew that kid's future was only cut short by an hour at most—that he would die by his own hand or someone else's—I was the one who saw him draw his last breath because I made it so.

For now, I have to let it go. The list, the need to fix what's broken because it's breaking me. I have to accept what I'm capable of.

Of what I'm not.

My limits have been repeatedly shown to me as of late, and I feel that defeat start to settle low in my gut.

Opening my laptop, I press my palm to the keyboard, and it lights up in a fiery red welcome before I start to file it all away, temporarily laying it to rest—for a time when I can do something about it. It feels like nothing short of bloodletting as I allow it all in. All of my failures in the last few months and the guilt that multiplies daily because I can't get them all. No matter how much I want to.

Maybe this is how my brother felt, waiting all those years for us to catch up to where he was. If he did it, so can I. Because whether I've outgrown them or not, this is my family, and the men surrounding me are the only men I trust to help me see this through. Until the time comes when we're aligned on the same path, ready to pull the trigger, it can't happen.

Purging as failure runs down my face, I drown in it, allowing the emotions to take over while I mourn for the path I can't travel until I'm freed. I make peace with it because I don't want my eyes to ever match the void I saw in the eyes that are starting to haunt me.

"Dom, when you . . . feel this way, you can come to me . . ."

But I can't anymore. That's the hardest part to swallow.

Exhaling due to the sting that truth brings, I plug in my earbuds and scroll through my playlist for a beat before tuning into the mics planted in Cecelia's bedroom. Lengthy seconds of silence ensue as I lay back in bed, her room just as quiet as mine.

Just as I go to switch it off, I catch a faint drum in the distance. *Thunder.* The light pattering of rain follows, the clarity of the sound telling me she left her French doors open tonight. Turning my volume all the way up, I settle in for the restless hours ahead but manage to drift away just as her storm catches up to my roof.

Shrouded in the dark, I search the wall for a way in as cries sound from the other side. Pushing against it, the screams grow louder, as if I'm hurting them by trying to break through. But that's not the truth of it—that

rings clear as echoes of pain and torment fill my ears, elevating my panic. Exhausted, I continue to try to force my way through, to make it stop. Terror filters in when one by one, the screams start to cut off abruptly. A spark of fire flashes in the distance, and I turn to look for the source, seeing Sean's profile before he clicks his Zippo closed. My shout for help is absorbed by the pitch dark, my fists useless as I pound on the wall, exertion futile as they bounce off the impenetrable stone. The more their cries die, the harder I hit and fail. Gritting my teeth when the last wail is stifled, I sag against it, knowing I'm too late. Lingering silence sucks every ounce of hope from me while midnight shadows start to weigh me down, paralyzing me slowly in their grip. Sinking against the wall, I land in a puddle, palms splashing before sinking to the ground beneath. Lifting my hands, I run what's covering them between my thumb, my roar swallowed by the blackness as my mother's voice reaches me. "It's only a storm—"

"—storming, I hope that's okay." My eyes pop open from where I lay on my stomach, facing my bathroom. Cecelia lays on top of me, just out of my line of sight, her weight covering me like a security blanket, her tender whisper in my ear. "I came in from my shift, and you were already out. I'm sorry I woke you."

The sound of rain patters outside as I try to get my bearings, her whisper pulling me back toward her as the shadows disperse.

"Were you dreaming? Your arms were jerking a little."

Coming to fully, I realize I've got the forearm she has wrapped around me in a tight grip and release it. I move to get up, and she presses against me, pinning me to the mattress.

"No, stay in bed," she orders, running her fingers through the damp hair at the back of my neck.

"I fucking hurt you," my voice sounds like sandpaper and exertion.

"No, you didn't. Not at all," her tone fills with concern. "You okay?"

"I'm good."

Even as I lie, I take long drags of air until the pulse pounding in my ears starts to even out.

"Better," she whispers, "was it a nightmare?"

"I don't remember." More like my definition of hell.

"Consider yourself lucky," she murmurs. "Just sleep, okay?"

Feeling raw and more exposed than I can ever remember, all I can do is nod against my pillow. Hearing the rustling as she sheds her uniform, I lie in wait—eyes closed as the thin veil of sweat produced by my dream cools on my skin.

That was most definitely my subconscious's warning of too much to process, the dream far too easy to pick apart. I'm still somewhat between worlds when the bed dips a second before her bare thigh slides over my lower back, her arm snaking around me before the soft skin of her breast is pressed against my bicep. My body becomes lax as her scent, her skin, and her soothing touch lull me along with another gentle whisper, "You're so warm. Always so warm. I missed you."

She's come for me again, constantly showing up for me without motive because she's worth my time, effort, and attention. Something I've known far longer than I've let on. The urge to lose myself in her begins to hum, but I don't move, too weak, drained from my dream while knowing the illusion I'm feeding into with her is about to come to an end.

My throat constricts at the comfort she brings and the fact that this is the last time I can lose myself in it. But I do lose myself one last time as her nails gently rake up and down my spine, pulling me into a blissfully deep, dreamless sleep.

Waking a few hours later, dream forgotten, my room lit in a deep shade of purple, I rouse her with the soft press of my lips. A slow smile appears before her eyes do. Slipping between her legs, condom already secure, I take her mouth, the need to drive inside her taking over.

Cupping the back of her head to cradle it, I don't break our kiss as I part her thighs and ready her, swallowing her noises and soaking every bit of her in as I slowly press into her.

Palming her thigh up with one hand, cradling her head with the other, I fuck her nice and slow, to the point I'm barely moving inside her. Even without friction, we're deeply fed by connection. What was meant to be a thank you turns into something else entirely as she washes away all remnants of what haunted me. Rain ticks against the window as I tip over, losing myself in rapture for the last time. It's only when I'm forced to come up for air that I lift to hover. Keeping my hand beneath her head, her thigh firmly at my waist, she stares back at me, caressing my bicep. Wordlessly, I roll my hips, chest detonating with tiny explosions as she gasps my name. It's the first time I've ever wanted to rip my condom off and fuck a woman bare. Even though I keep it on, I know I'm as close as I'm ever going to get.

I know I'm in love with him. I just don't know how much of him I know.—Cecelia, *Flock*

THIRTY-SIX

F EELING THE SHIFT IN TEMPERATURE SWEEP THROUGH THE garage, I tighten the last bolt on the piece of shit Subaru I've been pumping life into for the past six hours. Rolling my neck to ease the tension, I glance past the hood to see splattering rain collecting on the grease-stained cement inside my open bay.

Ignoring the increasing thud in my chest, I inhale the stench of Mrs. Wellers' Dachshunds, who all have embroidered names in their designated car seats, and turn the ignition, satisfied when it starts with ease.

Pulling the key, I close and lock the bay door before heading into the lobby to finalize the ticket. Rain pounds the roof as the steady thud inside increases—a reminder I ignore as I pull my phone from the safe to see a missed text, hours old, from Sean.

S: She's here.

Fuck.

The sky cracks above, rattling the ground beneath my booted

feet, reverberating throughout the garage and grounds as I pull the door to, and lock it, pausing when my eyes land on the name etched into the glass. The sight of it only adding to the guilt festering in my gut.

As it turns out, Tobias *is* searching for his phantom birthfather, Abijah. The raven following him confirmed it within twenty-four hours after landing in Paris.

Which makes the only deceptive brother in this equation *me*.

Deep down, I knew that. Maybe I wanted his guilt to make me feel better. A crime I accused Sean of, which now makes me a hypocrite.

Behind the wheel of my Camaro, I scan the interior, and in the next second, I'm not alone. I can picture Cecelia so clearly next to me, her long legs taking up the floorboard, her tight body tucked into the seat, and dark, fire-kissed hair floating on the breeze.

Cranking my car to warm it up, "Tennessee" starts to blare through my speakers. Turning up the volume, I scoff at the lyrics as I wait, gaze drifting back to the window, specifically to the name.

Shooting out of the parking lot, song ringing in the cabin, irony strikes that my predicament is almost fucking prophetic at this point. A part I accused Sean of playing as the quilled pen swivels back in my direction, mocking me.

I'm no Romeo, but everything about this shit show has to do with our last names, our parents, a vendetta, and the reason why we're destined to implode.

So, what's in a name?

Everything.

Everything's in a name. A name I take pride in because my brother made it that way. He made us future rulers from a pile of discarded fucking rubble, and every time I get drunk on blue flames, I ruin a part of what he gifted me.

Speeding down the main road, I accelerate as my mind wars with my chest.

At twenty-six, I see things so differently now than I did when I demanded so much of him. Throwing tantrums in my early teens, insisting he be more present when he was killing himself, and risking his life to provide for me, and not just the necessities. He struggled for years to give me a life neither of us could have imagined after starving for so many, both *together and apart.*

The feeling growing up in that house—especially during those years without him—was exactly like Cecelia described. Desperation vibrated from those walls. The atmosphere was so bleak that, at times, I thought I would just evaporate. My brother did his best to shield me from it, and to this day remains my protector.

He toed the line between parent and brother well, as he does everything else. Everything except women.

I'm almost positive he'll never care about their place in my life—or *his.*

So now, in his eyes, I've taken part in the only unforgivable sin.

Because what *Roman Horner* did is *unforgivable.*

Fucking his daughter and ruining her should have been a given and would have done some collateral damage if Roman bothered to care enough about her ruin. As it is, she's an orphan like me.

I'm incapable of going that far, even if my blood can run cold. For the most part, it still runs warm, and Cecelia keeps reminding me of that.

But I am doing a cold thing—just because I'm not deceiving her with malicious intent doesn't mean I'm not hurting her or won't.

She's done exactly shit to deserve it, too. For me, she's accurately what Tobias predicted a woman would be—a sanctuary.

I can practically hear the sarcastic "I told you so" dripping in French as I spin out on the first turn—this call close enough to have my adrenaline spiking and sweat dotting my brow.

"Naw, Sean, *this* is me *spinning out,*" I spit, gassing the Camaro, taking another curve, the car catching on the rising water before I shoot forward. In an instant, my brother's voice cuts through my thoughts with a warning to calm the fuck down.

Something I haven't been able to do successfully for long since my anger gained a sort of razor's edge with his continued absence over the years. Anger no soul on this earth has been able to fully curtail—not even Sean. Cecelia's been fruitless at times, too, walking on eggshells, and even for her, I haven't always succeeded.

For her, I wanted to.

I really wanted to.

But I have to keep that anger and edge. With what we're up against, she can't soften that for me. She's stolen too much already. At this point, I resent her as much as I want her, and right now, that's a fucking lot.

Taking another curve, I hydroplane, only able to correct the wheel just in time to avoid certain fucking death.

I used to question why I don't fear for my own safety. At first, I thought it was because I believed I was trash, or at the very least, the charity case I saw in the eyes of those who witnessed our neglect growing up. Now I know I'm not, but I'm determined to take out the true wastes of life, the scum of the earth, the real threats, and there's a cost to being that type of garbage man.

A cost I know will come sooner than later. Just as that notion strikes me, the familiar urgency sets in—we're wasting time.

I could fucking end this right now. Right fucking now.

With a bullet.

I can't blame Cecelia, and I can't blame my brother.

But I *can* blame *Roman.*

I can blame Roman for being the barrier between the life I could be living—unshackled, untethered, and freely reigning down punishment. A life I want more than any other.

I click my signal at the stop light while eyeing my glove box.

My ignorance is no longer bliss but *blistering* me, hindering me from the progression just as much as her father.

One-point blank shot to that arrogant prick's skull will put my brother's drawn-out mission to rest and grant me the freedom I need.

Even if I could kill him without remorse, I could never look at her, let alone touch her again with his blood on my hands.

A simple solution to an overly complicated problem.

Banging my head against the back of my rest, I shake my head in dismissal. Because of both Tobias and Cecelia, that bullet can't fly.

Trapped by the stoplight, I glimpse Maman through the haze clouding the windshield, dancing and waving her hand in encouragement to join her before sweeping me into her hold and swaying with me all over the kitchen floor.

A blink later, Cecelia takes her place—hand outstretched for me to dance with her where I sit beneath my windowsill as she sways in a cloud of smoke emitted by my exhale.

What I've allowed to happen between us is an illusion, one I bought into—that, as of late, I started feeding.

Tobias surpassed it all. Bulldozed past Delphine, our fucked situation, all of it, while managing to stick to the game plan without entanglements holding him down. Yet, I can't make it past the daughter of the man I hate with every fiber of my being?

For my brother, I will, or else I'll ruin everything we've collectively overcome to get to where we are.

I have to let her go.

Decision made, I speed toward the end of the secret I can no longer participate in and park on a dime when I reach the house.

It ends now.

Stalking through the front door and up the stairs, I'm stopped at the door by the sight of her lying face up at the end of my bed, wearing nothing but one of my black T-shirts and tiny boy shorts. Hair spilling over the side of the mattress, knees drawn, a book hoisted at eye level. She spots me, turning on her stomach, her smile lighting up the room as her soul-filled eyes meet mine. "There's my motherfucker."

Fuck.

THIRTY-SEVEN

"HI," SHE SAYS, EYES ROLLING DOWN MY FRAME BEFORE SHE bounds toward me where I stand, dripping at the door. "You're soaked." She lifts, pressing a chaste kiss to my lips. "What took you so long?"

"Business," I lie, taking a step in as she blocks me playfully, matching my footing.

"What business?" She asks.

I lift a brow, and her brow quirks before she rolls her eyes. "Fine. Whatever."

"Whatever means you're not an accessory after the fact," I snap, "secrets keep you *safe*."

"Secrets keep me *insane*." She shivers at the chill from the rain droplets spilling onto her while clasping her hands around my neck. "I missed you," she whispers, "been missing you ... where have you been?"

"Busy." Gripping her hands, I release her hold as my stunted heart thunders back in a determined rhythm while her expression draws in confusion. Destruction has been my sole focus for so long that I don't know how to slow my desire for chaos enough to fully give her the few peaceful parts of me I have left. I've educated myself to the point that it's maddening. I know too much to ever know peace like other people do. Where Sean sees a glass half full, I can only imagine shattering it. I'm too enraged, too fucking frustrated with all that's wrong. All that needs to be fixed, all that I want to fix—to change that for anyone, let alone a nineteen-year-old girl.

End this, King.

Frowning, she runs her finger along my drawn brows. "There's too much going on in there. You were just with me. What happened?"

I shake my head and try to move past her again, and she refuses to let me pass. "No. Talk to me. What's wrong?"

"You know I fucking can't."

"Agh," she groans in irritation. "You're the worst conversationalist in the history of ever."

"Talk feelings with your girlfriends, Cecelia. I'm not one of them," I remind her as I often do. Guilt threatens as hurt flits in her eyes, but I bat it away as I walk over to my dresser and grab some boxers. The second I unbuckle my belt, Cecelia plants her elbows on the bed and palms her face, her eyes following my every movement, and I stare back at her, annoyed. "You just going to watch me?"

"Less talking, motherfucker, more stripping. And when you get those boxers down, make sure you walk away *nice and slow.*"

I pause, jeans dangling on my hips. "You're making this weird."

She grants me an exaggerated eye roll. "Everything's weird for you, right? Because God forbid you let a second of intimacy linger when you're not fucking me. You can kiss me so tenderly as you take down my panties and stroke my face when I'm sucking your dick, but a second outside one of us coming, you clam up as though you're incapable. So," she turns her finger around, "if I'm stuck with minimally invasive conversation and the fact that you barely take your jewelry off before you fuck me," she adds as I unclasp my watch, "the least you can do is entertain me."

"I'm not here for your fucking entertainment." I slam said jewelry on the dresser.

"No? Then stop holding back every time we start getting closer."

"If you aren't happy here," I shrug, "the guy you need is a bedroom over."

She leaps from the bed, expression drawn with contempt. "Frankly, I'm sick of fucking hearing that, Dominic. It's a pathetic excuse. If you ever say that to me again, this is over."

She might as well have stabbed me with the threat. And because of that, it needs to be over. It has to be.

"I have to work tonight, so," I nod toward my bedroom door in dismissal as she stares at me for a few beats before moving to sit on the edge of the bed.

"Huh," she says, staring at her toes, "I'm guessing you'll have to work on the next rainy day, too?"

She slowly lifts her eyes, and I stare right back at her as I answer. "Yeah, I will."

Ignoring the tightness in my chest, I walk into the bathroom before snapping the door behind me to make my message clear. A second later, the knob nails me in the ass as she opens it, and I reel on her. "What the fuck?"

"What the fuck is right," she snaps. "That's the second time you've slammed a door in my face in a week, Dominic. I've been waiting for you half the night, missing you every day in between, and *this* is how you treat me?"

"Like I said," I point toward Sean's room.

"Don't," she warns, "because I'm not bluffing. Don't finish that sentence. You don't want this to be over. I know you feel for me . . . I just don't know why you're fighting it so much." She blows out an exasperated breath. "I don't know what the hell is going on with you two this week because you're both acting like you're on man periods. So, I'm just going to assume there must be something in the fucking water that needs to run its course."

I remain mute as she inhales a deep breath of patience. "Just . . . take a shower, and I'll . . . order us some food, okay?"

We stare off for several seconds, and I slowly nod.

Goddamnit, King!

She walks over to me and lifts, pressing her lips to mine as she slowly tugs my boxers down. My cock points directly to her as she searches my eyes, gripping my hand and rubbing off a grease stain from the meat of my palm. "Business, huh?"

Making it clear she's onto me, she searches me for a reason for the distance, and I give her nothing.

"I'm fine with whatever you're capable of giving me, Dom, but I don't think capability is your issue. You won't, or," she rakes her lower lip with her teeth as I fucking rattle inside with the need to touch her.

"Or maybe you don't want to, or can't take me seriously because . . . because I'm with Sean too?" She sighs. "If that's the case, then I guess that's the way you feel, but when we're together, I only *see you.*"

Pressing a kiss to my chest, she drags her nails along my dick, and it's all I can do to keep from fucking her.

What the fuck are you doing, Dom? End it!

"Cecelia," I rasp out, the cadence in my voice taking me aback as the low-lying burn in my chest ignites at the thought of what future rainy days would look like without her. Cutting words linger on the tip of my tongue, and sensing them coming, she gives me a firm shake of her head—refusing them from me for the first time.

"Pizza? I know what you like," she releases me, and I grip her wrist and tug her back to me.

Her navy blues volley and glisten, her voice a plea. "Dom, if we could stop this, we would have already. You think I don't feel guilty? You think I *wanted* to feel for you? You're holding back with me," she emits, "but I can tell you don't want to no matter how hard you push back . . . I can tell. Lie all you want to me, to yourself, but I know better. I know you better."

It's the truth. The totality of it. I'm fucking fooling myself into thinking that there's still a tipping point. I'm already past it. But my brother can't suffer for it. My club can't suffer for it. There's too much at stake.

"What the hell do you really know?" I snap, stepping out of her reach. "Let me clue you in . . . what I allow you to *know*, which is *nothing*."

I can see the second my venom hits her and ball my fists as the burn starts to singe the whole of my chest.

"I know you're guarding yourself with me to the point it's starting to bother you. You want to be with me, and you won't let yourself. Just tell me why. And I know enough," she says softly, eyes still pleading.

"Obviously, you don't. Do we really need to have this conversation again? I'm not bitter, or jaded, or fucking broken." I roll my eyes down her frame. "I'm just not interested. So, let me sum it up for you." I point to my chest. "I'm just another busy criminal that fucks you, and you're a convenient fuck. Get your head out of the clouds. There is *no us*."

She closes her eyes and presses her lips together to absorb the sting before they open. It's the smug uplift of her lips along with the clear 'you stupid bastard' in her expression that tells me she didn't believe a word I just fucking said—and we both know it.

"Okay, Dom, okay," she exhales resigned, chest pumping along with the slight shake of her head in a call of bullshit before she turns and leaves me there, annoyed, frustrated, naked, hard, breathless, and . . . fucking enamored.

THIRTY-EIGHT

Tossing my stress ball from where I lay on my bed, with every catch, I begin to tick off the reasons for letting her go as my limbs grow heavy, no doubt due to my long shift at the garage.

Toss.

Brother.

Catch.

Club.

Toss.

Hindrance to progress.

Catch.

Liability.

Toss.

Fucking her the first time was *fucking up*.

Catch.

Allowing her into my space, my bed . . . all of it was senseless, pointless, and unnecessary.

Thunder rumbles as the storm continues to rage outside, and

concern spikes that she drove home in this weather. Resisting the urge to ask Sean if he's heard from her or tune into the mics in her room, I slap off my bedroom light and resume my place on my mattress.

I gave up my right to know.

Facts.

Ended it.

Point blank.

Had to.

Watching my bedside clock, a low spike of adrenaline starts to zing through me as the minutes tick closer to midnight.

Putting my earbuds in, I press play on one of my go-to lists. When "Three Little Birds" rings out, I rip them out like they're on fire.

Nope.

Eleven-fifty-four.

The day is almost over.

I shrug against my pillow.

Swallowing against the increasing tightness beneath my rib cage, I turn on my stomach to get some shut eye.

Facing her pillow, I run my eyes down the vacant space beside me.

Normally, she'd be lying there, talking randomly, animatedly, droning on about something while running her fingers along my skin, laughter filling my room when she finally drew the reaction she wanted from me.

Even if I'm grounded in the club capacity, I have plenty to do. A thousand books to read, minimum. Bird business to conduct, which means we probably won't run into each other. Then again, we likely will. It's inevitable. I'll have to get Sean to give me the heads-up when she's around to make things easier for her. Not that it will be hard for her since I just ensured she'll hate me.

Toss.

She's got the plant and Sean.

Catch.

She's got *Sean.*

Squeeze.

Discarding the ball, I move to sit at the edge of the bed, ears perking up for any sign she's with him.

Is she with him?

That thought begins to gnaw at me as a rare, raw type of jealousy threatens at the idea that he's stealing my fucking time with her.

She wouldn't do that.

It's not his day.

But as of a few hours ago, the time is no longer mine.

I did this.

Made it this way.

No choice.

Craning my neck toward the wall that separates our rooms, I glare at it.

If she is with him . . .

Fuck that noise.

Denial is ripped from me completely when a foreign type of possessiveness overtakes me, and my heart starts to thrash in confirmation. Jerking on some sweats, I walk over to the wall and cup my ear, straining for any sound.

Nothing.

Fuck this.

Stalking down the hall, I slap open Sean's bedroom door with my palm to see him alone, flipping channels, boots crossed on his bed, a beer in hand. He flashes me his signature smirk. "Sup man?"

Relief skitters through me as I jerk my chin. His lips quirk further as his eyes drift back to the TV. "I'm thinking maybe someone doesn't want to say he's sorry."

"Fuck you."

I turn to leave, and he calls to my retreating back. "She's worth a lot more than an apology."

I turn on a dime. "Yeah, what's she worth to you?"

He uses my own tactic against me with silence—stupid question.

I glare over at him as he sips his beer. "What the fuck are we doing?"

"You know what you're doing, same as me. We're crossing an uncrossable line." His shoulders roll forward with the weight of the admission. "But the difference between us is that I've already made peace with it," he states in a tone that contradicts that declaration. "It's harder for you, Dom, and no big mystery why." His expression hardens into a look reserved only for those he's about to pull the trigger on. "So, I'll give you a fucking pass, brother, just this once, for thinking you'll *ever* be able to rip that woman from my arms—especially if you so recklessly ever push her into them."

"Oh, it's like that?" I ask, tilting my head as if I didn't hear him right.

"She's my fucking girlfriend, asshole, and she's destroyed right now because of *you*. She wouldn't let me console her, so what the fuck kind of reception did you expect?"

He pulls on his beer as if he didn't just threaten me for the first time in our lives, and I let that shit resonate before realizing I'm in his room for the exact same reason.

Regardless, the resentment that he did threaten me kicks in just as he speaks up. "I love you, brother," he sighs, "more than any other, that's the truth, but it's not *me* you're fighting. So, please don't twist me into the enemy to justify the turmoil going on in that brilliant fucking brain of yours. It's the decision that's killing you softly, so make it and make your own peace with it, for all our sakes." The warning returns in his eyes. "But know this. Your decision no longer has any bearing on mine. The time for that has fucking passed."

I linger in his doorway for a beat, seeing the toll the decision is taking on him before turning, gut lurching as I recall the damning words I hurt her with.

Do I even have a decision to make peace with anymore?

The realization that that choice is no longer mine takes hold as the ache I've been dismissing slams into me.

By the time I reach my room, I'm on fucking fire with regret. Shedding my sweats, I pull on some jeans as perspiration dots my hairline. Shoving into my boots, wallet tucked in my back pocket, keys in hand, anxiety propels me down the stairs as a nauseating unease sets in.

If I have to break into Roman Horner's fucking house to take those words back, I will.

Reaching the foot of the stairs, I'm freed of that burden when I see her on the couch stroking Brandy with absent fingers as she stares up at the ceiling. The sight of her tear-streaked face and blotched cheeks has remorse doing its thing.

Fuck this.

I open my mouth to speak, and she beats me to it. "I'm going to have a dog of my own one day," she utters faintly as if talking to an empty room. "They're so much nicer than people." She leans down so she's nose to snout with Brandy. "Definitely nicer than criminals who like convenient fucks." She laughs, but it's lifeless. I've hurt her, knowing her heart, gutted her, and I wouldn't blame her if she wrote me off for good.

You don't deserve the decision and never have.

"But I guess things would be easier if I were more like you, Brandy, huh?" She coos to the dog. "*Silent, obedient,* just waiting idly by for someone to order me around and tell me *when* and *where* to *lick.*" She lifts to sit without a glance my way, and it's then I see her resignation. "I was going to leave, but it was raining too hard." She slides into the flip-flops on the floor in front of her, "looks like this rainy day is over."

She stands and folds the blanket we've huddled under a handful of times—a blanket she brought from home—deeming it our movie night cover. A blanket we've wrapped up in after doing a lot more than watching movies. That's *our shit* she's holding for ransom and threatening to take out of this house along with her and away from me.

I stand there, like a fucking idiot, mad that I want her, boiling because I can't fucking have her—not the way I want to . . . and pulsing to the brim with whatever the fuck is refusing to let me watch her walk out.

But I do know . . . I know exactly what it is.

I've been struck fucking stupid by the four-letter curse.

I'm. So. Completely. Fucked.

She grabs her purse and stops in front of where I'm standing. "I'll see you around, Do—"

Snatching the blanket from her and tossing it on the couch, I ram into her like a linebacker and lift her, catching her harsh exhale as I whisk her up the stairs like a mindless fucking idiot before dumping her on her side of the bed. She bounces on the mattress, eyes wide, lips parted, gaping at me incredulously before her face twists with fury. "It's not raining anymore."

"I don't give a fuck," I say, damn near pointing to her side of the bed in instruction.

"Well, I do!"

"You're not a dog," I offer.

"Thanks, I guess that's a step up from *convenient whore!*"

She rattles with fury where she stands, and it's all I can do to keep from pushing her back down on her side of *my* bed, where she belongs.

Who the fuck am I right now?

She glares at me, her hostility visceral. "If I ever gave you the impression that I'm *fucking desperate*, you got the wrong one, Dominic. Because, trust me, you are no woman's first choice." She surprises herself with her venom, and I can practically see the hand she denies cupping over her mouth in horror as her eyes flit with regret. As the pain of that statement singes me, I feel sorry for the bastard that will deserve and eventually claim her for good. She's going to give him hell. In the next second, I fucking hate him because it's not me, and maybe I'll never be worthy of being in the running with the way I've deceived her. "You didn't go to him. Why?"

"To Sean?" she shakes her head. "Because this is our fucking rela—" she stops herself from saying the word she thinks scares me. That's not the word that scares me. Not anymore.

It's another word, a decision-making word that worries me.

"Let me clarify this for you," she asserts furiously. "I'm not desperate, but I'm becoming jaded because I'm the girl who really wants to fucking be with you, and you're the busy criminal that's fucking me because I'm convenient."

"I didn't mean it."

"Maybe you didn't, but because it's so easy for you to demean me that way, I don't want you anymore."

It's another knife to the chest, and fuck me, I deserve it. When she steps toward the door, I block her. "I'm sorry," I whisper. "That's not who I am."

She snaps her head up, her eyes searching. "I thought I knew that, but you told me differently." There's truth to that, a whole wealth of shit she's clueless to, and I can't even fault her for that because we're too good at what we do. She's already so tangled in our web that I don't know if she can get out. But all I want to do is sink my fangs in deeper, keep her tangled—with me.

"What, Dom . . . what is it that's holding you back? I mean, if it's Sean, I understand . . . I guess—"

I jerk my chin. "It's not Sean."

"Then what?"

That decision-making word.

Brother.

And it's too fucking late because I want her on her side of my bed no matter the weather.

Fuck.

Fuck.

Goddammit.

"I won't ever mistreat you like that again."

"That was too easy for you," her voice rattles with hurt.

I jerk my chin. "No. It fucking wasn't."

Her eyes mist, but she lifts her chin defiantly. She's not going to give me any tears. Good. I don't deserve them. The need to bridge this, to make her believe me, to touch her and ease the roiling in my gut, intensifies as my palms start to sweat. She couldn't have meant it. With the way I feel—if she's feeling it too—it hurts too fucking much. Why can't I say it?

Why can't I just admit that?

Because I can't tell her shit without backing it up, and I'm already too far into a corner that won't allow it.

"Tell me what to say."

She jerks her chin. "No."

"Tell me what to do."

"No," she scoffs, "You're a genius who was also blessed with common sense, and you damn sure know how to treat a woman a lot better than this—shitty temper or not. There's nothing to say. You ended us."

"No, I didn't, or you would have already left," I point out, which I note wasn't the best idea as her nostrils flare.

"And you want this, or you would have let me. That was me you were coming after, right?" She spouts smugly.

This. Fucking. Girl.

"Fine. I want this. You."

"Nope," another jerk of her chin.

I grip the back of my neck. "You want what? A declaration or something?"

"No. I just wanted *you*, and you've made it a lot less appealing now."

Fuck me.

"I told you that I would take whatever you could give me, and I meant it, so give me *something*, Dom."

I search myself frantically because I know she means it.

"French bulldog," I blurt, and she jerks back in confusion.

"*What?*"

"That's the dog you should get," I say.

She crosses her arms. "I'm listening."

"They're companion dogs with good temperament—easy going, alert, sociable, patient, smart. They're so ugly that they're cute. It's the dog Sean should have gotten, but he got an idiot instead."

She bites her top lip to stifle a smile.

"I won't ever talk to you like that again, Cecelia. I mean it."

"Yes, you will," she counters. "You can't promise that. So, don't.

Being with you is like being in a constant state between venom bite and cure. But with you, it's just another weekday, and I can handle that as long as you're honest with me . . . at least about us." She steps toward me and delivers her next words point-blank. "But I wouldn't suggest ever talking to me like that again."

"Did you just threaten me?" I can't help my smile.

"Yes." She deadpans.

Lifting a hand, I run my thumb along her jaw before brushing the divot in her chin. Her eyes penetrate, and her words soothe the ache. "But you are worth it for me, Dom."

My shoulders relax slightly as I circle her waist, my heart still pounding with the truth—there was never really a fucking decision. There was only giving into the one I'd already made. "I plan to make this apology much better."

"Well, you haven't set a high bar for yourself," she harrumphs.

"That changes the minute you get back on your side of the bed."

THIRTY-NINE

THERE'S INDESCRIBABLE FREEDOM IN FALLING.

"Dom," Cecelia moans, her perfect lips parting as I pin her wrists with one hand and pull out partway to deny her orgasm—killing her protest with my tongue by thrusting it into her mouth. She sucks it with abandon, spurring me on.

When I've pulled back enough to keep her edged, I burrow back in, rolling my hips, rubbing the ridge of my cock against her clit. Her orgasm rolls through her within a few thrusts, her release vibrating on my tongue as she tightens around me. Gripping her hips, I pull her to straddle me in the middle of my bed. Mattress clear aside from the two of us, sheets and pillows strewn, I thrust up, impaling her, and she cries out my name. When she attempts to move, I still her, commanding her eyes by gripping her jaw, demanding the acknowledgment that I'm the one giving her this pleasure—that this connection is with me.

She gently rocks against me as she stares back at me.

"You're so fucking beautiful," I whisper, as her eyes search mine in an attempt to find deeper meaning in my words—meaning that's there—that she knows I feel but refuse to put a voice to.

When she again tries to move, I keep an iron grip on her. I won't be the man who makes promises I can't keep, but I'll be dammed if I don't make it clear that in this room, this bed, it's all us and what we create when we're together.

We both know it and have known it since this started. It runs so much fucking deeper than physical. For me, it's a place of bliss, peace. A place I both liberate and find more of myself that I know is only for her. Holding her in muted intimacy is the only way I can effectively relay to her without words that I feel it, too. I'm not going to let her miss a second of the truth, even if it remains unspoken.

"Let me move," she pleas, pressing kisses along my jaw. My cock pulses as she attempts to gain the friction we both want—her need throbbing around me as my body thrums with hers. Heart pounding, I hold out as long as I can, for as long as possible, because it's with her that I feel the most alive. I'm so close to coming, just from seeing her staring back at me, explosions detonating in my chest as everything I feel attempts to break free.

"I need you," she murmurs, raking her nails down my sweat-slicked back.

We've been fucking for hours. I've felt nothing but frantic during that time, the compulsion to keep her with me becoming more finite with each release. The panic due to the notion that if I allow her a single inch of space, she'll discover the reason for my urgency, and I won't ever get this feeling back.

"Dom," she whispers as she reads my fear in my refusal to release her, "you can tell me anything."

Fisting her hair and pulling her neck back with my grip, I whisper the truth at the base of her throat. "I am."

And I am.

Telling her what I can.

Showing her how being with her revives me and that every day we're together, she brings me back from the brink, collecting pieces of humanity and empathy I felt I lost.

That she alone is the pinprick of light that brings me back when I get lost in the dark.

That she's the only being alive that has ever been able to make me feel so much at once.

That we're told to love our enemy, and I'm faithfully obeying.

Fear and lust war as I claim possession of her physically, but even as I take her body, she continues to steal and own pieces of me I ignored I possessed.

Before her.

Before this bliss.

Hellbent on making us both suffer for perfection I have no right to have with her, I take her mouth, and with just a kiss and one deep thrust, we both come.

Collapsing at the head of the mattress, we lay in a sweaty heap, face to face, stroking the other's skin, eyes locked. Even with my barrier of silence, we feel solidified—like a drop of black ink tainting the surrounding water, creating our own cloud. But it's within it where we're most comfortable. Where we can maintain this perpetual state until we inevitably end, by way of me, my brother, or however this plays out because I can't protect her from either of us. I can only prepare her. But looking at her now, I can't remember why I'm not allowed to love her. I can't think of a single fucking reason why I shouldn't have her or silence the words.

She's not her father.

I'm not my brother.

All these things make sense here, under the cover of the storm roaring outside—a cover we created that keeps us safe and hidden away.

It's just us. And it's here I can be myself with her, and I don't want to hide it anymore or from anyone—which is not only detrimentally fucking foolish, but impossible. Which brings me back to the only conclusion I can draw.

This is love, and I'm dangerously consumed by it.

Not a question I have to ask myself as the truth of that is beating steadily in my chest. Staring into her eyes as we share breath, I'm filled with the conviction that I'm looking back at my twin flame. Attracted to her in a way I can't escape. Even when I'm inside her, the need increases tenfold—especially then—I can't get close enough. I can't keep my hands off her or my thoughts from straying toward her constantly when we aren't together.

It makes sense to me now why twin flames are a love addict's choice, and since we've been together, she's drawn an addiction I didn't know I had out of me.

But we're the caustic kind of identical flames, and there's nothing that can change that.

It's already written.

So, while there might be freedom in the fall, there's consequence, too.

Delphine's words echo in my head as that truth sets in.

"She'll be the end of you."

What I didn't tell her was that I already knew it.

By fire or water.

Either way. So fucking be it.

Until then, I'll wait for the change in air pressure, the gathering of the clouds, the streak of lightning in the sky, the rumble of thunder, and rain.

So, this is the honeymoon phase.

Struck down with the four-letter curse or not, I'm still a motherfucker, and embracing it. I'm feeling cursed by the day and taking full advantage of the weather. It's stormed every single day this week, and my cock has been singing in it, splashing around in its raincoat. The forecast continues to guarantee that it's not going to dry up anytime soon. Eyes closed, I don't dare look down because I know exactly how far I've fallen into oblivion along with it, and I don't want to glimpse how much distance is left before I land. I have zero guilt over Sean's current state of neglect because he had plenty of time with her before I claimed my rightful place. Just as the thought crosses, my phone rumbles, and the devil I'm thinking of flashes as the caller on screen. Unable to help myself, I answer it, putting it on speaker and sensing the hesitation in the air.

"Dom?" Sean asks, due to my lack of greeting. "The fuck you doing, man?"

"What am I doing hmmmm . . . fucking your beautiful girl-friend's mouth," I answer, thrusting in deep enough that her eyes water.

I hold the phone out to her with the choice to end the call, keeping our eyes locked—she resumes sucking and grinning, and I tangle my free fist into her hair.

"What?" Sean croaks on the other end of the line as Cecelia clamps hard around my dick, drawing a groan. Fire licks up my spine, and it's all I can do to keep my knees from buckling.

"I said I'm fucking your girlfriend's perfect mouth, and you should be proud of her because she's . . . fucking hell," I rasp out as Cecelia's head bobs, "she's owning the fuck out of it."

Silence. A second ticks by, then two.

"You're such a fucking dick."

"I'd say more than a *mouthful*," I muse, grinning before Cecelia wipes it from my face, hollowing her cheeks and taking a deep pull.

"Fuck, baby," I croak, lowering the phone so Sean gets the full effect. "She's ravenous, bro. Shame the weather isn't putting out in your favor."

"Goddamnit," Sean grits out, his voice hoarse. "I miss that mouth."

I know he's getting off on this as much as me. Cecelia knows it too, which has her ditching the last of her foreplay and going all in.

"Keep talking," I grunt, "it's turning her on."

"I'm in the middle of a shift," his reply is gravel.

"Then I suggest you get somewhere private and f-fucking fast," I chop out, nearly losing my shit when she cups my sack and tugs. "She's in one of her moods."

The plant noise lowers, and I know he's taken heed of my suggestion.

"I feel for you," I say, massaging her scalp with my fingers, "and your current view," I taunt as she engulfs me, "because she's wearing nothing but fire-red panties . . . perfect nipples at attention." She bobs again, taking me prisoner by digging her nails into my ass. "I'm thinking maybe she bought these panties to wear for you." I run my finger along the stretch of her mouth. "Did you buy those to wear for Sean?"

A strangled confirmation is hummed around my dick as Sean curses over the line.

"Too bad you aren't here to see them," I say, pumping my hips. "She knows red is your favorite."

"I'm going to *redden* your perfect ass for that, Cecelia," Sean threatens, tone rough. Cecelia noisily pops me out of her mouth, her voice liquid desire.

"Looking forward to it."

"Fuck, baby," he whispers. "Are you wet for me too?"

I lift my brows and grip her chin. "Tell him."

"You know I am," she moans, gripping my cock so hard at the base that my hips jerk. "I miss you," she murmurs.

"This is torture."

"I'll say, she's licking me up and down like she's fucking starving, brother," I relay as she flattens her tongue along the bottom before swirling it along my head, our eyes locked.

"I was just minding my own when she drove over, stripped down, dropped to her knees, and started sucking my cock . . ." I run my thumb along her cheek, "She looks so fucking beautiful doing it, lips stretched wide. Too bad you're missing out," I grunt as she takes another hard pull before taking me down to the base.

"Fuck you," he growls as the noise at the plant dies with the snap of a door.

"I think you're making him hard," I whisper as she starts to edge me—to make it last. After another thorough pass, she pops me out of her mouth, whispering like I imagine a siren would. "Are you hard for me, Sean?"

"Fuck yes," he groans. "Always."

"Are you in our office?" She asks, pumping me while scoring her nails over my abs.

"Yeah, baby," he grunts. "Do you need me to come home and help?"

"That's not the way this works," I remind him.

"It's been raining all fucking week," he cracks out raggedly.

"It's up to her to share, but," I grunt again, "I would say our girl is owning it," I report as she takes me back down to the base, and I can't help my sharp exhale. "*Fuck, Cecelia.*"

"Baby, will you save some for me?" Sean rasps hoarsely.

"Always," Cecelia murmurs.

"Don't worry. I'll make sure she's well fed and taken care of." Using my grip on the back of her head, I thrust enough to gag her for him to hear. Sean's rapid hard breaths sound over the line. "Fuck, I'm already there."

"She's licking my crown," I report as fire ramps up my spine. "She's teasing me, Sean. Maybe I should teach her a lesson."

"Don't you fucking dare hang up," he grunts. "Baby, talk to me."

"I'll be in your bed," she noisily sucks the tip, "as soon as the sun comes out," she assures, cutting off my protest, gagging herself for us both as my cock jerks in warning.

"But her ass will already be red," I declare.

The second she digs her nails into my thigh, I come, groaning hard as I pulse into her waiting mouth while she blunts her nails down my thigh. She takes every drop as I grip her chin after filling her mouth.

"Open," I order, and she does. "She's got a mouth full of me, Sean. What should she do?"

"Swallow," he orders without hesitation.

"You heard him," I say, releasing her cinched mouth from my grip before her throat bobs. "She missed a little." Taking my thumb, I push it into her mouth, "but she's sucking it off my thumb."

"Jesus Christ," Sean curses.

"Don't worry about grabbing me dinner," I taunt, grinning down at her, "because, by the time you get here, I'll already have eaten."

Ending the call, I pull her to her feet, and Cecelia shakes her head, mock scorn in her eyes. "You're horrible."

"You'll thank me for that, and you know it."

"Yeah," she grins, "I probably will."

"You're finally owning it," I state, gripping her hair and pulling it back to expose her throat.

"Yeah, I am," she whimpers as I flatten my tongue at the divot of her throat before running it to her mouth, thrusting my tongue in for a little preview.

"Dom," she grits out, body rattling with anticipation, chest heaving, eyes dilated, expression needy.

"Need something?"

She narrows her demanding navy blues. I love it when she gets like this because she's almost impossible to keep satiated. Gripping her jaw, I take her mouth, tasting myself while walking her back toward the bed. Pushing her back, I tug down her panties and sink to my knees. Spreading her soaked pussy, I stroke it with my fingers leisurely, and she's so fucking ready after what just went down that she comes. Gazing down at her, I send up a selfish prayer for more rain just before I bow my head and worship.

"One day, I watched the sun setting forty-four times . . . You know . . . when one is so terribly sad, one loves sunsets."—*Le Petit Prince*, Antoine de Saint-Exupéry

FORTY

THE NURSE ROLLS DELPHINE TO MY OPEN PASSENGER DOOR before helping me situate her in the seat. She surprises me when she calls after the nurse with a seemingly appreciative goodbye. Scrutinizing her when I'm in my driver's seat, I notice a difference in her demeanor. "You good? You seem . . . good."

She gives me an easy nod as I turn the ignition over, eyes the same rare gray staring back at me. "You seem good, too."

"A rarity for us," I jest.

My quip dims some of the light in her eyes before she speaks. "Can we . . . can we go somewhere?"

Her request has me pausing my hand on the gearshift. "You don't want to go home?"

"I would like to see a sunset," she declares, her attention darting out of the windshield and back to me. "Do you know of a place?"

"We live in a mountain town. There are plenty of places to choose from." I glance at my dash clock and see we have two hours at most before sundown.

"Take me to one," she orders, clicking her belt and settling in.

"You don't feel sick?" I ask, pulling out of the circular drive.

"I have cancer and poison pumping through me to chase it," she expels a breath, "I always feel sick."

An ill feeling runs through me as I question her motive. "Planning on dying today?"

"Non, why?" She reads my expression. "I'm just trying to make good use of the time I have."

I mull that over. "Did the doctor tell you something?"

"Non."

"I can call the oncologist, Delphine," I remind her.

"Non," she sighs. "I only had my treatment."

If I hadn't caught her wiping a tear away, I would never believe it was there. The only tears I've ever seen the woman shed were when I was still of single-digit age, and those were for my parents and her ex-husband.

"You can take me home if you want to, I just wanted to spend some time with you. Is that such a crime?"

"Considering you never have, it's surprising."

"We are . . . friends now, are we not?" She asks.

"If you say so," I jest.

"Fine, take me home."

"I've got a place to take you if you tell me why you're leaking," I prompt, spotting another fast tear trailing down her cheek. The sight of it jogs the memory of Cecelia that day she came to me. Her eyes were pouring, just as emotional, because something significant had happened, and it appears to be the case for my aunt.

"Why are you so upset, Tatie?"

"I don't want to talk about me." She appraises me as I pull to a stop light. "You are a handsome man. So much of Celine I see in you."

"Are we seriously having a heart-to-heart?" I ask, utterly confused.

"You have found love," she states, not at all a question.

I blink back at her. "Why would you think that?"

"We are so alike, Dominic. I know you might not want to hear it—and maybe do not believe it—but we are. In many ways. I'm happy if you have."

"Happy if I found love with Roman's daughter?" I query incredulously.

She stares back at me, lips quirking. "You deny you are?"

"That wasn't the question," I redirect.

She turns back to stare out of the windshield. "I am happy you are capable, that you embrace it."

"Wouldn't go that far," I mutter, almost inaudibly, but that's not exactly true anymore. We spend the first of the drive making small talk, which makes me feel a little like I've entered the *Twilight Zone*. She laughs, twice, and *loudly*. The unease increases, and I start to wonder if she's lying about her treatment progression and is now on borrowed time.

A little under an hour later, we're coasting up the narrow, winding road to the top of the mountain with twenty minutes to spare for the sunset. Delphine remains quiet, trusting me to get her there, anticipation radiating from where she sits with a rare hope in her eyes. When I pull into a parking lot which consists of nothing but a small building sitting to the right of us, she looks over to me skeptically. "Here?"

I nod and walk around the car to help her out. She practically falls against me when she hits her feet, sweat beading her brow and upper lip as I grip her tightly to keep her upright. "You okay?"

Her lips tremble, her pride at stake as she eyes the distance to the building. "I'm weaker than . . . we don't have to—"

"I'll walk you," I assure her. Her eyes again mist and I clutch her to me, walking her toward the building. When we reach the steep stairs leading to the door, she looks at them warily, shaking her head. "Dominic, I'm too wea—"

"I've got you." Sweeping her securely in my arms, I take the stairs toward the doorway just as a man opens it and spots us, quickly ushering his wife through and holding it for us to pass.

"Thank you," I mutter, and Delphine echoes it. Her eyes trail the couple, who curiously stare back at us as I step in, cradling her to my chest.

"Don't be embarrassed, Tatie," I tell her just as she buries her face in my shoulder before I slowly start descending the heavily inclined steps passing the vacant pews which sit to our left and right.

Once I reach the bottom, I glance around satisfied before nudging her with the lift of my shoulder. "Just in time for the show. Look at your sunset, Tatie."

She slowly lifts her head and gasps when she sees the view before us. Feet ahead stands a twelve-foot cross secured in a brick foundation, and to both sides of it lies a low-lying border wall. Beyond that is an endless sea of Blue Ridge Mountain peaks, which are quickly becoming saturated in various hues of orange, gold, and pink.

"Mon Dieu!" *My God!* She exclaims, her voice shaking as I lift her gently to her feet. She soaks in the scenery for several quiet seconds, her hand still clutched to my bicep as we watch mist and color steep through the mountaintops. "What is this?"

"It's called Pretty Place Chapel," I answer, just as taken aback by the sight before us, which is almost too surreal to believe.

She shakes her head, shock and awe in her expression, appreciation in her voice, and follow-up question. "How do you know about it?"

"I've been here a few times," I admit.

She narrows her eyes in suspicion. "You do believe."

"Still in negotiations," I tell her.

We spend a few quiet minutes as I glance around the small chapel and back to the blocked out view the size of a theater screen. It's when I look back and glimpse the fear that's been crippling her expression since she was diagnosed that I speak up. "I did a little research a few years back . . . when I was curious."

"Curious about what?"

"Your *good book of morals*," I grin, "the climactic ending, and what happens after."

She nods in encouragement for me to continue.

"During my dive, I read a dozen or more stories and testimonies and came across one that took place back in the eighties. It has kind of stuck with me since."

I glance over to see her focus on me.

"It was an account from a Texas housewife who was driving a station wagon on her way to JCPenney to pick up some curtains she'd ordered. Her two young daughters were coloring in the back of it." I search my memory for the details that stuck out. "What that housewife didn't know as she sped down that highway to run her everyday errand was that she would die *three times* that day."

Delphine's eyes widen.

"She didn't know that just ahead, an eighteen-wheeler had stopped on the highway due to some debris—rolls of chicken wire. He hadn't turned on his signals or laid out traffic cones, so she didn't slow or brake and slammed into the back of it at full speed."

Delphine listens, rapt, her eyes drifting back to the view.

"The woman was considered medically dead three times. Twice on the way to the hospital—once while waiting for the helicopter, once in transit, her longest flatline took place on the operating table. The medical staff wanted to call her death, but the doctor who'd been working on her refused to stop trying to bring her back—he was thinking of her two daughters being stitched up just a few rooms away. She was considered medically dead for longer than acceptable to have a decent prognosis if revived—to ever fully function again—but the doctor tried one last time and brought her back."

The chapel fills with a misty pink hue as I relay the rest. "She had significant brain damage, had to learn to walk and talk again, read and write, but she made a full recovery." I turn to Delphine and see she's hanging on every word. "And do you know what her only complaint was?"

She gives a subtle shake of her head.

"That they brought her back." I grin. "She'd seen what was waiting on the other side and didn't want a damn thing to do with the world anymore."

Simmering tears fill her eyes.

"She claimed that in the time she was down, she experienced

enough of the afterlife that she never wanted to exist anywhere else. That for the entirety of the time she spent there, she was enveloped in a perpetual state of love—nothing like the human love we experience, but magnified by a billion and then some. That every being there reverberates that love, and the second you brush against them or pass through them, you know every single thing about them, every detail of their lives. That the first time it happens, you become part of a collective consciousness. There's no judgment, no shame, no suffering, regret, or pain. Nothing but an inconceivable type of feeling no human mind could ever begin to comprehend. She swore that no living soul should ever worry about the question of an afterlife."

Delphine breaks at that moment, crying in her hands, and I whisk her to sit in the first pew, leaving a palm on her back as her body shakes with her cries.

A few beats pass before whispered apologies are amplified by the hands covering her face, and I'm just able to make them out. "Je suis désolé, je suis désolé, Dominic," she gasps, before lifting red rimmed eyes to mine. "Truly, sorry for the way I treated you." Tears of regret roll down her face. "I was so horrible to you both in the beginning."

"You can still beat it," I tell her.

"Maybe, but this apology is long overdue," she sniffs. "It is one of my biggest regrets."

"You were young, heartbroken, and penniless, and don't forget I know what got you to the place you were in. This life hasn't given either of us very many breaks. In that we are alike."

"You were just a little boy . . . you shouldn't have had to suffer for it. I was selfish," she admits hoarsely. "I've been selfish for a very long time."

"You were, but I forgave you a while ago."

"You did not," she dismisses.

"Okay," I grin. "I've been trying."

"I will understand if you don't," she stares back at the view. "I do not deserve it."

"Maybe . . . but you could have abandoned us, which could have separated us. I keep that in mind when memories of you piss me off."

She grins. "You grew into a good man, Dominic. I do not take any credit for that. Though I should warn you again that we are *very much* alike."

"Think so?"

"Sadly, I know so," she turns back to take in the last of the setting sun. "Do not let your heart harden you like mine did. I've lost too much because I could not forgive."

"I'll do my best."

We watch the last of the sun sink before we stand, and she turns to me. "Thank you for that story."

"There are hundreds, if not thousands like it, all claiming that there's something waiting. For every person fiercely claiming there's a deity, there's another hell-bent on proving nothing exists. At the end of the day, both are so bloated with ego, so firm in their beliefs that neither can prove it. It's the world's best-kept secret, one that none of us become privy to until we become a part of it. But there's got to be some truth to some of those stories, right?"

She nods.

"So, try not to worry too much," I nudge her shoulder, and she gives me a rare, full smile.

After a silent but peaceful drive home, I lead her into the house to get her settled, my chest aching a little at her admissions and the isolation she's endured for so long. We dwelled in the same state of desperation, both recluses for fucking years, never mending the bridge even as we both suffered the same type of existence. She wasted half her life as an alcoholic recluse to heartbreak because every single man in her life had failed her—robbed her of security at every turn. It started with her father and ended with her husband and every man between those two. Despite her admirable resilience up until her husband left her, that final blow had her withdrawing, drinking her secrets silent with her daily bottle until her existence was nothing but background to others who were living.

The idea that we are a lot alike in some of those respects starts to instill a sort of fear in me.

The minute we step into the house, the scent of lemon and other household chemicals hit hard, jarring me. Clicking on the light, I spot a notice on top of an empty plant stand for a recent extermination. Glancing around, I see that the house is spotless—the shelves are dusted. Walking into the kitchen, I open the cupboard and see the dishes have been washed and neatly stacked. Glancing over at Delphine as she settles in her recliner, she answers my unspoken question without so much as looking at me. "She didn't want you to know, but now you do."

Cecelia.

Instantly, the liquid passing through the beat in my chest solidifies her name inside before passing through to the other.

Whoosh. Whoosh.

Whoosh. Whoosh.

I can't even imagine the reception she was met by when she showed up.

Chest aching with the need to get to her, panic briefly seizes me. "Fuck, did she—"

"No," she squelches that fear, reading my thought. "His room is still locked."

When she finally looks at me, I see that same guilt I saw the night Cecelia knelt at her feet begin to seep into her expression.

"What?" I ask, walking over to where she sits and crossing my arms. "We've been sharing bluntly all night, Tatie. Why stop now?"

"I've wronged her," she whispers low, gaze distant, "in the past."

"Wronged Cecelia?"

She nods, her eyes watering.

Fuck.

"It's the most despicable thing I've ever done." Her eyes gloss with memory. "When I," she shakes her head as a sharp pang of protectiveness thrums through me.

"Tell me," I demand.

"It was a long time ago," she assures.

"I'm listening."

"When I worked at the plant. I told you . . . I was close to her mother, Diane, for a short time."

I nod.

"After they died, I knew she knew what happened and that Roman had something to do with it. I was angry."

"Delphine, what did you do?"

"Cecelia was an infant," she whispers as if her timbre will have any bearing on the delivery. "I got really drunk and broke into her mother's house."

"And?"

"I put a loaded gun in Cecelia's crib," she grimaces, "while she was sleeping in it."

"Jesus Christ, Tatie."

"I wanted to send a message to Roman that we knew that fire wasn't an accident."

"What happened?"

"Nothing. Absolutely nothing," she assures. "I left the safety on."

"Oh, well, that changes everything." Fury seeps into me as I pull the keys from my jeans pocket when lightning flickers just outside the living room window.

"Dominic," Delphine calls behind me, but I ignore her, my chest thundering as the rain begins to pour off her roof. Whatever confessions Delphine has left, I decide she can take them to her grave or find a priest to confess to. The image of Cecelia with a loaded gun at her head sends a shiver through me, making me physically ill as I pound down the steps and start my Camaro. Tearing out of the drive, the need to come clean surges through me as I race toward the townhouse—toward her. As much as I fucking hate Roman, as it turns out, my own family is just as guilty of the same malicious intent concerning her. It strikes me on the drive that no matter who guards them, secrets—especially those that are most fatal—have a way of poisoning those who keep them, as well as those on the receiving end of discovering them. When it comes to my tie to Cecelia, we were damned before we met—through no fault of our own—and in discovering each other, we're both slowly being poisoned.

Pulling into the drive, relief covers me at the sight of Cecelia's car. Thunder rolls as I exit, and get drenched in the seconds it takes to get to the door. Cracking it open, I see Cecelia bundled on the loveseat facing the sliding door, earbuds in as she reads along with the audio on her Kindle. Closing the door with a soft click, I creep in, ducking behind the couch when she senses she's not alone. Waiting until she's comfortably reading again, I pounce from behind, soaking her with my dripping hair as I grip her and pull her over the back of the couch.

"Dom," she shrieks, palming and pushing against my soaked T-shirt as I shake my head, shedding water and soaking her in the process. Twisting her to face me, I scoop her into my hold before resting her ass on the edge of the couch.

"You're terrible," she laughs as she sinks into me, and I shut up the rest of her protests with my kiss. When I break it, I pull back to admire the heat in her eyes, lids hooding, breaths coming fast, a slow smile spreading across her face with her greeting. "Hi."

Her legs tighten securely around me as I lift her up and walk us toward the stairs.

"God, you're soaked. Let's get you dry," she says, squirming in my hold.

"Let's get you *wet*," I counter.

When she bites her lip, the divot in her chin brings my cock full mast.

"How was work?" she asks.

"Work."

She rolls her eyes. "How are you?"

"Still me," I jest.

"Motherfucker."

"Only the once," I taunt.

Her body tenses. "I didn't need to know that."

I widen my eyes. "But you seem to need to know *everything else*."

She sobers and takes offense. "You really just want me pliable and mute?"

I press my lips together as she slaps my chest playfully and tries to pry herself away when we reach the top of the stairs. "Such an asshole."

"Told you I was."

"You can tell me many things, but you'll never convince me of that, sir. Not *that* way."

"You should believe me," I warn.

"Stop trying to scare me away from you, Dom. I'm not going anywhere."

I set her on her feet as she surveys my room. "So, what's it going to be tonight? We could read . . . I could make you dinner or breakfast? How about runny eggs and a movie?"

I nod.

An hour later, we're stretched out beneath our freshly laundered blanket—inhaling the fresh scent I can't place. I glance around the townhouse. It's just the two of us, with Sean working his night shift at the plant and Tyler unaccounted for—as he has been the last week—spending both his days and nights elsewhere. I suspect that if I drive back to Delphine's, I'd find his truck in the driveway, but I don't bother trying to draw that out of him.

I'll make peace with Delphine for her confession at some point, but that's not happening tonight, as the same surge of protectiveness sweeps me. Swallowing, I fixate on Cecelia as she watches the movie, completely rapt, hand still in the popcorn bowl. Grabbing her hand, I lift it and suck the remnants of the cheddar from her fingers. She turns my way briefly, and I release her, feigning interest in the story playing out on screen. When she turns back to the TV, I keep her hand in mine, running my thumb along the back of her delicate hand before splaying my palm next to hers. Mine rough and calloused, hers smooth against it. My digits thick in comparison to her slim, delicate fingers. Mine covered in blood and wrath, while hers remain unsoiled.

Whoosh. Whoosh.

"You have found love." *Delphine's whisper trickles in.*

It found me.

Whoosh. Whoosh.

"I love you," I whisper in declaration just as thunder rattles the sliding glass doors, the confession dying with that warning as she looks over to me in question. "Hmm?"

Whoosh. Whoosh.

Whoosh. Whoosh.

I jerk my chin slightly as she turns back to the movie. I soak in her profile, taking note of the length of her lashes, the utter perfection of her nose, and the fullness of her lips. Legs draped over my lap, she sinks further into the couch as I watch in wait.

Eventually, it happens. Her chest begins to pump, emotions emanating from her, a whimper leaving her throat as tears form in her eyes. Turning back to the screen as the clueless asshole professes his love, I glance back to see Cecelia buying every second of it.

It's so easy to see that love is her life force, her reason for being—what drives her. I didn't need to witness her watching this to know it because she's just as emotional with me. When I lose myself in her, when she lingers after every spoken sentiment and the way she looks up at me when I fuck her slow and deep. She's a hundred percent fucking heart, and it leaks everywhere, no matter where she is or what situation she's in. She's incredibly brave in that respect.

For that, I admire her.

For that, I respect her.

For that, I fucking fear for her.

When her tears finally spill over, I lean over and snatch one with my lips. Her breath hitches, and her watery eyes zero in when I sweep the salt collected away with my tongue. Biting back the words that were never supposed to slip from my lips, I give her another truth.

"You're beautiful, Cecelia." It's the first time I've said it without anything physical happening between us, and her eyes widen a little with the sentiment. This woman has completely consumed me in every way that matters, and she needs to know.

Instead, I press a promise into her as I take her lips in a kiss—a vow without words that I'll protect her perfect heart as much as I can.

A vow without words but a promise just the same.

A promise I'll do everything in my power to keep.

Looking into her eyes, I vow she'll never know about the monsters she can't see because I'll slay them all before they have a chance to get to her.

Even if that monster is me.

FORTY-ONE

THE SKY DELIVERED TONIGHT BEFORE THE SUN FULLY SET. Endless stars litter the vast expanse above from where we lay on my hood, where Cecelia rests, cradled in my hold. My heart beats steadily as she gazes up with me, music filtering from the cabin of my Camaro. Crickets chirp around us in offering with the rest of the budding night noise as contentment blankets me in a way I never thought possible.

"Dom?"

"Yeah?"

"What do you want, you know, for the future?"

Too much to explain, but she means personally, and that answer is simple, despite the inkling she's given me of something different. I have no way of navigating that inkling in the present, so I stick to what I do know. I've never been able to picture a personal future beyond the minute I exist in.

"It's not a stupid question," she prompts with mild scold. I opened this can of worms minutes ago by telling her what I remember about Maman and Papa, giving her pieces of the truth while skirting our parents' merged pasts and how they factor into the puzzle.

This question I can answer truthfully. "Nothing."

She audibly sighs. "I guess it's a good thing you won't be disappointed."

I can't help my chuckle. "Am I supposed to ask what you want now?"

"Not if you don't care."

I do, but I can't offer it to you.

I tuck my fingers into her silky hair before voicing more truth. "I'm not future centered. Plans don't make the man."

Because I tried that tactic and was blocked at every turn.

"I know, I know. Live in the now. Take each day as it comes," she recites, "I get it, but isn't there something you want?"

I'm holding it.

"No," I jest, "but there's obviously something *you* do."

She stays silent for long beats, stiffening slightly in the crook of my arm. We've been copacetic since I accepted my fall, but something tells me what's stirring inside her now has nothing to do with my refusal to give her promises.

Knowing she's getting lost in her thoughts, I gently nudge her. "What?"

"I don't like putting a voice to my fears. Because then, I can only expect them to come true."

"That's bleak," I mutter.

"It's better than not wanting anything in the future," she counters dryly.

"I already know what happens," I whisper.

"What do you mean? You can predict the future?"

In a fleeting second, I conjure the blueprint I tucked away for when the time is right. "I can predict mine because I make shit happen."

"What is it?" she questions.

"Whatever I decide."

When I'm finally unshackled.

"Just for once, can you give me a straight answer?"

I can't help the twist of my lips as I run my eyes down the length of her. She floated down Roman's porch steps hours ago, looking every bit my realized fantasy for our date.

Our first, and mine. A secret I keep to myself. But a secret I share with her. Only her. Her greeting as she entered the Camaro was soft-spoken, "*I missed you.*" A genuinely whispered sentiment I've come to rely on—which keeps me aching to return it.

I did everything I could to make it memorable. I denied the easy affections I give her behind closed doors because right now, I'm no longer in daily communication with Tobias—I think it's because he may be onto us. He didn't answer my last text after I ghosted him briefly when the weather permitted. But if he has caught wind of our deception, we may very well be under a watch we haven't detected yet, which has me up in arms.

The familiar, ill feeling starts to sink in, and I banish it by craning my neck enough to peer over at her. Spotting a smear of black beneath her eyes, my gaze slowly drops to her swollen, thoroughly kissed lips, focus drifting between the faint marks on her neck and chest. Evidence of when I ravaged her the second we pulled up. *Twice.* Fixating on the freshly fucked look of her, I revel in the slight imperfections I created and how they got there. "What was the question?"

"Do you ever get jealous?"

"No." A white lie. But not for any conclusion she may draw.

"Why?"

"Because he can give you things I can't," I admit honestly.

Sean can freely express himself to her, whereas I'm limited. His ink is etched skin deep, and though his promise is genuine, it's ultimately up to him to keep stock in it. Even if the words are there for me, too—along with the need to claim her in totality—both of us have withheld staking that claim and putting a voice to it with so much deceit between us. Until she knows the whole truth, I can't utter them—where Sean might. Because underneath my ink is a blood tie made with my brother, which binds me from being anything more than what I am to her now. That's where any jealousy I harbor lies.

"I'm not complaining," she whispers, "please don't think that, but why can't you?"

"Because I'm not like him. I'm a lot simpler." Even now, it remains the truth.

"I don't believe that," she insists.

"It's true." The guilt gnaws deeper, eating away at my resolve. At this point, I'm struggling daily to count the number of lies I keep to hold my secret to the truths I can reveal, and it's fucking crippling.

Sensing my discomfort, she traces my jaw in a caress that has me aching while voicing her declaration. "You are anything but simple."

"My needs are. I don't want things like other people." Even if I could imagine a future for myself, I don't see anything resembling the type of personal future so many others strive for.

"Why? Why train yourself for such simplicity when you are worth so much . . ." My chest caves in with the look she gifts me, the one that makes me feel invincible. "You are so much more than what you let people see—than what you give yourself credit for."

"That's the point."

She holds my eyes hostage with her next question. "Why won't you let people know you?"

You're my people. "You know me."

Her eyes soften to the point I almost look away, the deceit tearing at my insides as she speaks again, nailing me with right-hook sentiment. "And I'm lucky."

Jesus Christ.

"You are anything but."

"Please just stop that . . ." she cuts herself off before digging in. "You don't have low self-esteem. What's with this glib shit?"

Because if I voice my own fears, I know they'll manifest by my own fucking doing, and I'll lose you.

I swallow. "There is so much you don't know."

"I want to, Dom. I want to know all sides of you."

"You don't, Cecelia, you think you do, but you don't." The vow

I made strengthens within me that she will never glimpse the dark I do embrace.

"You think I won't care for you like I do?"

"Things will change." It's the absolute truth, and even as knowledgeable as she is thanks to Sean—and as strong as she's becoming—the flipside of our reality and the life I live under her radar is sometimes too much *for me* to handle.

"I don't care," she declares, palming my chest. "I want in. Please let me in."

I can barely contain the sting building in my throat as I remain mute. After several beats of my forced silence, she relents. "Okay, okay." She presses a kiss to my jaw. "It's hard being with you. It's just hard sometimes."

The burn that statement causes has me losing my grip briefly as I let her in on the most important truth, a truth she made fact. "You are in."

She looks back up at me, and I see it so clearly.

She loves me.

Words seem meaningless compared to what thrums between us, but I see those damning words forming as we gaze at each other, my pulse spiking as I soak in her expression and see it so distinctly, so intently, it's unmistakable.

She loves me.

Whoosh. Whoosh. Whoosh. Whoosh.

Covering her mouth with my palm, I stop her attempt to voice them because if she utters a single one, I might not ever come back from it. "Don't waste good words on me."

She loves me.

Knowing is enough. But I refuse to recite those words unless I can act on them. As of right now, I can't.

Her eyes search as I keep my palm in place to silence her and think of any way to offset the sting I know I'm causing. "It's okay, Cecelia. I'm as close to happy as a man like me deserves."

It's all I have left for her until I sort through the debris collecting daily between us.

Chest alight with the awareness of her unspoken declaration, we stare back up at the sky, which feels like it's peering back at us, laying witness. Getting lost, my mind wanders as I engage them, questioning whether the cosmos really has anything to do with our life path—if destiny and fate truly play a role in anyone's life. Tobias forged our path, and I latched on. I wonder briefly if he saw me with him when he did or if it was his destiny alone that he invited us to be a part of. If that's the case, it's always felt right. Felt like mine, just as the woman beside me does. Wordlessly, I ask the visible galaxy comprised of sentinel stars what the future holds for us while knowing I'm stuck in limbo for an answer.

Which is fucking torment.

Tobias's return is imminent. I can feel it with every fiber of my being. With that coming, our future remains unknown. Even so, I feel the steady beat of my heart driving me forward to face whatever is waiting on the other side of this. What Cecelia and I have is worth standing ground for, but coming clean means exposing Tobias completely and endangering the club—I could never do that. Our purpose is about so much more than our selfish needs and we have livelihoods that rely on the success of our club and lives literally dependent on it. I can't throw that away or be that selfish.

Therein lies the crux of falling, giving merit to Tobias's consistent warning of entanglements and this mindfuck of a situation with no viable solution I can conceive of. In this case, the truth will not fucking set us free, but damn us.

"Have you hurt people?" Cecelia asks, bringing me back to the hood, to her.

I answer with silence. That truth and those details are something I might eventually confess with time—if her place is claimed and accepted amongst us. If, somehow, she can forgive me for the lies.

"Do I make you happy? Even a little?"

Stupid question. But I answer it with a slow, deep kiss, pressing that truth into her until she's thoroughly convinced.

Gathering her from my hood just after, I hoist her to wrap

around me, carrying her toward the passenger door, ambling slightly until her breath catches.

Fuck.

"Dom, did you just *sway* your hips?"

Busted.

Though shrouded in the dark, I see her eyes bugging wide along with her smile. "O.M.G. Did you just *dance* a little with me?!"

Sighing, I press my forehead to hers. "Cecelia?"

"Yes?" She beams back at me.

"When you call me out for this shit, it stops. Haven't you *figured* that out by *now?*"

"That you're a closet romantic and *love it,*" she drops drastically. "Yes. I figured that out ages ago. You're really not *that smart* nor smooth, King."

Opening the passenger door, I dump her unceremoniously into the seat. "*Date over.*"

Her laughter trails me even as I slam the door on it, hiding my grin until I'm in the driver's seat.

Sean summons us by text just as I hit the main road. Shifting, I turn in that direction catching a flash of Cecelia's hair in my peripheral. Ripping my eyes from the vacant street, I glance over to see her head resting against the seat, head tilted toward the breeze, gaze trained up at the sky.

This is happy.

Sensing my stare, she looks back at me, a smile cracking her face, and with it, she steals the last unchartered piece of me.

As that elation scores through me, it's muted slightly by the anxiety that's been trickling in for the last few days. I'll make it a point to get ahold of Tobias soon and talk to Sean about how in the fuck we're going to sort this. I just have to believe my brother will hear me when the time comes.

When we pull up to the garage, Cecelia spots Sean's car and hops out, tossing a look my way as I trail her, noticing his is the only one in the parking lot. I assumed his text was a summons to join whatever festivities were going on. Knowing we're alone, Tyler absent, and wondering why he summoned us both, every step becomes heavier as I follow her into the bay. Striding in, my heart fucking stops along with my footing when Sean locks eyes with me while Cecelia races toward him.

He knows.

Dread filters through me as Sean forces a smile for Cecelia while blood pulses in my ears.

Whoosh. Whoosh. Whoosh. Whoosh.

Every bit of the contentment I just found gets ripped away as my heart thrashes with the knowledge—*he knows.* Sean and Cecelia's conversations partially muted with the erratic beat.

"... up to no good?"

Whoosh. Whoosh.

"Always."

Whoosh. Whoosh.

"... my girl."

Those words crush me as she inquires about everyone else's whereabouts, and Sean tells her he's taking her home so we can talk. Her confused eyes dart between us as my insides start to rattle, feeling like they're about to break apart.

Whoosh. Whoosh. Whoosh. Whoosh.

Cecelia reads us both easily and puts a voice to it. "Are you safe?"

Whoosh. Whoosh. Whoosh. Whoosh.

"... is an illusion, baby."

Whoosh. Whoosh. Whoosh. Whoosh. Whoosh. Whoosh.

"... for once, can you lie to me?"

Whoosh. Whoosh. Whoosh. Whoosh. Whoosh. Whoosh.

"... hate the ground you walk on."

Whoosh. Whoosh. Whoosh. Whoosh. Whoosh. Whoosh

Sean's eyes find mine once again.

"When?" *When did you find out?*

"Now." *When I texted you.*

"Fuck," I sweep Cecelia from head to foot as anxiety takes hold. "Get her home."

Sean moves to usher Cecelia away, and she refuses him, rushing toward me instead as our cloud starts to disburse. When she reaches me, I sweep her into a kiss, feeling the break start inside as she surrounds me. Clinging to every second, desperation laces the last press of my lips. "You gotta go, baby."

I keep her gaze for as long as I can, burning it in, knowing the next time our eyes meet, that look may only be glimpsed in memory.

Sean whisks her away, and it's the brush of our fingers as she literally slips through my hands, and our cover disappears that does me in. As she vanishes from my peripheral, the loss consumes me, and I boil over.

Destroying everything in my path, the crashes fuel me as I fucking rage against the laughing heavens who duped me into thinking this reality was possible. A reality where I got to keep the girl and everything else I hold close. But I can't exactly blame them because I called on them too late. I can't blame fate or the fortune that's never been on my side, or anyone . . . but myself. I forged my own future from the minute I was capable and chose this fate. It was only inevitable that after ignoring every crackle of warning in the sky and every rumbling step that followed outside my window, the heartless giant I helped to create would finally appear.

Trying to reason with love is fucking pointless. It doesn't care about your reasons, right or wrong. Love has no regard for circumstance, nor does it give a fuck what state it puts you in. It's a relentless and unforgiving emotion that will never let you lie to yourself.—Tobias, *The Finish Line*

FORTY-TWO

"**P**LEASE, DOM. PLEASE DON'T GO."

Hell exists.

Hell's current geographic location? *Paris*

The city my brother conquered in his early twenties and declared our righteous prison.

Hell's definition? Replaying the last year and change on a loop while questioning my decisions and the choice I made every second of every day since.

Because the Giant didn't appear.

No, Tobias waited three agonizing weeks to come home. Weeks in which we pleaded with him to return our calls and texts. Weeks where Sean and I lost our goddamned minds, completely unaware of where his own cognizance was at—along with his whereabouts and intentions for us—Tyler included.

Tobias either figured it out before he made the bird I charged to watch him or spotted his feathered tail just after—because he dropped off the radar. This left us scrambling in his wake, only to imagine and prepare for the worst.

For two of those weeks, Cecelia fled to Georgia with a broken heart—a heart that we shattered by design in an attempt to get a message to him. The mystery of who spilled our secret remains unknown. It was a bird outside of our inner circle, of that much we were certain as we formulated a plan.

Said plan was as much of a fool's plot as the one we used to betray Tobias. Which, in turn, cleaved me in two—leaving me in dual, measured pieces burning in the aftermath. One part was on fire for her, the other, sifting through the singed remnants for any remaining bond with my brother.

Watching Cecelia crumble in the garage while realizing what vindictive actions we're capable of was one of the most brutal experiences I've ever endured.

I broke my own vow to guard her immaculate heart in a stupid fucking attempt to distance her from our deceit and keep her safely away from my brother's wrath.

Witnessing her spiral—which felt like it played out in slow motion—further widened the fracture inside me, especially when her deep blues beseeched us for any sign it wasn't the truth. Sean had given me the ammo to make it convincing, and it was. *Too convincing.*

For me, at the time, it was the only way to try to distance her from the path of destruction coming our way. While also attempting to mask the truth until we had a chance to explain ourselves.

When Sean broke at the sight of it, his punch felt like a bee sting compared to the gutting I felt as she cried openly—which further drove the slow sink of the knife into my chest as it pierced her own due to our gift of precision. Every agonizing second of watching her fall apart in that garage will forever be ingrained in my memory.

Those weeks of torment have only led to more in those that followed, heading up to the minutes that now haunt my every waking hour.

"Please, Dom. Please don't go."

After two weeks of deserved silence from the two people we

annihilated for our selfish gain, Sean and I decided that when and if Cecelia returned to the plant, Sean would come clean about Roman. Thus revealing him as the prime suspect in my parents' death and our revenge plans while omitting Tobias. A way to further prepare her while giving her leverage in an effort to gain some of her trust back.

A risk we decided was worth taking if we only implicated ourselves. We'd already given her access to the club, how we worked, and our trust.

Decision made, when she returned from Georgia, we kept our distance from Roman's house. We were flying blind, unknowing if he was already back in the States or who might be watching and reporting our every move.

The mindfuck of my missing brother felt like a punishment in and of itself. Despite the burn her absence caused, I hoped Cecelia would stay in Georgia to avoid being on a collision course with whatever was coming until we could do some damage control. Her reason for returning was selfless, and I knew it had everything to do with her mother—which only intensified my guilt.

The day after her return, I lost my shit and went AWOL, straying from every thought-out decision Sean, Tyler, and I had agreed upon. Sean was set to intercept her first with parts of the truth, but I allowed my need to take over—starving for the sight of her. I knew my behavior was fucking borderline as I drove like the four-letter cursed man I'd become. I was driving down the road next to Roman's mansion, hoping she would hear my engine before idling nearby on the off chance she came out of hiding.

Eventually, she did, spotting me on the side of the road before leading me on a street chase, intent on losing me.

After realizing it was a pointless crusade I was not backing away from, she pulled over and came out swinging with war in her eyes. Delivering death blow after death blow, her stinging heart voicing every brutal delivery. My emotions were so all over the fucking place that I acted a fool by allowing them to cloud my judgment. Instead of behaving or saying what I should have, I was apologizing one second, filled with pride the next for her fiery return, and rock fucking hard after her wicked display of backbone and voicing as much. *"You've come a long way."*

"Is that supposed to be a compliment?"

It was, and admittedly ill-timed. Her reception pulled me in and drove me to kiss her venom away, while her vicious backlash fueled me to try and bridge the separation.

During that exchange, I knew I would love her through every bit of whatever our future brought—owning it to Tobias and taking any penalty my brother doled out. I told her as much with my declaration. *"I have to let you go for now, but I don't fucking want to . . . I don't have a choice, but everything I do now, it's for you."*

She fought me brutally, but in the end, I knew there was forgiveness there—in both our hearts, we were far from over. Even with the hard-edged, internal change in her makeup from the damage Sean and I caused, it was evident she was ready to face my brother—if it happened—and whatever hell he brought with him.

That I was *ready for*, that I was *prepared for*. What I wasn't prepared for was the complete and utter devastation that greeted Sean and me when Tobias finally arrived back in Triple Falls before he, too, openly cracked in front of us.

"This was for Maman and Papa, Dom. We were so close, brother. Why?"

His voice was ragged and broken—decimating. Even as we stood, lined up like the soldiers he raised us to be—chins lifted to accept our fate while determined to plead our case—in seeing the damage we'd done, we both faltered. The more he unraveled, the more our argument paled, our fight lessening as he leapt between agony and fury—both devastating. *"Tell me, brothers . . . word for word, how you deceived me for three months."*

Our sentence passed? Ten months. Ten fucking months.

Three times as many as I admitted we'd been deceiving him, adding another to ensure we knew just how much his faith in us had been destroyed.

"Tell me every single thing you did, every purposeful lie you told

me, every move you made to betray me this way, to keep me in the dark, and then . . . tell me how you love . . . tell me you love me."

With our every objection refused and dismissed—even after openly admitting we loved her—we agreed to his soul-crushing sentence.

What he told us next had us reeling. Before we'd had a chance to intercept, Tobias had outed himself to Cecelia. Sean and I firmly believed at the time that collision annihilated any hopes we had of convincing him of her place with us. That he saw what I saw when he laid his eyes on her. That he perceived her as a naïve and innocent girl with no business in our business, no place in our world, and no promise. He had not a single fuck to give about any of our admissions because he couldn't see past his devastation.

"I can't even fucking look at you!"

He hasn't since. Not once.

Drunk to the point of nearly passing out, his words and mindset were crystal clear. As Tyler drove Tobias away, we chose his sentence and the club, our brothers, and our purpose, believing if there was a way to get her back, to lessen its length, we'd find it. That Tobias would forgive us, reduce our time, and bring us home.

It was his ultimatum of no contact with her that had us raw as we tied up any loose ends before we broke our lives down into boxes. Sean and I turning over our townhouse keys to Tyler as movers herded our shit out to storage until our future was decided. My suspicions were that Tyler was already living elsewhere and remained tight-lipped about it during the move. Neither of us gave him shit about it because he spared us his own backlash for his strained relationship with Tobias, along with a promise to vigilantly watch over Cecelia.

This is all we could ask for because even as he did promise to guard her, we didn't get to know anything else.

But it was the last day—the day we were leaving for the airport, that refused and still refuses to release me.

"RB just texted," Sean says, *checking his burner behind the wheel*

before turning his engine over. "Cecelia's at the Apple Festival. Alone. I'm going."

"No," I jerk my head, even as my heartbeat ramped up.

"I have to, man," his voice a plea. "I have to see her. Give her something," he snapped as he pulled out of King's garage, turning in the direction of Main Street—decision solidified. "Ten fucking months, Dom."

I lost that dispute before it started, too lost in my own shit to put up much of a fight—all of it drained from me with the dread of the months ahead. My real battle began as I sat idle in his Nova, hand on the handle as hellacious minutes ticked by and our flight time drew closer. Mere blocks away, she was somewhere in the crowd, aware of the truth about my parents and Tobias's existence, aware that we lied and manipulated her, but unaware of where we were going and for how long. Forbidden to make her cognizant unless we want our wings clipped. The only thing I urged Sean to tell her and he refused before exiting. "I've already told her that day is coming, and she'll wait, Dom. She will."

After ten minutes in that fucking car, the overwhelming urge to leave her with something from me had me stepping out just as Sean stalked back down the alley to his driver's door, looking as fucked as I felt. His return had my heart hitting concrete that I missed my own window. We had a plane to catch, and if we missed it, we may never fly again. My dashed hopes had me spiraling until I turned and saw Cecelia racing straight toward us.

Toward me.

Stopping feet away as she looked up, and our eyes connected.

"Please, Dom. Please don't go."

Turning toward the window, instead of the late-night backdrop, all I can visualize is that sun-drenched day in an alley thousands of miles away. A moment in time I can't get back, no matter how fucking much I want it. I don't even have to close my eyes to see it vividly—long hair blowing around her face, watery blue eyes pleading as tears for me roll down her cheeks, hands pressed to her chest with her confession.

"I love you."

It was the opposite of what I expected.

It wasn't anger that greeted me when she cornered Sean and me in that alley but a mix of determination and vulnerability in her expression before she fell apart with her confession. We'd readied her as much as we could without the full truth, but judging from the look of her, she was suffering as much as we were. She knew the truth about our deception, and she still loved us.

Loved me.

There was no trace of hatred for the fact we'd wronged her so horribly, lied to her, deceived her. She tracked me down. She'd followed Sean to make sure I knew she loved me. That no matter where I was taking that love, she was willing to let me pack and part with it, even if I didn't deserve it.

All I can see is anguish twisting her flawless face, the desperation in her voice as she moved toward me, and I jerked my chin, refusing her, denying us both as my brother's warning played barrier.

But the true reason was, if I so much as took another step toward her, I never would have gotten back in that car.

But I made the decision. I chose my brother and the club. I left her there without returning the sentiment or giving her anything she deserved after she did the impossible and forgave me.

Leaving those words unreturned is a regret I'll carry until the day I die, even if I do get a chance at redemption. I never once truly deserved her love, trust, loyalty, or faithful heart.

Fuck my brother for denying me that moment, for being the very reason I'm ripped right down the fucking middle and have been for these long torturous fucking months. It's been far too many days since I've laid eyes on her, heard her voice, her laugh, drank in the look in her eyes, touched her, fucked her, let myself love her.

Every mile between us ripped me apart as we sped toward the airport. Sean remained wordless the entire ride. It was only when we silently commiserated in wait for the plane that Sean again tried to console me, surety in both tone and delivery. "She'll wait for us, Dom. She will."

It was as our flight was about to board that it occurred to me that Tobias and Cecelia might have collided at Roman's house. It's when I voiced as much to Sean—realizing that I was still privy to the camera feed—that he perked up as I frantically searched the recorded storage of that day. Seconds later, my throat burned as we were granted a parting gift.

As our flight was called, Sean and I watched the soundless standoff play out from every angle at the pool. Mortified as Tobias hovered over her and tried to humiliate her by hiding her bikini top, which had us both fucking fuming.

It was after enduring a few tense minutes of his berating that she came back swinging with the same ferocity, hitting him with the lotion bottle in the back of the head as Sean and I shared a pride-filled expression and loud chuckle, both of us in fucking awe of her. Though we couldn't hear a damned word of it, we didn't really have to, the body language between them telling enough from what we caught. From the second they collided—our worst fear playing out before our eyes—we knew that conversation was damned. Hostile posturing took place on both ends, and the back and forth was intense before Cecelia finally snapped and engaged him with her real power—pleading with her heart to his retreating back. Sean's eyes reddened as we both watched her while dragging our suitcases down the jetway, knowing that whatever she was saying was for us—while she hoped her heart-filled plea would somehow sink in.

After watching it again, Sean spoke up, red-rimmed eyes on mine. "Leave it to our girl to have us lusting after her one second, terrified the fucking next, and laughing before leaving us aching and in awe of her. We never had a chance, Dom." His next words were jarring, part serious, part joke, as he glanced back at the screen with a love-soaked expression. "*If she ever fucking forgives us, let's fucking marry her.*"

We watched the footage twice more before we were forced to power down the burner, both of us equally as fucked up. Guilted by the fight she gave for us—which we failed to give for her—we shared a long look before manning up to start serving our sentence.

His words mimicking my thoughts as we sped down the runway. *"She's worth it."*

Never truer words spoken.

But where time used to blur for me, and days and dates passed without remembrance, the days and nights I spent with her appear with every beat in my chest, an engraved timestamp.

I swore I would try to forget her the minute Tobias looked at me the way he did the night he confronted us in the parking lot— face etched with devastation. It was as if he realized we weren't worth it—that *I* wasn't worth it.

It was the worst I've ever felt in my life, next to leaving her in that alley.

It was as if Sean and I had broken him, and in a way, I think we did.

All I wanted to do was make it right, fuck my heart, and the trouble it caused me. Fuck me for knowing what getting involved with her would do to him and falling anyway, but I haven't been able to bring myself to regret it.

"I love you."

My eyes pop open as though she's whispered it directly into my ear. Those last cutting seconds paralyze me to a place, in that alley, thousands of miles away, to an unreachable point in time, where I exist—in purgatory.

"I want in. Please let me in."

"You are in."

"You're in too deep, baby. Fuck," I whisper as a flash of lightning fills the room, and sleeping forms light up around me.

Another rainy day. Without her.

Running my hand through my cropped hair, I move to sit at the edge of the bed—skin slicked with sweat due to the useless unit recycling moldy air in the corner. Clenching my fists, my heart jogs into panic mode at the idea that she'll be leaving Triple Falls when the summer ends.

She's twenty now, her future about to kick off, and if Roman kept his word, she's a millionaire. Her world is still wide open, her options limitless, while mine feels like it's starting to close in on me. As promised, I cut every communication with her.

We've been flying in the dark for the entirety of our time here, and the kicker? It's voluntary.

If a case for a silver lining could be made, it's that we've made good progress in our time here. I've met relatives who've enlightened me further about my parents—before they became parents. The stories are wild and, at times, unbelievable. About Delphine as well, who had a colorful past, too. I now know she omitted parts of it to spare me, but those details had me making peace with a lot, and I'll make it a point to let her know that. Tobias and I had it breezy compared to her. To this day, I can't believe she survived what she has—for that, she's earned my respect.

Lightning flashes again, filling the room. A rumble of thunder follows as I crack my neck, muscles fatigued from my earlier struggle today. We successfully executed our last coup before our return to Triple Falls. One we've been planning for weeks. I had a close call, wrestling with a fucker twice my size, who spit putrid breath and French in my face before I managed to get my barrel to his chin and end his tirade permanently.

Sean and I both passed on the celebratory dinner and drinks offered, much to our chaperone's dismay. While Sean sleeps above me, our designated babysitters—Julien and Albert—snore in their equally lumpy bunks on the other side of the room. All of my roommates are in an exhausted sleep that I've failed to follow.

Julien has been my biggest ally in my last six months here since we made our way from the southern coast of France to the outskirts of Paris—and, as of a week ago—moved to this dumpster hostel within the city. Even though our stint in France is voluntary, as the months passed, we seemed to go from remote areas to eventually graduating to a city. Maybe a tactic of Tobias's to inform us wordlessly that we're gradually earning his trust back.

In that respect, we've fucking earned it.

Credit where it's due, Julien is the one who's made this time for us most fruitful. Fresh out of his five-year stint in the French military, Julien was brought in, in consideration of getting inked by Ormand, one of Tobias's French raven partners. Julien sparked my interest immediately with his calculated moves and the fact that I got little past him—not that I tried much. After doing a little digging by way of Albert—who, frankly, is too fucking slow on the uptake to cover Sean and me—I found Julien's military training and impressive education made him a prime candidate and recruit for *me* and the purpose I armed myself with when I got to France.

That said, Julien's a stubborn son of a bitch, so much so, it's sometimes comical. It took me almost a week to get his attention in private to try and convince him of whom he was guarding during his grunt work phase as a recruit of the club. To convince him that I was the brother of the man behind the curtain, the half-French half-American ringleader running this show. He clearly saw us as no more than two arrogant American assholes in their mid-twenties that he had to monitor for reasons unknown to him.

I let him in on that secret.

He's not much of a romantic and comically berated me and Sean for it for hours. It was hilarious.

Once I finally got through to the fucker, my instincts paid off in spades. By day as we did our recon on raven marks, he also helped me gather some much-needed intel I'd been lacking and in search of for years.

It was also when I realized how far Antoine had his hooks into my brother and what leverage he holds over his head. Tobias not only strengthened the French fuck's organization in return for minimal help, certain connections, and privileges but he's also made it the strongest and most feared underground kingdom in France. By reputation alone, no one will dare cross Antoine, and it's Tobias's goddamn fault.

He's fucking created a near indestructible army, and if he so much as steps in the wrong direction with Antoine, the land mines my brother himself set will blow up in his face. We aren't going out like this. I refuse to let him be beholden to this sick fuck. He wants me nowhere near Antoine. It's clear why—I'm my brother's only weakness.

I believe Antoine knows it, no matter how good Tobias's poker face is. In turn, Tobias has become a monster's puppet—*for me.*

A fact I cannot turn my back on. A fact that hammered that guilt nail in, cementing me here to serve my time and rectify the situation.

Julien is key.

Because he's not at all on Tobias's radar—a grunt on the bottom of the bird chain—Julien can slip out at any time unnoticed. We don't work like other organizations with death threats until the ink dries. Even then, it's not a blood-out situation. With Julien and I diligently working to put a plan in place, as of today, we cemented a long-term strategy to get my brother out of Antoine's clutches and bring him down while taking over the army Tobias himself built.

In a matter of a year or two, Julien will be the first undercover raven to infiltrate Antoine's army. Once established there, he'll start the recruitment process to lure in other ravens to create an effective sleeping giant. When awoken at the most optimal time—sadly for Antoine—it will be game over. This giant to serve the same purpose and be just as effective if executed properly. It will take time, but it will work.

Sean's aware of it, and as soon as I can safely brief Tyler, he'll be the only other to know.

But the sadder truth of discovering the flipside of my brother's world is the condition in which he lives. A soldier without a true home, with absolutely nothing but the moves he makes and the hands he continually plays. I full-on fucking cried when I realized what lengths he's taken to get us to where we are—along with the depth of his perpetual loneliness. That the luxuries he claims to love might be a mirage or an attempt to mask the isolation he must feel.

A hobby that came out of necessity to bide what little time he doesn't spend taxing himself with keeping Antoine happy and our noses clean back in the States. Though Tobias's warmth isn't perceptible to any naked eye, its existence is far more prevalent than mine—and these people he surrounds himself with *aren't* his fucking people.

His heart is useless because it's only his mind he fuels.

Fourteen months ago, that was me.

I hate every facet of his world here, and I'm convinced he does too—suffering in silence and trapped with no sanctuary.

No comfort in a sound like the scratch and flip of a new page. No cloud to immerse in—limbs tangled in damp skin, hair tickling my nose, fingernails raking my chest, and soothing murmured words. He's never had the escape of getting lost in love's deep blues, in sinful lips, in a scent so addictive, it immediately gets him hard, or the gift of how breathy moans that reek of praise make a man feel invincible. If he only knew what it felt like to be looked at the way she fucking looks at me. Her dark blue eyes searing through flesh and bone as if she could see every part inside and appreciate each one—no matter how well some of it works and some doesn't.

Of having a woman who fucking understands him and refuses to let him back down from who he truly is, of freeing him.

She sought me out, fed my starving heart, and resurrected it. She dragged the weakening organ out, kicking and screaming . . . but it's out, and it steadily beats for her.

Whoosh. Whoosh. Whoosh. Whoosh.

There's no going back. This shit's not reversible.

You can't unlove someone because you're ordered to. His belief that it's possible shows how immature his heart is.

He may have posed the decision, but my heart had already made the fucking choice before I began serving a minute here.

I chose my brother the night he sentenced us—and every day since, the guttural burn that I carry keeps telling me it was a mistake.

You chose wrong.

Hell's true definition is living out the wrong decision.

My jaw clenches with the realization as I stare up at the black-molded ceiling of my prison.

My shackles invisible but there.

If I walk out of this hostel, I'm free. But if I do, I'll never be let in again.

It's a mindfuck, and one I no longer want to participate in.

Hurting him that way broke something inside of me, too. Something between us we may never be able to get back. And that's on me, so I've done what I can to fix it, but he's tearing me apart in seeking satisfaction.

Because he doesn't have a fucking clue what it's like to feel it, so he doesn't understand his current demand.

Cecelia would never let me forsake my relationship with my brother. Her heart is far too evolved. But sadly, Tobias's isn't.

Lightning flickers through the shadows, and I rip my earbuds out, listening for the thunder. It inevitably sounds a few beats later, rumbling throughout the room as the faint stream of David Bowie playing between my fingers reminds me of a time I lay beneath a starlight sky with the woman haunting me.

With our silence, has she washed her hands of us altogether?

Quietly dressing, I slip into my boots, grabbing Julien's burner, which he now leaves for me every night.

In my mind, these days, weeks, and months have been pointless, and every single one has felt like the sentence it is. I feel like my heart can only resume its rightful beat when I'm back in Triple Falls, and my brother can look me in the eye—until I can find her hand in the midst of this shit.

The time we spent together is starting to feel more like a distant daydream. And the worst part is, the longer I stay here without her, the more it will remain one. Even when we get back to Triple Falls, I won't find her on that street—waiting.

Or is she?

Shutting the door behind me, I trek down the hall, making my way out of the hostel and into the storm. She probably hates us both for deserting her without promise. For not fighting Tobias harder. For remaining silent. We aren't helpless. We could have refused to come and engineered a new way to move forward and around my brother. Being here is a choice, remains a choice, a pledge of allegiance, and most importantly, an apology. One he deserves.

But at this point, I'm getting pretty fucking sick of apologizing.

I'm not afraid to go head-to-head with whatever waits around the corner, but I'm terrified her hand will no longer be there when I reach for it.

Abandoning cover, I let the rain surround me, my skin eagerly soaking it in like it's been starved.

Every day is starting to feel like a day too late. There's a panic that's snaked its way in the last few weeks and is beginning to fester in my chest.

And it's changing—right now.

We left her mind racing and her confused heart gaping. Any vulture that comes along now is likely to devour her, to pick at her piece by piece until there's nothing left. The idea of her moving on makes me physically fucking ill. The thought of that has jealousy rooting deep.

I have to get to her.

Tobias is just going to have to accept it. She deserves more than being left on a deserted street with a shady explanation. If this time has taught me anything, it's that I know exactly who the fuck I am and what I want, and I don't have to have my brother's permission to have it.

Time. Fucking. Served.

Sentence over.

Without another thought, I press send on the burner phone, and he answers on the second ring.

"Dom?"

"Tyler," I rasp out, freely bleeding as her voice whispers through the rain.

"*I love you.*"

"Tyler, I fucked up," I relay, as the water sheets down around me, thunder rolling down the quiet residential street.

I hear the concern in his voice. "What's going on?"

Muting myself until I can speak, I feel his anxiety spike over the line. "Dom?"

"I need a favor," I croak.

More silence. And we both know why. He's already walking a thin line with Tobias and knows exactly what I'm about to ask for.

"You'll be home in a week," he reminds me.

"I don't give a fuck! I've done nearly ten goddamn months. Don't you think that calls for a little fucking acknowledgment? He was here yesterday and didn't fucking bother speaking to us. I don't even know if it's worth this shit if he won't even talk to us anymore. Things won't be the same no matter what we do. Why the fuck am I even here?"

"Dom," he says in a tone that insinuates I should know better. And I do but fuck this. "You saw him."

I did. And he was inconsolable. Aside from the day of my parent's funeral, I've never seen him cry. Even then, he was alone when I caught him, but my decision is made. "If he wants to live like a fucking monk for the rest of his life, that's on him."

"You know that's not why."

I slam my fist into the mailbox next to me. "What the fuck am I supposed to do?"

"You're doing it. Hang in there, seven days, and you're home."

"It's not just me," I snap, thinking of Sean and how the time here has altered him. I'm not even sure he recognizes the changes in himself. "Sean's . . . he's not doing good, okay? I wonder if he even gives a fuck."

"He does. It's been all over him," he assures.

Closing my eyes, I try to reason with myself to wait. What we're doing fucking matters and matters a lot. We broke the rules. You can't break the rules in our club. No exceptions. At the same time, my pockets are empty, and the price is getting too high.

"I need this, Tyler. I know what I'm asking, man. But I need this."

"Name it."

I grip the back of my neck in relief. "Get us the fuck out of here. Right now."

"Dom, it's a week."

"And I'm calling it!" I snap. "Time served for good fucking behavior, but I'm telling you right now, if I'm not on a plane in the next few hours following him home, that will no longer be the case. It's time to have this out with him and figure it out. I'm not asking him for permission anymore. You know we've done our part. Get us the fuck out of here." Closing my eyes, I hear the guttural plea in my request. "Please."

I feel it—the urgency, the crushing itch to get back to her. It's been there, but it's never been this strong. Even as I think it, my gut tells me it may already be too late.

"If he finds out . . . it won't be good. You sure about this?"

"That's where you come in. Just mute our watchdogs for enough time to get us home so we don't have to deal with it. I need you to work your magic and make it quiet and painless. I'll explain myself to my brother when the time comes—if I fucking feel like it—but I'm telling you, the longer I fucking stand here, the more I resent him for it. I honestly don't give a fuck what his reaction is anymore." I man up in a way I never thought I would or be inclined to. "I fell in love, and it's not a fucking crime, and you of all people know it's nondiscriminatory about the fucking who . . . how is she?"

Silence.

"We're fucking grown-ups, Tyler. Let's stop with the bullshit. I don't fault you, the same way you aren't faulting me right now. How is Delphine?"

"She just got her last scan done, and we get the results tomorrow or the day after, but she's gone almost eleven months without a sip," he relays, pride clear in his voice.

"You're fucking kidding me," I rasp out, emotion getting the best of me.

Eleven months. Which means she was already sober when I took her to Pretty Place. *That* was the change I noticed in her, and *Tyler* was the significant thing that happened.

Emotion burns in my chest, my eyes stinging. She was sober. "I . . . I don't know what to say."

"*She* kicked it, Dom, not me, and she's still fighting . . . she's fucking happy."

The back of my throat burns. "Good, you both deserve it, especially her," I say honestly. "We all fucking do," I tell him, "And my bill here is settled. I'm not paying for it another goddamn day for loving her. Do you hear me?"

Tyler's lingering silence sends my mind racing. "What? What aren't you telling me?"

"There's a direct flight leaving in a few hours," he offers.

Relief washes over me as my eyes catch on a woman taking her dog on a late-night walk. She's carrying a Louis Vuitton umbrella and matching leash.

I decide I'm never coming back to France.

She draws closer on her heels, her mile-long legs encased by thigh-high shorts. Her thin top has a little bow that lies in the middle of the cut in the chest, showcasing ample cleavage. Primed and packaged. She looks buzzed as she passes me, her gaze lingering enough to know she's fair game. When our eyes meet, she smiles in invitation as she passes, her frizzy dog leading her down the street. I can't remember the last time I really looked at any woman—save one.

"Dom?"

"Book it."

An hour later, Albert is hooded as Julien gives me the dip of his chin in farewell before he's covered, just as Sean lands next to where I stand. Glock trained on those apprehending our babysitters as I bat his arm away before he can focus and fire.

"Little slow on the reaction time, brother," I chuckle as I pull my duffle from beneath the bed as our babysitters are dragged from the room. Sean turns to me, eyes wide. "What the fuck is happening right now?"

"Get dressed and packed. We're fucking going home."

"I'm the man who would step in front of a bullet for either one of you, no questions asked, but I'm also the man who held your fucking hands before I shaped them into fists. I'm the same man—up until I met her—who put you both above everyone else. But right now, who am I right now? I'm the man who loves her enough to not let anyone or anything in front of her."
Tobias, *The Finish Line*

FORTY-THREE

SLUMPED AGAINST THE DOOR, HEAD TILTED BACK, EYES FIXED, I absorb the night noise. Cicadas sound in the distance, in serenade with the crickets. The rustling of trees announces the light wind before it filters in, cooling my skin as the scuff on my outstretched boot becomes magnified by the filtering moonlight.

I miss none of it.

Where the world used to blur and time lapsed past me unnoticed, I'm fully attuned to it now.

Aware of every ragged breath I draw along with the distorted beat that steadily drums in my chest—despite its current inhabitable state. The overwhelming burn in my throat intensifies as I keep my focus while the ache webs its way through every vein, pumped further in by every broken beat.

The cool breeze whispers in again, gliding over my profile and arms, cruelly denying a shift in temperature, lacking any sign of a storm.

There's not a single cloud in the moon-absorbed sky, a

convenient view accessible to my right. A view that I reject with my whole being to keep the one I have. I have no use for the heavens anymore, no more questions to ask the cosmos, no future to ponder because they delivered my fate today.

A future without rain.

Without her.

As it turns out, hell isn't discriminatory about geographic location but is, in fact, a state meant for me to endure wherever I may roam. That truth made evident today when it faithfully followed me home to watch me shatter on impact.

It was the sight of his Jag parked behind what we could only assume was Cecelia's Jeep that tipped us off. After Sean and I shared a loaded look in the driveway, Tobias's laugh reached us where we stood, ringing out from somewhere in the backyard. The sound of it drew us in and had us creeping through the gate, past the pool and garden, only to be slammed by the sight of what greeted us.

Closing my eyes, the sting intensifies in my throat, the thump in my raw chest serving as a reminder while the image of them surfaces.

Cecelia lying beneath my brother, wearing next to nothing. Tobias, bare-chested, in his briefs, staring down at her like she was everything he ever wanted.

It was apparent by the intimate exchange that they were more than familiar with the other physically. With timing being everything, it seemed Sean and I arrived in the nick of time to witness them in the midst of falling and confessing. My brother's declaration being the first. *"You warned me not to fall in love with you. You said you wouldn't make room for me."*

"You told me you wouldn't." Cecelia's heartfelt reply served as a sledgehammer, driving in the reality playing out in front of us.

I didn't have to see the look in her eyes to know she was giving her heart to him . . . a heart that could never be mine again. So, when he opened his mouth to voice his reply, I took the opportunity to personally deliver his karma.

Grunting through the pain, I shake my head to try and disburse the sight of them—to no avail.

So, this is heartbreak.

The word seems weak in comparison to the feeling.

Obliterated feels more fitting. *Insignificant* as well, in the sense that it seemed our time together meant fuck all to her—at least from where I stood this morning, watching her give her love away . . . to my brother.

My gut feeling in France had proven to be on point, and as I feared and deep down *knew*, I lost my place with her during and because of my absence.

"Where have you been?"

That question hadn't surprised me as much as the discovery that the man I looked up to my whole life—whom I respected and revered—was only too happy to keep that answer hidden so he could take my place.

My brother stole my ignorant bliss.

The hardest part?

I let him.

Eyes stinging, I scrub my face against my T-shirt sleeve to clear my vision, unwilling to lose a second of the time I'm stealing.

My anger for my brother can be easily conjured, but my fury for her is much harder to find. Cecelia had been just as blindsided today.

If I hadn't seen her learn of his deception—hadn't witnessed or heard firsthand the lengths Tobias went to in an effort to keep her in the dark—then maybe I could hate her.

But I did see it, along with her fight to remain upright, visibly shaken by the sight of Sean and me. There was longing mixed with incredulity in her eyes—like she had been starving for the sight of us but never thought the day would come. That was proof enough that Tobias failed to take either of our places in her heart.

Even if that's a fact, *it's too late.*

Too late.

Keeping my focus, I draw another jagged inhale as her confession rings clear in my ears. *"I waited for you. I made myself sick. I cried for you both every night for months. I waited and waited, and you never came for me."*

Though I credited myself with personal growth before we landed, I lashed out at her in a mix of hurt, anger, and jealousy—which Cecelia rightfully called me out for. I turned my back on it all then, and she cried out. She called after me, begging me not to go—the same way she had in that alley—pinning me with the same words. *"Don't, Dominic. Please don't go."*

Even if I lost my place with her, she still didn't want to give up on me. She wanted to understand what happened and, more so, how I could walk away from her—from us. *"You mean to tell me you've been waiting this whole time to come back to me?"*

"I chose wrong," I admit hoarsely, drawing my knee up and resting my forearms on them while gritting my teeth through another blow.

My brother purposefully led her to believe we left her by choice, making her think it was our decision. That was the last nail in his coffin, and we all felt it hammer home. I thought that was the worst of it until Sean nailed Cecelia with both accusation and statement. *"You love him."*

She didn't deny it . . . because she couldn't.

It was obvious my brother found his salvation in her the way I had—his refuge. Only last night, I was in that hostel feeling sorry for him. Pitying the fact that he had no idea what it was like to experience reciprocal love.

He knows now, along with how terrifying the idea is of losing it.

Especially losing her affection, *her, period.* Which is my current reality.

"I fucked up," I choke out, palming the back of my head, trying my best to absorb the break happening inside me.

My brother's heart may have matured, but by his actions tonight, it was obvious that when it came to Cecelia, it had grown into something dangerously possessive. He had come to King's frantic, begging us not to withdraw our protection one second and condemning us the next.

". . . you two idiots parading around like men, like soldiers, when you don't know a fucking thing about sacrifice. And with her, you

sacrificed nothing! Not a fucking thing! Until you know what that is, you aren't capable of being the man she needs . . . and you know all too fucking well that you lost her the minute you shared her." That blow was for Sean, and I knew he felt it before Tobias fixed his gaze on me. *"And chose this life over her."*

Guilty.

Of all of it.

Tobias had succeeded where Sean and I failed—he chose her. He put her first, before himself, before the club, before us.

I lost the best thing that ever happened to me because of that failure while discovering one of the most damning truths about the four-letter curse—about love, which is that you don't know how significant or powerful it is until you lose it.

The breeze kicks up, increasing the sting on my face, and I'm thankful for the physical pain, even for a second, to detract from what's happening inside me.

Gathering myself from the floor, limbs heavy, I walk over to the bed. With every step, she comes more into view, and it's the sight of her, so unnaturally still, that crushes me. Moving a pile of folded clothes to perch at the edge of it, I soak in every inch of her sleeping form, knowing she won't rouse because of the drugs pumping through her.

Because Tobias carried through with his threat and marked her.

I pulled up in an attempt to stop it just as I spotted Jimmy's SUV. Jimmy was the one who inked us all, and I knew the second I saw him pulling out of Roman's gate that I was too late.

Too late.

Too late, and my brother wasn't even fucking here.

He didn't even give her the choice.

He just . . . claimed her.

More to add to the list of shit I can't forgive him for.

Staring down, I drink in her perfection the way I have a dozen times or more as she sleeps. As she dreams, and for a time, she was mine.

She was mine.

Visions flood in as I watch her chest rise and fall . . . the second our eyes locked in my backyard, the flash of surety I initially dismissed but still rang true through every fiber of my being.

She knows you.

The long looks we shared across every space, to the minute we snapped on that float before we collided and were created. The same continuous buzz thrumming steadily as we stole glances of each other between the flip of pages as storms raged outside my window.

Her fingers tracing my skin, wonder in her eyes, to running my palm reverently over her back—in awe of the heart that beat inside of her, wrapped in her mystery.

To the burst of sun that lit her up in my passenger seat as she adjusted her honeysuckle crown. The laughter spilling from us where she lay beneath me, tangled in the sheets before our smiles faded. Hearts raw and aching as we locked together, lost in our connection, chests bouncing in unison due to the tie that bound us.

That still binds us.

A fate we created together.

A story I'll continue to relive without regret.

Falling for her was worth hitting bottom—and every single ache that comes with it.

Reaching out, I trace the curve of her cheek.

"You gutted me, baby," I croak in confession as my chest caves. "But I can't say I don't deserve it . . ." I falter, grunting through the pain consuming me. "You thrive on love, and I . . . we fucking starved your heart . . . we just left you here."

Crushed by the weight of that truth, I lift her hand and thread my fingers through hers. "We both know I didn't deserve you . . . but you made me feel like I did . . . even if I wouldn't fucking hold your hand," I admit. "I was going to," I sniff. "I was going to try to be that guy. I was that guy. I just . . ." I slide my thumb along hers, the burn unbearable. "I would give fucking anything for one more day. Just one."

She doesn't stir, her hand lifeless in mine, breaths shallow but steady as she lays beneath me, looking every bit the sleeping beauty she is. But her eyes won't open for me because they're no longer mine to lose myself in.

No more escape.

No more fire and water to drown out the noise.

No more flame.

No more rain.

No longer mine.

Cracking wide, I bend over her, pressing my forehead to hers, "I'm sorry." Feeling the shatter of finality, I press a salty, damp kiss to her temple, my whisper for her ear, my last confession, far, far too late. "I love you too, Cecelia."

No more rain.

FORTY-FOUR

A FTER TWENTY YEARS OF OBSERVING ALCOHOLISM, I FINALLY fucking understand the *why* of it. Drunk brings with it a state of numbness I hadn't realized I could reach so easily. I can now appreciate how it helps to lessen the pain by blurring reality.

A reality where I stand in the garage surrounded by birds in a celebration I want no fucking part of.

Another homecoming party, bringing me full circle in this living hell—a reminder of the day it started. The day I locked eyes with the woman who's forever altered me for better and worse.

The birds gathering around us pop beers, cracking smiles, and chattering noisily. Most of them are oblivious to the soul-crushing karma Sean and I have endured the last two days—where I exist in a present I can't handle. A present only made bearable for the moment thanks to the half-drained pint in my hand. As I dwell in it, the future ticks on by the second—its taunt is cruel and unforgiving. Cecelia was right. When you don't demand anything from life, that's exactly what it delivers, *nothing*.

I never asked this life for anything but took everything it denied me. That tactic worked for me just fine—something my brother and I share in common . . . along with our taste in women.

I told my brother Triple Falls was mine, but as of now, I no longer want to play my part. I can't even imagine what a life outside of the club would look like, but the question remains . . . how in the fuck are we supposed to resume our roles, our lives?

Tobias stole the one thing that made mine bearable. But in doing so, he finally discovered the value of something he practically forbade us all to take part in—love.

His rattled expression last night and panic-filled pleas to put Cecelia first were all too familiar because they mimicked the panic I felt when I was worried about *his reaction*—mostly of his reception and treatment *of her*. An ironic laugh escapes me, getting lost in the crowd, but it doesn't go unnoticed by Sean, who nudges me from where he stands beside me. "What's so funny?"

"Nothing you would find humor in," I retort, taking another mind-numbing pull from my bottle before offering it to him. He shakes his head, full beer in hand, surveying the party.

"Let's shut this bullshit down," he says, "I'm not feeling this."

"You should celebrate. You're your own boss now," I quip.

"I still can't fucking believe it, any of it," he sighs, eyeing the bottle I'm rapidly draining.

"I can."

Sean's head whips toward me as I stare back at him, unflinching, and his gaze hardens. "Don't tell me you're going to let this go. I can't believe he went through with it."

It occurred to me, as I drove away from Cecelia last night, the possible *why* Tobias would go to such lengths and mark her. I relayed as much to Sean this morning.

"You really think it's Antoine?" He asks.

"Has to be. Antoine is the only one that can instill that kind of fear in him." *Swig.* "Even if he's not, the ink will protect her, but if that piece of shit ever discovers Tobias has a weakness—and Tobias doesn't heel when commanded—she'll be his first target," I relay grimly.

A long minute passes, and I know that Sean's doing his best to accept it and make peace with what he can before he speaks up. "I don't think I can forgive him, Dom."

Scrutinizing me, he takes a long drag of his smoke.

"Then don't," I tell him. "But if we're being one hundred, he was right about a lot of what he said. We could have and should have done so much shit differently."

"We did it to protect him," he points out.

"That's fair, but he's no more guilty than we are."

"Fuck no," he refutes, "he purposely—"

"What?" I interject. "What exactly did he do that was so different? Fall in love with a woman he wasn't supposed to fall for, put his life and our club in jeopardy, lie to his brothers about it, and do what he could to keep her by deceiving her?" I look over to him, "sound fucking familiar?"

"It's different," he snaps.

"It's not," I swallow, "It's not different."

"I can't believe you're taking up for him. He knew we loved her."

"That might be the only thing you can justifiably hate him for, but you fucking know a lot of what he called us out for was true."

"Reason away all you fucking want, but I'm not feeling any of them," he states in blunt delivery.

A loud clatter erupts, and we look over to see Jeremy flailing as Russell pummels him playfully. Sean manages to crack a smile as I pin him with my next question.

"You were serious, weren't you, when you said you wanted to marry her?" His eyes dart to me, and I can see the answer without him voicing it.

"I just wanted to love her." I hear the crack in his voice, even over the noise surrounding us. "I just wanted it to be okay to fucking love her without the guilt."

"You're justified now," I tilt the bottle toward him, "but I can't fight with you about him. I'm exhausted, Sean." My vision blurs briefly, and I shake my head to clear it.

He cups the back of his neck and nods.

"It's your choice," I relay in whatever tone I manage to muster. "It's your choice to honor your ink or to walk away. I'm with whatever decision you make."

A long silence follows as he turns back to me. "Can you forgive him?"

"Not tonight," I answer, polishing off the bottle before lighting up my blunt.

"Jesus, you're on a mission, huh?" He remarks, eyeing the bottle dubiously.

I shrug. "I've recently found myself in the position of having absolutely no fucks to give."

He lights up again and exhales a plume of smoke, scanning the garage. "You think . . . think he was right?" he asks, "you think we're a bunch of fucking idiots parading around—"

"Like soldiers? Taking Halloween dress up too far?" I finish, and he nods.

"All the time," I shrug. "But I always come back to the same conclusion."

"What's that?" He asks, tone contemplative, and I know why.

"Why *not* us?"

He nods in understanding as we both ponder clipping our wings for the first time. As if sensing our collective predicament, Tyler catches my eyes where he stands feet away. I lift my chin to him, knowing he's here in silent support, knowing he'd rather be somewhere else. Tyler had scraped us from the floor of the bay yesterday after Tobias left and whisked us to Delphine's. We were so fucked up after the day's events that we'd forgotten we were temporarily homeless.

But as of this morning, the three of us are commiserating together.

While Sean and my annihilations were swift, Tyler's happiness will be stolen by the day.

Delphine's last scan results came back, and her brief remission is over.

The stars have been generous in doling out more future, and I curse every one of those mother fuckers. For their unapologetic theft from Tyler and for allowing me a glimpse of heaven I can't steal back. Tilting my bottle in defiance of them, I softly whisper, "fuck you."

Pain spikes, and the consumed liquor attempts but fails to dissolve it in time as it spreads like the thrumming bass through the bay.

Getting swept in by the threatening burn, it's the sudden *thwack* ringing out through the bay, cutting through the noise, that brings me somewhat back into the present. Tyler whips his head in our direction as all of us perk. It's when the crash rings out again, the shatter of glass registering, that Tyler races into the lobby.

The music is cut abruptly, and all movement ceases as every bird in the garage postures up, their attention on the bay door just as Tyler announces the source from where he stands in the lobby. "It's Cecelia . . . and she doesn't fucking look happy."

Another crash and shatter outside has Sean's eyes darting to mine before he stalks toward the door, speaking up. "I've got it."

Tyler joins him, and just as Sean lifts it, glass shatters inches from his face. He shields himself at the last second, expelling a "Jesus, fuck."

Cecelia hurls more bottles toward us, and a few birds manage to dodge them as I flick my blunt. Sean takes a step toward her as her eyes dart from him to me—a flash of hurt flits through her livid gaze when she sweeps my whiskey-muted profile. Layla speaks up, caution in her voice, as she tries to reason with her while stunned by the state of her. "Cecelia . . . baby, what's going on?"

Layla—who's not in the know about any of what's transpired in the last twenty-four hours—looks between Sean and me. "What did you fuckers do?"

The better question is, what haven't we done to her?

The look of disgust in Cecelia's expression, the wrath in her posture, says it all as she darts her focus around, betrayal and vengeance warring in her eyes.

I know the feeling, baby.

"Don't bother," she snaps in response to Layla's gentle coaxing. "Don't pretend to give a damn about me."

"You know I didn't have a choice," Layla replies in a guilt-riddled tone.

"Oh bullshit," Cecelia counters with a vicious bite, "you had a choice. You chose them. And guess what? You deserve them."

"I'm sorry," Layla offers in apology.

"Save it," Cecelia refutes it, "you've all made your point. I think it's time I made one of my own." Lifting the gas can in her hand, she pours the rest of it into a large puddle in front of her, which serves as a barrier between us and the idling Jeep behind her. Between the beam of the headlights behind her and the light in the garage, I drink in every detail as the consumed whiskey fails to stifle the budding ache.

"What the fuck are you doing?" Sean snaps, surveying the damage to our lot as she lifts a bottle, rag soaked.

Tyler speaks up next, just as taken aback. "Jesus Christ, Cecelia, what the hell are you doing?!"

"Who did it?!" she demands as confusion sets in as to why Tobias went through with it—and apparently didn't cop to it. Sean takes another step forward as she lifts the bottle in threat. "Take another step before I get my answer, and I'll light this, and we'll all see where it lands. Don't fucking push me, Sean."

"Put it down," Sean orders, stunned by her wrath, but I know better.

Have known.

"Who did this to me?!" She shrieks.

Even as she declares war on us, inciting a one-person riot, tossing accusations, I know she's barely scratched the surface of who she'll eventually become. She looks so goddamned beautiful—even in her rage-induced state—that no amount of buzz can dull that. Pride floods me as she refuses to back down even as she hurls accusations and insults between Sean and me.

Whoosh. Whoosh. Whoosh. Whoosh.

"... You want me. Here I fucking am!"

Whoosh. Whoosh. Whoosh. Whoosh.

". . . speak up, and you can come get your fucking prize!" With that, she strikes a Zippo in threat as Sean calls out to her in panic. "Cecelia, don't!"

I can see it all over her. She has no intention of listening. Pushing off the wall, I start to move toward her, birds parting, a few of them tossing insults and ill-timed jokes at her expense.

"Bitch has lost her mind."

"You must've dicked her good, Dom."

Fixed on her, I steadily make my way toward her as they start to realize what she did before announcing her arrival.

"What the fuck? . . . She slashed our fucking tires!"

Raising a hand to shut them up, I keep my pace as she zeroes in on me with her threat. "I swear to God, Dominic. I'll light this place up."

Of that, I have no doubt, baby.

"Stop!" she orders, and I do.

"Why?" she looks between us, "Why?!" She turns then, giving us a view of her fresh ink. In my peripheral, I see Sean stiffen as the sight of it nauseates me, and she hurls more insults.

". . . cowards! You're both fucking cowards!" She lashes between us before delivering a guttural blow. "I was *never yours*, and I never will be. Stay the fuck away from me!"

Hurt leaks through that declaration even as she seethes, and it's evident Tobias isn't going to be forgiven anytime soon.

Good.

Give him hell, baby.

Tyler looks to me for any clue as to how to handle this, but we created and nurtured the raven within her, and it's starting to spread its wings as her ink settles in. That isn't something that can just be *handled*.

Ha! You are so fucked big brother!

Question is, why isn't Tobias here to clean up his own fucking mess?

Even as I think it, an unsettling inkling kicks in.

Something's not right.

Tobias wouldn't just mark her and abandon her.

Not a second later, the hairs on my neck lift as buzzes and pings sound around me.

Cecelia, too consumed by her tirade, continues to rage feet away. Tyler barks my name, and I pause my footing a second before he presses his burner to my ear, my brother's voice ringing out. "Miami took a fucking contract on Roman! Get her somewhere safe! . . . Miami is coming!"

The adrenaline spike has me rushing her just as she tosses the cocktail down in a puddle of gas, igniting it and blocking me with a wall of flames. Jumping through them, they lick my forearms before I break through to see her already in her Jeep. Lunging forward, I manage to slam my fists on her hood for a second before it disappears beneath them, and she tears out, racing away.

Fuck.

Whoosh. Whoosh. Whoosh. Whoosh.

In an Instant, Tyler is next to me inspecting my skin, and I jerk away, knowing the damage is minimal as he starts to shout orders at the birds already scrambling around us. "Use whatever you can!"

Tyler speaks rapidly into his phone as my heartbeat ramps, filling my ears.

Whoosh. Whoosh. Whoosh. Whoosh.

". . . came here in a rage, asking who fucking marked her, T. She shredded every tire and threatened to light the place up. She looked fucking possessed, man. Why doesn't she know? . . . Where the fuck have you been?!"

Whoosh. Whoosh. Whoosh. Whoosh.

A long pause follows, and I know my brother is rapidly relaying a worthy explanation. As ruthless as he is, he wouldn't have left Cecelia so exposed if he didn't have a choice. Even as my brain reasons in his favor, I feel the resentment simmering beneath.

"Dom," Tyler says, stretching the phone out to me.

"Don't we have a track on her Jeep?" I ask, and Tyler jerks his chin.

"The fuck?!" I roar. "Why?"

"They were living together," Tyler says on harsh exhale, "At Romans." Sean visibly flinches from where he stands a foot away as I snatch the phone and curse the fact that I'm too drunk to fucking function properly. "What the fuck is going on?"

"Dom," the panic in his voice has my fear elevating. "Listen to me, I'm begging you, listen to me."

"I'm listening," I snap.

"Roman didn't do it. He didn't kill Maman and Papa. I got it all wrong . . . Jesus Christ," he roars.

"What?" It's barely a whisper.

Whoosh. Whoosh. Whoosh. Whoosh.

". . . Dom! Are you there?"

"I'm here," I say, as my focus flits to Tyler and Sean, who can hear every shouted word, their wide eyes glued to me as I put the phone on speaker.

"Roman didn't do it."

Whoosh. Whoosh. Whoosh. Whoosh.

"How do you know?" I ask, my voice barely audible.

"Because he just fucking told me," Tobias croaks.

"What?" The ground starts to feel like it's moving beneath me as my breaths become labored while the weight of his words sink in.

My head starts spinning with answered questions while more begin to circulate.

"Dom?!"

"Yeah," I croak as he talks over me, and I pinch my temples, a headache forming behind them.

". . . his office, Roman knew we were coming for him, Dom. He's fucking known."

Tyler, Sean, and I stare in disbelief at the burner in my hand.

"It was an accident," Tobias says, tone rattled, "Dom . . . it was Diane . . . she was pregnant with Cecelia. Roman didn't do it."

Why would he allow us near her? Why would he . . . I gape at the phone as the answer snakes its way in. Because we couldn't even fool our fucking enemy of our affection for his daughter.

What confounds me just after that is that he was never our enemy.

Head racing as the missing pieces we've been searching years for lock into place, the first car fires up feet away. Turning toward the sound, I spot Jeremy speeding past us and out of the parking lot, flying in the direction Cecelia fled. As another car fires up, Denny shouts orders along with Russell as they call out a map of roads to search and set blocks on.

"Keep your goddamn phones close," Tyler shouts as a final order before starting his truck and waving toward me. "Get in. You're fucking drunk."

"Dom!" Tobias shouts over the phone. "Brother . . . I'm begging you, talk to me!"

"I hear you," is all I can say as panic rises and emotions start to burn away at my alcohol-laced blood by the second.

"I'm in Roman's car," Tobias relays, and I catch on to why.

He's trying to lure them in.

"I'm following," I tell him as I desperately try to break through the whiskey haze.

"I can't speed, or they'll suspect we're onto them. That's if they're not already here. We're flying completely blind. I have no clue who ordered the hit, and the two birds on watch said they don't know how long they've been missing. They followed them home last night and must have slipped out undetected this morning. I'm going to try to lure them in."

Alarm shoots through me as panic sets in for him. As I go to speak my objection, he beats me to it. "Don't send a single bird to me. She's all that matters, Dom. Do you hear me? I don't matter. Find her!"

My anger abates a little because I feel just as fucking helpless right now. My brother is begging me to help save the woman we both love. It's right up there with the other worst few seconds of my life—when we were told we were both all we had left. That was the case up until Cecelia Horner.

The pain thrums, and it's then I know. No matter how this ends, everything has already changed, and we can never go back.

"Tell Denny to unpack," Tobias shouts in order. "Everything. Every fucking thing we have, do you hear me?"

Sean nods, having heard it as I take the phone off speaker. Pulling out my keys, I hold them out to him as I do my best to cut through the slow-motion haze I'm stuck in. "I've got two spares in my trunk," I tell Sean. "Get mine going and have Denny grab *everything* we lifted from the warehouse."

Sean turns without a word, his expression mixed. Taking the passenger side of Tyler's truck as my brother shouts in order and plea, I watch Sean retreat and briefly close my eyes at what he must be feeling. He dedicated his life to helping us avenge our parents' murders and gave up the love of his life to help us see the quest through.

And now he knows it was all an accident. So does Tyler.

Staring after Sean as he pops my trunk, I have to believe he'll forgive us and reason that the ink still means something. That the purpose we spun from where it stemmed is enough to hold him—not to regret his ink any more than he does right now.

That he'll forgive us both for our ignorance and pointless vendetta.

Along with the fact that he could have loved her freely, without guilt—and so could I.

It's that blow that nearly does me in, but the fear for her and what she's been put through—for our parent's fucking mistakes—has me tensing at Tyler's side with my request. "Take me to Delphine's."

Without a word, he nods and tears out of King's as I lift the phone to my ear.

". . . have to find her! Dom!? Brother . . . please." The terror in my brother's voice has me sobering considerably as we speed out of the parking lot.

"I'm here. Start from the beginning."

"And now here is my secret, a very simple secret: It is only with the heart that one can see rightly; what is essential is invisible to the eye."—*Le Petit Prince*, Antoine de Saint-Exupéry

FORTY-FIVE

INTUITION ISN'T SOMETHING I'VE BEEN GRANTED THE SAME way others have. A gift that sparks up at certain times for guidance. It's never been that way for me. For the entirety of my life, it's been my daily fuel and has never failed me. Not once.

The thing that's kept me exactly where I need to be. In the right places, at the right times.

So how did I get here?

How in the fuck did I get here?

By ignoring my intuition long before I allowed myself to fall.

By blurring the sand streaming through the hourglass to multiply it, make it last, even as I saw it slipping away.

By playing deaf to every whispered sign and, instead, reveling in the fire she ignited inside my heart.

By ignoring the roar of warning that told me to hand her the gun, tossing it instead, if only to dim some of the fear in her eyes. A look I feared all along. A look that comes with the knowledge of what I'm truly capable of.

A look that told me she was finally convinced that I was the bad guy I told her I was.

A look of terror that ate me alive as she cowered from me when I entered her bedroom. In mere seconds I recognized the realizations I had failed to protect her from. The truth that this was never a game, and we hadn't exaggerated the stakes—but underplayed them. A look that told me she thought I would be the one to deliver those consequences.

A look that annihilated me enough to toss my gun too far out of my reach.

It was when her eyes cleared, and she truly saw me as she had all those months ago, that I was gifted those few precious seconds of exchange. A collection of minutes where I was able to confess my fears, apologize for my deceit, and finally deliver my ill-timed declaration wholeheartedly.

"*Yes.*"

"*Yes, what?*"

"*Yes, I've been in love.*"

A declaration I fucking refused to hold inside another second, knowing it was too late. A confession that gave me a bittersweet sort of peace, along with the notion that one day, I might be a worthy man deserving of the love I selfishly took.

And now?

Now I'm standing front row and dead center to the consequence of feigning ignorance to those instincts.

But in doing so, I was rewarded with a piece of paradise, a minute more with my ignorant bliss.

And I took it.

That's how I got here.

Even if my gun now resides in enemy hands.

"What brings you here, Matteo? It's a little late for company."

I spike my tone enough that if Tobias is anywhere in the near vicinity, he'll come. But I feel the intuition I've overlooked one time too many kicking in as my entire being erupts in awareness.

It's too late.

Intent on keeping Matteo a safe distance from her, I engage in pointless back and forth while maintaining the focus of the monster in front of me. The threat in his eyes and posture looming mere feet away from the one thing I refuse to be robbed of.

I've lost enough to life's hand. It doesn't get to have her.

Feeling it when Cecelia emerges from her bedroom, I calmly tell her to step back. I don't want her seeing the depravity radiating from this motherfucker. Though alike in some ways, this sick fuck considers spilling blood a pleasure.

We're entirely different in that respect.

At least I have that. Even if I can identify with him in a few ways, I won't lose sleep over spilling his blood.

For her, I'll become the goddamn boogeyman. Matteo reads as much in my eyes, of that I'm sure, even as he threatens her in an attempt to rattle me.

Before I can take another step, Tobias sounds up behind me.

"What's good, brother?"

"Got this handled," I relay before asking Matteo about his brother's whereabouts—my confidence in Tobias. Refusing to think about the half-dozen ways this has already gone wrong, I'm reassured when I hear Tobias address Cecelia to come to him. Just as relief briefly filters in, Andre's voice sounds. The three of them go back and forth in meaningless exchange as Tobias tries to reason with me to wait. But I voice my objection because of what I know and see—no longer ignoring my instincts. It's so fucking clear in Matteo's eyes that he's salivating for this.

That makes two of us, motherfucker.

Knowing I can take this piece of shit out through sheer will alone—whether he has the advantage or not—I assure Tobias I can. It's the threat behind the front door that I'm wary of. It's going to take time, even at top speed, for our birds to get here.

When Tobias snaps at Andre to back off, I take another step down, separating the monster from her. With each one, I feel the chains that have bound me start to strain and break, one by one. Cecelia is at the forefront of my mind. The noise surrounds me, the collective screams of the other innocents I've sworn to avenge pro-pelling me forward. Getting lost in the void of the eyes staring back at me, adrenaline starts to take over.

Whoosh. Whoosh. Whoosh. Whoosh.

This monster is going to pay for them all, even as my brother pleas with me, and I assure him there's no deal to be made. This was inevitable, and another unmistakable inkling tells me that I knew it well before now.

Whoosh. Whoosh. Whoosh. Whoosh.

It's Cecelia's call that stops me from embracing the dark snak-ing its way into me. Focusing on her, I allow myself the chance to tell her that briefly, she gave me a glimpse of a happiness I hadn't thought I was capable of.

"Cecelia," I address firmly, my heart lurching into the rhythm she created.

Whoosh. Whoosh. Whoosh. Whoosh.

Tobias attempts to cut in, calling my name, but I refuse him.

"I'm talking to Cecelia."

"Yes?" she replies, voice shaking with fear.

"After this, want to watch a movie?"

Ignoring any outside noise beyond our exchange, I tell her of the memory that kept me going in France.

Whoosh. Whoosh. Whoosh. Whoosh.

Of a time I felt complete and whole.

"You can make that cheddar popcorn I love, and we can crowd under that blanket that smells like . . . what's that smell?"

"Lavender," she releases in a shaky rush.

Whoosh. Whoosh. Whoosh. Whoosh.

Of a life we might have had . . . if I didn't have so many fuck-ing monsters to slay.

"Yeah, and I'll watch a chick movie because all I really want to do is watch you watch it. Your face gets all dopey when you get love drunk."

Whoosh. Whoosh. Whoosh. Whoosh.

"We love rainy days, don't we, baby?"

"We do," she croaks, voice breaking.

Tilting my head at Matteo in challenge, I make my declaration clear to Tobias to ready himself. "We don't fucking negotiate with terrorists."

Taking another step toward Matteo, Cecelia's voice reaches me in elevated panic. "Dominic."

"What is it, baby?"

"S'il te plaît, ne fais rien de stupide. Je t'aime." *Please don't do anything stupid. I love you.*

"Je sais." *I know.*

Her declaration fuels me as I stand between her and the monster I swore to protect her from while her love sets me free. For a brief time, she was my solace—my reprieve. The only dream of a future I allowed myself to have, but she can't be. Not anymore.

Too many monsters.

"Dominic," Tobias orders gruffly. "Stand down, right fucking now. We're still talking." I feel the desperation in his order, in him, as he rattles behind me to stop and think it through. But I have, for far too long, and I'm finally ten steps ahead.

Sorry brother.

Whoosh. Whoosh. Whoosh. Whoosh. Whoosh. Whoosh. Whoosh.

Irony strikes me then that I've been waiting for what seems like a lifetime to start this war. But with my brother's confession about Roman—about Cecelia's mother—I waited in vain.

As I inch closer, my intuition grants me a revelation that ignites me.

All this time, I've been waiting to *pull* the trigger when I *am* the fucking trigger.

Feeling the truth of that to my core, I lift my chin, eyes mirroring the black gaze of the monsters I've battled my whole life and everything they represent—the system that set us all up for failure. That put us at war with each other as they watched on in amusement while creating more power-hungry predecessors. All of it's there—the poverty, the pain, the suffering, the division, and all for one thing that has never been successfully bought or retained in human history—*control.*

It ends here and starts here.

I might not be able to take them all out, but *this monster . . .* this fucking monster is mine. With a head full of vengeance and a heart fueled by blue fire, I feel the last chain break free as I take my next step and engage the abyss. "Care to dance?"

"Honored, my friend," the evil replies.

"Make it a good one."

"Dominic, no!"

White hot pain blinds me as it shoots through my limbs as I'm struck forward by another bullet—this one ripping through my shoulder. My eyes find Cecelia, relief covering me to see her whole and untouched as a wave of pain blinds me, and I reach for her. A second later, she's in my arms as I collapse against the wall, fire circulating in my belly as a chill skitters up my spine.

Whoosh. Whoosh. Whoosh. Whoosh.

Pain takes hold, breaths hard-earned as Tobias appears, cursing while trying desperately to plug the holes running through me. Cecelia's cries drag me back to her as I take relief in seeing them both unscathed.

"Go," I tell them both with what energy remains as their words blur, my pulse slowing as the pain takes over.

Whoosh . . . Whoosh . . . Whoosh . . . Whoosh.

Feeling myself slipping, Cecelia pleads for me to hold on, apologies pouring from her lips. "I'm sorry, baby. I'm so sorry."

Focusing on my brother, I see my fate solidify in his eyes and, in return, give him words I know he'll understand. Words that, deep down, he's always understood and a truth I've always known. "Nous savions tous les deux que je n'allais jamais voir mes trente ans, mon frère. Prends soin d'elle." *We both know I was never going to make it to thirty, brother. Take care of her.*

Seeing the promise in his eyes, I feel the urgency of the threat waiting behind the front door, and voice as much. "Go," I manage through a cough, tasting the blood coating my mouth as I wheeze through the pain. "Please."

"No," Cecelia shakes her head furiously, demand in her deep blues. "Sorry, you can't go, Dominic, because I dreamed your future up for you. Hang on, and I'll tell you all about it."

Staring up and into the soul of the woman worth warring over—who gave me a glimpse of heaven on earth, aware of just how much power her love holds—I again curse the fucking fate that allowed it to be taken from me. But just as that thought drifts in, what I thought I'd been robbed of is gifted in the way it always has been, through her, because it was never about the weather, time, or place.

Whoosh . . . Whoosh . . . Whoosh . . .

Her warmth engulfs me. The atmosphere shifting as tumultuous storm clouds gather in her eyes, and her rain begins to pelt me—all burden lifting, along with any remnants of anger. A bone-deep chill sweeps through my body as the pain abates, and her turbulent blues pierce and hook me, sweeping me away.

Denny

E**VERY UNMARKED MOTHER FUCKER IN THAT HOUSE IS ABOUT** *to die.*

It's my only thought as Tyler emerges from the trees, Cecelia's blood-soaked clothes in hand. Discarding them, he nods toward me, pulling twin Glocks from his sides as he starts toward the house at a dead run. My gun at the ready, I cover him, and within seconds we've breached the trees at the side of the house near the pool—the roar of gunfire sounding around us.

Pop. Pop. Pop. Pop. Pop.

The rapid fire only fuels me, letting me know it's not too late to join the party, and frankly, I can't fucking wait.

So, I don't.

Covering Tyler, I shift when a man appears in my peripheral just outside the tree line. It takes a split second before I identify him, my gun already trained on him.

Not a bird.

Squeezing the trigger, he goes down in a heap.

Pop. Pop. Pop. Pop. Pop.

Most of the gunfire comes from inside the house, a window shattering as we approach, and another figure enters my peripheral. I turn to see Jeremy backing away from the gate, eyes trained as he lifts his gun.

Pop. Pop. Pop.

Another down.

He turns to me just after and gives me a dip of his chin, expression murderous, but the message is clear—he's got our six.

Making my way to the back door, Tyler already inside, I start to toe it open and hear a struggle ensuing on the other side. After rolling in, guns raised, I catch sight of Sean on the kitchen floor, feet ahead. He's straddling one of the Miami crew, blood lust in his expression as he presses his gun against the fucker's throat in an effort to crush his windpipe.

It's no mystery why he wants to prolong his death. He wants him to suffer the way he is—the way we all are.

Dom.

None of us will ever be the fucking same.

Tossing away the threatening grief for when I can allow it in, I fight to stay hyper-focused, scanning the massive double kitchen. Anxiety spikes when I see one of Miami's creeping in from the hall, gun trained on Sean. My fear is quashed when, without looking, Sean lifts his Glock and fires two shots, taking him down. Losing the advantage with the man beneath him, Sean takes a right hook and grits his teeth before turning back and raining down a few death blows before delivering a point-blank shot to his head. Standing, Sean kicks his lifeless body, his thirst nowhere near satiated as his eyes briefly meet mine. What I see in his return gaze is beyond anything I have before. In the next second, Sean disappears from view, no doubt in search of more.

Glancing to the other side of the massive double kitchen, I spot Tyler rushing toward an overturned kitchenette, one of the Miami crew barricaded behind it. As Tyler moves in, the asshole frantically fires around him.

Tyler stalks toward him, not stopping his footing, even when he's struck by a stray bullet to his vest. Gun lifted, I start to head their way. A second later, Tyler's there, pushing the table back like it weighs shit and cornering the fucker against the wall. Within a blink, Tyler hovers directly above him, unloading both his guns.

Pop. Pop. Pop. Pop. Pop.

Sensing me behind him, Tyler turns, guns trained, but it's his expression that has me retreating a step.

Goddamn.

Tyler disappears within a breath as the need to stake my own claim overruns me. A few steps into the corridor that leads from the kitchen to the foyer, I spot one of the Miami crew cowering in a coffee station. Sneaking up behind him, I make my presence known with a tap on his shoulder. The second he turns, I shove my gun into his gaping mouth and fire.

The sight of his body hitting the tile floor does nothing to prevent the ache in my chest.

He's gone. My closest friend. Fuck, my only friend.

Stalking toward the foyer, I see the front door ajar just as a few of the Miami crew slip out. Lifting my gun, I stalk toward them when I hear a bullet expelled from a silencer above, and an unmistakable "thunk" follows.

Pitching forward in a race to get to those out front, I'm stopped by the sight of a falling body before it crashes into the table a few feet in front of me. The man groans as he rolls off and hits the floor.

Miami.

I move in to finish him off and am stopped with a growl, "he's mine." Turning toward the source of the voice, I spot Tobias slowly taking the stairs, dragging the lifeless body he just silenced behind him by the collar. Expression lethal, Tobias's eyes remain fixed on his target, who's now using his forearms to army crawl toward the open front door. Hitting the foot of the stairs, Tobias discards the body, stepping over another to get to the screaming asshole trying to crawl out of the front door. Within two steps, Tobias is crushing what vertebrae the guy has remaining with his shoe. He screams out in agony as Tobias rolls him over before silencing him forever.

Pop.

"They're trying to run!" Russell calls from somewhere outside. Tobias's head snaps toward the driveway before he stalks out the door, grabbing a discarded M16 lying on the porch as he goes. Tyler appears at his side in an instant, flanking him. Trailing them both, I walk backward from the house, gun lifted and scanning as more birds emerge from all sides, mimicking my stance. Russell joins me to help me cover them. When we're at a safe enough distance, birds surrounding the house, I turn to see Tobias open firing on the retreating Miami crew scrambling to their cars.

Pop. Pop. Pop. Pop. Pop. Pop. Pop. Pop.

"Go," Russell yells to me, "go help him!"

Running toward them, I catch sight of two cars speeding toward the gate as Tobias gains on the last one, riddling it with bullets. Tyler clears the gate, open firing on the car speeding away.

Pop. Pop. Pop. Pop. Pop. Pop. Pop. Pop.

Tobias's aim pays off when the car crashes into a nearby tree.

By the time I make it to him, Tobias is ripping one of the Miami crew out of the car and makes quick work of dropping his gun before breaking his tatted neck with his bare hands.

Checking the cabin of the car, I spot one of them coughing up blood, trying to hide in the divide in seats between the two blown airbags and take him out with a single shot.

A second later, I hear a scream and look over to see Tyler taking out his grief in a way that nauseates me before he fires.

Pop. Pop.

Just after, an eerie silence blankets the house and surrounding grounds.

Long, tense seconds pass.

It's over. *For now.*

"Get back to the house," Tyler snaps as he passes me, trailing Tobias, who's already halfway there.

I silently follow, my eyes scanning the lifeless bodies littering the porch to see if any of them are our own. I'm thankful when I come up empty, but I know the zero count isn't true.

Layla's face crosses my mind along with her order to come back to her, and all I can do is thank whatever fate decided I deserved to make it home today. Knowing it may not be the same fate tomorrow.

For any of us.

Because a war has just started, and we all know it.

Prepared or not, it's coming, and that's not the only thing in store for my future. As of last night, Layla gave me even more incentive to return to her—as if she wasn't enough.

I'm still reeling about the fact that I'm going to be a father.

As the exhilaration of that knowledge flits in, it's overridden by another—*he'll never know my son or daughter.*

Feeling the weight of the loss start to cripple me, I silently step into the foyer to see birds gathering—one by one from different directions as the rest file in from the porch. Corpses lay scattered around us, blood seeping into the floors, bullet holes littering the walls. It's a fucking bloodbath, but I can only be thankful that most of what's been spilled isn't ours.

Russell joins Tyler and me where we stand next to the front door, equally assessing. Sean appears to my right and joins us at the foot of the stairs as Tyler looks over to me. "Compound ready?"

I nod before asking my own question. "They broke through one of our borders?"

He nods in reply. "Four birds gone. They didn't have time to send a warning."

"Any other company coming today?" I ask.

"We think this is all of them for now, but we're going to make fucking sure." He elevates his voice to everyone gathered. "No head hits a pillow until we are. I want every fucking bird and their closest at Denny's within the hour," he jerks his chin toward me. "No fucking exceptions."

Wordless nods and chin dips are all we can convey as we all glance around at the carnage.

It's when Russell looks up to the second floor and freezes that I follow his line of sight and still—chest seizing. Tobias stands at the top of the stairs, Dom's lifeless body cradled in his arms, drawing every eye to him before he slowly starts to descend. An anguished mewl erupts from Sean before he hits his knees, palming the top of his head, body bent as if taking cover while his grief echoes around us.

One by one, heads start to bow as Tobias draws closer, face twisted in agony, tears spilling from his lifeless eyes.

My own eyes spill over as Tyler clips out a hoarse request. "Russell, grab your—"

"On it," he says, turning and making a beeline for his car.

When Tobias hits the bottom of the stairs, we all step back, giving him a wide berth. Unable to look away, I lift my head just as Tobias passes, staring straight ahead as he walks down the porch steps. It's the sight of Dom's limp hand that has my throat closing as Sean's agonized grunts fill the air. With the slam of Russell's car door, the morning birds begin to sing as if our whole world didn't just fucking stop.

My only friend.

Tyler

THE WIND KICKS UP, THE BREEZE RUSTLING THE TREES ABOVE, creating a calming atmosphere just as the sun peeks out, highlighting the solid white casket before us. The roaring in my chest emanates in unison with the grief of every single one of us gathered—inked arms motionless at their sides.

No one speaks. No one wants to. There is no ceremony because our brother would have hated it. We don't need words spoken because I'm certain we're all lost somewhere in time with him. Our individual memories flooding us—a comfort to some, excruciating for others.

I'm the latter.

Most of us are banged up, bandaged, or in physical pain in some form or another due to the battle that started the minute Dom lost his. A fight we all lost, no matter how many of us escaped breathing because the aftermath is fucking excruciating.

Our new reality surreal.

One in which our magnet no longer exists.

Flashes of my brother shutter in. The day we met. Our first late-night bike ride. Sharing our first stolen beer. Coughing through our first joint. Our high school homeroom theatrics. The shared pains of growing from boys to men.

Homing in, I attach myself to a few that stick out. One being the day Sean, Dom, and I stood outside the newly purchased garage—rattling inside with the inkling that we were on the precipice of something bigger, better than the simplicity of our current lives. The wordless looks we shared before we stared up at the building. The satisfaction in Dom's eyes when he fixed his first car. The day he left for Boston, hesitating briefly with his duffle on his shoulder—not turning back to face any of us, the same way I hesitated the day I left to train as a marine. Because we knew we wouldn't be able to take another step forward if we did.

Staring at my brother's grave, I travel through rips in time between us all, and the tie that bound us—brought us all back together. Our bond first and always before our purpose, reason, and agenda. It's the very thing that made us that feels as though it's breaking us now.

In my peripheral, I catch the slow lift of Sean's head and turn to see his watering eyes zeroing in on Tobias, filled with a contempt I never imagined I would witness. Tobias stands on the other side of the coffin, dressed in an immaculate black suit, not a hair out of place, his expression that of a man utterly destroyed. Feeling Sean's gaze, he lifts his eyes to meet his judgment. As they stare across Dom's casket, I feel the true break set in between them, along with the knowledge that they will never be the same.

That crippling realization lodges a thick ball in my throat. Next to me, Delphine squeezes my hand, having missed none of it. Needing her, I grip hers just as tightly as Dom's casket starts to lower. It's with that finality that Jeremy bursts where he stands, grunts of pain leaving him as his tears flow freely. With Jeremy's break, grief starts to disperse in spurts throughout the crowd. It's then Tobias visibly fractures from the weight before turning abruptly and stalking toward his Jag.

Pressing a kiss to Delphine's temple, I whisper a low, "I'll be—"

"Go," she whispers, her gaze fixed on Dom's casket as it sinks further into the hallowed ground.

I'm ten steps behind when I snap out Tobias's name in vain, knowing exactly where he's going and to whom.

"Tobias . . ." I manage, my throat thick. "You can't go," I swallow, jogging to catch up with him as he quickens his pace. "You know you can't—"

"Where is she?" He snaps, not sparing a glance back as he pulls his keys from his pocket.

"You don't want to do this," I warn. "It will only—"

He turns on a dime. "Where is she?!"

"At school," I exhale, exasperated.

Within the minute, he's inside his Jag, speeding toward Georgia, toward Cecelia. But even this far gone in his grief, we both know he won't make it past the state line. He'll protect her, even if doing so destroys what's left of him. When his car is out of sight, I turn and start my climb back up the hill and through the gate. The sun disappears beneath a blanket of clouds as the crowd begins to disperse in scattered waves. Delphine remains the only one left, looking so small as she stands isolated at the edge of the grave, eyes cast down. Standing nearby with shovels, the two men at the ready look to me for permission to start, and I jerk my head, refusing to allow her to see it. Her grief and fear are too much of a combination to endure. Or maybe it's mine.

It's when I reach her that I see the true toll in her posture—which looks more maternal, like that of a grieving mother—as she stares down at her nephew's grave. Standing idly next to her, it's when the last car starts and begins to pull away that she finally turns to me and allows herself to fall apart in my arms.

Russell

POTTING THE KID PEEKING BEHIND THE TREE AS THE LAST of the soil is patted in, I wait at my car until he starts to approach Dom's grave.

He looks to be no more than twelve or thirteen, but I can see in his posture that he's matured far beyond his age. It becomes even more apparent as I approach, and he turns his watchful gaze toward me. His eyes are filled to the brim, a thousand emotions flitting through them. His lip is cut, and there's a yellow bruise beneath one of his eyes.

I stand beside him in wait, sensing some familiarity but unable to place who he is.

"Hey," I say, lining my footing up with his.

The kid's chest bounces as he stares down at the fresh soil, and I appraise him. He looks like he hasn't bathed in days or eaten well in months, his skin sickly.

"He was . . ." the kid starts, "he was the only . . ." he tries again and fails before deciding to allow his grief through—though he bats away a few of his tears. "He was the only person who ever saw me," the kid sniffs and falters, face crumbling as though he's lost everything.

My eyes burn as I stare down at the dirt and nod. "I can relate."

For me, Dom was a mentor, a friend, and the only human being who truly saw the struggle going on inside me. He pinpointed it early, talked it out with me when I wanted to, and sat it out with me when I didn't.

It was our secret.

Getting lost in that thought, the kid speaks up again, his voice filled with utter devastation. "I-I went to t-the garage last week, and that g-guy Peter told me," he shakes his head, "never mind. I'm sorry for your loss. I shouldn't be here."

The kid moves toward the gate, and on instinct, I palm his

shoulder. He flinches, instantly pulling himself from my grip when it dawns on me. A conversation Dom and I had before he left for France. "You Zach?"

He nods, eyes widening a little. "He told you about me?"

"Yeah, he did," I nod. "And I can tell you right now, you're *exactly* where you need to be." A soul-crushing relief covers his face as I nod toward my car. "Let's go."

Sean

"**A**LFRED SEAN ROBERTS, GET YOUR ASS BACK IN THIS HOUSE *right now!*" Mom yells at my back as I race out of the driveway, one of my shoes slipping on my pedal as I call over my shoulder. "I'll be right back, Mama!"

"Now, mister!" Mom hollers after me, and I know she means business.

If I get my Sunday school clothes dirty, I'm going to get an ass-whoo-pin'. I pedal faster, my shoes slowing me down as my dad hollers my name from the porch when I turn the corner.

I pretend not to hear him. If I go back now, he might not be there.

I saw him when we passed on the way home from church—sitting on the curb. He's always on the curb and never plays. Turning onto his street, I see he's still there, sitting next to his mailbox. He sees me just before I ride up and stands up fast, looking both ways.

My shoes slide a little when I put my feet down to stop. "Hi."

He stares at me as if I didn't talk to him.

"You want to ride bikes with me?" I ask.

He just blinks at me. He's got dark hair and skin. My cousin Bradly said his family are fortuners.

"Where's your bike?" I ask, and he doesn't say anything.

"If you get your bike, we can ride." When he doesn't talk, I try again. "Bradly said you were a fortuner!" I shout. "Are you weird?!" I tilt my head. "You don't look weird."

He squints at me.

"Can you hear me?!" I yell.

"I crashed my bike," he says, squinting harder like I'm stupid.

I step off my bike and start rolling it toward him. He's got a T-shirt with a car on it. I like Batman better. "You can ride mine, but only for a bit. I have to change out of my Sunday clothes."

He jerks his chin and looks back at his house. "I can't leave the yard."

I tilt my head. "You can't ride on your street? I can ride on my street, your street, all over."

"No," he shakes his head.

"Why? Where is your mom? I'll ask her."

"She's dead."

"Oh. Can I ask your dad?"

"He's dead."

I kick at a rock. "Then who do you live with?"

"Tatie," he says, looking at my bike like he wants to ride it.

"What's a Tatie?"

"Tatie means aunt in French."

"You're French? That's what fortuner means?"

"You talk a lot," he says, tilting his head.

I laugh at him. "I talk the same as everyone else. You talk funny."

He squints at me again.

"You can ride mine, but just for a bit," I hold the handles out to him. When he doesn't take them, I sigh. He's hardheaded.

"Okay. Well, I have to go." I turn and walk slowly, knowing Daddy will meet me at the porch and skin my hide.

"I'll get on, just for a . . . bit," he says it like me. I turn back to see him rushing toward me before taking my bike by the handle. He sits on the seat, puts one foot on the pedal, and waits.

"Are you scared because you crashed?"

"I'm not scared," he says through his teeth.

He's scared.

"I crashed before, too, cut my hand good and bloody." I hold it up for him. He doesn't look mad anymore but still doesn't push on the pedals. "Just . . . push the pedals really fast and hold the bars straight. You can do it."

"Dom?" I hear called from inside his house. "Dom!?"

"That you?" I ask. "You Dom?"

He nods and drops his head. "That's my brother," he says as he gets off the bike and holds it out to me. "He won't let me ride with strangers."

"Okay," I say. "Well . . . meet me tonight, after bed."

He jerks his head. "He won't let me."

"Don't tell him." I smile.

"Oh." His eyes go wide. "Okay."

"It will be our secret."

He nods.

I point to the streetlight. "Meet me over there. I need to get home. I'm going to get an ass-whoopin' for coming to meet you in my church clothes."

He throws his head back and laughs.

"You think that's funny?" I smile. "That I'm going to get an ass-whoo-pin' to meet you?"

He nods again and again, smiling, and I smile too.

"Okay, Dom, see you after dark."

I look back as I push the pedals. "I'm Sean."

He nods again, still smiling. The front door opens at his house as I turn the corner. "Dom, what are you doing? Get out of the street!"

"You were fearlessly flying down that street by midnight," I say, ripping at some of the grass near his headstone—chest roaring as it has been since I saw his lifeless body on Cecelia's bedroom floor nearly three months ago. "Not that you asked, but I did get an ass-whoo-pin' just to come and meet the boy who sat on the curb every day."

A wave of pain crashes into me as my eyes sting. "Best decision I ever made. I won't ever regret it," I choke out. Waves of anguish rush through me as I lower my gaze to the definitive dates. The dates that mark the beginning of his life and the end of it. I come here as often as I can to convince myself that this is real.

That he's gone.

Something inside me refuses to believe it.

Our last words weren't at all sentimental in nature or anything memorable. More transactional and out of fear.

But he knew. He always knew of my affection for him and vice versa. I used to wonder why people were so worried about last words after someone passes because the relationship is what matters most, but I get it now. I get it. I would give anything to have those seconds back, but I still have no idea what those words would be.

Then and there, I decide there won't be.

I'll never stop talking to him.

"Fuck," I rasp out at the sting of the memory of the day we met. Seeing that kid on the curb, seemingly lost and waiting for anyone or anything to come along. The second time I saw him, I just knew that someone he was waiting for was me. Just as that surety settles over me, the breeze kicks up, and the trees rustle above, the foliage floating slowly toward the ground around me. The hinge of the gate squeaks as I focus on a gold leaf as it lands on top of his headstone.

"You always knew how to help me make sense of things, and you left me here to figure it all out. You did that for me. You always put things into perspective. I can't," I swallow, "... I need you because I can't make sense of this, brother. No matter how hard I try, I can't understand how you not being here will ever be the way things were supposed to play out." The ball in my throat chokes me silent momentarily as I grunt against it.

"I'm so fucking lost, Dom." I fist my eyes as the merciless crack ripples through me as it has every single day since he left.

"How in the hell am I supposed to do this without you? The truth is, I can't ... but you're going to make me, aren't you?"

The breeze blows steadily, and I close my eyes in an attempt to gather myself. Face stinging, I take a few deep breaths, and inside them, somehow conjure an image of a freezing January night. A glimpse of Dom and me a few years after we met, flying down the street on our bikes. The shine on his, which was brand new as he flew past me, arms raised just as it started to snow.

"*We're flying,*" he yells, *looking back at me, eyes bright, a smile taking up the whole of his face. I'm flying with him. Head tilted up, snowflakes pelting my nose and lips as he whizzes past me—past the streetlight and into the darkness, his high-pitched voice filtering back to me,* "*Come on, Sean!*"

My cellphone vibrates, jarring me out of the most vivid memory I've ever had, and I'm strangled with agony at the loss of it as his voice echoes through time and back to me. "*Come on, Sean!*"

"I'm right behind you," I whisper in promise, "I'm right behind you, Dom."

"I'm glad that you loved him, and I'm glad he knew what it felt like to be loved by you before he died, and it's because of the way you love, Cecelia."—Tobias, *The Finish Line*

Tyler

"**N**E ME PLEURE PAS. PROMIS MOI."

Delphine's whispered plea echoes through me as I stand at the large window in my suite. Gaze trailing up the glittering Eiffel Tower to the high beam shooting straight up into the clouds above. Thunder sounds nearby, light rain trickling down the four-squared windowpane as the rumble of my phone follows.

T: What were his exact instructions?

Sighing at the sight of the same message I've gotten a dozen times or more, I type my reply.

Working on cracking that top again?

T: Always.

I swear I relayed every word to you verbatim.

T: Humor me and tell me one more time.

In a blink, I'm re-living the day I gave the laptop to him. A day I've lived through one too many times.

"Wake up, asshole," I snap, pushing through the door, still furious about the hand he dealt Sean and me yesterday when he woke up in the hospital. A moment I prayed for every second since he was gunned down on the street and spent a week in a coma. The upset in his eyes when he realized he survived broke me in a way I can't ever see being repaired. Not after all the loss we've suffered.

Sickly pale and dressed in a hospital gown, his head lolls in my direction, eyes glazed over. A glaze that hasn't cleared a single fucking day in the last year. "I'm awake."

"No, you aren't," I snap, "but you're about to be." I drop the machine onto his lap, ignoring his pained wince. It's a dick move, but it's the pain churning in my own chest that has me giving zero fucks about my theatrics or his discomfort. It's past time he acknowledges he's not the only one suffering.

Sean's refusal to speak a word to him when he woke—though he sat by his side the entire time he was unconscious—had us close to exchanging blows in the hospital parking lot yesterday. I've done nothing but fight for a year and a week since Dom died, trying to salvage what's left of us.

A year and a week later, and I'm out of fucking patience.

"We've lost twenty-five goddamn birds," I remind him, "and I'll be damned if your casket is next to hit the ground. It's time to wake up!"

Lifting the heavy laptop in his hand, he extends it toward me to take it, and I bat it back down to where it crashes painfully against his chest. He curses but doesn't lash out, and we both know why. His selfish absence has cost us enough.

"Tyler," he croaks hoarsely, "I can't. Just—"

"His instructions were clear. I don't get to 'just' anything."

"Instructions?" He asks, eyes lowering to the sleek machine.

"Yeah, that 'if the worst happens, I was to put it in the right set of hands.'" Opening the laptop to demonstrate, I press my finger on it, and nothing happens. Gripping his finger, I press the pad in the same place, and it lights up instantly. I lift my palms. "It's obvious that set of hands isn't mine."

"I can't," Tobias chokes out in a plea, his voice tethered from the tubing they removed yesterday that pumped breath into him while Sean and I sat back, terrified he would never draw his own again. When he roused, and the realization set in that he'd survived, it was immediately followed by despair . . . the truth was made clear. He wanted to die.

Anger boils over as I lash out at the memory. "Fuck you!"

His eyes snap to mine in confusion, so I set him straight.

"You raised soldiers," I pound my chest. "And right now, you have an army you're not fucking commanding. At this point, we're just as aimless as you've been since we buried him! I can't do this alone. Correction, I won't do this alone, and you're not the only one going through shit."

He stares through me. I haven't made a dent. Nothing has.

"I've lost every fucking thing right along with you, you selfish prick!"

I see it the second it registers with him.

Delphine.

I swallow as what strength I have disperses. Aside from watching the woman I love lose her battle to a sickness I couldn't fight for her, *my brothers are all walking shells at this point. His eyes slick over with grief as he studies me.*

"Tyler, I know that I'm—"

"If I don't ever get my brother's back, I guess that's one thing, and maybe, one day, I'll make peace with that." I relay, choking on the fact that may be the truth. "But that's not happening today. So, I'm not carrying out another fucking task for this ink until I have the man back who put it there. Wake the fuck up, T," I stalk over to the door.

Gripping the long handle, I glance back to see him looking at me. If anything, I've earned his attention. "You take for granted the breath in your body while I watched her struggle for every single one. She wanted those breaths because it meant having another day—with me. You want to line up with the rest of your family, go right on ahead, but I will not fucking be there to witness it if you don't fight for your own breaths anymore. They deserve better . . . I deserve better. So, if you give a fuck about me at all," I plead with him for the last fucking time, "wake the fuck up!"

To my surprise, Tobias texted me back to the hospital the next day. Sadly, my plan to motivate him with Dom's laptop and target list bit me in the ass when Tobias was unable to crack into it.

Eight years later, we're no closer than he was the day I delivered it, hoping it would restore his fire and give him a renewed sense of purpose.

He's found that purpose and is more determined than ever to see the rest of his mission through. But knowing Tobias, he won't be able to rest until he's made good on the promise he made to Dom years ago.

To be fair, we've already seen a lot of those through. If he is watching, I doubt Dom would be disappointed. Tobias's renewed sense of mission has him anxious to get started. One is because of the position we're in with the US Government. Two, so at one point, he can claim his newly architected future with Cecelia.

I can't blame him at all for the selfish quest to end it prematurely. I had the same selfish need in savoring the seconds with the love of my life.

If given the chance, I'd do it all over again—even knowing the outcome. Though, I went in knowing it.

After years of selfless deprivation, Tobias is wise to that—of how precious a currency time is, and in no way do I disagree that we need to see the last of this through before either of us can hang it up.

Our sacrifices are too fucking many, too great—it's our time to reign.

This time, with the addition of a queen.

Her wings and upgraded status rightfully earned.

Even as Dom's plan to overthrow Antoine took a back seat to our war with Miami, the reforming of our organization, the election, and the destruction of loose ends—Julien never forgot. Tasked with the unimaginable, Julien recruited carefully and masterfully, strengthening the birds hidden in Antoine's ranks. Dom's plan hatched just in time for Cecelia to swoop in and set off a chain of events to take Antoine down.

In our short stint working together since, Julien has quickly become one of our most trusted assets, surprising us all with his capabilities. Though Dom is irreplaceable, Julien has proven to be worth his weight in fucking gold.

We've been maiming those remaining in Antoine's defective army in the months since Cecelia took him down. Clearing a path for the next phase.

Some of the fuckers Antoine had under his rule were ruthless to the point they in no way wanted to change their ways to suit having wings, and so, we've had to put a few down. Thankfully, through Julien, we've been able to track down the hardest cases.

But because we've had to wipe so many of Antoine's thugs from our docket, we've made new enemies, and they're making their presence known.

Many of them have become bold in their quest to retaliate. As a precautionary measure, we've moved residences every day for the last week. Tonight, we rented out an entire boutique hotel and have armed French ravens on watch taking sweep shifts on every floor.

We also have Secret Service on every block within a quarter mile—added aid from my boss and our current President.

We have no plans to go quietly, or for that matter at all, especially with the recent drastic increase in the size of our movement.

After pulling on a T-shirt, I tuck a gun in the back of my jeans and exit my room, nodding at the two birds standing guard just outside their suite door before knocking.

Seconds later, Tobias answers in nothing but his pajama bottoms, his posture wary from another day of clean up.

He opens the door just enough for me to slip in with his whisper, "Cecelia's sleeping."

Nodding, I bend to greet Beau, allowing him to sniff my hand before scratching behind his ears. As cute as he is, he's a temperamental, needy little shit who will make a fuss if he's not acknowledged or doesn't get the love he feels he deserves. He is also the second apple of Tobias's eye.

Scanning the large suite, I spy the open laptop at the end of a solid oak dining room table that seats a dozen and make my way toward it. Tobias takes a seat behind the table and types in the first of two passwords. The first password he created was enclosed in the note the day I delivered it.

ALWAYS BROTHERS

It's the second we've never been able to get past.

"I don't understand why he would make it so fucking hard," Tobias groans.

"Why wouldn't he?" I counter.

"I get that, but it's something I'm supposed to know," he frowns at the screen. "Tell me what he said."

"We've gone over this, man. He said to put it in the right set of hands. Your prints are the only ones that fire up this fucking thing." Just as a thought occurs to me, Cecelia speaks up from behind us.

"That's Dom's," she whispers hoarsely, and we both turn our heads to see her standing just a few feet away, tightening a long, floor-length silk robe as she stares at the laptop like the fucking ghost it is. "That's Dom's laptop."

"Did we wake you, Trésor?" Tobias asks, his eyes roving over her in the way they always do—a way that conveys *exactly* what she means to him—*life*.

"I couldn't sleep," she replies before bending to scratch her attention-seeking whore of a dog. "Today was . . . long."

Understatement.

Today was fucking horrific. Cecelia's body count climbed substantially in the months since she and Tobias left Atlanta, her wings spreading and strengthening by the day. The innocence of the girl I met at eighteen is long gone and replaced by a fiercely made, forged by fire fucking warrior.

"You've seen this?" I ask, nodding toward the laptop. She nods, her eyes traveling over the piece of Dom sitting on the table in front of the three of us.

"What's on it?" She asks.

"We don't know, Trésor," Tobias sighs. "That's what we've been trying to figure out. For too fucking long."

"You can't get in?" She asks, peering at the image on the screen— Santa holding a waving American flag.

Tobias grips her hip and looks up at her from where he sits. "Remember when we met, I told you Dom and I were having a lot of problems seeing eye to eye on his extremes?"

Cecelia nods as Tobias looks back at the screen, his gaze somewhere in the past. "He was in the midst of building files of incriminating evidence against a lot of the corrupt. Somehow, he's tapped into what no one should be able to. I sent him this laptop to help put his list together."

She palms his shoulder in encouragement as he searches his memory. "I was searching for Abijah, so it was not long after you arrived in Triple Falls."

She nods again, sadness etching her features, concern in her eyes for him. I see it the minute he recognizes it, and his eyes soften with devotion.

Her focus darts back to the screen. "So, Santa means a list, right?"

"Right," Tobias nods.

She reads the little square box inside the flag. "And the hint is N-enemy?"

"Yes, we've exacerbated everything we can think of in that respect. We've even called in experts to calculate a list of possibilities, but *my fingers* have to be the ones to type the answer. There's no way around it, and I haven't exactly had the time to devote—"

"Tobias," she interjects, "the N stands for natural."

"Yes, Trésor, we've considered that, but—"

"That's what it is," she presses. "Natural Enemy."

"Jesus Christ," I utter as I look between them, the inkling growing stronger.

They both turn to me, alarmed as the image of Dom scanning his room the night he died, his back to me, shutters in. He wasn't *looking*—he was *thinking*.

Tobias speaks up first, hope sparking in his eyes. "What?"

"I'm such a goddamned idiot." I turn to Cecelia. "Have you ever typed into Dom's computer?"

She nods.

"Do you remember what?" I prompt.

She shakes her head. "No, it was just a bunch of his codes, letters, and numbers."

"No, it wasn't," I say.

"Tyler," Tobias snaps out of patience.

Gripping Cecelia's finger, I press it to the newly darkened keyboard, and it lights up like Christmas. Tobias's eyes widen in shock as I exhale. "He was encrypting your fingerprints and programmed them to this keyboard."

"*When?*" Tobias asks.

"It's all about timing, isn't it?" I sigh, shaking my head.

Tobias nods, knowing exactly when he encrypted them.

"What am I missing?" Cecelia asks.

"The night he died," Tobias answers for me. "He told Tyler that if anything happened to him, to get the laptop into the right set of hands."

"The right set of hands," I whisper, "As in *two sets of goddamn hands*."

Tobias had the first passcode, she had the other, and even if he figured it out, *Cecelia* had to be the one to type it in.

"Do you know the answer, Trésor?"

"I do," she replies as we both tense up. She positions herself behind his chair before running her palms up his back along the expanse of his raven tattoo. "He and I had the conversation in passing one day. I'm sure you've guessed a thousand government-based terms, right?"

"Right," Tobias nods.

"You're thinking of a *man's* natural enemy." She bends to whisper in his ear. "What is a *Raven's* natural enemy?"

Fingers hovering over the keys, Cecelia types in each letter.

BALD EAGLE

In the next breath, the screen springs to life. A list of files lines up, and one name, in particular, catches my complete attention as Tobias stares up at Cecelia, incredulous. Seconds of stunned silence ensue as Tobias tries to make sense of it. "It was you, Trésor. He knew—"

Cecelia's eyes fill and I glance over at her.

"We had to be together," Tobias rasps out. "It was the only way in."

She nods in perfect understanding, a grief-filled tear sliding down her cheek.

Elation quickly turns to alarm when I recall my conversation with Dom years ago—the day Cecelia arrived in Triple Falls—and Dom tried to explain what he was dealing with.

"*That bad?*" I ask.

"*Worse, these aren't acts of war.*"

I ready myself mentally for whatever we're about to see as Tobias and Cecelia remain staring at one another, bewildered.

"Please, man, please," I plead. "I know this is heavy, but I have to know. After all this time, I have to fucking know."

Tobias stares back at the screen, his own fear coming out to play. "Trésor—"

"Don't waste your breath," she shakes her head adamantly, her eyes relaying enough, and he nods. He's been completely transparent with her since she took Antoine down.

But even I have to voice my objection—at least to warn her. "Cecelia, this is different. This is something you can never unsee."

"I shot three men today. Don't fucking preach to me, Jennings," she snaps, giving us both a pointed look. It would be comical if Tobias and I weren't truly concerned. This is what tortured our brother and had him acting out of pocket up until his death.

"Okay, Trésor, but please—"

"If it's too much, I promise to walk away," she assures us both before Tobias turns back to the laptop, trepidation littering his profile.

Bracing myself, I feel it coming. I know that whatever we're about to discover will irrevocably change the three of us as Tobias clicks the first file, and a video pops up.

Mere minutes later, I have Tobias pinned to the floor, using every bit of my strength as I press my knee into his back while he roars beneath me in a mix of torment and fury. Agonized cries leave him as Cecelia quickly lays on the floor next to him on her stomach, gently calling his name over and over to bring him out of the darkness that engulfed him. Doing what I can, I chime in as he flails physically and mentally.

"We'll get every single fucking one of them, T," I grit out as he struggles against me. "I swear to you, man, we'll get them all. Every single fucking one."

"I'm right here, Tobias. Look at me. Please, my love, look at me," Cecelia begs, her tear-streaked face an inch from his, the horrors we've witnessed reflecting in her eyes. She peers back at him, voice soothing as she palms his jaw.

"Trésor," he gasps just as he goes limp beneath me.

"Tyler, let him go," Cecelia whispers, not looking away from him.

Unable to think past the second I'm in, I watch them for endless minutes as Cecelia coaxes her king forward in the way only she can.

Like everything else, *Dom just fucking knew.*

With the way Dom set this up, there was no other way to task Tobias with a future he couldn't survive without *her* to fall back on. A plan that was impossible for Tobias to execute without her strength. An undertaking he refused to let him near without Cecelia there to bring him back from the dark places in his mind.

Because that was what she did for Dom.

Cecelia's always been a reprieve, a safe haven, and had the resilience many of us didn't.

It's what none of us could pinpoint inside her because we were the ones who eventually tested it and brought it out of her.

Dom figured it out at some point and gave her the position before she earned it.

Staring back at the start of the video that set Tobias off, nausea churns in my gut at the memory of each horrific second, but I manage to tamp it down.

Our agenda for the foreseeable future is sorted.

The idea that Dom shouldered this on his own is too much to fucking bear. We'd all condemned him for his behavior while daily, he struggled in his own skin. Knowing that there were monsters like these sick fucks out there, doing these things for their own amusement, and worse . . . getting away with it.

But like with all things, knowing or suspecting is one thing, but Dom has always known the value of seeing to believe. I stand shaken to my core by the amount of strength and discipline he had to have mustered, even with the way he acted out.

Inhuman strength.

When our wheels touch down on American soil mere hours later, and we're safely in the car, I marvel at my chosen brothers—both of them.

From orphans with absolutely nothing to the men they became

to this moment. I feel a sense of pride for having witnessed such a miraculous transformation—including the revolution of the woman currently at Tobias's side. The difference between the beginning of then, to the beginning happening now is mind-boggling. As I study them both in wait for what's about to transpire, Tobias unlocks eyes with Cecelia, swiveling his head in my direction. After hours of disconnect from him, he's back, and there's only one fucking way to discern what's so clearly written in his eyes. The same look that was in his brothers years ago—*Vengeance.*

Tyler

HEARING THE STRAIN OF MY POUNDING FEET ON THE treadmill of my office, I click the channel and browse through Fleet Media news stations.

Click

"*. . . twelve trafficking hive leaders were found murdered in their homes last month, thirty additional arrests have been made. Authorities have reported that over six thousand children have been recovered in the last two weeks—*"

Click

"*The A-list is under cyber-attack today, and it's not pretty folks. New evidence has been circulating the web regarding several studio moguls, pop singers, producers, acclaimed actors, and even sports giants taking part in a disturbing ritual. Warning, the brief clip you're about to see is not at all recommended for sensitive and younger viewers—*"

Click

"*This just in. Two military officials were discovered today, having been gunned down in their homes. Investigators at the scene reported looping video footage on every screen of the official's houses, including incriminating correspondence between the two officers. The two men were under investigation nearly a decade ago when charges were brought against them due to the discovery of a re-routed shipment of military-grade guns. One of which was found in the hands of Joshua Brown, the twenty-year-old who was shot dead outside of a North Carolina auditorium on the Fourth of July. Next to Joshua's body was a duffle bag filled with military-grade guns and ammunition, along with printed online correspondence of his plans for a mass shooting to take place later that day. Though the second suspected gunman was never found, shell casings of the same weapons were discovered during a North Carolina crime spree which led to the arrest of both military officials. Both officials were charged but found not guilty due to insufficient evidence. But in light of investigators' new findings—*"

Click

"In the last two months, numerous reports have been flooding the airwaves in what officials, government agencies, and media alike have deemed the most methodical retribution plot in US history. The common ties to each, substantial and indisputable evidence, which has perplexed authorities. Many reports have labeled this movement the 'Smoking Gun.'

"The FBI, CIA, DEA, and other government agencies are baffled by the surge of vile acts and crimes that have been brought to light but have not been able to identify a single suspect in connection to this phenomenal string of vigilante justice. The suspects, who took it upon themselves to act as investigators in addition to judge, jury, and executioner, still remain at large. These eye-opening events have since set off a chain reaction around the country, and many have come forth in aiding these vigilantes—"

Clicking off the TV, I slow the treadmill to cool down before walking a full minute in silence, his words echoing through me.

"You would think at least one of you would understand my struggle."

My chest cracks in recollection as I absorb the domino effect Dom set into motion a year before he died.

Though satisfied with our progress since we left France, it's as though not an ounce of the weight has left me. It's no big surprise why. I memorized every detail Dom left us, along with his methodical plans to both expose and dispose of the trash. It's the amount of planning that remains the most disturbing. The painstaking detail in which he laid it all out. The amount of time he spent with this in his head. Alone. Utterly alone in it all.

Feeling the burn in my chest and making peace with the fact that I may never know peace again, I make my way to the shower.

Minutes later, I wrap a towel around my waist as I pick through more than a dozen suits, expertly tailored to fit the President's right-hand man. Today, I'm not him, and I won't be until my task list is complete. Mine is much longer than everyone else's—not out of spite but because Dom knew what position I would be in at some point.

Exhaustion tries to sneak its way in, but a little over two years into Monroe's first term, I marvel at the fact that Dom's next gift will help us exterminate enough in DC to win Monroe his next election. As invisible as Preston's ink might be, he's a raven through and through.

Allowing the day to settle in, I remember my brother for who he was and what he hid.

His secrets were always kept with the purpose of being our gateway.

He didn't just shield us from the burden of knowing. He was biding his time for all of us so that, piece by piece, we got everything we needed to press forward and do it in the most impactful way.

I'm convinced now he felt his imminent death on those stairs all those years ago and no doubt started preparing in the year before he left us.

Whether he knew it or not, he knew enough and mapped our start.

Plucking a suit from my closet, I walk inside my bedroom as my cell rings. "Jennings."

"Mr. Jennings, your car is here."

"Thank you, I'll be right down."

Walking out of the hotel ten minutes later, I'm met by the sight of my temporary driver as his lips quirk up, eyes dancing with mirth.

Clint holds the door open, his driver's uniform laughable as he greets me. "Good morning, Mr. Jennings."

"Cut the bullshit," I clip, my own lips lifting at the sight of him, looking whole and healthy compared to the night I drove him into an unknown future.

"Today's the big day, huh?" Clint asks.

"Yeah, so let's not keep him waiting."

"Yes, sir," he says, smirking as he closes the door and gets in the driver's seat. Twenty minutes later, we pull up to the airport in wait.

"Heard the news," Clint says while my eyes frantically search the terminal for any sign of him.

"Yeah?" I say as we share a smile in the rearview.

"It's unbelievable, man, what you guys have accomplished," he says with nothing but admiration in his voice.

"By someone else's design," I say, straightening my sleeve beneath my shirt jacket as Dom's words strike me again.

"*When we wait for someone to do something, no one ever fucking shows up.*"

Just as his words reach me, Zach appears outside the terminal, civvies on, his hair only an inch thicker than when I picked him up from graduating basic. He cracks a smile a mile wide when I step out of the car, and I head in his direction. Neither of us breaks our stride as we embrace. My heart alight as we hold on a little tighter than the norm, and his whisper hits my ear. "Hey, Dad."

Chest roaring with the sound of it, I clamp his broad shoulders and pull back slightly, eyes roaming over him. "You look good."

"Feel good," he says as Clint relieves him of his duffle, tossing it in the back of the SUV.

"You ready?" I ask.

"Been ready," he reminds me. We've had a few arguments about when he would get inked, but we always agreed this day would come. What better place to commemorate the occasion than the place where it all began.

Three hours later, the three of us stand graveside as I scan the headstones lined up just past the iron gate—one belonging to my first and only love, and the other, my chosen brother. The two of them were so alike in so many ways that it was uncanny. Ways I never pointed out, but they were both aware of. Both of them were intuitive and fueled by their hearts, but those hearts were often stunted by their brilliant mind and need for independence. Impenetrable until they weren't, and once you got in, you were made to feel it. I experienced the love of both those hearts, and it was incredible.

We all stare for a few beats at the headstone that reads PRINCE DECHU. Three generations of birds paying homage to the man who irrevocably changed each of our lives for the better. Who gave us purpose and made us part of the most valuable thing that continues to survive his death—*his legacy.*

Allowing the ache to have its way with me, I watch as Clint steps forward. He pulls his latest annual sobriety chip from his pocket before bending down to Dom's grave, his words drifting back to Zach and me.

"I wanted you to have this one." He pushes the chip into the ground in front of the gravestone. "You saved my life, brother. In more ways than one. Thank you."

He slowly stands and lingers briefly before turning to Zach and me, palming my shoulder as Zach steps forward. Plastic wrapped around his fresh ink, he kneels, no longer resembling the gangly boy we collectively took in and sheltered, and brushes some of the debris from the weathering headstone.

"I," his voice wavers slightly, and I understand every shake inside it. It's been a long, hard road for both of us. Zach became a permanent part of my life at the worst imaginable time. At the brink of war, and while Delphine was losing her battle with cancer. His father hadn't bothered looking for him, and I had to pin the fucker down and get persuasive for him to sign for the adoption. Even as my own hand trembled a little while finalizing the papers, I knew it was the best decision I would ever make. He became my son legally at fifteen—now a man, a fourth-generation marine, and a raven. I've never been more in awe of how things work out.

"You were right," Zach tells Dom. "I'm nothing like him," he relays hoarsely. "Dad says I'm a lot like you, and all I can say to that . . . is I fucking hope so." He runs a hand along the top of the stone. "You gave me a family, and for that, I can't thank you enough, Dom. We'll be back."

Zach stands and looks over at me with a reverent glaze in his eyes. I return his stare, hoping he sees the pride shining in mine as the burn keeps me mute.

Zach reads my expression and gestures toward Clint. "Let's give him a minute."

Zach and Clint both nod and take off through the gate and down the hill. Taking my time, I allow the memories to flood me, emotions churning as I stare at the etched date of the days I lost them. It feels just like yesterday, then again, a lifetime ago.

His words kick back to me as I stare down at his weathering stone.

"When we wait for someone to do something, no one ever fucking shows up."

"I always believed you," I whisper as every hair on my body stands on end. "You were the someone who did something—still are," I choke around the burn in my throat. "I hope you're seeing this, brother."

Dom

"**D**ON'T YOU DARE LEAVE ME HERE. I WANT THAT DATE WITH you," Cecelia demands tearfully, roping me back to her as the past, present, and future collide and intermingle. Within the next heartbeat, I'm blinded by another flash of light and pulled back through.

Whoosh. Whoosh.

Anger and resentment between two fighting brothers who refuse to turn their backs on the other.

A ceaseless war.

Love lost and found.

"*I'm right behind you, Dom.*"

A battered heart pushing a ring on a new love's finger.

More grief as a presence brushes against me.

"*I see you found our back door, nephew.*"

A hospital door.

"*Wake the fuck up, T.*"

A faithless man healed by a fatherless son.

An intake of a baby's first breath. "*I told you I'd give you my firstborn, but I gave him your name instead.*"

Another crack of a baby's first cry . . . echoed by another, and another.

Flags waving as millions gather with renewed hope.

"*We're waking ghosts up, Rye.*"

A lost love retrieved on a cobblestone street.

"*I wish you would have taken me with you, but I guess, in a way, you took us all with you.*"

A burst of music, a paintbrush dipped in red, a distant bark.

Healing.

"*Je suis désolé. Je suis désolé. Je suis vraiment désolé.*"

"*Fireflies.*"

The coronation of a queen.

Unification.

More presences brushing against me, our governing view the same.

The click of pool balls.

Endless laughter.

Boundless love.

A solid beam of light piercing into a cloud-filled sky.

A long-awaited reckoning followed by an awakening.

Vengeance.

Revelation.

"You were the someone who did something—still are. I hope you're seeing this, brother."

Endless dawns and sunrises.

Foamy waves rolling toward cliff rock as clouds gather above a turbulent sea.

"We did it, brother."

Life given and life taken away, and every moment in between. I live it all, *with them, through them, as them.*

Whoosh.

"If you leave, we will be brothers wherever you go, right, Maman?"

Whoosh.

Tobias presses his forehead to mine as I relay through stunted breaths that there is no separation—one last secret to take with me. "Frères pour toujours."

Whoosh.

Cecelia's storm engulfs me fully, sweeping me into the blissful state only she could ever take me as my brother's whisper reaches me, "Mother greet you, Father keep you. I love you, brother."

Whoosh.

"It's time to sleep, Petit Prince."

Whoosh.

Whoosh.

Who-osh.

Whoo

DEAR READER,

Hey you . . . was that ending a little *out there*? For me, it felt fitting, but let me preface my reason for it with a little explanation of where it stemmed from.

You know that woman that Dom mentions in the eighties, who flatlined three times and was brought back with a vivid recollection of the afterlife?

That was my mother.

Every detail of her description of the afterlife came directly from her memory of the brief time she swore and faithfully believed she visited. Due to the substantial injuries she sustained in that horrific car accident, she was considered medically dead for a long period. However, the doctors refused to give up on her because she had three young daughters—two of whom were in the accident with her.

I was one of them.

I gained consciousness in the middle of that highway on that sunny day and saw the cloudy sky hovering above before a medic popped into view. My first question was, "Is this heaven?"

All I remember was his smile, but I can't at all recall his reply.

Ironically, during that time, it was my mother who was taking that brief journey. After coming back, she learned to walk, talk, read, and write again. Once she could, the first thing she expressed was that she was not at all happy about being brought back.

My mother lived another thirty or so years before cancer took her back. Every minute I spent with her leading up to her passing, she never seemed afraid. Maybe she was trying to protect me, but honestly, she wasn't that selfless, which convinced me she was looking forward to her return trip.

Since that accident, she always remained firm in her testament that an afterlife exists, and it's better than we could ever imagine. For someone like me, who fears the inevitable, it brings me some comfort. Not to mention her description seems pretty sublime—like a place I wouldn't mind going.

That said, I hope you'll forgive my 'what if' indulgence, as we truly have no idea what's waiting because it's a secret none of us will ever be privy to and can only faithfully believe in until we discover it for ourselves. But if such a place truly exists, I can't wait to see you all there and feel that unimaginable love, compassion, empathy, and forgiveness we seem to be abundantly lacking.

Despite that, there's still so much good left worth fighting for, and *someones* are still abundant, living every single day as a testament of that. I'm forever grateful for those people, and this book is my way of acknowledging them. If you took the time to read any part of this, I thank you from the bottom to the top of my heart.

All my love,

XO
Kate

THANK YOU

Thank you, incredible reader, for the gift of your time and attention. I cannot express enough how grateful I am to you for your continued support. It is a gift, and I will continue to thank you for it as often as possible and will never take a single one of you for granted.

Next, I want to profusely thank the little girl who was coloring in the back of that station wagon with me. Kristan, you have saved me in every way imaginable this year. Thank you isn't enough, but I'll say it anyway, thank you, little sister. I love you dearly.

Thank you to the three wise women who sat with me on that porch for hours and helped me summon the strength and nerve to finish this novel—Amanda, Kristan, and Alta. If it hadn't been for your encouragement and enthusiasm, those crucial twenty-nine days behind the keyboard to kick this novel off wouldn't have happened. End of.

A huge thank you to my ride-or-die best friends, Donna, Ally, Irene, and Erica. You continue to amaze and inspire me. I'm so grateful to each of you for who you are and who I am because of your friendships. You have my love and devotion till the wheels fall off.

To my best friend and editor, Donna, I can't thank you enough for reminding me of our journey as I went through the gauntlet with this one. "You always do this" was exactly what I needed to keep going. Thank you for answering those Facetimes and bouncing the ball with me until the wee hours. You are a true Trésor.

Nadine, you had me at "Let's talk, kid." Thank you for your endless support and unwavering belief in me. For being an amazing teacher and partner and all-around badass. Our strengthening friendship has changed my life for the better and brought me so much joy.

To my KLS PRESS TEAM, you know who you are, but shout-outs never hurt. Bex, Cassie, Donna, Marissa, Christy, and Beth, thank you ladies so much for being strong and steady, and for your hard work and dedication. I'm so very grateful to every one of you.

Thank you to Sara and Kristi of The Book Bar, you two are absolute geniuses and weave magic, and I'm so grateful for your partnership and friendship. I love you both dearly.

Thank you to Amy of Book Shelf Production for bringing my vision to life and for your friendship. I adore you.

Thank you again to Amy Queau and Stacey Blake for again knocking it out of the park with the cover design (Q-Design) and format (Champagne Format.)

Last but not at all least, I want to thank my husband, Nick, for the last twenty years, but especially the last ten I've been a writer. Your unconditional love is the foundation on which I stand, and I'm so richly blessed to call you, my husband. I love you, Nick Stewart.

ABOUT THE AUTHOR

USA Today bestselling author and Texas native, Kate Stewart, lives in North Carolina with her husband, Nick. Nestled within the Blue Ridge Mountains, Kate pens messy, sexy, angst-filled contemporary romance, as well as romantic comedy and erotic suspense.

Kate's title, *Drive*, was named one of the best romances of 2017 by The New York Daily News and Huffington Post. *Drive* was also a finalist in the Goodreads Choice awards for best contemporary romance of 2017. The Ravenhood Trilogy, consisting of *Flock*, *Exodus*, and *The Finish Line*, has become an international bestseller and reader favorite. Her holiday release, *The Plight Before Christmas*, ranked #6 on Amazon's Top 100. Kate's works have been featured in *USA TODAY*, *BuzzFeed*, *The New York Daily News*, *Huffington Post* and translated into a dozen languages.

Kate is a lover of all things '80s and '90s, especially John Hughes films and rap. She dabbles a little in photography, can knit a simple stitch scarf for necessity, and on occasion, does very well at whiskey.

Other titles available now by Kate

Romantic Suspense

The Ravenhood Series
Flock
Exodus
The Finish Line

Lust & Lies Series
Sexual Awakenings
Excess
Predator and Prey
The Lust & Lies Box set: Sexual Awakenings, Excess, Predator and Prey

Contemporary Romance

In Reading Order

Room 212
Never Me (Companion to Room 212 and The Reluctant Romantic Series)
The Reluctant Romantics Series
The Fall
The Mind
The Heart
The Reluctant Romantics Box Set: The Fall, The Heart, The Mind
Loving the White Liar

The Bittersweet Symphony
Drive
Reverse

The Real
Someone Else's Ocean
Heartbreak Warfare
Method

Romantic Dramedy

Balls in Play Series
Anything but Minor
Major Love
Sweeping the Series Novella
Balls in play Box Set: Anything but Minor, Major Love, Sweeping the Series, The Golden Sombrero

The Underdogs Series
The Guy on the Right
The Guy on the Left
The Guy in the Middle
The Underdogs Box Set: The Guy on The Right, The Guy on the Left, The Guy in the Middle

The Plight Before Christmas

Let's stay in touch!

Facebook
www.facebook.com/authorkatestewart

Newsletter
www.katestewartwrites.com/contact-me.html

Twitter
twitter.com/authorklstewart

Instagram
www.instagram.com/authorkatestewart/?hl=en

Book Group
www.facebook.com/groups/793483714004942

Spotify
open.spotify.com/user/authorkatestewart

Sign up for the newsletter now and get a free eBook from Kate's Library!

Newsletter signup
www.katestewartwrites.com/contact-me.html